RED
BOUNTY

J.N. CHANEY
TERRY MAGGERT

VARIANT
PUBLICATIONS

LAS VEGAS, NV • PORTLAND, TN

CONNECT WITH J.N. CHANEY

Don't miss out on these exclusive perks:

- Instant access to free short stories from series like *The Messenger*, *Starcaster*, and more.
- Receive email updates for new releases and other news.
- Get notified when we run special deals on books and audiobooks.

So, what are you waiting for? Enter your email address at the link below to stay in the loop.

https://www.jnchaney.com/backyard-starship-subscribe

CONNECT WITH TERRY MAGGERT

Check out his website
http://terrymaggert.com/

Connect on Facebook
https://www.facebook.com/terrymaggertbooks/

Follow him on Amazon
https://www.amazon.com/Terry-Maggert/e/B00EKN8RHG/

JOIN THE CONVERSATION

Join the conversation and get updates on new and upcoming releases in the awesomely active **Facebook group**, "JN Chaney's Renegade Readers."

This is a hotspot where readers come together and share their lives and interests, discuss the series, and speak directly to J.N. Chaney and his co-authors.

facebook.com/groups/jnchaneyreaders

CONTENTS

1

I LEANED back in the *Fafnir*'s pilot's couch and grimaced at the planet below—barren reddish-purple rock sheathed in a nightmarish shroud of methane, ammonia, and water vapor, all of it dully lit by the ruddy glow of the system's dwarf star.

"You know, I'm starting to think outer space isn't as full of wonders as I was led to believe. How many hunks of bare rock orbiting dim, little red dwarf stars are there?" I asked the cockpit and the universe beyond it.

"Red dwarf stars *are* one of the most common types in existence, at least in this part of the universe. And given how small the Goldilocks Zone is around even big stars to begin with, rocky worlds are by far more likely to be frozen and airless, or superheated and airless," Netty, the *Fafnir*'s AI, replied.

"Yeah, but I grew up on a steady diet of glowing nebulae, and supernovae, and spatial anomalies, and temporal distortions, and—"

Perry interrupted my rant. "Van, let's assume for the moment we kept running into stuff like that out here. Do you really want to spend your time desperately trying to escape things in the nick of time? Or working out intricate scientific puzzles to avoid ending up trapped forever in some alternate dimension, or something similarly desperate and uncertain?"

"But exciting," Torina put in. "Don't forget exciting."

I shrugged. "As long as everything reset back to normal at the end of the episode, sure."

"You don't want outer space, Van. You want Hollywood."

Torina frowned. "What's a Hollywood?"

"A place where dreams are born and souls are crushed, my dear," I said. "Also, a place in Southern California where a lot of entertainment is made."

"Oh. California. Wait." Torina frowned into the distance and slowly moved her finger around in midair. Finally, she brightened. "California. That's the one on the bottom right corner of the United States that sticks out like a guy's—"

"That's Florida," I said, then stopped. "Although, there *is* a Hollywood there. Huh. Though Hollywood, Florida is where old folks used to go to die, and Hollywood, California is where dreams go to die. Anyway, no, California's on the west—er, left-hand side of the states, right on the coast, at the bottom."

"Damn."

Torina and I had agreed to get to know more about one another's homeworlds. I had a distinct advantage, since hers, the moon named Helso in the Van Maanen's Star system, had only a dozen different jurisdictions, and only two of them resembled conventional governments. The rest were privately owned, either by corporations or, in the case of Torina's home, by her family. The system was otherwise considered a supposed protectorate of the Seven Stars League. And that was it. I'd memorized it all in basically one sitting.

On the other hand, Torina was trying to figure out Earth, which was… complicated. For now, I suggested she concentrate on North America, then branch out from there. I mean, I was from Earth and knew its geography pretty well, and there were *still* edges and corners that were as alien to me as Helso was.

"All of which is to say that we're here, the poor bastard who we're looking for is down there, so what's next, boss?" Perry said, snapping us back to the job at hand.

Which was essentially a rescue mission. We'd been hired by the family of one of the many names on the dreary roll we obtained that listed the people who'd been chipped—that is, had been murdered, but not before being uploaded into a memory chip—by a nasty little criminal enterprise we'd uncovered. The chips were sold to buyers who wanted to use them for all sorts of nefarious, and in some cases truly horrifying, purposes. The unfortunate victim below us was a Nesit, a race hailing from a star known on Earthly star maps by the romantic name HD4628. The Nesit, which was also the common name for the star, were members of the Seven Stars League, the same outfit that had failed to stop the illegal mining on Torina's homeworld. He'd gone missing several months ago, and we'd located his name,

Erflos Tand, on the list—family name first, then given name, as was the custom for his people. His family, the Erflos, had given up on help from the League. Instead, they'd retained us to retrieve Tand from whatever awful predicament he'd landed in.

So here we were, orbiting a planet in the midst of terraforming. A consortium of large corporations had decided that, despite orbiting the shrunken, crimson corpse of some ancient star, the planet had merit as a terraforming operation. I was no expert, but I couldn't see it, and neither could Netty, who *was* an expert on all things astronomical. The series of domed habitats that had been laboriously constructed contained plants and trees, even crops, sure. But they only thrived because their environments were rigorously controlled, powered, and lit by fusion generators. Netty was pretty clear that there was no reasonable path forward to making this toxic hunk of dim rock habitable otherwise—not without staggering amounts of money, resources, and effort.

Torina had summed it up in two words.

"Tax dodge."

The consortium was losing huge sums of money here, which were no doubt being written off against somebody's taxes somewhere. The best anyone could say about it is that some novel terraforming methods were being tested out.

But we weren't here to critique terraforming science or engineering. We were here to—

"Found him," Netty said, putting an icon on the tactical overlay. She'd been looking for the unique electronic signature of the chip containing Tand's stolen mind and had discovered it plugged into a mining tractor working outside dome number 16. I zoomed the image, an oblique view that slowly scrolled across the screen as the *Fafnir* orbited past. Several small, tracked autonomous vehicles were busy chewing into the rock alongside the dome, apparently preparing the foundation for something. The icon highlighted one of the tractors.

"I don't know what's worse—the scumbags that install these chips to power some mundane piece of machinery's AI while it carries out mind-numbingly tedious work, or the ones that incorporate them into their sicko fantasies," I said.

Torina shot me a glance. "Really? You don't know which of those two things is worse?"

"Okay, yeah, I do. But being stuck doing something like poor Tand here, or Fostin back in that fuel-processing plant, is still pretty bad."

"No argument there."

Perry spoke up. "Van, I've done the background research on this operation, and also made some discreet queries to its traffic-control AI. This whole planet is under a blanket restriction enabled under Article Five, Section Three—you don't care, do you?"

"About the chapter and verse? No, I trust you on that part. What sort of *blanket restriction* are we talking about?"

"Any descent below one hundred klicks altitude is forbidden. Ships breaching it are liable to be engaged with lethal force."

"Is that legal?"

"Well, considering it's signed off by Master Yotov, it is as far as the Peacemakers are concerned."

I scowled. Yotov was one of the seven Masters of the Peacemaker Guild. She was also, as it was becoming quite clear, fully immersed in a slimy pool of corruption and power-mongering. We'd brushed up against her name in intelligence related to criminal syndicates like the Salt Thieves and the Stillness and the Arc of Vengeance, as well as more sophisticated schemes like this sham terraforming operation, which involved wealthy and powerful patrons. Every time, though, she came up on the right side of the law—just.

I'd asked my own Peacemaker patron of sorts, Lunzemor Nyatt, aka Lunzy, about her. All I'd gotten in return was a hard look and a warning.

"Best to give her a wide berth. I know I sure as hell do."

I turned to Perry. "And what, exactly, does *lethal force* mean?"

"That would be force applied with the intent of inflicting—"

"Yeah, Perry, I know the definition, duh. What does it mean *here*, in the context of *this place*?"

"Actually, not as much as you'd think. There are three orbital security platforms equipped with mediocre missile launchers and point-defense batteries. There are also some security bots down on the surface, armed with large caliber small arms, and that's about it."

"Still enough to chase off casual visitors," Torina said.

"I think I should point out that even small arms can inflict serious, and by serious I mean *expensive*, damage on the *Fafnir*," Netty put in. "They might just ping off the armor, but they could damage scanner transceivers, comm arrays, and other external systems. And then there's what your grandfather called *the golden bb*."

I turned to Torina, who was already opening her mouth to ask what a golden bb was. "That's a single, small projectile that normally wouldn't be a problem but just happens to hit that one, specific spot where it causes all *kinds* of problems."

"Ah."

"Okay, well, all of that is duly noted. But we're here on a legitimate Peacemaker mission and have a duty to perform." I tightened my harness. "Netty, take us down."

NETTY INDEED TOOK US DOWN, electing a screaming power dive from orbit that strained the *Fafnir* to the thermal limits of its atmospheric abilities. The orbiting security platforms came to life, lighting us up with their fire-control systems. But they decided their chances of hitting us while we were impersonating a meteor were too small to be worth expending the ordnance.

After all, it looked like we were going to hit the ground at Mach 3 or so.

The security bots were a different matter. There were four of them in range when we descended into the vicinity of Dome 16. They all opened fire, making us the apex of four converging streams of high-velocity slugs. Rounds pattered against the *Fafnir*'s armor and pinged off in all directions in arcs and crazy loops of tracer ricochets.

"There are four more security bots en route," Netty announced. "They'll have range and line-of-sight in two to four minutes."

"So what's the plan?" Torina asked, raising her voice over the rattle of incoming fire.

"Plan? Were we supposed to have one of those?"

Honestly, I'd expected to just hover, snag the tractor containing Tand's chip with the *Fafnir*'s winch, then haul it away. Once we'd broken orbit, we'd have plenty of time to extract the chip. There was a flaw in my half-assed plan, though.

"The tractor doesn't have a standard lift point for the winch," she announced.

"I thought they were standard for a reason," I snapped back.

"I can contact the manufacturer's customer service department if you'd like to lodge a complaint."

I cursed and unbuckled my harness. Torina shot me an alarmed look. "Van, you're not planning on going out there, are you?"

"I wasn't, no. But it looks like we have no choice." I stood up. "Netty, Perry, remind me next time to do some proper damned reconnaissance."

"Van, next time, do some proper damned reconnaissance," they both said in unison.

I snorted in resignation. "Just what I need, smart-assed AIs."

BY THE TIME I'd cycled the airlock and admitted a swirling cloud of poisonous fumes, the first four security bots had run out of ammo. They'd managed to do minor damage to the high-gain comm antenna and two maneuvering thrusters. Frankly, though, it wasn't the *Fafnir* that worried me as much as my own frail, pink skin. A hit that penetrated my Peacemaker armor wouldn't just hurt, it could potentially let methane, ammonia, and other toxic gases leak into my suit. That would hurt, too, though not for long.

Because I'd be dead. I reminded myself again that *space is fun*.

As soon as I felt the *Fafnir*'s landing gear touch down, I leapt out of the airlock and hurried toward the tractor containing Tand's chip. I had a bad moment when I found myself facing a half-dozen identical tractors, but Netty helpfully painted an icon onto my heads-up, indicating the right one.

I raced toward it, dodging another tractor as it scraped up rock shattered by earlier demolitions. Tand's tractor was busy drilling holes into the bedrock for the placement of new charges to blast out the next round. I clambered up onto it just as Netty came on the comm.

"Van, two of the—"

Streaks of light flashed past me, and I heard sharp pings against the tractor's chassis, distorted by the properties of the noxious atmosphere.

"—new security bots have taken up firing positions and opened fire."

I ducked as a round clanged against the chassis a half-meter to my right. "No shit?"

I had the sturdy bulk of the tractor between me and one of the bots, but the other had an enfilade position on me, forcing me to hug the chassis and cower behind a hydraulic cylinder. I'd already loaded the tractor's schematics off what amounted to the interstellar version of the manufacturer's support website, and flashed it up onto my heads-up. Tand's chip was installed in the tractor's logic center, a series of modules that acted as the machine's autonomous brain. That, of course, was buried deep inside the chassis for protection. I found the access port, scowled at the locking mechanism, then swept out the Moonsword.

"The hell with it—"

More fire came pouring in. A third bot had joined the fray, and this one also had a clear line of sight. I was now taking fire from two directions, tracers snapping past me and sparking off the machine around me.

I hacked at the metal but realized I was on borrowed time here.

"Hey, can you guys do something about those bots?"

"We could destroy them," Perry said. "However, the consortium would have a case to make a claim against—"

"I don't care!" I shouted, as a round clanged off the Moonsword. It didn't even scratch the blade, but I was nowhere near bulletproof.

"Van, are you authorizing an override based on—"

"Yes, dammit! I'll override the Ten Commandments if that's what it takes to get some covering fire!"

"Stand by."

A moment passed, then the *Fafnir's* point-defense system opened up and loosed a torrent of counter battery fire on one of the bots. Our rail gun—it still had that *new weapon smell*— slewed around and snapped out hyper-velocity slugs at the other, turning it and the small, rocky rise upon which it sat into a fountain of fragments, vapor, and dust.

"Huh. Guess that was bonds well spent." I gave the railgun an appreciative glance and turned back to my work of finally hacking away the cover plate. The whole logic center was a single module. I unplugged it and yanked it out. The tractor shuddered to a stop, and an alarm shrilled. I ignored it, jumped off the tractor, and raced back to the *Fafnir*, clutching the logic module like a running back with a football.

Another deluge of fire snapped around me. The fourth new bot had appeared and now poured fire after me in a flickering storm of rounds. For some reason, whoever was firing the rail gun slammed several rounds not into the bot, but into the bedrock between it and the *Fafnir*. More pulverized rock flew amid a churning cloud of dust.

Tracer rounds kept flashing out of the dust all around me, but they were far more scattered. I made it back to the airlock, and Netty lifted off even before I'd hit the cycle command.

I watched the ground fall away, then the outer door closed and sealed. The pumps sucked out the toxic atmosphere that had also come aboard the ship, then shoved in fresh air in its place. I looked down and noticed something red and wet spattering on the floor between my feet.

"What the—?"

My left leg was fine, but my right calf was a mess of blood and damaged armor.

Oh. I'd been hit.

As soon as I realized it, pain seared through me like a lightning bolt. I groaned as I stepped—actually, fell—through the inner door when it opened.

Perry was waiting for me. "Van, did you—"

As I toppled forward, he leapt out of the way.

"Van!"

I leaned against the bulkhead, gave him a weak smile, then held up the logic unit.

"Success," I said, but it came out as a slur of vaguely S-shaped noise, and then everything went black.

I'M A PRETTY SMART GUY. I'm definitely smart enough to know that the way Hollywood portrays things like gunfire is often grossly exaggerated for dramatic effect. Being hit with a shotgun blast will *not* fling the target bad guy back a dozen feet because, you know, Mister Newton and his physics. Grenades do not explode in huge gouts of flame, like small napalm bombs, but detonate with a surprisingly underwhelming WHUMP, followed by a small cloud of smoke and dust.

But it never even occurred to me that you could be *shot* and not even realize it.

Apparently, though, it was very much a thing, particularly in high-stress, high-focus situations like combat. Many of those hit felt, at most, something like being poked or prodded, then they just carried on without stopping. But as soon as they realized they'd been shot, the pain and shock would hit them like an avalanche. That's what had happened to me.

I was lying in my bed in the *Fafnir*, which could, by design, be repurposed as a fully functional medical unit, complete with monitors, oxygen, the whole works. Waldo, our service 'bot, hunkered next to me, and Perry the Combat AI perched on the end of the bed between my feet. Torina stuck her head in through the door, a look of inquiry on her face.

Waldo held up a slightly deformed projectile. It looked a hell of a lot bigger than the hunting rounds I'd used as a kid-- and in my leg, it *felt* like a round from a battleship's main gun.

"That's what hit me?"

"It is. Standard fifteen millimeter auto-gun slug," Netty, who'd treated me via Waldo, said. She had a complete suite of medical skills programmed into her, for the treatment of everything ranging from minor injuries to serious trauma—even major surgery. And Waldo had all the doodads and attachments to do the actual cutting and stitching. According to Perry, while the *Fafnir* was sitting on Earth, Netty was probably among the best surgeons on the planet.

I took the slug from Waldo. "And you—holy shit, you extracted this from my leg?"

"Actually, it was embedded in your armor, which stopped it from being a through-and-through wound. Which, incidentally, would have probably taken off your leg."

"Good thing it wasn't an armor-piercing round, or Torina would probably be alone with her favorite mechanical bird now," Perry said.

She grinned. "Ooh. Would I take over the *Fafnir*? Is my path to Peacemaker over Van's corpse?"

"I am lying *right here*," I said, then shook my head at the big

13

projectile. "So my armor stopped this? Well, shit. If I had any doubts about it before, I sure don't now."

The wound had still been a serious one, but between the immediate first-aid effect of the armor's sealing foam, and Netty/Waldo's tucking and stitching and application of potent tissue regenerator, I'd probably walk away from it with nothing but a slight scar. It still hurt, but not enough to keep me from dragging my injured ass to the cockpit for the flight back to Anvil Dark.

"Best part? Every Peacemaker in *The Black Hole* has to buy you a drink next time you're there," Perry said.

"So you get to swap the pain in your leg for another one in your head the morning after," Torina said.

I shrugged. "At least I'll be alive to feel it, so it's all good."

2

WHILE NETTY OVERSAW repairs to the *Fafnir*, and my armor got
fixed by Anvil Dark's Quartermaster Stores, we brought Tand's
chip to Lunzy. She handed it over to the techs who would
"awaken" Tand in preparation to return him to a functioning
Nesit body, which was already being made for him on Spindrift.
His family was waiting, overjoyed and anxious, for his return.

"Needless to say, they're ecstatic that you recovered Tand's
chip," Lunzy said as we settled comfortably into her ship's study.
"They've requested that you bring it to Nesit personally so they
can pay the fees they owe you, plus what I have to say is a
generous reward—fifty thousand bonds."

"Hey, that means we'll be able to afford those upgrades to the
Fafnir we've been waiting to make," Torina said.

Lunzy gave her a curious look. "You know, Ms. Milon, I'm

surprised you're not subsidizing Van and his ship. That's half the reason most Peacemakers look for wealthy Seconds."

I answered. "I've actually asked Torina not to do that. I don't want her—or me—to feel obligated to her family. That can lead to problems, believe me."

"Sounds like you speak from experience."

"Second-hand experience, yeah. Back on Earth I had a friend, another hacker, who got himself generously bankrolled by a Russian oligarch. Best computers, best software, enough cryptocurrency to buy his way into some of the most closely guarded corners of the dark web—basically, whatever he wanted."

Lunzy gave a thin smile. "I take it the bill came due."

"It did. And it involved some pretty bad stuff. He refused."

"What happened to him?"

I shrugged. "No idea. One day he went offline, and I haven't seen a sign of him since."

An ominous moment of silence followed, which Torina broke.

"Not that I'd ever expect my family to demand that Van do anything untoward, but I'm happier this way, too. There's a downside to growing up rich. You know you've got that soft cushion to land on, so nothing ever really feels… challenging. Every time we complete a job, I feel like we've genuinely earned it. And that feels good."

"Can't argue with that," Lunzy said, then stopped and picked something up from the table alongside her overstuffed chair. "Right. Almost forgot this. Here you go, Van."

She handed me a small box. I opened it and found a crimson Wound Badge inside.

"Wear it proudly," Lunzy said. "But try not to earn any more."

"I notice you've got four of them," I said, smiling wryly.

"I do. But I'd have been quite content with just one."

LUNZY ACCOMPANIED us to *The Black Hole*, slower than normal, as I limped along. When we reached the bar, she walked up to the end of it, rang the bell reserved for special moments like this one, and announced my injury and recovery to the patrons.

A cheer went up, and what followed was a blur of alcohol, hearty congratulations and knowing commiseration, alcohol, other Peacemakers' stories about being wounded, alcohol, a few hands of a poker-like game that cost me a hundred bonds, alcohol—did I mention alcohol?

At one point, I saw Carter Yost walk in. Once he found out what was going on, he shot me the evil eye. I raised my glass back to him, and he just scowled and left.

"Rude. Doesn't even want to come shake his cousin's hand," were the words my mind put together, but what came out was a lot more slurred.

The next day, I woke up on the *Fafnir*, opened my eyes, and groaned as a star went supernova somewhere behind them.

I sat up, clutching my temples. When I spoke, my voice sounded like a rusty hinge. "Damn it, sci fi promised me booze I could drink forever without getting hungover."

"This ain't sci fi, Van, sorry," Perry said, not sounding sorry at all.

Torina smiled brightly. "Look at this way—your leg doesn't bother you anymore, does it?"

I glared back at her. "How come you're Little Miss Sunshine? You were right there, drinking with me?" I held up a hand. "Wait. Don't tell me. Expert pilot, martial artist, crack spaceship gunner, lethal sniper—and you don't get hungover, either. I hate you."

She put a companionable arm around me. "Actually, Van, I stuck to soft drinks after the first couple of rounds. No one was buying drinks for me, after all." She then grimaced and pulled away. "So you drank way more than I did, and I can smell every one of those drinks on your breath. Make sure you shave your tongue before you hit the cockpit. You're kind of… ripe."

Netty came to my rescue. She had me breathe pure oxygen for a few minutes, which made me feel a whole lot better. I showered without falling over or crying—both very real possibilities—got dressed, then headed back into Anvil Dark to retrieve Tand's chip.

But there was a problem.

"We're having trouble waking him up," the tech, an insectoid creature from a race with an unpronounceable name but whose name was, for some reason, the very pronounceable *Steve*.

"We've run diagnostic checks on the chip itself, and everything checks out. So it's something psychomechanical," Steve said.

"Psychomechanical? There's a new word for me."

"It's a new and burgeoning field. I've got a call in to an expert based in Tau Ceti but haven't heard back. So we're not ready to release his chip to you yet."

I shrugged at the fact, then spent the next day wandering Anvil Dark, making a stop at the Quartermaster's shop to price out the detailed upgrade package we intended to buy for the *Fafnir*, and checking on the ship's repairs. I braced myself for an unpleasant bottom line, but by using some reconditioned parts, we saved a bundle and ended up with a manageable bill. And, by then, Tand had awoken.

"He's—I guess groggy is the best way to describe it, but not in the sense you and I would understand it," Steve said.

I glanced at him, wondering if a giant anthropomorphic grasshopper and I would understand *groggy* the same way. But I let it go and focused on Tand.

"You... rescued me," he said, speaking through the external speaker attached to the chip reader. The memory chips were a novel technology, so the reader systems being used for them were cobbled together by clever engineers and techs like Steve. However, Torina informed me that three corporations were rushing to get dedicated units to market, which proved that, as long as there was suffering to alleviate, there were parties anxious to profit from it.

"I had help," I replied, then introduced Torina, Perry, and Netty, who joined in over the comm.

"But you... were wounded."

"Most of the damage was to my armor, not to mention my pride."

We conversed a little longer, then Steve interrupted to explain that he needed to package Tand's chip for transport. We said goodbye to him for now and then, chip in hand, returned to the *Fafnir* for our flight to Nesit—the planet *and* the people.

THE NESIT WERE HUMANOIDS, bone-thin and quick, and vaguely reminiscent of Koba, the sleazy alien who'd been running his murderous little shuttle scam out of Dregs on behalf of the Salt Thieves. But that's where the similarities ended. Koba had been obsequious, greedy, manipulative, and scummy. The Nesit were the opposite—effusive, good-natured, and generally charming. We grounded on their planet, surrounded by a vista that could have been a postcard. Even the spaceport was charming, no mean feat given it was mostly concrete, alloys, and glass.

I drank in air that was a little thicker and humid than I was used to, then wandered to the edge of the landing pad. Beyond a railing was a plunge of several hundred meters into a canyon, along the bottom of which a river rushed along, foaming over rapids toward a waterfall, with a long drop into an even deeper chasm. Upstream, another spectacular waterfall roared over a towering cliff. Mountains rose on three sides, capped with gleaming white snow, their lower slopes furred with trees ranging from dark rust to brilliant red.

I've heard the term breathtaking before, and the land around me made that word seem—pale.

The spaceport itself sat atop a colossal spire of rock whose top had been truncated and graded flat. A long, somewhat terri-fying suspension bridge connected it to the terminal complex built into the base of one of those mountains. A procession of Nesit were crossing, approaching us.

"That looks pretty formal," Torina said, shading her eyes.

It did. A Nesit carrying a complex banner led the way, with other Nesit following behind in two orderly rows. All were dressed in flowing robes in a riot of colors, as though each was trying to do a better job of approximating the rainbow than the Nesit next to them. And yet, somehow, it all seemed to fit together.

They reached the pad, crossed to the *Fafnir*, and stopped. I saw that the banner, which hung from a wooden pole that was itself an intricately carved work of art, was embroidered with what seemed to be many overlapping generations of symbology. Like the strangely coherent display of wild colors, the embroidery somehow seemed both discordant and yet also formed a whole, both at once.

Two of the Nesit at the head of the procession approached us.

"Welcome to Nesit, honored guests. I am Erflos Gosk, first progenitor of Erflos Tand. This is Erflos Nara, second progenitor of Erflos Tand."

I'd done some crash reading on the Nesit on our way here, so I knew what these terms meant—sort of. As much as any human could, anyway. The Nesit didn't have sexes in the way we under-stood them, so they didn't have mothers and fathers. They had progenitors, Nesit who had contributed their genetic material to forming a new Nesit. However, the number of progenitors could consist of as few as two to as many as a dozen. Those with the most progenitors also had the highest social standing. Tand, it turned out, had eight progenitors, the other six of whom I assumed made up at least part of the procession. It actually made Tand part of what, in its closest Earthly approximation, was the nobility.

I greeted the two and introduced Torina, Perry, and Netty. Once I'd done so, the Nesit all suddenly relaxed, as though once the formalities were out of the way, everyone could be more casual. It was, I thought, like the stiffness of a wedding ceremony, followed by the blowout of the reception.

"We want to thank you for all you've done, Van," Gosk said. "May I call you Van?"

"You certainly may. And I'm glad we were able to help. I understand that you already have a new body being made for Tand," I said, handing over his chip.

Gosk made a sharp clicking sound—anger, I recalled. "Actually, it has been completed and brought here, and we're ready to return Tand to it." Gosk looked up from the chip. "I hope you intend to run down whoever did this to him."

"Oh, you can count on it. We've already nabbed one of the bastards, named Hoffsinger. He's spending the next hundred years watching the gauges on a sand runner on Srall."

"Bah. You should have just tossed him out the airlock."

"I know, right?"

The Nesit wouldn't hear of us leaving until Tand had been restored, and that was going to take a day or two. It left us enjoying the Nesit hospitality, which was, to say the least, generous.

The terminal built into the side of the mountain contained luxurious quarters, a suite of rooms assigned to Torina and me. We each had our own room that opened off an expansive common room full of comfortable furniture and beautifully ethereal works of art, and there was a large balcony that protruded over the river gorge. Sitting on a soft chair, staring out across the stunning landscape, we nibbled on snacks that managed to be both sweet and spicy. As we sipped smooth, delicious drinks, Perry wheeled and soared in the distance.

I could get used to it, and said so to Torina.

She'd kicked off her boots and propped her feet on the railing. She glanced at me, then nodded and sipped her drink. "Same here. This is wonderful."

"Isn't this the lifestyle of the rich and famous, though?"

She gave me a sidelong glance. "Like I told Lunzy, when you just end up with this kind of luxury as part of your normal day, you don't appreciate it. This"—she smiled and sipped her drink again—"we *earned* this."

She paused, then smiled at me. "Especially those of us who got shot doing it."

"It's all in a day's work for a Peacemaker, ma'am."

"TAND, you look—well, like you, I guess. Still, looks way better on you than a computer chip."

"I've said it before, those Flesh-Merchants on Spindrift do damned good work," Torina agreed.

Perry hopped onto the back of a chair. "Hey, being electronic isn't *all* bad."

Tand laughed. "No, I'm sure it's not. It's just not for me." He looked from Torina, to me, then back, his face a pastiche of emotions.

"Thank you. All of you. I understand that my family intends to pay you a bonus. I've asked them to increase it by half."

"Cha-ching," Perry muttered, and I threw him a warning glare. But Tand just laughed.

"No amount of bonds will suffice to show my gratitude to you, Van—and Torina, Perry, and Netty, of course," Tand said.

Gosk, his first progenitor, stepped forward and offered me a piece of golden thread encased in crystal. "This is for you. We are going to embroider our family's spirit banner with Tand's tale. This thread is from that tale, yet unmade. Please, take it as a token of our appreciation. Any Nesit will recognize its significance immediately and will do their utmost to render whatever aid or assistance you need."

I looked up from the thread, a little choked up, just as I'd been when So-metz, the Srall princess we rescued, adopted Torina and I into her family. The bonds were certainly nice, but these gestures meant so much more.

We thanked the Nesit and returned to the *Fafnir*, almost reluctantly. I'd found the cliffs and chasms and crimson forests around the spaceport peaceful, even comforting, in a way that few other places had felt. The only other similar experience I'd had was a few years earlier, in Ireland, when I took a few days after a cyber-security job to tour the country. I arrived at the Giant's Causeway in County Antrim, a unique geological formation composed of hundreds of regular columns of basaltic rock, on a day when virtually no one else was around. For an hour, I sat on the rocks, watching the ocean boom against them, raising fountains of spray, the wind rushing around me from an empty horizon of water. It was peaceful in the way this place had been peaceful, with a sense of age, grace, and dignified warmth.

That was it. There was a touch of home. Even though I wasn't from Ireland, I'd felt a welcome that went beyond the greetings of people. It was an ineffable resonance, calling to me with the tone of an old friend.

I felt the same thing now.

I was actually a little reluctant to board the *Fafnir* and leave, so I made a decisive mental note to return here someday and take some time to myself doing nothing but getting to know the Nesit better.

Torina gave the land a final, longing glance. She understood.

I STOPPED AS SOON as I entered the hangar on Anvil Dark and stared at the *Fafnir*. She looked *different*.

Our upgrades included more bolt-on applique armor, a new ablative coating on the exterior, and some reactive armor add-ons over critical parts of the ship. The reactive armor was basically explosive boxes that would detonate outward when impacted by a solid projectile, reducing its kinetic energy and, therefore, it's potential damage. They were one-shot systems, though, and had to be replaced after use.

We also added a second point defense system and upgraded both of them with better fire-control AIs and larger capacity magazines. The *Fafnir* was now one *tough* little ship. We'd debated at length whether we wanted to focus on improving her defenses or upping her offensive punch, and decided on the former. As a general rule, we usually didn't want to outright destroy whoever we were fighting and were more than happy to run from opponents who were just too strong. We did, however, round out our upgrades with a pair of EMP warheads, which could be used to disable ships not hardened against them, while hardening our own systems to prevent us from knocking ourselves offline.

Which left us, ironically, at a loose end. We had a much more capable ship—but nothing to immediately do with it. There were three jobs coming up we'd bid on, and we'd already gotten accepted for one. But it was nearly a week from starting, which meant either hanging around Anvil Dark or going somewhere else. I wasn't thrilled with the first option, simply because Anvil Dark is a bland, functional place to spend downtime, plus I really didn't want to enjoy the pleasure of Carter Yost's company. We considered returning to Earth, traveling to Torina's homeworld, or even going back to Nesit. We ruled out Earth because there were hints of intelligence suggesting our capture of Hoffsinger brought attention—the bad kind, from bad people—to Earth. And heading right back to Nesit seemed a little—I don't know, overeager, maybe?

So Torina's homeworld it was.

"THIS IS, what, like our fourth visit here? And this is the first time I've actually been in your house," I said to Torina.

"Actually, this is the guesthouse. The main house is up the hill."

"That's the main *house*? I thought it was a nearby *town*."

"To be fair, a lot of it is given over to corporate offices. My family's business enterprises are all run from here." She looked around. "I thought the guesthouse would be a little more, ah, cozy."

I looked around at a sitting room that could have swallowed my apartment back in Atlanta and not even burped. And that was *just* the sitting room. Of the guesthouse.

We ambled out onto the terrace. I'm not sure at what point *patio* becomes *terrace*, but this one had passed that line at least five hundred square feet ago. We leaned on the balustrade and stared across Torina's family estate. I could see the hill where we'd landed the *Fafnir* during our very first visit here, far in the misty distance. The rolling, forested lands around it glowed with vibrant life, so much so that if I hadn't seen the illegal strip-mining going on myself, I'd have never even suspected it.

"This is beautiful," I said, enjoying the breeze over my face. Torina had an AI servant bot bring us drinks—fizzy, citrusy things with a finish of a good pale ale. I've never been a fan of that, but this somehow worked.

"Not your natural habitat?" Torina asked, looking around and then raising a brow at my drink.

"No, and no. I accidentally went to a fancy restaurant two or three times, but nothing like this. We weren't poor. Just—"

"Practical?"

I tilted my glass toward her, smiling. "I like that term better."

Torina sat on a lounger, while I claimed a chair upholstered in *squishy*. For a moment, we just sat, enjoying the sun, the breeze, and the silence. It was similar to the balcony on the Nesit homeworld, but while that had a hint of splendor about it, of rugged, wild beauty, this was more—pastoral, is the best way I could put it. More tailored. A well-tended park versus untamed wilds. It was like the difference between upbeat jazz and the smoother variety. Both could be relaxing, but in different ways.

"I could get used to this," I said.

Torina smiled. "I am used to it."

"And?"

"And what?"

I sipped the fizzy drink, which Torina had named *echee*, which was also a variety of native fruit vaguely similar to a pineapple. "And what's it like being used to, well, this? All this space, all this land, all this—"

"Money?"

"Yeah."

She shrugged. "Like I've said, it's fine. Fine… and a little empty."

I'd never talked to someone truly wealthy before, at least, not on a casual basis. So I was curious as to what she meant, and asked.

"Why empty?"

"Because this is what I grew up with, Van. It was all I really knew. When I was a little girl, that was my backyard." She swept a hand at the pastoral vista. "I was a picky eater because I could afford to be. If I wanted something different for dinner than whatever my parents were having, I could have it." She offered a rueful smile. "When we were walking through Hoffsinger's neighborhood in Indiana—"

"Illinois."

She frowned. "Really? I thought Chicago was in Indiana. Why put two states with such similar names right next to each other?"

"To foil nosy aliens trying to memorize the map of America. Anyway, you were saying…"

"Right. When I was looking at those houses, I wondered how many of them could afford to make separate meals for their kids, just because they didn't want what was being offered."

I didn't tell her that Hoffsinger's neighborhood had actually been fairly affluent, where the people probably *could* afford to make separate meals for their kids, at least in terms of money, if not time. But I got her point.

"So you don't like being rich?"

She sighed. "It's not that. It's—" She frowned for a moment, obviously putting some thoughts together. I waited.

"Do you know what it's going to take for all of this to be mine?" she finally asked, again gesturing around. "Time. That's it. I just have to live long enough. When my parents are finally gone, then, as Perry would say, *cha-ching*. The only qualification I need to inherit a business empire is a beating heart. And that—" She shrugged. "It's not good enough for me. I want to become whatever person I'm meant to be through *my* choices, *my* accomplishments, *my* failures and missteps. I don't want to just inherit someone else's."

"Hence the martial arts, shooting, piloting, and all that stuff?"

"Yeah. That, I admit, was very much enabled by being rich. I could afford to take the time, pay the instructors, all of that. My father, in particular, thought I was nuts, but he and my mother just kind of rolled their eyes and went with it."

She suddenly sat up. "Which reminds me. There's one unique aspect of Helso's culture—as much as it has a culture of its own, anyway—that I want to show you."

I assumed she meant something like local folk art, or regional music or something similar. Instead, she led me back into the guest house, to a side room apparently devoted to things martial —weapons of all sorts, from primitive clubs to fearsome swords and axes—even ranged weapons. There was also armor, including a set of intricately worked plate mail inlaid with complex golden filigree, stylized renditions of cherubs in metal, a true work of art that had to originate on Earth. Sure enough, the little plaque mounted beside it proclaimed it to be the work of Fillipo Negroli, one of the most innovative and celebrated armorers of Milan. This particular set had apparently been made for Alessandro de'Medici, the Duke of Florence, in 1534. Every item in here was similarly cataloged and described on a small metal plate.

"I gather that someone's a collector," I said, brushing a finger across a leering medusa face glowing from the armor's breastplate.

"My grandfather was," Torina replied, retrieving something from inside a cabinet. "But it's this I wanted to show you."

She held a knife with a large handguard and a slender, slightly curving blade reminiscent of the shape of a katana.

"Elegant. Is it rare? Notable? Worth a small planet?"

She snorted with laughter, then grew serious. "No. It's probably worth a few hundred bonds. That's on a good day, and as to age? A few years. No older."

I had no idea why Torina had selected such a mundane weapon out of all the military artifacts in this room, which must have been evident from the blank look on my face.

She grinned. "Follow me, and I'll show you what this is."

Intrigued, I followed her out of the fascinating little armory.

3

SHE LED me all the way to a small building on the outskirts of the nearby town after a twenty minute walk. It was two stories, maybe half again as large as a typical single-family house. Like most of the buildings here, it was a hybrid of modern construction materials, and a few uniquely local elements, like dressed stone and even a pale, cream-colored clay made into both stucco and bricks.

For the fifth or sixth time, I tried to get her to explain what this was all about. And, like all the other times, she returned a slightly smug grin and stonewalled me. This time, she added a finger-crook to gesture me into the building but stopped me just inside the threshold.

"You need to take off your shoes and socks," she said, stripping off her own.

I gave a bemused sniff and toed off a shoe. "Why?"

"Because you do not bring the outside world into these walls. It is a world unto itself."

"What?"

She shrugged. "It's symbolic. Taking off your shoes symbolizes leaving the outside world behind."

"Of course it does."

We padded into a large space near the back of the building that was two stories high. The floor was covered with clean, white sand, which had been raked into an intricate set of geometric forms, like crop circles. I paused to admire it, but Torina just walked across it, spoiling somebody's hard work with her feet. She stopped in the middle of the room, stabbed the knife into the sand between her feet, then straightened and clapped three times.

"Torina—"

"Shh."

I crossed my arms and waited to see what happened next.

An older man wearing nothing but baggy trousers emerged from another door. He held a knife similar to Torina's. He walked across the sand design, wrecking more of it, and stopped a few paces in front of her. Then he stabbed his own knife into the sand, faced Torina, and likewise clapped three times.

A moment passed, the two of them facing each other, apparently staring intently into each other's eyes. This was clearly some sort of martial arts thing—but those looked like real knives. They couldn't be, of course—

Without warning, both of them exploded into action, snatching up their knives, dodging, leaping, sometimes even dropping and rolling and coming back to their feet in one smooth, unbroken movement. As near as I could tell, they weren't holding back, either. They seemed to be genuinely trying to gut one another. I took a step forward, about to raise my voice, to put a stop to what could easily be very fatal, very fast.

Before I could speak, though, Torina was down, pinned by the man, his knife to her throat. I held my breath.

They both suddenly relaxed, disentangled themselves, then stood. Torina knelt and bowed her head, while the older man again clapped three times.

He then turned and grinned brightly at me. "You must be Van, the one Torina's been talking about." He strode across the room with a friendly hand extended, showing not even a flicker of the man who'd just a moment ago seemingly been trying to kill Torina. She stood and followed him.

"Do they still shake hands on Earth?" he asked, his hand extended but looking a little uncertain.

I nodded, accepted his hand, and shook it. "With respect, sir... a bloodsport?"

The man, who'd introduced himself as Cataric Innsu, laughed. "Oh, no. Quite the opposite. If you draw your opponent's blood, you immediately lose your bout of *Innsu*."

"Innsu?" I tapped my chin. "So familiar."

Cataric gave a laugh that was young and bright, despite his years. "Indeed." His eyes danced with merriment, but he said nothing.

I ventured a guess. "You are the inventor, um... sir?"

Another laugh. "Oh, no. Innsu is hundreds of years old, and is based on earlier fighting styles going back thousands. I'm actually the one named after *it*. You see, when a practitioner reaches the rank of Most Deliberate Learner, they shed their family name and take the practice as their surname instead."

"The objective is to get as close to inflicting harm on your opponent as possible without actually doing it," Torina said. "And it's really not as dangerous as it looks." She offered me her knife. "See? No edge."

I brushed my finger gently across the edge, not along it, and made a *huh* sound. It wasn't even remotely sharp.

"At its highest levels of mastery, though, Innsu is performed with true blades," Cataric said. "That is the purest test of control. It's very easy to chop someone down with a blade. It's much harder to *almost*, but not *quite* chop them down."

"Give it a try, Van," Torina said.

"I know absolutely nothing about, uh, Innsu or any other sort of knife fighting. You guys will either win instantly, or I'll manage to get in a blow and hurt one of you, although I think that's rather unlikely on my part, given what I just saw."

But Cataric waved away my protests. "I can assure you, Van, that neither of us will come to any harm. You are quite correct in assessing our skills, though I both respect and applaud your small streak of optimism."

I glanced at Torina, who gave me an encouraging nod. So I shrugged and followed Cataric into the sand. The grains were warm under my feet and firmer than I expected.

"You must start by placing the blade into the ground, precisely halfway between, and no more than a blade's length away from each of your big toes," he said.

I did, then clapped three times, which apparently constituted a challenge.

Cataric's face turned grave. He planted the blade between his feet, then clapped three times, accepting my challenge.

And then he simply stared at me.

I stared back. "So what—?"

I didn't even see him move. There was a blur, and the blade was at my throat. I'd barely twitched a muscle, then flinched in surprise.

Cataric laughed. "That was unfair of me, but it serves to illustrate a point. The First Stance is Focus. We study one another, seeking to understand our opponent, to read the cues they give in even their most minute movements—changes in their breathing, movements of their eyes. That leads to the Second Stance, which is Strike. Strike lasts until one of us is defeated. Here, let me show you."

We spent the next hour practicing Innsu, interspersed with bouts between Cataric and Torina, while I caught my breath. I quickly learned that no matter how hard I tried, I could never get my blade into the last and decisive part of Strike, the so-called Finishing Blow. For that matter, I couldn't even get it anywhere near his body. No matter where or how I slashed or jabbed or struck, Cataric was somewhere else.

It was absolutely fascinating. The hour passed far too quickly. And I'm proud to say that by the end of it, I managed to land what would have been a Finishing Blow on Cataric—if his forearm constituted such. But Finishing Blows were reserved for the so-called Vital Points, the eyes, the neck and throat, the heart, and the groin. But it didn't matter. I came up from it slathered in sweat and sand, gasping, and grinning like an idiot.

"Okay, I really want to learn this," I said, kneeling for the dozenth time while Cataric clapped his victory over me.

"You're well-suited for it, Van, except for one thing. You've previously injured your knee, haven't you?"

"Actually, it's a flexion deformity. It's a defect I've had since birth."

"But you haven't made it part of you."

"I—what?"

"Your flexion deformity is part of who and what you are. But you haven't accepted that yet. You—" He paused and studied me for a moment. "You see it as a weakness. A shortcoming. It has held you back before, and you let it hold you back now. You need to learn to incorporate it into yourself, perhaps even find advantage in it."

He shrugged. "That, or go get it fixed. Prosthetics and tissue regeneration are things, you know."

I laughed. I liked this man and his irreverent sense of humor. I now had a place to come back to when I was free of other obligations. I not only wanted to learn Innsu, I wanted to learn it from this man.

"Now, you have one more thing to do," Cataric said. He padded to one side of the airy room and returned with a wooden rake. "Ordinarily, it is the victor who grooms the sand at the conclusion of a bout. But I am passing that honor to you."

I took the rake. "I—thank you. May I ask how?" I felt a sense of reverence there, sweating on the sand, and wanted to show respect to the space. And to Cataric and Torina as well.

"Whatever you wish. The actual form of what you draw in the sand doesn't matter. What matters most is this—you, and only you, must be the artist. The creator of the shape, or line. In that moment it becomes uniquely yours. But the next challenger will tread upon it, destroying it, and setting the conditions for a new design to be drawn by a new victor.`` He smiled beatifically. "Such is the impermanence of things. And such is our impact on the world, causing that impermanence."

At one time, I might have regarded Cataric's words as so much psychobabble, just as I'd dismissed the Synergists as space hippies. But there was a weight of meaning to his words that made sense to me, that I *got*. So I used the rake to begin making marks in the sand, lines and curves, swirls, piles, depressions— whatever occurred to me in the moment.

For the time that I did it, everything else ceased to matter, or even exist. There was just me, the rake, the sand, and nothing else.

I finished my task, feeling a bit... empty.

Torina stayed carefully away from what I'd drawn. "I think this spoke to you," she said.

"Don't take this the wrong way, but—"

Torina lifted a sculpted brow, smiling. "Generally, that phrase is followed by something that is usually taken the wrong way indeed."

I laughed, thinking of how many times I'd seen that very scenario play out in conversations before, but this time, there truly was a difference. I lifted my hands in surrender, then let my thoughts come tumbling out in a rush. Honesty was best, especially there, on the sand, surrounded by the weight of tradition.

"When I found the ship, and this life, I'd just lost something—wait. That's not true. I'd just lost almost *everything*, and I don't think I was grieving, at least not like I needed. And then you were here, and Perry, and," I waved at everything, feeling the press of a new life come rushing in.

Torina touched my shoulder. "I'm sorry you lost him, Van. I don't know if I ever said that."

"Thanks. Truly. I'll grieve when I need to, maybe, I don't know, in between stars, where it's quiet. But I'll do it as it comes to me, and in the meantime, things like Innsu help patch me up."

She turned her head, one hand on a hip. "Are you saying I'm a patch?"

"You? No, no... I... "

She touched my face, and her fingers were warm. "I'm kidding. I know how serious you are about the job. And I think, all things considered, you've opened yourself to a reality that goes far beyond anything you could *ever* have prepared for."

"Now *there's* an understatement."

She chuckled, a low, warm sound that sent the hair on my neck to attention, and then I saw how she was looking at me, and I liked it. "I'll be here. Does that answer the question you were going to ask?"

I held out my arm, and we stepped off the sands in unison. "Like you read my mind."

THE CHANGE WAS JARRING. From the mindful peace of Torina's homeworld and Cataric's Innsu, we were plunged right back into the tension and chaos of a Peacemaker job. We'd bid on this one because it seemed like a good combination of lucrative and easy. Basically, all we had to do was find a guy who'd defaulted on some gambling debts, indulging himself in a few scams and acts of forgery, embezzlement, and extortion, and take him into custody.

And based on how much this guy lost, and to whom, we were doing him a favor. Prison was *safer* for our target. If his creditors caught him, he'd be dead. Or worse.

His creditors would make him an *example*, which was a bland word for *spectacularly dead*.

"Just to clarify, this guy owes money to *nineteen* different banks, casinos, and organized crime syndicates? And he has the audacity to call himself *Hot Hand?*" I whistled softly, looking over some details of his habit—or addiction. "Likes playing the tables, huh?" I sniffed and shook my head as the *Fafnir* broke orbit from Helso. "Had a friend, a computer science guy I used to hire as a consultant when I needed his specific expertise. He liked playing the tables, too—Vegas, Atlantic City, even a stint in Monte Carlo—"

I realized Torina was giving me a blank look, while Perry—well, he really only had one look, *AI bird with glowing amber eyes.*

I smirked. "Las Vegas is in Nevada, and Atlantic City is in New Jersey."

41

I saw Torina examining her mental map. She brightened. "I know where both of those are! Not Monte Carlo, though. Which state is it in?"

"It's… not. It's not in the United States at all, with apologies to your growing knowledge about my planet. My point wasn't about geography. I was just saying, I knew a guy like Hot Hand, who got caught up in gambling. Way over his head, and he ended up in jail, asking me to bail his dumb ass out. I did."

"Did you do it legally?" Perry asked.

"*Parts* of it were legal. Does that count?"

"I expected nothing less from you, given your creativity," Perry said with a small, avian bow. "But how does this relate to he of the poorly-chosen name, Hot Hand?"

"Well, it stands to reason that we'll find our guy someplace that involves gambling. A casino, a horse or dog track—or whatever the alien equivalent of horses and dogs are—something like that. Perry, how many casinos are there currently operating?"

"Legal, registered ones? Four hundred and sixty-five across known space, as of today."

I sank back in the pilot's seat. "Four hundred and—okay, we need to narrow that down."

"How many illegal, unregistered ones are there likely to be? Does anyone even know?" Torina asked.

Perry shook his head. "That's anyone's guess."

Torina called up the Peacemaker job file, and we scanned it, looking for ideas.

"This guy has come close to death any number of times," I said.

Torina pointed to the last part of the report. "Says his last brush with the great beyond was just a month ago, when he almost drowned in a swimming pool in a casino in the Eridani system."

"Probably not an accident," Netty observed.

"No, I'm sure it wasn't. Somebody was probably trying to persuade him to make good on some debt." I shook my head as I scanned the list. "This guy has had some amazing escapes. He must have horseshoes up his ass."

Silence. I looked up into more blank expressions.

"Okay, guys, if I happen to use some Earthly idiom or phrase you don't understand, just file it and ask me to explain later, okay? Like over a drink?"

Perry looked at Torina. "I'll keep a log."

She nodded gravely, fighting a smirk.

"The reason he seems so lucky—which is what the horseshoe thing means, by the way, and I know that because your grandfather used it once—is that he's a Tophin, and they're shapeshifters," Netty observed.

"So he, what, changed into a fish when someone tried to drown him?"

"No. The Tophin ability to shapeshift is mostly cosmetic, so they can change their appearance. However, they can change their shape enough that they can often escape restraints, and they can alter themselves sufficiently to, say, grow functioning gills, if they've prepared themselves for it."

I lifted an eyebrow. "Netty, I know you're the authority

around here on astrophysics and spaceships and stuff, but you don't usually have such detailed knowledge of our bad guys."

Torina nodded. "That's usually Perry's job."

"I know all this stuff, too," Perry snapped back, sounding petulant. "Netty just beat me to it."

"One of my key systems programmers was a Tophin. I got to know the race pretty well," Netty replied.

"Okay, that's all good to know. But it doesn't really help us find the guy," I said.

But Netty spoke up again. "I might be able to help with that, too. I was a little surprised that a supposedly down-and-out gambler has a ship as high performance as his, the *Lucky Number Four*."

I blinked at that. "Lucky number four? Isn't it usually seven?"

Torina shot me a wry smile. "Now who's derailing the conversation with unrelated questions?"

"Ouch, but yes. So how does that help us find him, Netty?"

"His ship uses a two-stage fusion drive. It gives terrific acceleration, but it also has a much higher power demand. Two-stage drives normally use a boosted fusion powerplant."

"Oh… I see where you're going. He needs fusion fuel with a lithium-7 additive and a tritium kicker. That stuff is only available at maybe a dozen places in known space," Perry said.

We brought up a map of the sources of the boosted fuel, then compared that to Hot Hand's known movements. Less than five minutes later, we had a pretty sound idea regarding where he was likely to go next.

"WISE J035000.32−565830.2, eh? Now *there's* a magical name," I said, grimacing at the star chart.

"That's why it's generally known as Reticulum. More to the point, it's a system essentially owned by a criminal syndicate, the Reaver's League," Perry said.

"Or, more correctly, the Reaver's League Incorporated, aka Reaver Enterprises Interstellar. They actually went at least semi-legit, incorporating and engaging in a bunch of up-front business ventures. Lucrative ones, too," Torina said.

I gave her a questioning look. "You just knew that off the top of your head?"

She shrugged. "My father knows a good investment when he sees one. Reavers ended up sitting on some valuable asteroid mining leases in Reticulum and realized they could make more money licensing them off and collecting royalties than engaging in all the… unsavory crime stuff."

"Alrighty, then. Netty, let's go pay a visit to the criminals-not-criminals of WISE J03-whatever-the-hell," I said.

"Very inspiring, boss. You're really blooming as a speechifier," Perry quipped.

"That's not a real word, you talking weathervane."

Perry managed a robotic sniff. "It is now."

4

RETICULUM WAS ANOTHER BROWN DWARF, similar to the one where we'd met Lunzy to talk about rescuing Carter Yost. Unlike that one, though, Reticulum clearly wasn't a rogue planet, booted out of another star system in the distant past. It was a full-fledged star —almost. According to Netty, the system formed in the usual way, a disk of dust and gas accreting into planets around a star, except that Reticulum had been just a little too small to actually ignite its fusion furnace. Instead, it was just a hot ball of hydrogen, helium, and a bunch of gases that had collapsed as much as their gravitation would allow. It was, Netty said, like a fuse that had been lit but sputtered out before lighting the charge.

It meant that the three rocky planets orbiting Reticulum were uninhabitable, at least without using tech to create a stable environment. And the Reavers had done just that, building a domed city on the second one, a roughly Earth-sized rock coated in icy deposits of frozen gas. The only other developments in the system were mining operations on the asteroids that formed a thick belt just outside the orbit of the third planet. Unlike Wolf 424, though, where the asteroid mining business was a wild west of competing interests and even claim jumpers, Reticulum's mining operations were all owned by the Reavers.

Crime pays, it turns out, but not as well as being a large corporation.

The domed city, also called Reticulum, was effectively the Las Vegas of known space. Governed only by loose laws and even looser morals, pretty much anything went here. What made it different from the seedy sprawl of Dregs, or the grubby compartments, corridors, and modules of Spindrift and Crossroads, was *glitz*. When I say Reticulum was the Las Vegas of known space, I mean just that. From orbit, the city was a glowing beacon of neon-bright color. We decided to play it low-key, dock the *Fafnir* at an orbital transfer station—essentially, a parking lot for spaceships —and take a shuttle down to the surface. We also kept our transponder in off-duty mode, indicating to anyone who might raise an eyebrow at the presence of a Peacemaker that we weren't here on business.

"Not that anyone's going to believe that," Perry said. "But Peacemakers do come here on their, uh, personal time, so people should be generally happy to leave us alone."

The plan was that, assuming we could find Hot Hand, we'd take him into custody and have Netty bring the *Fafnir* down to collect us and our prisoner. We also traveled in civilian clothes but kept our Peacemaker credentials handy. We brought Perry along with express instructions to be smug, aggressive—but not militaristic, and no gambling.

"I'm not much of a gambler anyway," he said, apparently not especially fussed about being kept away from the tables.

"Let me guess, you prefer musicals?" I prodded.

He turned to regard me with a level gaze, then twitched. "Actually, yes. For my birthday may I suggest you get me tickets to—"

"Your birthday? You have a birthday?" I turned to Torina, spreading my hands. "I didn't know. And I'm still processing the idea that you like musicals."

Torina pointed at Perry. "I hear him humming the songs from that stupid dance with the singing cats. I do *not* know where the cats came from, but I wish they would go home. I *hate* those songs."

I cut my eyes at Perry, then Torina, and gave a small shake of my head. "Um, yeah. It's a mystery to me, too. Perry, no more showtunes," I said, making a cutting gesture with my hand. "Ship's policy."

He managed to look aggrieved. "I can't work like this." Then he started humming a song I recognized.

Torina rolled her eyes and flopped into a chair while slipping headphones over her ears. That was certainly one defense against earworms. And musicals.

The shuttle grounded Torina, Perry, and me at a bustling terminal whose neon clamor engulfed us as soon as we stepped out of the arrivals port. Customs was about as rigorous as you'd expect customs to be in a place like this. When Torina handed over an unsolicited "administrative fee" of five hundred bonds, with the understanding that the agent, an alien that resembled an animated hat rack, would simply record us as Mr. and Ms. Tudor, here for a brief getaway.

"Oh, right, and there's a departure fee as well when we leave, isn't there?" Torina asked.

"Why… yes. Yes, there is. Now, you have a good time, Ms. Tudor."

I'm sure the alien would have winked if he had any wink-capable anatomy to do it with.

We pushed on into a huge, sleek shopping center, brightly lit, with choreographed fountains shooting water that threw spume over massive crowds of people in every shape, size, and numbers of limbs. Or no limbs at all.

Or three heads.

Perry saw me looking at the alien. "Do you think they fight over who gets the last slice of pizza?" he asked.

"Bold of you to assume they eat pizza."

"I don't know anyone who doesn't like pizza, Van, and more importantly, I don't *want* to know anyone who doesn't like pizza," Perry announced.

"Same," Torina said with a single nod. She tapped Perry's left wing in what passed for a high-five, proving that some things—like pizza and high-fives—seemed to be universal.

I was wearing my duster coat again, and Torina her stroller coat. We decided to go unarmed, bringing only two sets of restraints. This made me a little nervous, but Perry quite rightly pointed out that gun play in a crowded casino would not go over well, while the Moonsword, if anyone saw it, would be a dead giveaway that I was a Peacemaker.

We spent the next several hours wandering mall-like concourses, past shops and kiosks that reminded me of the types you find in airport departure terminals, except even more over-priced. But our real objective was the casinos, of which there were four. One was devoted to the high rollers, while the other three were for the masses. Games ranged from things I recognized, including something that seemed to play like poker, and an honest-to-goodness roulette wheel, to things that were entirely alien except for one thing—I recognized people losing to the house.

Even in the galaxy, the house always won.

I eyed one game that seemed to involve people picking up small, glowing crystals and quickly sorting them into piles. "What, exactly, is the point of that?" I asked Torina.

She shrugged. "No idea."

"Not your area of expertise?" I sort of assumed Torina knew everything about culture, so this gap in her baseline was new to me.

"I've never been into gambling. I just don't get the appeal of betting your money against a system designed to take it from you."

I smiled. It was the most apt description of casinos I think I'd ever heard.

I was studying a table game that involved circular, transparent cards that were overlain on one another, both on your own table and those of your opponents. It actually intrigued me, and I think

I was starting to discern the logic behind it, when Torina appeared beside me.

"I was off doing some scouting, and guess who I found?" she said.

"Our boy?"

She nodded. "He's four tables down, with his back to us. Dark red tunic, high collar. He's currently engaged in a tense game of *tandow.*"

"Of what now?"

"It's an area control game. You—" She stopped. "How about I explain it to you when we *don't* have someone to take into custody?"

"Good idea." I studied our surroundings, and Hot Hand's, and the layout of the casino in between. We were in one of the more downscale casinos, which was where we'd expected we'd find Hot Hand. The hoity-toity, upscale casino had too much surveillance, too much security, and, most important of all, too many people with the means to exact a brutal revenge on someone who cheated them. Hot Hand was smart that way. I'd never frequented casinos back on Earth, but even I knew that if you wanted to cheat at games and get away with it, you did it among the common masses at Vegas or Atlantic City, and not in the rarified environs of Monte Carlo.

"Okay, looks like the easiest way to do this is to just walk up behind him, grab him, and slap on the cuffs," I said.

But Torina curled her lip. "He'll try to raise a stink about it, probably claim we're trying to shake him down or something.

Anything to get the crowd riled up, cause a ruckus while he shapeshifts and makes a break for it."

"So what do you suggest?"

Torina smiled. "This time, I'm the one with an idea."

I TENDED to forget that Torina was wealthy, and had grown up as a *rich kid*.

With a transition in body language alone, she assumed the role of *idle rich woman at play* flawlessly, changing her manner, her body language, her whole *attitude* as though she'd flicked a switch. She didn't walk toward Hot Hand's table, she glided. She didn't gawk about, or even react to the clamor and neon, but just kind of deigned to occasionally let her attention settle on someone or something, then look bored and just move on. She somehow even managed to make her relatively plain outfit seem... slinky.

It was hard to reconcile this figure of bemused, slightly contemptuous ennui with the tough, smart, and funny woman I'd come to know. So, add *one hell of an actor* to her resume of martial artist, expert pilot, crack marksman, savvy business person, and all-round charming badass.

She slid up to Hot Hand's table. The—dealer, I guess, because they were playing another of the many games I didn't understand, this one seemingly about stacking colored disks—offered her a place at the table, and Hot Hand edged away, clearly swayed by her presence. I saw her look at Hot Hand as though noticing him for the first time and then look away, as though she hadn't even seen his attempt at being gallant.

Her disdain was flawless. I was embarrassed *for* Hot Hand.

I circled the table at a distance, trying to pretend interest in everything around me, and not just Hot Hand's table. I spent a moment studying a craps-like game that one guy seemed to be dominating, then amused myself looking for the inevitable humorless casino thugs that would have moved in to watch for even a hint of cheating. And, there they were, two of them, one humanoid, the other a short, hulking alien with eyes on motile stalks that let him watch in every direction at once.

I turned back to see how Torina was doing and was surprised to find her approaching me. The plan had been that she'd look for an appropriate opening, distract Hot Hand, then give me an ear-tug to signal it was time to do the takedown. But she'd apparently aborted the attempt.

She stopped beside me but looked away. "Something wrong?" I asked.

"Uh-huh. He's eating Moretini bugs."

"Is that, uh, a problem?"

"Damned right it is. They have to be the most expensive item on the menu here. There's no way I'm going to let them just go to waste."

I glanced at Hot Hand. Sure enough, he'd just received a plate of what looked like crab legs, but much larger.

"So you would rather wait to grab a wanted criminal so he can eat his martini bugs than snatch him as soon as we have the chance," I said, keeping my voice as low as I could over the din around us.

"Moretini bugs. And yes, yes I would. I can hear my father saying, eat your dinner, Torina. There are people starving on Provosal."

"Why? Didn't you have your choice of, ah… everything?"

"Yes, but that was just a parental guilt trip. I'm sure those are universal."

"Even more so than pizza," I said, thinking that instead of Provosal, Gramps would use *Africa* as his example. Family psychological warfare was a constant, it seemed. "Okay, fine. We'll wait until he's—"

I stopped, seeing Hot Hand wave away a half-finished plate. Torina shook her head.

"He just wasted a few hundred bonds worth of Moretini bugs. The man really is a criminal."

I smiled. "Couldn't agree more. It's showtime."

She nodded and wended her way back to Hot Hand's table. I ambled around the table and slowly made my way toward her.

This time, she sat beside Hot Hand. He glanced at her, and she completely ignored him. I could just make out the dealer's question to her.

"Is the lovely lady going to join us in a round or two?"

"How much is the pot?" Torina asked.

"Currently, five thousand bonds. As much as two exquisite dresses for someone of your… shape."

I winced. Condescending sexism was, like starving people

being used to guilt kids into eating supper and the mass of a hydrogen atom, a universal constant.

Torina gave the bartender a cool smile. "The only shape I'm interested in is that stack of chips, you cretin."

That provoked some snickers, one coming from me. *Atta girl, Torina.*

She leaned back in her seat and tugged her ear. I immediately moved in.

I arrived just as Torina put her hand on Hot Hand's shoulder. "I am very interested in you, though."

"So am I," I said, grinning at the miscreant's startled glance back at me.

Torina's knuckles whitened as she tightened her grip just so. Hot Hand winced. The other patrons at the table started to react, while the dealer obviously pressed a button under the table.

I swept out my credentials. "Nothing to get alarmed about, folks. Just a Peacemaker doing Peacemaker stuff—in this case, taking in an *inveterate cheater.*"

It was almost funny, the number of patrons that suddenly remembered they needed to be elsewhere.

"Like kicking over an anthill," I said, then turned to Hot Hand. "And speaking of insects—"

Hot Hand made a sudden break, trying to dive into the crowd and, no doubt, shapeshift and escape. Torina slammed him back into his chair and held his bony wrists while I snapped a set of restraints onto them. I looked him in the eye, pinning him with my full attention.

"I've got a set for your ankles, too. So unless you want us to drag you on your ass back to my ship, I'd suggest cooperating."

"Kiss my—" he snapped, the first words I'd heard him say. He had a whiny voice that grated on me like fingernails on a chalkboard.

Torina leaned her face close beside his. "And these restraints have trackers built into them, so even if you rearrange that ugly face of yours into something else, well, we'll still just be tracking the guy with the cuffs on him, now won't we?"

Someone tapped me on the shoulder. It was the chunky alien with the eyestalks I'd seen earlier. He had a trio of security thugs in tow, trundling obediently behind him. He was in charge.

"What... do you think you're doing?" he said, his voice an absolute contrast to Hot Hand's. It was low and grating and made me think that if the word *menacing* were turned into a sound, this would be it.

"I think I'm making an arrest. Would you like to see the warrant?" I reached for my data slate.

"I don't give a shit about your warrant. No Peacemaker comes into our casino and starts making collars. It's bad for business. So, here's what's going to happen. You're going to uncuff this person, and you'll be on your way."

Hot Hand held his hands out to me with a smirk of triumph. At the same time, as if to underline their boss's words, the three brutes behind him closed in, two going left, one right. I braced myself and hoped I could remember what Torina had taught me about hand-to-hand, because this was going to get really ugly really fast—

"So tell me, how is Leonada doing?" Torina asked.

That broke through the security thug's wall of menacing. He turned to her. "So you know her name. Big deal."

Torina smiled and pulled out her comm. "Put a call through to Leonada Vaarcus, originator Torina Milon."

The thug's bravado crumbled a little more, but he still refused to back down. His stooges had boxed me in by then, and Hot Hand was looking a little less triumphant.

A new voice came over the comm. "Torina? Are you here on Reticulum?"

"I am. I'm actually on business, which I'd love to explain to you. But I've got one of your security personnel getting in the way of doing it." She managed to make *security personnel* carry the same connotation as *cockroach*.

The security boss immediately spoke up. "It's all just a misunderstanding, Ms. Vaarcus. I'm here to help these good people *uphold* the law, not *interfere* with it."

"Uphold the law? Torina, what have you gotten yourself into this time?"

"It's a long story," Torina replied.

"I need to hear all about it. Drinks in an hour, in my office?"

"That should give us time to finish up here and get freshened up. I'll see you then," Torina said, closing her comm channel while sporting a megawatt smile.

The big alien deflated. "I misspoke."

I patted his meaty shoulder as we slipped past. "Happens all the time."

WE GOT Hot Hand back to the *Fafnir*, locked him into our tiny holding cell, and left him for Perry and Netty to watch. Then we returned to the casino in Reticulum and met Leonada Vaarcus, for not just drinks but a sumptuous lunch that included Moretini bugs, which actually turned out to indeed be truly delicious. It made for a pleasant hour or so, followed by a tour of the casino that Leonada *owned*. Once we took our leave of her and started back to the *Fafnir*, I gave Torina a sidelong glance.

"Were you going to tell me? About Leonada?"

"No, I wasn't."

"Why not?"

"Because I didn't want us to build a plan that relied on me knowing the owner of the place. That's a card you can only play once, and I wanted it kept in reserve."

"Good point," I admitted.

"Also, I was hoping that we could get in, grab Hot Hand, and get out before security could interrupt us. Smooth, quiet, no fuss —and—"

"Keep your ace card in reserve. Ahh."

Torina tapped her head, then turned away, her body tight with anger. "You take this job seriously, right?"

"You know it."

"So do I. This isn't a day trip for me. And that means that my past—me, my family, their money, and all that goes with it—"

I stopped her with a gesture. "Torina, I owe you an apology."

"You do, but why? Kind of need to hear that part."

"Among other things, you're smart and tough and honest. But to be specific—Innsu."

"My training?"

"Yeah. I know what it takes to get where you are, and I know there's no monetary gain. It's a pure pursuit. It's an expression of your character, and so is your skill as my Second." I shrugged, then held out a hand. "I was wrong. Forgive me?"

"Forgiven. And let me offer a clarification. If my connections can ever help us, I'll offer them. No prying, no holding back. I'll know. Deal?"

She took my hand, and we shook with a grave formality before laughing as one. When we got to Hot Hand's cell, he was waiting for us, radiating petulance as we slid the door open. It wasn't like he was going anywhere. At least not on his own terms.

"Excuse me. Can we leave this general vicinity? Standing there in cuffs damaged my reputation," Hot Hand said, with unbelievable bravado.

I regarded him with a look of sheer amazement. "You've got balls, friend."

"Actually, I don't. I reproduce by—"

I held up a finger. "If you utter the term *fluid* or *moist*, you're going out an airlock." I smiled pleasantly. "Now, you wanted to share your means of reproduction?"

Torina snickered. Hot Hand paused, then stood straighter. "I believe I will keep that sacred rite to myself, thank you very much."

I gave Hot Hand a real smile. "*Excellent* choice. See? You're already on the path to rehabilitation."

LESS THAN AN HOUR from our twist out of Reticulum and back to
Anvil Dark, we received a priority comm message from one of
the Deputies to the Peacemaker Guild's Chief Magistrate. It
instructed us not to bring Hot Hand back to Anvil Dark, but to
take him instead to The Hole.

I glanced at Perry. "The Hole?"

"It's a prison barge orbiting another of those stars whose
names you find so sexy, L1159-16. It's where the Guild stashes its,
um, more difficult cases," he replied.

I frowned at that. "More difficult cases? Hot Hand was a
pain, but I wouldn't consider him a difficult case."

"Except he's a shapeshifter, remember? He's managed to slip
custody before. It's not so easy to escape a prison barge orbiting a
nowhere star. It's also for his own protection. He owes a lot of
people a lot of money, so in nearly any other place of incarcera-
tion, he probably wouldn't last more than a few days. He's not
likely to owe any of the inmates in The Hole anything at all, since
they're not the, ah, money-lending types."

"Well, I live to serve. Netty, new plan. Take us to The Hole."

"Why does that sound vaguely dirty?"

I flashed her a grin. "*Vaguely* dirty?"

WE HANDED over Hot Hand to the custody of the Warden
running The Hole, a Peacemaker named Ul'ats. He was a wiry

alien with an elongated skull whose race, the R'Shari, were famed throughout known space for being dour and inflexible doctrinaires. It made them useful in some jobs, like prison warden, and a massive pain in the ass in others.

I was glad to thumb Ul'ats' data slate, transferring custody of Hot Hand. The shapeshifter threw me a venomous look as he walked past. I just smiled back.

"Buh-bye. You have fun now."

His reply made it clear that he didn't really understand human anatomy, since it referred to parts I didn't even have. I got the underlying message, though.

We detached from the grim prison barge called The Hole and prepared to head back to Anvil Dark. Again, though, we were waylaid by an incoming comm message. This time, it was Lunzy.

"Van, you need to get back to the Nesit homeworld as soon as you can."

"Trouble?"

"You might say that. Remember Erflos Tand?"

"I do, yes." I shifted uncomfortably, not liking where this seemed to be heading. "What's happened to him?"

"We don't know. He's missing."

"So we have to find him again?"

"Well, that, and the fact his whole family has been murdered."

5

We landed at the picturesque spaceport on Nesit, but this time there was no formal procession. We were met by three Nesit with a much more officious attitude than those we'd met previously. One of them, dressed in a dark uniform that spoke of authority, introduced himself as Grisha Vorox, Chief Prefect of the Seventh District and the lead investigator in the case.

"Peacemaker Tudor, yes? I'm glad you got here so quickly. I wish the visit was under better circumstances."

So do I. I thought back to the easygoing members of Erflos Tand's family. Though our previous visit had been brief, his first and second progenitors, Gosk and Nara, had been delightful hosts.

And now they were dead. Inwardly, I seethed. Outwardly, I felt myself go still.

Vorox led us into the spaceport's terminal, to a meeting room that overlooked the plunging waterfall. I had no eye for the scenery, though. My attention was fixed on a screen, currently blank, but which I assumed would soon show us the horror of what happened.

Unfortunately, I was right. Vorox spared us the most graphic images and displayed none that showed the victims' faces. And that was good, because these people hadn't just been murdered, they'd been mutilated, even dismembered.

I gritted my teeth. I just couldn't reconcile Gosk's easy charm with the torn and broken remains on the screen. I glanced at Torina beside me. Her eyes were like chips of dark glass.

The presentation didn't take long, no more than ten minutes.

"The only other specific item of interest we have is Tand's final message, retrieved from his household's comm unit. It had been deleted, but we were able to retrieve the contents of the message, though not its routing information.

"What did it say?"

"Wrong unit."

"That's it?"

Vorox nodded.

"Does that mean anything to you?" Perry asked.

"It does not."

Earlier in the presentation, Vorox had mentioned some stolen items. I asked him about that.

"The Erflos are noted collectors of art."

"Okay. So was it art that was stolen?"

"It was."

I waited for Vorox to go on, to give more explanation, but he didn't. For some reason, his collaborative openness had slammed to a sudden halt. He was holding something back, and I could tell.

"What aren't you telling us?" Torina asked, apparently thinking the same thing I was.

"I've provided everything relevant to the case—"

"No, you haven't," I said. "There's something about this crime—or this family—that you're keeping back."

Vorox tried one more time to deny it. "It's sufficient for you to know that valuable items have been stolen—"

I stood. "Come on, Torina. Let's go talk directly to the rest of the family, any witnesses we can find—"

"You can't just start up your investigation here, on our home-world, without our approval," Vorox snapped.

Perry made a dramatic show of leaping onto the back of a chair, his wings fully spread for a moment, before settling into place with a soft, metallic rustle. "But we've got your approval. Your central governing body submitted a formal request to the Peacemakers to launch an investigation. It would appear that some of Tand's progenitors aren't willing to see the entire case-load fall on you, the local authorities. It's comm log number A98704-98A6Y, in case you want to look it up."

I headed for the door.

"Wait."

I turned back to a glowering Vorox. He seemed to study us for a moment, then gestured to the chairs. "Fine. But what I'm about to tell you is to be treated with the strictest confidence."

I returned to my seat. "Of course. We're Peacemakers. We don't go around blabbing about our investigations."

Perry returned to the floor so that his talons didn't damage the upholstery. "In fact, we can't. The Peacemaker Charter, Article Five, Section Three—"

"Stipulated," Vorox said. He turned back toward the screen for a moment, then back to us.

"The Erflos Progeny is one of our wealthiest and most influential. They not only have a seat on the Prefecture Council—"

"Your bosses," Torina put in.

"That's correct. They also have a seat in the Central Assembly."

"So they're powerful," I said.

"Very. They are also, not to put too fine a point on it, thieves."

I blinked at that. I hadn't expected quite so candid a response. I waited for Vorox to go on.

"Some of Tand's ancestral progenitors came into the possession of a large quantity of artifacts and relics that had been acquired—that is, stolen—from several existing civilizations, all of whom had recently been in a state of conflict. It would appear that whetted their appetite for the collection of rare and valuable items."

"So not just thieves, but art thieves," Perry said.

Torina shrugged "I guess that makes it classier. Still thievery, though."

"So the basis for the wealth, and therefore the influence of the Erflos progeny, was stolen art, yes. Needless to say, this was kept carefully concealed," Vorox said.

I nodded. "Wouldn't do to have one of your leading families to be outed as a bunch of crooks."

"No, it would not. So you can understand the need for discretion."

"Well, someone in that progeny wanted this investigated. And, with all due respect to you and your colleagues, it would appear that they wanted it investigated by the Peacemakers," Perry said.

"So it would appear. They likely thought we'd be susceptible to pressure from other elements of the progeny."

"And they were right. You weren't going to tell us any of this," I noted.

Now, Vorox was an alien, so my usual understanding of things like body language, and facial and vocal cues, wasn't as easy to apply to him. But it was still clear that he was pretty miserable about the situation. I actually felt a pang of sympathy. This was a Nesit who wanted to do the right thing and see justice done for Tand's family. But his hands had obviously been tied, so much so that he actually seemed relieved to have been able to fess up.

"So the implication of all this is that Tand's family was killed as part of a theft. I do notice that your report says some valuable pieces are missing from their, uh, collection," Torina said.

"And had it not been for the recent incident involving Tand, and that last message of his, I suspect that that would have been the accepted motive and you'd never have been called here," Vorox agreed.

"We need to see the crime scene," Perry said.

"Of course. I've got a shuttle waiting."

We stood to follow Vorox. I couldn't deny a bit of a drag in my feet, though. So far, in my short Peacemaker career, I'd been subjected to some pretty harrowing situations. Now, though, we were about to visit the scene of a grisly multiple murder, of people who I'd actually come to know.

I was not looking forward to this.

EVEN ABSENT THE BODIES, which had been removed, an oppressive menace hung in the air of the Erflos home. The Nesit version of blood, which I gathered consisted of several different fluids carried in multiple circulatory systems, still spattered the floors and carpets, the walls, and even a few stray droplets on the ceiling. Whatever happened here, it had involved tremendous violence.

We stepped carefully, avoiding areas marked off on the floor around particularly thick, dark accumulations of Nesit blood. Those had been the locations of the bodies. Vorox had already confirmed that the whole scene had been thoroughly scanned, and had uploaded all of the data they'd collected to Perry. He hopped from perch to perch, apparently doing a little scanning of his own. Meanwhile, Torina and I tried hard to be professional about this, comparing the scan and image data to the room and trying to assemble some sort of coherent picture of what had happened. It took a lot of willpower to just view the spatters as evidence and not imagine the horrifying moments when they'd been made.

"Van, Torina, something over here," Perry said.

We picked our way toward him. He perched on the back of a chair, facing a shelving unit whose doors had been forced open. Vorox's report noted that three items had been removed from it, but Perry said there'd been a fourth.

"I don't think the Nesit were trying to cover anything up, just to get that out of the way. I think they missed the fact something was sitting there, on the lower shelf, to the right. I'm reading a strange mix of metallic alloys from the surrounding dust and a few other, odd, chemical signatures."

"Any idea what it was?"

"Actually, yeah, I think I have an idea. The isotopic signature of trace amounts of lead in the alloys conforms best to an Earthly origin."

"You mean they had something on display from Earth here?"

"Earthly origin. There are some other traces whose best source match would be Venus."

I stared. "Venus? What the hell's on Venus?"

"Well, lots, but if you're talking about things of Earthly origin, then not very much. Fourteen missions, most of them Russian, have entered the Venusian atmosphere to date, some managing soft landings, others not so much. It would seem that someone recovered something from one of those missions, and it ended up on display here."

I shook my head. "Hard to believe anyone not from Earth would even be interested. I mean, to us, they're historical artifacts. But to aliens with spaceships capable of retrieving stuff from the surface of Venus, you'd think it would just be scrap."

"Oh, no, not at all. Lots of people are fascinated by civilizations just starting their first steps into space. There are tours to fly along with both Voyagers 1 and 2. Oh, and I don't think you've ever seen this."

Perry sent an image to my data slate. It showed Gramps, in his Peacemaker armor, standing on a rocky rise and giving a thumbs-up, Perry beside him. A greyscale panorama sprawled out behind him, a flat, monotone plane stretching off to a flat horizon beneath a black sky. Sitting in its center, just to Gramps' right, was a boxy contraption sitting on four legs. I recognized it instantly. Hell, I'd built a plastic model kit of it. It was the descent stage of an Apollo LEM, a Lunar Excursion Module.

"Is that—that's not the Apollo 11 landing site, is it?"

"It is indeed. It's actually registered as a 'site of significance' in the known space heritage register. This is as close as anyone's allowed to get to it," Perry replied.

Torina frowned over my shoulder. "Why did they put up a white flag?"

"They didn't. That was an American flag in 1969, when it was planted there. Solar radiation has just bleached it over time."

I could only stare at the image and marvel. I'd gone through a phase in my early teens of being fascinated by human space exploration. I thought I'd known everything there was to know about the Apollo program and just assumed that, to Gramps, it was something of historical curiosity. Strangely enough, it never occurred to me to ask him if he'd ever *been to* the Apollo 11 landing site.

But Torina's mention of the flag had tickled something deep in my mind. I've had this happen before, usually shortly before a breakthrough regarding a particular piece of code I was working on, or a new angle to approach a cyber operation. I knew better than to dwell on it, and just let it percolate while we went over the rest of the crime scene.

I was trying to puzzle out the order in which the murders had occurred when it hit me. I turned to Torina.

"If I sent you to the Moon, to the Apollo landing site in Gramps's picture, and asked you to retrieve a Russian flag, what would you do?"

She stared dumbly back at me. "Why would you do that?"

"Just bear with me. It's a thought experiment."

"Well, I guess I'd grab that white flag, since it's the only one there."

"Sure. But you'd grab it thinking it was a Russian flag, because that's what I'd asked you to find, right?"

"I... suppose." Torina cocked her head at me. So did Perry. "Where are you going with this, Van?"

"We assumed when we recovered the chip from that tractor that it had Tand's personality on it, because that's what we were told. But what if that wasn't Tand on that chip at all?"

TORINA AND PERRY stared at me for a moment. Perry broke the silence.

"Wrong unit," he said.

I nodded. "Yeah. We assumed that was Tand. But if this information we were given was wrong—"

"Maybe even deliberately," Torina put in, and I nodded at *that* ugly little thought. But I parked it for now and pushed on.

"Anyway, if it was wrong, or even if it was right, but the chip got swapped out for some reason—"

"Then we might have rescued the wrong guy," Perry said.

I took a slow breath, then let it out. "Yeah. Which means we brought a mass murderer into this progeny's home."

Torina held up her hand. "Before you start beating yourself up about that, Van, keep in mind that there was literally no way to know that."

"Yeah, I know. I just—" I shook my head.

But Perry stayed focused. "Whoever was on that chip, they still had to be Nesit. Otherwise, they wouldn't be compatible with the body made by the Spindrift flesh merchants."

That was a good point. And it hinted even more strongly at us being given deliberately incorrect information. And that pissed me off in a deep, visceral way. If it were true, then we'd been used as a vector for someone's nefarious scheme, which had ended up with several people dead in an especially gruesome mass murder. And for what? To snag some old space junk?

For a while, I just looked out at the wind-whipped plume of spray streaming off the waterfall.

"I don't get it," I finally said when I'd gotten my anger in check enough that I trusted myself to speak. "Is this stuff really worth that much? Part of some old Russian Venus probe is worth"—I gestured vaguely to the epicenter of the blood spatters —"this?"

"Actually, Van, yes it is." I opened my mouth, but Perry went on. "No, I'm not saying any artifact, no matter how valuable, is worth a life. And no, I'm not saying that part of a Venusian probe is worth much of anything at all, aside from historical curiosity. But do you remember Lunzy's stealth enhancement on her ship? That was a piece of ancient alien tech that someone was able to get working aboard a contemporary ship. Do you know how much that would be worth to, say, the Stillness? Or the Arc of Vengeance?"

I looked back at the waterfall. The ability to make a ship effectively invisible, even at very close range? I sighed and nodded. "Lunzy said a million bonds."

"She was being conservative, Van. She could probably sell it for millions, plural, to the right buyer. And that's just that particular device. The original twist drive was based on an ancient artifact recovered on a remote planet—which, incidentally, has been exhaustively scoured for anything else of similar value. The license has long-since expired, and now there are many variations on the original, but in its early days, that single piece of tech made *billions* of bonds for its discoverers."

"So are you saying the Erflos had something like that here?" Torina asked.

Perry shrugged. "At the very least, someone seems to have thought so. Of course, they might have had another reason to steal something here, like a sentimental attachment, or they were trying to complete a set of something. But my money would be on, well, the money."

I nodded at that. During my days as a cyber sleuth and operative, I'd run into a few bad guys driven by ideology, or simply a quest for revenge. But the vast majority, by far, were up to their various flavors of no good for the money.

When Vorox returned, I asked him about it, holding back nothing and letting him know that we may have been made unwitting accomplices to this crime.

"Needless to say, that pisses me off right down to my cells. Hell, right down to my mitochondria."

"Powerhouse of the human cell," Perry added.

"Um… right. Almost like you were in my eighth grade science class with me. Regardless, we know that whoever it was that we retrieved from that terraforming operation must have been Nesit. Do you have any idea who might have been behind it?" I asked him.

"The Darilos progeny," he said without hesitating.

"That was quick. I'm assuming you have a reason to suspect them," I said, trying to deliver it in a tone exasperated enough to make it clear that now was not the time to be holding yet more crucial information back, but not enough to be outright insulting. Vorox immediately picked up on it and shook his head.

"This wasn't me dissembling. My people and I have been working for the past few days on possible suspects, and we've only just learned that the Darilos were also collectors of rare artifacts, or at least they wanted to be. We've uncovered a great deal of hostility between the two progenies, most of it fought out through proxies like professional collectors and appraisers. I was just coming to tell you about this, in fact."

I nodded. "Timing is everything, I guess. Apologies if I made that come across as a little, uh, *assertive*."

"There's no need to apologize. I've begun a detailed forensic audit of the Darilos accounts to see if there are any significant in- or outgoings of funds that can't be readily accounted for. I've also contacted a number of artifact dealers to try to get a comprehensive list of what the Erflos possessed and, based on that, what's missing," Vorox said.

"That all sounds like it's going to take time. In the meantime, Van, there is something *useful* we can do," Torina said.

"What's that?"

"Well, we were hired to find Erflos Tand. We thought we had, but clearly we hadn't."

"Oh. Right. He's still out there somewhere."

She nodded. "It seems to me that we still haven't completed that job. More to the point, scummy artifact thief or not, he doesn't deserve to be stuck on some chip, digging ditches or whatever."

"Plus, he may have information that could help us solve this crime," Perry put in.

"Right. So we need to find the real Erflos Tand. The question is, where do we start? Do we try to go back to the terraforming operation?" I asked.

But Perry shook his head. "I've got a better idea. I've done some digging into that whole terraforming outfit, which, incidentally, is clearly just a big tax write-off. But I found the identity of the original engineer who designed the operation. Interestingly enough, once it was up and running, he seems to have been fired."

"So he's presumably not all that loyal to whoever's running that operation now. Do we know where this guy is?"

"We do now. Netty just informed me that she's located him, via her AI net."

"Her AI net?"

"Yeah. These ships all talk to one another. Most of what they share is navigational and flight performance data. But every once in a while, she learns something interesting. She's done some checking around with other ships she knows, and she's got a hit."

I shook my head, imagining a whole invisible network of ships all talking to one another, their owners and operators maybe wholly unaware of it.

"You know, I'm surprised you AIs haven't taken over the galaxy by now," I said.

Perry gave me his amber stare. "What makes you think we haven't?"

6

"So his name is Urnak?" I asked, watching as the gas giant, a swirl of cool blues and greens, loomed ahead. "And he lives... here?"

Here was a system known as Lacaille 8760, a red dwarf star about thirteen light-years from Sol. Aside from a few rocks, its only planetary companions were this gas giant, about the size of Saturn, and an even more distant ice giant similar to Neptune. The system was considered open, meaning that no jurisdiction claimed any particular sovereignty or ownership over it. That was mainly because there was virtually nothing here of significance. Netty informed me that the gas giant could be skimmed to retrieve deuterium and other useful gases, but since there were better candidates in more developed systems, no one had even bothered with that.

It was the system's lack of anything interesting that had

attracted Urnak here, to take up residence. And he did it not on a natural body, but aboard what was apparently an ancient battleship.

"And how the hell does someone end up owning a battleship?" Torina asked.

Netty replied to her. "The *Arcturus* class battleship he owns was surplused by the Eridani Collective, a forerunner of the modern Eridani Confederacy, a little over one hundred standard years ago. The *Arcturus* was, when it was first conceived three hundred years ago, one of the most potent weapon systems in known space. It was big enough to power massed batteries of main and secondary armament, while also providing a good balance of armor and acceleration."

"So why did it get surplused?"

"They… got old? Ships don't last forever, you know."

"True for all of us," I said, rolling a shoulder experimentally. No twinge. Good.

"Anyway, the *Arcturus* class still managed almost three hundred years of service. By then, they all needed major upgrades to their drives, powerplants, and internal systems—basically, everything but the hull. Over a period of fifty years or so, the various militaries using them phased them out of service since new designs were cheaper, smaller, more efficient, and just as effective."

"So our friend Urnak bought one," I put in.

"So it would seem. Some with hulls that were still sound were gutted, then sold for conversion into bulk carriers, although one became an orbiting hotel in the Tau Ceti, and two more went to private buyers. The rest were scrapped."

"Who the hell buys themselves a surplus battleship, then drags it out here to the middle of nowhere, parks it in orbit around a gas giant, and takes up residence?" Torina asked.

I glanced at her. "Somebody very interesting, I'm thinking."

———

THE OLD BATTLESHIP had no transponder, so it served up no name or registry data. Technically, it wasn't even a ship anymore. The only information we got was what we could see, and scan.

"You know, that old battlewagon isn't as dormant as she looks," Netty said.

She flashed the scanner returns, and her analysis of them, onto the tactical overlay.

"Huh. There's a working powerplant, a big one. And it looks like it's had a drive installed."

"So this old girl's been given a new lease on life," Netty said, sounding decidedly happy about it.

Perry spoke up. "And that somebody is the person we want to see. While you've been oohing and ahhing over that big old ship, I've been digging into Urnak's background. He's a Wu'tzur, an engineer who graduated at both the top and bottom of his class."

Torina turned to him. "Are your circuits misfiring? How can someone graduate at both the top and the bottom?"

"First of all, Ms. Milon, my circuits don't misfire, I'll have you know. Second, he managed to be an absolutely brilliant engineer —his school bio refers to him as a generational intellect. But he was also a massive pain in the ass—arrogant, contemptuous of authority, and more than a little narcissistic. Apparently, when his class position was announced, he complained that he'd even been lumped in with the rest of his class, and that a whole separate category should be created for him. The school obliged, happy to point out that he was both the top *and* bottom graduate in his class."

"Which consisted of him," Torina said.

"Well, now we know why he had to buy an old battleship," I said.

They both looked at me. "He needed it to carry his balls around."

Torina guffawed. Perry bobbed his head.

"Congratulations, Van," Perry said.

"For what?"

"For telling a joke as stupid as the ones your grandfather used to."

I smiled. "That does sound like something Gramps would say, doesn't it?"

"Yes. Yes it does."

The comm crackled abruptly to life.

"Who the hell are you?"

The voice was rough and terse, grating out of the comm in a decidedly *get off my lawn* tone.

I glanced at Torina, shrugged, and opened the channel. "This is Peacemaker Van Tudor. I'm looking for—"

"Trouble, that's what you're looking for. Now, haul your law-enforcing ass out of here because there ain't no laws that need enforcing."

"Uh, Van? Believe it or not, we've just been illuminated by a fire control system," Netty said.

"Shit. I thought you said that all they sold was the hulls."

"They did. All weapons were removed, for obvious reasons."

I switched back to the comm. "Listen, we are not here with hostile intent, and the only laws we intend to enforce are ones designed to bring some good people justice, and some bad people *to* justice."

"Not my problem. You've got one minute to show me you're coming about and hauling ass—"

"It's about the terraforming operation on Gliese 1," Perry put in, leaning toward the comm.

A long pause. Finally, the voice spoke again. "What about it?"

"The whole thing is a tax dodge. You got screwed over because of it, and now whoever's behind it is implicated in several major crimes, possibly including mass murder."

Another pause. I eyed the fire control alert nervously.

But it abruptly winked out, and the voice came back, low and hard.

"Come on aboard. I want to hear *all* about it."

———

As we approached a UDA on the flank of the massive battleship, I turned to Perry.

"How did you know that he got screwed over by the terraformers?"

"A little deductive reasoning. Urnak was retained to design, set up, and implement the terraforming operation, and then he promptly departed the project. Not long after, he filed lawsuits in just about every jurisdiction you can imagine, demanding damages from the terraforming consortium."

"He sued his former employers. I wonder if that's significant in any way. Hmm." I tapped my chin. "If only there were some way to tell—"

"Hah, and allow me to repeat, hah. Sure, make a joke at the bird's expense, when he's trying to be helpful."

"Apologies, my fine metal-feathered friend. Anyway, we just have to hope that this Urnak is more cooperative and less narcissistic asshole. I've already got one of those to deal with in Carter Yost, and that's my limit."

We docked and stepped aboard the old battleship. We were immediately hit by a wall of warm, stinky air. Not stinky as in neglected or dirty, but stinky in a mechanical way. The air reeked of welding fumes, hot electronics, and something oily.

We were greeted by a Wu'tzur with dark brown fur, grey-tinged, wearing a set of welder's goggles pushed up on his head and a voluminous apron, stained and even singed in a few places, festooned with tools. A mechanical spider contraption clung to the bulkhead beside him.

I offered my hand. "Hello, I'm—"

"A damned Peacemaker, I know. Where the hell were you people when I was being cheated out of my pay and having my life threatened?"

I shrugged. "Well, unless that all happened in the past couple of months, I was living in a slightly tacky apartment in Atlanta."

"Couple of months—no, hell, this all happened nearly twenty years ago now."

"Well, in that case, I was probably in first or second grade and playing with robot action figures. Which, now that I think about it, was kind of prophetic, me consorting with AI machines."

"What the hell are you talking about?"

I smiled and shook my head. "Let's try this again. I'm Van Tudor, a recent addition to the Peacemakers. This is my Second, Torina Milon, and this is Perry, my AI assistant—"

"Combat AI. AI assistant makes it sound like I shuffle around your paperwork," Perry cut in.

"But you *do* shuffle around my paperwork."

"Yeah, but I do it in a combat kind of way."

Urnak suddenly rumbled, deep in his massive chest. I started to get alarmed, then realized he was laughing.

"You folks are either putting on one hell of an act, or you really *are* as screwed up and disorganized as you seem to be."

I shrugged. "Um—sorry?"

"Don't be. Last thing I need is to be wasting my time on officious, bureaucratic assholes. I've spent enough of my life doing that." He suddenly stuck out a hand, one of his smaller ones on his two lower limbs. I shook it and pulled my hand away covered with grease.

"I'm Urnak, and grease is just a fact of life aboard the *Nemesis*."

"The *Nemesis*?"

"Yeah. It means *the inescapable agent of someone's or something's downfall*."

"I know that. I'm just wondering about the name. Does it have anything to do with that terraforming consortium?"

"It has everything to do with that terraforming consortium. I won't rest until I've made them admit that they wronged me and pay what they owe me—plus interest."

"I thought you sued them. And did it all over the place," Torina said.

Urnak snorted. "Yeah, I tried to play the game by their rules. But they've slithered their tentacles so deep into every government out there that I can't get anyone to hear the case. So, it's plan B."

I cocked my head. "And what's plan B?"

"Well, if you can't win in court, then the next step is a battleship."

I think Urnak might have missed a few steps between *court case* and *battleship*, but I wasn't going to get into that. We were only here for information, so I just nodded along, pleasant as could be.

"I couldn't agree more, friend," I enthused.

Urnak nodded. "Damned right. Now let's get out of this reeking corridor and sit, and then we can talk about how we're going to turn the tables on those terraforming scum."

———

As we followed Urnak and his robotic spider along a corridor, Perry's voice sounded in my ear bug.

"Van, this guy seems to think we're going to become part of his vendetta against the terraforming consortium. We can't—"

"*I know* this ship is pretty old, but you've done some amazing work on it," I said, accentuating the *I know* for Perry's benefit.

"Yup, I figure I'll have her battle ready in just another few years," Urnak called back, over his shoulder.

I exchanged a look with Torina and mouthed the words *battle ready?* She just shrugged.

Urnak had clearly become obsessed with exacting revenge on his former employers. And that was fine, until you threw the word *battleship* into the mix. Given that he was a genius-level engineer, the idea that he might actually get this old beast back into some sort of fighting form wasn't really that far-fetched.

And *that* raised the possibility of this mad genius flying around known space in a massive battlewagon, determined to seek vengeance on those who wronged him.

Urnak led us into a surprisingly comfortable suite of compartments that formed his home. In contrast to the starkly mechanistic character of the rest of the ship, these spaces were almost cozy. They were carpeted, the walls were covered with hangings, some tapestries, and some intricate macrame designs, and the seats were upholstered and quite comfortable. I gave Torina a wry look.

"I'm starting to feel like the only guy in space that doesn't have wall-to-wall carpeting on my ship."

"I'll buy you a throw rug for your cabin."

"Don't make it any bigger than a facecloth, or it won't fit."

Urnak plunked himself down facing us. "Okay, what's this all about?"

I filled him in on the situation—the stolen identities, the use of memory chips as what amounted to slave labor, our rescue of Tand, and the subsequent murder of his family by whoever it was we had rescued.

"So, I'll be blunt. Our main focus right now is finding Tand. He's out there somewhere. He doesn't deserve what happened to him."

"Damned right he didn't. And on top of what happened to him, now you have to tell him his family is dead."

"Yeah."

Torina leaned in. "So, Urnak, what's *your* story?"

"I was hired by a bunch of assholes to design a terraforming operation for them. I did that, and they paid me my design fee. Then they retained me to oversee the construction and get it all working. They offered a generous fee, one quarter up-front, the rest on successful completion."

"You never saw that outstanding three quarters of your fee," I said.

"Oh, no, I did, and then I lived happily ever after." He scowled. "What do you think—"

"Dad, don't be an ass," a new voice said. A Wu'tzur, a young female, had just entered the compartment. Like Urnak, she was festooned with tools hanging from a complex harness. And, like him, she was matted with oily stains.

Urnak sighed. "Sorry. I don't get much company out here, so I'm out of practice when it comes to social graces."

The other Wu'tzur, obviously Urnak's daughter, shook her head. "You've never had social graces."

"Don't disrespect your elders."

86

"I'm not. I'm disrespecting you."

It was all delivered with an undertone of playful fondness, like these two had had similar conversations many times before. The younger Wu'tzur stepped forward, and I stood.

"And about those missing social graces, here's exhibit A. Since my father isn't going to introduce me, I'll have to do it myself. I'm Icrul, but call me Icky."

I shook her hand—gaining another layer of grease in the process—then she sat on the arm of her father's chair.

"Well, since I'm apparently a social clod, I guess I should remember to introduce Bucky." He gestured to the mechanical spider-thing.

"Uh, hello, Bucky."

The spider raised a foreleg and waved it.

"He's not much of a conversationalist—no voice processor. It's a future upgrade. My initial focus was on getting his chassis worked out. It's made entirely of what you Earthers would call Buckminsterfullerene. So, he's Bucky."

"Huh. I've heard of that stuff—wait, you're familiar with Earth?"

"Well, sure. I've stolen some ideas from you folks. BMF is one of them. A damned good one, too. I've managed to stabilize it by adding some specific impurities to tweak its molecular structure. Bucky's chassis is as hard as diamond, but flexible enough that it's nearly impossible to break. I've subjected him to everything from nearly absolute zero, to well past the melting point of most conventional alloys. In short, he's pretty much indestructible."

I stared at the innocuous little spider construct. "Why haven't you... ah... capitalized on that? It must be worth a fortune."

"I'm sure it would be. And if it didn't cost an even bigger fortune to make, I might." He waved a hand at Bucky. "For what it cost me to make him, I could probably buy two ships like yours out there."

Again, Torina and I exchanged a glance. Okay, so if Urnak was in the midst of restoring a battleship, while also fiddling around with ultra-expensive experiments, where was his money coming from?

Icrul saw the glance and obviously knew what it meant. "My father runs a vast criminal enterprise. We do drugs, prostitution—oh, lots of prostitution—gun-running—"

"Children are meant to be seen, not heard, Icky," Urnak snapped, but using a nickname that revealed his anger was hollow.

Icrul laughed. "Actually, my father owns about a million different patents and makes lots of money off the licensing fees."

"I see," I replied, but that just raised another question. Again, Icrul seemed to almost read my mind. The girl was definitely sharp.

"You're wondering why he's so obsessed with collecting the money those terraformers owe him if he doesn't even really need it."

But Torina spoke up. "I get it. It's the principle of the thing. It's not about the money, it's about the agreement they made with you, and their obligation to uphold it."

Urnak stabbed one of the fingers on his big upper arms at her. "This lady knows the score."

"Those bastards didn't just refuse to pay my father what they owed him. They tried to kill him."

I raised my eyebrows. "Really?"

Urnak nodded, his eyes sizzling with latent anger. "They did, the bastards. They set some mercenary thugs on my trail. Took me forever to shake them. That's part of the reason my old girl, *Nemesis*, even exists. Mercenaries want to come after me? Fine. Oh, and by the way, how do you like my battleship?"

I laughed, and the conversation carried on. It quickly became apparent that Urnak was, indeed, obsessed with righting the wrong that had been done to him, to an almost pathological degree. But he wasn't actually crazy. He was abrasive, yes, but he was also insanely sharp and insightful. His daughter, Icrul, wasn't far behind.

As we talked, it became clear that Urnak would be a powerful ally in any effort to crack open the terraforming scam and, hopefully, the identity-theft operation in the process. The first stirrings of a plan started taking shape in my mind.

"So your old girl, as you call her, the Nemesis? Can she move?" I asked.

Urnak's eyes narrowed. "She can. Why?"

"Because I think I have a chance for you to get your justice—okay, your revenge—and earn some pretty good bonds doing it."

"Don't care about the bonds. Tell me more about the revenge part."

"Well, it starts with you relocating to the Gamma Crucis system."

"That's where you Peacemakers have your base—Anvil Dark, I think it's called?"

"That's right. That'll be our base of operations, too, while we track down the missing Nesit, Erflos Tand, and any more of the poor, chipped bastards along the way. It'll also be our base for prying open the bad guys' operations, starting with your terraforming friends."

"Oh, you want to dig into the terraformers? Well, that part's easy. The person you want is my former partner."

"Your former partner? And who would that be?"

It was Icrul who replied.

"That would be my mother."

It DIDN'T TAKE MUCH to get Urnak to agree to our proposal. And it took him only a few hours to get the *Nemesis* ready to fly.

Which, of course, raised a serious issue.

"Quick question—what are you going to do for a crew?" I asked.

Urnak smiled. "Don't need one. I've rigged the old girl for completely automated flight. Basically, whoever's sitting in the pilot's seat on the bridge can fly her the way you do your *Dragonet*."

And, sure enough, when the time came, the big ship's engines lit, and she burned out of orbit, leaving the blue-green splendor of the lonely gas giant behind.

Icrul begged passage with us, aboard the *Fafnir*. "I've never had a chance to see one of these from the inside, so this is my chance," she explained, and with that, I had a new passenger as we burned hard away into space, chasing the big battlewagon toward our twist to Anvil Dark. In moments, Icrul was bustling around the *Fafnir*, calling up technical specs and chatting with Netty. I gave Perry an uneasy glance.

"Should she have access to the technical manuals for a *Dragonet*?"

"*Now* you ask that, after she's been rooting around in them?"

"If it is a problem, you could have said something, you know."

Perry gave one of his one-winged shrugs. "Actually, there's nothing really special about the *Dragonet* itself. And Netty won't give her access to anything Peacemaker-specific, any weapons schematics or anything like that."

That didn't seem to matter, though. While Netty was configuring the *Fafnir* to twist, Icrul popped her head into the cockpit and handed me a data slate.

"There."

"What am I looking at?"

"Improvements."

I scanned the list. It wasn't anything big but rather a multitude of small things. Her proposed tweaks would increase efficiency one or two percent here, shave off a fraction of a second of time there, and generally offer a host of tiny improvements. But when I got to the bottom and saw the end result, I whistled.

"You can improve the overall efficiency of the *Fafnir* and her systems by fourteen percent? Really?"

"Whatever the numbers say, Mister Peacemaker."

"Netty, what do you think of this?" I asked.

"I think that Icrul, or rather Icky, is absolutely delightful, and I highly recommend you let her get to work."

I looked up from the slate, at Icky. "Wait. You mean you want to make these changes yourself?"

"Who else would do it?"

Scanning the list again, I asked myself the same question. Some of the tweaks were esoteric to the point of meaning almost nothing to me. There was clearly engineering expertise, and then there was the father and daughter combo of Urnak and Icky. One of them had turned a *battleship* into a one-man operation, while the other proposed myriad, miniscule changes no one had thought of previously and came up with an aggregate improvement that even impressed Netty.

I offered a sheepish smile. "Well, we can pay you, but probably not what this is really worth. If you're willing to wait—"

She raised one of her lower hands. "I'm not looking to be paid. I'm happy to do it for—to pay for my passage, I guess. But really, because you're offering to help my father."

"Yeah, but that might all amount to nothing. We might never even get close to those terraformers," Torina said.

"Doesn't matter. The point is that you've given my father some focus for his life. What was going to happen was that he was going to work forever on the *Nemesis,* adding one more system, mounting one more weapon. And then he was going to die and take all of his bitterness and anger to the grave with him, and that would be that." She smiled. "So can I get started?"

I looked around the cockpit, saw no objections, and nodded. "Sure. Go ahead. Just let us know if anything's going to go boom."

"That almost never happens," she replied, turning and heading back towards the *Fafnir*'s engineering bay.

I turned back to the flight controls, then stiffened and looked back.

"What do you mean, *almost* never?"

WE MADE the trip to Anvil Dark uneventfully. I couldn't say the same for our arrival. The sudden appearance of the Nemesis in the system provoked an explosion of comm traffic, with Lunzy finally taking charge. She cleared all of the channels, then came back on ours.

"Van, looks like you found a friend. Care to explain?"

"He's a valuable asset, with a legitimate axe to grind. In short, he got screwed by the very people we want to take down. He's owed money, he's angry, and his solution was to buy a battleship and use it against them. His daughter is a superb engineer, and he owns an array of patents," I said.

"Battleship?" Lunzy asked, eying Urnak with respect.

"Among other tools, but yes."

Lunzy gave Urnak another long, measuring look, then waved at Urnak. "Aside from his skill and anger, is there—"

"Because I think he might be key to breaking open this case—or, rather, these cases. And if the bad guys find out about that—" I began, but Lunzy interrupted.

"They might have decided to pay a visit to him where he was, and do it in force."

"Honestly, he might actually be able to fight them off in that battlewagon. But maybe not. So I figured the best way to protect him was to bring him here," I said.

Lunzy gave a dramatic sigh. "Life sure isn't boring with you around."

"Is that a bad thing?"

"Sometimes, yeah, it is. Anyway, just stand by. I'll clear this with the Keel. Wait here."

Her image vanished.

Torina shifted uncomfortably. "That's a point, Van. The Keel. If one or more of the Masters are compromised and are actually involved in this—"

"Then seeing the Nemesis show up with Urnak on board will not make them happy, I know."

"Oh. And you're okay with that?"

I gave a fierce nod. "Damned right. First of all, it might make someone nervous. It might even make them panic. And when people are nervous, they make mistakes."

"And when they panic, they make even bigger ones," Torina said, nodding.

"Exactly. Plus being parked outside a corrupt Master's

window is probably the safest place for Urnak to be. Could you imagine if the Nemesis was attacked here? At Anvil Dark?" I asked, incredulous.

"Yeah, that'd be a public relations nightmare," Perry said. For a moment, he leveled his amber gaze on me. I sensed he was about to say something, but that the pause was for dramatic effect. Perry's "thoughts" occurred on the scale of nanoseconds. So I wondered if waiting a few seconds before speaking would be like me having a thought and then sitting for a few days.

"You really are your grandfather's grandkid," he finally said.

"How so? The good looks and charm?"

"Hell no. The sneaky, duplicitous way you have of thinking."

I blinked. "Was that a compliment? Because I'm really not sure."

"Why, of course it was, Van. How could you even think otherwise?"

7

THE *NEMESIS* WAS GIVEN a parking orbit that would keep it at least a million klicks from Anvil Dark. That was unnecessarily far, and was probably intended to send us the message that it, and Urnak, weren't really welcome here. But that was fine. In fact, it was a good thing. It was petty, which meant we'd gotten under someone's skin. Now we just had to figure out whose.

In the meantime, we returned to the *Nemesis* and dug into the whole terraforming operation in a lot more detail, all of which Urnak was happy to provide.

"This consortium is really just a gang of thieves. They got their wealth from any and all illegal means. Name it, and they used it. The Gliese 1 terraforming project was more of an elaborate way of laundering money, while avoiding taxes," he said.

"Well, we nailed the second part," Torina noted.

But I gave Urnak a hard look. "Did you know this for sure? That it was all being financed with dirty money?"

"For sure? As in, could it prove it in court? No. They were way too cunning for that." He scowled. "Maybe early in the project I could have grabbed proof. But I was stupid and naïve and just tried to stupidly do my actual job—put together an effective terraforming op, like I'd been retained to."

"But you suspected it."

"Very much so."

"So if you suspected it was a racket, why did you continue with it?"

Urnak smiled thinly. "Because I didn't give a shit. I just wanted to do the engineering. And if you think that makes me an accessory to it, well, the line forms behind me on that. If I could go back and do it differently…"

He trailed off into a shrug.

I nodded, appreciating his honesty.

"What about the whole identity-theft, chip-slavery thing? Did you ever suspect that?" Torina asked.

Urnak shook his head. "I like to think that was a line even stupid younger me wouldn't have crossed. But that doesn't surprise me. Scumbag behavior has a way of attracting more scumbag behavior to itself."

I gave a grim chuckle. "Tell me about it," I said, then went on to describe how we'd crossed swords with the Salt Thieves, the Stillness, the Arc of Vengeance, and the mercenary company led by the mysterious Pevensey.

"And you've done all that in just a few months?" Urnak shook his head. "I think there are still a few criminal organizations out there that don't hate you yet, so you'd better be on your way."

"I'm quite happy to deal with the ones I've already pissed off, thanks."

Urnak gave a tired nod. "Yeah, not that it matters anyway. The names might change, and they might be found in different places, but when it comes to being criminal assholes, they're all the same."

I opened my mouth, but my comm cut me off. It was Netty.

"Van, you should get back to the *Fafnir*."

I sat up. "Okay. Why?"

"Best if you see this in person."

I sighed as I stood. "Ah, yes, the old, *you'd better come take a look at this* cliché". I offered Urnak an apologetic shrug. "Duty calls."

He returned a sage nod. "As it always eventually does."

ICKY SHOWED me an image on a data slate. It depicted a small device located between the *Fafnir*'s inner hull and outer, armored hull.

"What is it?"

"No idea. If I had to guess, some sort of tracking device."

"Yeah, we found one of those attached to the *Fafnir* after we left Crossroads. I had to go outside to get it."

"Which was a lot of fun to watch," Perry said.

I glanced at him with a poisonous smile. "Why don't you go find Bucky and play? You might make a new friend."

"And why don't you go—"

"A tracking device," Torina said. "Do we know how long it's been there?"

"It had to have been installed after our first armor upgrade because we would have seen it when swapping out the outer hull plate. I've gone back through all the logs and have pretty much narrowed it down to our last visit to Spindrift," Netty said.

"And what is it tracking? What sort of information is transmitted?" I asked.

Icky shrugged. "Right now, it doesn't seem to be transmitting anything."

"Maybe it's just a passive recorder and someone's planning on eventually retrieving it," Torina suggested.

"I don't think so. It clearly has a comm unit built into it. But it would be constrained to sub-light transmission, so it probably deactivates itself when it knows it's somewhere it's not likely to be talking to anyone—like here, at Anvil Dark," Netty replied.

"Okay, can we configure it to send out *misinformation*?"

Perry bobbed his head. "Leave it to me, boss. You decide what you want it to say, and we'll make sure it says it."

"So now we just have to get it out of there," I said, grimacing at the thought of disassembling a chunk of the *Fafnir*'s hull.

But Icky just grinned. "Leave that to me. I've developed a few tricks over the years to get at things in tight places." She turned away, then stopped and turned back. "Oh, if that sounded kinda dirty—it was meant to."

I laughed and shook my head. I liked this girl, I really did.

WHEN I MET WITH URNAK, the mood was somber. I had to broach the touchy subject of his wife. The woman had apparently not only broken his heart, but she'd also robbed him blind and had likely been complicit in attempts to kill him—betrayal in the most epic way possible. It was no wonder he'd taken it all so personally, to the point of obsession.

"So, Urnak, I need to know more about this consortium that hired you to design and build that terraforming operation. And that means I also need to ask you about—"

"My wife, Axicur."

Everyone present in Urnak's "living room" aboard the *Nemesis* shifted a little uncomfortably. I couldn't resist a glance at Icky's face, but aside from maybe having hardened a little, it didn't change much. Which made sense, I guess. Her mother had done what she'd done while Icky was still a toddler, essentially. She probably had no real memories of the woman. More than that, whatever she did know about her mother had been filtered through a lifetime of her father's pain.

And speaking of Urnak and his pain, I braced myself for a passionate reaction, anger or misery or something similar. But he just crossed both pairs of arms and looked at me as I nodded.

"Well, she loves money more than her own child. More than me. And more than her own soul, I think."

I raised a mental eyebrow at Urnak's mention of a soul because it made me realize that was a whole aspect of interstellar culture I'd barely brushed against. How many religions were there across known space? What did they all believe? It was something I'd have to get at least passingly familiar with if I was going to be making this Peacemaker gig my career, but not today. Today, I was more interested in sin—specifically, greed.

"She doesn't sound much different from many humans I've unfortunately known."

"Oh, greed is far from being owned by humans, a fact I'm sure you've come to know as a Peacemaker. Even when Icky was still creche-bound, Axicur was never—" He paused, and I realized he was playing memories in his mind. I just waited.

"She was always cold. Always looking past us when she spoke," he finally said.

"So, if you don't mind me asking, why did you marry her?" Torina asked.

"Because I loved her. Not sure why, but I did, from the time I first met her. I was getting close to completing my graduation and inductance into the Engineering Caste, and she was doing the same in the Commercial Caste. And, if I'm honest, for those first few years, she was actually a wonderful mate."

He shrugged. "But I guess she'd had greed bubbling away deep inside her, and it just couldn't be contained. And, well, you know the rest of the story. We went into the terraforming job not just as husband and wife, but as a commercial partnership. Once the bonds started piling up, she—she *changed*. That greed was finally released, and it totally consumed her."

Silence toppled off the end of his words, threatening to become truly awkward. But I really didn't need to know anything more about his relationship with Axicur, so I pushed on to matters that were both more practical and more pressing.

"So what are we going to find if we pry apart the secrets of that planet? We're already looking for thousands, if not tens of thousands of stolen beings."

"Oh, I have no doubt at all that you'll find the two are related. There might be wealth that spans star systems, and greed to match, but it still takes work. You'll inevitably find needs that are every bit as monstrous as the desire for power and wealth that drives them. Money doesn't corrupt by itself, but put it together with a long life, a lack of justice, and a general contempt for others, and you've got the schematic for the most horrible things one being can do to another."

I knew that Urnak was still talking about his wife, as much as he was about all of the other avaricious assholes behind all this.

But I couldn't help noticing Torina looking at me, and I knew what she was thinking. Was Urnak just pontificating, or did he actually know something about this? Had he been aware of the identity theft operation? I'd previously assumed he hadn't, but if he had—

I really did *not* want to arrest this man.

I leaned forward. "Urnak, did you know—"

"No. Of course not. I've already told you I didn't," he snapped.

Okay, time to back away from that particular idea. But Icky spoke up.

"Father kept a close eye on the terraformers. Closer than they'd ever think. And when I got old enough, I helped. So yes, we eventually started to realize that something *evil* was going on. Something that was much, much worse than greed."

"Greed that also inflicts pain," Urnak said, nodding.

"So why didn't you tell anyone about what you knew, or at least what you suspected? Why didn't you inform the Peacemakers?"

"We did."

Stunned silence followed. I exchanged a wide-eyed look with Torina. Even Perry perked up, lifting his wings slightly.

"You did? When?"

"It must have been almost ten years ago now. We didn't have what you could call hard evidence, but there was a lot of circumstantial stuff. We handed it all over to a Peacemaker and assumed that they'd take the case from there. And having heard nothing until now, ten years later, I assumed it had just either hit a dead end or gotten buried for some reason."

I leaned even closer. "Do you remember the name of the Peacemaker you told about this?"

I tensed so much my toes pressed into the soles of boots hard enough to hurt.

Please—not Gramps.

Urnak nodded. "His name was Groshenko."

I SLUMPED BACK. So did Torina. Perry slowly lowered his wings back into place. None of us said anything.

Urnak and Icky picked up on our reactions immediately.

"You know this man, don't you?"

"He's one of the Peacemaker Guild's seven Masters," I replied.

Urnak stared back at me for a moment before finally nodding, slowly, and only once.

"I see."

I glanced at Torina, who shared my same rueful expression.

What a *mess*.

"I'm thinking that you need to start watching where we step *very* carefully, Peacemaker Van Tudor," Urnak said.

"No shit."

"If it helps, there's always a place for you on the *Nemesis*."

I offered an appreciative smile but saw immediately that Urnak was offering more than just refuge. If we needed the power of the big old battlewagon, we could have it. Which was good, because I was pretty sure we were eventually going to need it.

But Icky brought us back to the immediate problem. Or, at least, the most immediate one we could actually work on solving.

"Just like we told Groshenko, not all of those stolen people are in slave units, scrubbing the domes clean. Father and I got glimpses of what else they're doing with them. Some live on in the bodies of criminals, but only the important parts. And by parts, I mean mind *and* body. We're pretty sure they harvest some of their victims for their organs—"

"But they also have a way of disassembling their minds, too," Urnak said. "No idea how, but it seems that they can extract skills and memories from people and then implant them, if that's the right word, in other people. It can apparently give them new skills, abilities, let them know things they otherwise couldn't know—"

I swore viciously under my breath, slamming a fist into my open palm.

I felt Torina staring at me. "Van? What is it?"

The room was still, but charged with my sudden anger. I felt my chest rising and falling, each breath draining away a spike of rage, triggered by a single word—

"Crossroads. The Peacemaker memory implants Gus and Gabriella injected into me. *Where did they come from?*"

I wheeled on Perry, who recoiled back a bit. "Van, listen. Those *memories* are artificial. They're generated by an AI, synthesized from huge studies of best practices. You didn't get the memories of one spaceship pilot. You got memories manufactured from studying hundreds, maybe thousands of pilots, and they were all distilled down into what was injected into you," he said.

"You sure about that?"

Perry opened his beak but paused and finally shook his head. "*Sure* of it? No. I've never been involved in any of that. It's just… how I understand it works."

I slumped back into my seat. "I don't know if I want to know the truth."

But Urnak snorted.

"I thought you were tougher than this, Van."

I glared at him. "Pardon?"

"Let's assume some or all of those memories the Peacemakers

gave you were stolen. Fine. So you're going to honor the poor wretches they were stolen from by, what? Giving up?"

"Father's right. If you just give up, then anyone whose memories might have been stolen will have just died in vain. This way, they didn't. Their deaths will mean at least *something*," Icky said.

Torina put her hand on my arm. "Look at this way, Van. If that's what happened, if some of those memories you were given were stolen from people, then they can help you find justice for it."

"Good point. Not too many people get a chance to help solve their own murders," Perry put in.

I looked around the room. "You guys should go into business as motivational speakers. You're all pretty damned good at it."

"Especially the bird," Perry replied. "If this doesn't work out, I'm selling timeshares in Alabama. Got a standing offer from a guy who still uses a *lot* of hair gel."

Chuckles rattled around the room, scattering the growing tension like so much smoke. I still had a lingering horror at the possibility I had stolen memories lingering in my brain. My concern grew deeper as I thought about the ranks of Peacemakers knowing about such vicious practices—but Perry clearly hadn't, and when I thought back to Gabriella and Gus, I didn't think they would have, either.

That alone stilled my rising worry.

But Groshenko? Gramps' best friend? We were already suspecting Master Yotov, but could the cancer of corruption have spread among the Masters? And if it had, how far and wide had it insidiously inserted itself in the Peacemaker Guild as a whole?

Thirteen hundred years was a long time for an organization to exist. Hell, back on Earth, most governments only managed a tiny fraction of that before the various scandals and outrages started to pop up.

"Actually, those who just get dismembered, mind and body, might be the fortunate ones," Icky said.

I looked at her, my face flushing anew with anger. There was something *worse?*

"What do you mean?" I asked.

"Father and I caught hints—"

"Just hints, mind you. Nothing firm," Urnak interrupted.

"Hints that some people might end up alive but used for... other things. If they didn't have usable organs, then after they were stripped of whatever memories these bastards wanted, they were tossed into nutrient tanks, becoming slurry, fertilizer to feed the crops in the domes." She released a long sigh. "Talk about a death so vile, so pointless—"

She stopped and looked at me. "I think it's going to take people like the Peacemakers to make it right. And by that, I mean Peacemakers like you, Van."

I sat back, feeling despair lapping around my boots as our task came into focus. This wasn't a simple job for a few bonds. This was... war. Sort of. "These crimes are linked somehow. There's something much bigger at play here. It's like we've started putting together a jigsaw puzzle, and we're beginning to get the first idea of what its showing us, but we have a long way to go yet—"

I stopped and glanced around at blank looks. "Let me guess. Nobody here knows what jigsaw puzzles are."

"I do," Perry said.

"Yeah, well, someone keeps telling me the bird is really smart."

"Someone's right."

I looked at the others and shook my head. "Doesn't matter. There's a picture, but we're only seeing little bits of it. All of which means our life's work just got... bigger."

I let my head loll back for a moment and closed my eyes. I suddenly felt overwhelmed, like I had the first time I pushed myself out of the *Fafnir*'s airlock and stared into infinity all around me.

Okay. Enough of that. One thing the army had taught me, and coding had reinforced, was that the way to handle big problems was to break them into little problems and solve them one at a time. So I gritted mental teeth and made myself focus on what we needed to do next.

"Tell me one thing. Where can we find Axicur?" I finally asked.

Icky looked at her father, but he seemed lost in thought—or memories.

She finally turned to me and answered. "We don't know where *she* is, but her banker is on Spindrift."

I nodded and stood.

"Okay. It's a start. Next stop, Spindrift."

8

I FLUNG the *Fafnir* through the hardest turn I could manage, Netty controlling the thrust, while Torina targeted the attacking ships. We held off on firing missiles—they were expensive after all—and used only laser and rail gun fire. But our attackers were proving nimble and elusive targets.

The *Fafnir* lurched under a hit. I glanced at the damage control display, but everything was still green, aside from one of the applique armor plates, which had absorbed something.

"Perry, any idea who these assholes are yet?"

"Pirates, I'd imagine."

"As usual, thank you for the illuminating details. I was thinking more along the lines of, *which* pirates. Are they anyone we know?" I asked because of something Torina had said as we were about to twist to Spindrift—a warning that getting too close to the truth might be hazardous to our health. Her words echoed as we twisted, then emerged in the searing glare of the Sirius system.

And then we got jumped.

Two ships, each ranked by Netty as level five or six. They'd been lurking among some asteroids we needed to navigate, and had seen us as a target of opportunity.

Or were we? Were they actually waiting for us?

But Perry quickly dispelled that idea. "As near as I can tell, matching their power signatures to our database, they're just freelancers. There just aren't any ships with those signatures that match anything we know about."

"On top of which, if the bad guys were going to send someone after us, I think they'd—" Torina said, then paused, lining up a shot and triggering the rail gun.

A moment passed, then a searing flash marked a hit as the rail gun slug's kinetic energy instantly turned to impact and heat.

"Got you, you bastard," Torina mumbled around a ferocious grin.

The stricken pirate started spinning, trailing vapor. If they didn't regain control, then in about thirty seconds they were going to smack square into one of the asteroids they'd been using for cover. Torina was unconcerned.

And so was I.

"Anyway, if the bad guys wanted us dead, I think they'd have sent more than two little ships."

"Good point," I said, then spied an opening. The pirate had slammed into a hard turn, its drive burning fiercely. One of my implanted memories moved my hands by instinct, executing a nifty combination of roll and turn, flipping us upside down and momentarily motionless relative to the other ship. It was the perfect setup for a shot, and Torina didn't waste it. She triggered both lasers and rail gun and hammered the pirate into a slowly dispersing cloud of wreckage.

"Good flying," she said, shooting me a grin.

"Thanks," I replied but took a moment to think that, if that memory of that maneuver had been stolen, then the one who should be thanked was whoever it came from.

I definitely had to get that resolved, one way or another. Otherwise, it might distract me at the worst possible moment. For now, I mastered the memory—and source—and stilled my breathing with a will.

"Where's our other friend?" I asked, looking at the tactical display. I spun the *Fafnir* so we pointed that direction, and saw the second pirate just seconds away from impact on the asteroid. They weren't going to hit especially hard, but it would be hard enough to smash them to debris.

"Sucks to be you," I said, and there was nothing cheery in my tone.

Out of morbid curiosity, I watched the impact. The pirate ship spun into the surface and—

Didn't shatter into fragments that rebounded back into space. Instead, it just kind of *stopped*.

"Uh—is that supposed to happen?" I asked.

"Sure, if that asteroid is made of marshmallow," Netty said.

I saw Torina mouth the word *marshmallow* and smiled, making a mental note to add it to the lengthy list of things I needed her to try.

"Okay, assuming that isn't marshmallow and it's actually a rock, what else could do that?" I asked.

Perry shrugged his wings.

Netty was just as mystified. "No idea, Van. Asteroids aren't supposed to be soft and squishy," she said.

"Gang, we have a genuine mystery. And I think Spindrift can wait a bit."

I WASN'T sure what to expect when we grounded on the asteroid. I'd kind of assumed some interesting natural phenomenon, a geological oddity that just happened to be the impact point of the pirate ship. What I certainly hadn't expected was finding the wrecked pirate ship embedded in ice, apparently formed when they'd struck a massive bladder full of water.

And I *really* hadn't expected to find a fistfight going on.

Torina, Perry, and I piled out of the *Fafnir*, keeping our weapons ready. The asteroid was big enough to offer a little gravity, but not much. We did the scooting, shuffling gait that offered the best locomotion in such a low-g state, making our way toward a scuffle. Three suited figures were being beaten on by a half-dozen more, while another half-dozen looked on. Beyond them, I saw a blast door set into the face of a rocky cliff.

This airless rock was *inhabited*.

Two of the figures watching the tussle turned and loped

toward us. Both were humanoid, but we got close enough to see through their visors and I could see that they weren't human. The faces peering back were chubby, jowly, and the color of pea soup.

"So—who the hell are *you?*" one of them asked.

"Uh, Van Tudor, Peacemaker—"

"Oh, shit!"

They both turned and ran. One fell and immediately bounced, which sent him sailing at least ten meters up. The other managed to keep his feet but ended up zigzagging erratically in whatever direction each bound left him facing.

I looked at Torina. She looked back.

"This looks fun," I said, and we continued toward—

Whatever the hell this was.

I STARED. "A DISTILLERY? HERE?"

The chubby, yellowish face nodded. He'd introduced himself as Fizz. He was the leader of this weird, asteroid-bound little commune, which existed to operate a still.

On an asteroid orbiting Sirius.

"It's a private op-operation." He gave me a goofy grin. "We're just a small group of folks who... who want to be left alone."

"Are you drunk?"

"How d-dare you! Implisicating that I'm drinking—er, drunking. No, wait. Drinking alcohol." He frowned. "Or is it drunking."

"Actually, I kind of like *drunking*," Torina said, grinning.

Fizz turned his bleary gaze on her. "So do I!"

"I meant the word, *drunking*."

"What about it?"

She chuckled and shook her head. "Never mind."

Perry came on the comm. "Van, I've placed these guys. They're Arbosians, a race from Eridani."

"What the hell are they doing here?"

"Making booze, it appears." Perry then added, "A *lot* of booze."

"Yeah, I know that. But, why?"

"So they can spend their time drunking, I guess."

"Ossifer—officer. You aren't going to shut us… down, are you? We can pay!" Fizz started patting himself down. "You can pay us—no, wait. *We* can pay *you* the fine."

He suddenly laughed. "You pay me a fine. Wouldn't that be… be nice."

"Perry, are they breaking any laws?" I asked.

"Well, they're avoiding *somebody's* taxes and excise charges. But other than that, no. These asteroids are considered open territory, probably to encourage mining development."

"Which is fine, except these asteroids are entirely devoid of anything interesting. Well, except for all the drunking going on," Netty said.

"I am going to be hearing that word forever, aren't I?"

"Oh, I'd say you can count on that, Van," Perry said.

I turned back to Fizz, who'd been muttering and digging through pouches on his suit the whole time.

"Fizz—"

"I'm broke. I hafta—have to go get you some money—"

"Fizz, no, you don't. There's no fine. I'm just wondering, well, why? Why are you here? On this rock? Making hooch?"

"Hooch? Who's that?"

"It's a name from Earth for, you know, booze. Rotgut. Moonshine."

"Moon—oh, moonshine. I like that!"

I laughed, then looked past him. The three pirates had been sitting at the base of the cliff, just outside the blast door. I gestured for Torina and Perry to follow me and walked toward them.

"Well, hello there, people who just recently tried to kill me. I'm Van Tudor, a Peacemaker. And guess what you are? That's right! Under arrest." I took a small bow, then waved grandly. There are moments that I truly enjoyed being a Peacemaker. This was one of them.

Despite their beating, the three looked to have only minor injuries. One was human, a scruffy character with a face scarred as though by fire. The other two were, unsurprisingly, Yonnox. Leave it to them to be involved when something shady was happening.

"Fine. Arrest us and take us away from these assholes before they try beating us up again. With their fists. Us in these suits. It was more annoying than anything else."

Fizz reappeared beside me. "We want repar-repa-preparations! That was all our water! We'll be dry in… in just a few weeks!"

I glanced back at the chaotic, impromptu ice-sculpture that embraced the wrecked pirate ship. "They're storing water on the surface? Why didn't it just freeze solid?"

"That bladder they were using was heavily insulated and heated. I guess they don't have room to store it inside," Perry said.

"Whatever works, I guess." In a way, I admired their ingenuity.

"Van, Netty did a query and found out an interesting little fact about the Arbosians that might help explain why they're here. The reason they have that yellow-green thing going on is because they're always on the cusp of alcohol poisoning."

"Wait a minute—you mean they're dying?"

Perry shook his head. "Not at all. They can metabolize alcohol, but they can also *store* it. It just keeps accumulating in their system, making them more and more inebriated. They eventually get to the point they're sweating and urinating what amounts to pure ethanol, one step ahead of their organs being utterly pickled."

"Without killing them?"

"Yep. They can do as much drunking as they want, get severe alcohol poisoning, and just carry on. They don't even get hungover. If they stop drinking, their body's alcohol content slowly drops as they burn through their reserve tank, if you will, and that's pretty much it."

"So these miserable fools can get as drunk as they want, for as long as they want, with absolutely no ill effects?" Torina asked. "Other than the, um… skin the color of a dead toad, that is."

"Sounds pretty appealing, doesn't it?" I asked, my eyes misting over with the possibility of never knowing the exquisite self-hatred and near-death experience of a true five-alarm hangover. The kind where you cry on your steering wheel on the way to get french fries only to realize you're not wearing shoes.

That kind of hangover.

I thought about my college years, when I could get utterly shitfaced, sleep it off after some greasy food and a two hour nap, and still show up for work in the morning. Granted, my breath could jumpstart a nuclear reactor, but still—I was more or less in one piece the next day, an ability that faded a bit with each passing year.

That was appealing, but it was also a blueprint for getting absolutely nothing accomplished, so I was unsure if I should envy these Arbosians or feel sorry for them. Maybe some of both would be appropriate.

Something smacked my arm, then went "WOAH!" over the comm. It was Fizz. I braced my feet and caught him in mid-spin, then eased him back down to the surface.

He gave me a boozy leer. "So who's gonna fi-fix our still? And get that damned crashed... crashed ship outta here?" He followed this with the kind of belch that a doctor would call *rich and productive*, and once again I thanked the stars we were in separate envirosuits.

Sometimes, technology is magical.

I put a hand on Fizz's shoulder. "Fizz, I'll tell you what. There are probably some usable components on that crashed ship.

Those, plus the scrap value for the rest, should set you up with some pretty good money."

Fizz blinked at me for a minute, then grinned. "Hey, everyone, he says we... we should start grabbing ships and... and selling 'em for scrap!"

Ragged cheering erupted over the comm.

"No, Fizz, that's not what I said at all." I pointed at the crashed wreck. "That ship. That one in particular. You can sell it for money. But that's it. No other ships, okay?"

I heard Torina chuckling over the comm and shot her a poisonous glance.

Fizz gaped, then nodded. "Hang on. He's says we can't... can't do that."

This time, a chorus of disappointment rang out.

"But we can still... still sell this one!"

Cheers again.

It took a while, mainly because our translators weren't very good at interpreting drunk, but we eventually worked out what was going to happen. We'd take the three pirates to Spindrift and hand them over to the authorities there.

"Which means they'll be *released on their own recognizance* the instant we step out of sight," Perry said.

I shrugged. "Three riffraff pirates ain't the hill I want to die on, Perry."

We'd also contact a bonded salvager to come and pay the Arbosians what they had coming to them for the wreck. Finally, I told them I'd arrange for them to get a replacement thermal bladder for their water supply.

"Wha-what about the water? It's all gone!"

I put a companionable hand on Fizz's shoulder. "Fizz, my friend, I am not here to solve all your problems."

He peered at me, frowning. "So we getting the water or not?"

I slapped his shoulder a couple of times, then made my way to the three pirates.

"So, boys and girls, you're coming with me to Spindrift. And you're going to be very, very good about it, or—"

"Or we'll bring you right back here," Torina said.

"We'll behave, believe me," the apparent leader of the three said. The others just nodded.

They stood and shuffled along with us toward the *Fafnir*, giving their wrecked ship some rueful glances as they walked by.

While Perry and Torina got them bundled aboard for the trip to Spindrift, I found Fizz standing among a group of his fellow Arbosians, arguing about—something. I wasn't sure what and had no desire to get involved in a debate with a bunch of pickled aliens.

"Fizz, we're leaving now. You'll see that salvage ship sometime in the next couple of days. Meantime, you guys take care out here."

He turned, blinked at me, then grinned. "Did you see... see that Peacemaker that was just here? May-maybe you know him!"

I nodded gravely. "I do. I'll tell him you said hello." But Fizz was already starting another argument with his crew about who was... taller. Or something.

I waved my goodbyes to the squabbling aliens, then returned to the *Fafnir*. As I clambered aboard, I was shaking my head.

"So, we've had space hippies. Space pirates. And space gangsters—lots of those. And now, space hillbillies."

"I think the term Space Rednecks is slightly less offensive," Perry said gravely.

"I'll make a note of it. What's the difference between the two?"

Perry's eyes flashed with mischief. "Rednecks drive bigger trucks."

9

"Technically, The Quiet Room is the only official bank in known space. They set the value of the bond, and the exchange rates of all other currencies against it." Torina gave me a shrug. "Keeps things tidy."

"By which she means space would be commercial chaos otherwise," Perry said.

I peered around the corner of the bulkhead. "So, like Earth, you mean."

"Oh no, not that bad. I hope."

We staked out the bank where, to the best of Urnak's knowledge, his wife still did business. I was surprised to find it wasn't part of The Quiet Room, which had prompted Torina's explanation. It seemed that there were lots of banks across known space, some well-established, noble, and trustworthy institutions, and others not that at all. They essentially functioned as repositories for bonds so that everyone in the galaxy wasn't loaded with cash all the time. Most of them also reinvested their depositors' funds and paid out part of the interest to those depositors as a return on investment. And that was great, as long as the next time you visited your bank, you didn't find it was just empty compartments, a few scattered papers, and no forwarding address.

This bank, the Spindrift Commercial Investment Trust Depository and Savings Reserve, was somewhere between *time-honored institution* and *scruffy guy with a box full of cash*. I couldn't get past the name, though.

"Spindrift Commercial Investment Trust Depository and Savings Reserve? Were there any synonyms for *bank* that they didn't use?"

"Coffer, countinghouse, credit union, exchequer, fund, hoard, repository—"

"Perry. Seriously."

"Why ask the question if you don't want the answer?"

I glanced around the corner again. Still no sign of our guy, yet another of our Yonnox friends, named Klelos. Urnak had been pretty sure that his wife, Axicur, still used Klelos to handle most of her finances. Or she had up until at least four years ago, which was the last time he'd managed to get any up-to-date information. Still, this was our best lead. If Klelos didn't still count Axicur as a client, then he could, we hoped, at least point us in the right direction.

"Have to admit, *Commercial Investment Trust Depository and Savings Reserve* sounds a hell of lot more—I don't know, *financial* than The Quiet Room."

"This place is trying hard to make sure everyone knows it's a bank. The Quiet Room doesn't have to," Torina replied.

"Ah. Well, I suppose—"

A pudgy Yonnox appeared, one who reasonably matched the description of Klelos, as Urnak recalled him anyway, right down to a brightly colored Mohawk. He exited the Spindrift Commercial Investment Trust Depository and Savings Reserve, then locked it up and walked away.

"That's our boy. Come on."

We set off in a low-speed pursuit, Klelos taking his time as he ambled through the concourses and corridors of Spindrift, us following. I kept apart from Torina and Perry as we did. Technically, any number of people could have a combat AI, often for personal protection, so it wasn't just Peacemakers. But, while not everyone who carried a gun was a cop, when you saw someone packing one, the possibility would at least occur to you. This way, Torina could legitimately say she was *not* a Peacemaker and that Perry was just her bodyguard.

Klelos stopped and talked to a few people along the way, including one of the Cloaks, the breathtakingly corrupt Spindrift security force, and a couple of other sketchy characters, one of whom was an actual human wearing jeans and sneakers that looked rather Earthly. I'd have liked to have been able to overhear a few of these conversations. But we were following this guy for a specific reason, so I stuck to the plan.

We carried on, entering the most affluent part of Spindrift, a gated section called Rapture. I thought it sounded a little more apocalyptic than necessary, but whatever, I didn't have to live there. What I did have to do, though, was get inside, which meant passing through a heavy blast door. Klelos unsealed it by touching a plate mounted into the bulkhead beside the big door and sliding smoothly aside, then closing it behind him again.

But we were ready for this, too. I touched my comm.

"Torina, you're on."

She strode past, Perry hopping along with her, *ting-ting-ting* against the deck. She touched a comm panel and had a brief conversation with someone. Then she stepped back, and the door rolled open.

I hurried to catch up to her, my badass duster coat flapping dramatically as I strode along. Snippets of Ennio Morricone spaghetti western music played in my head as I did. Wearing the thing had given me a passion for the genre, so much so I'd uploaded all of Sergio Leone's movies to the *Fafnir* and watched them in my spare time. I absolutely did *not* sometimes stand in front of the mirror in my cabin, sporting my duster coat, holding a pen in my mouth like a cigarillo, and squinting back at myself.

I did not because I have dignity. Sort of.

The atmosphere on the other side of the blast door was very different from the rest of Spindrift. And by that, I mean the atmosphere was literally different. It didn't carry the faint but pervasive and perpetual stink of electronics, lubricants, mingled odors of food, and various species' versions of sweat the way the rest of the place did. The air here was far cleaner and fresher, smelling of nothing at all.

"Rapture has its own entirely separate life support system,"

Torina explained. "The rest of Spindrift could decompress, and they'd be fine in here."

"It's rumored that Rapture can actually be detached from Spindrift in an emergency and move itself off to a safe distance," Perry put in.

I glanced at them both as we strode along a brightly lit corridor lined with potted flowering plants. "Really?"

"The life support thing, yes. The ability to detach wouldn't surprise me a bit," Torina replied.

"By the way, who exactly is this person you know that lives here?" I asked.

"An old friend of my mother's. By the way, when we're done with our Yonnox banker friend, we have to stop by for tea."

"Tea? Really?"

"Yes, tea. Oh, and by the way, you're my husband."

I stopped. "What?"

Torina laughed. "I'll just assume that stunned look on your face is one of great joy."

"You do that." I blinked at her. "We have to pretend we're married?"

"Just for a little while."

"In that case, we need to practice, as I take my role seriously." I stopped, closed my eyes, and pursed my lips with all the romance of an English governess.

Something hard and cold touched my lips. I opened my eyes, then pulled back.

"Be gentle, I'm new to this," Perry said, perched on Torina's arm. "You handsome devil."

"Sorry, Perry, you're not my type. I prefer my significant others to be a lot less metallic."

He dropped back to the carpet lining the corridor with a soft thud. "Ah, well, it is better to have loved and lost…"

We continued through Rapture and stopped at a corner around which we'd seen Klelos turn. Rapture was far less busy than the rest of Spindrift, so we'd had to fall back a long way. This time, though, we didn't see him. Moreover, this side of the corridor was a dead end, with two doors each left and right. One of them had a pair of bodyguards standing outside.

We pulled back a short distance to confer.

"Urnak said he's quite paranoid, so I'm assuming his apartment is the one with the—what the hell are those, anyway? They look like crash-test dummies," I said.

"They're synthetics, security model. Humanoid form, cheap AI with limited cognition. They're good at standing around and fighting, and that's about it," Perry replied.

"How good are they at the fighting part?"

"Very."

"Shit."

"I do have an idea, though, Van. Your grandfather acquired an, um, piece of software uploaded in me that might, hypothetically, be used to break into a security synth's operating system and take temporary control. In theory."

"Wait. On top of everything else, Gramps was a *hacker?*"

"Oh, no, no, no, no. Not even a little. I was *his* hacker."

"So you can hack into those two synth things and take command of them?"

"Hypothetically, could—"

"Perry!"

"Yes."

"Okay. Do it. Shut them down."

Perry's eyes glowed. "They should have an access channel for things like software updates, routing maintenance, that sort of—ah. Yup, there it is. One moment please while the bird does his thing."

While we waited, a blowsy woman, who resembled Fizz and the other Arbosians, strolled past, walking a—thing. If this had been Earth, it would have been a yippy little dog, a miniature poodle or Pomeranian or something similar. This was a pale, pinkish slug as long as my forearm that slithered along the carpet in a vaguely obscene motion. With a leash.

She gave us a suspicious look as we passed.

"Afternoon, ma'am," I said.

She said nothing, just turned up her nose and carried on, her designer gastropede squelching alongside her.

I glanced at Torina. "That sound you hear is my skin crawling."

"Because of the… the sticky creature?"

"No, because escargot isn't meant to be pink. Or weigh ten pounds."

"Humans eat slugs?" Torina asked in horror.

"Only if they used to live in a shell. Like a house, but on their backs. Oh, and we like them with garlic and butter."

She considered that, then gave a slow nod. "I'd eat *Perry* if he was in garlic and butter."

"Done," Perry said. "Our synth friends are now in safe mode, and no, you will not prepare me in any manner whatsoever, although I commend your tendency to favor French peasant cooking."

"I don't know if peasants eat snails, but I know—hey, the android on the left just frowned. Or, rather, its face went slack," I noted.

"It's safe to approach them," Perry reported, then spread one wing experimentally. "Dad, will you let the mean aliens eat me if there's butter?"

"Enough sass outta you, bird. Let's go," I murmured.

Torina snickered and we moved as one.

We rounded the corner and headed directly toward the synths. I kept a hand on The Drop, my nasty little shotgun, and got ready to draw it if Perry's safe mode turned out not to be. But the two synths just stood, still as statues, as we approached. Perry leapt up with a flap of wings and landed on the head of one of them.

"May I have your attention? These security bots are now glorified doorstops." He lowered his head in front of the synth's face, until he was looking right into it, upside down. "How's it feel, bud, to be beaten by a space chicken?"

"You're too hard on yourself, Perry. You're a space turkey, at least," I said, reaching for the door chime. I was tempted to switch my hand to the Moonsword, but there was nothing non-lethal about it, and I didn't want to kill this guy if he put up a fuss. I drew The Drop instead, ensuring the underslung energy gun was calibrated to stun a Yonnox. Torina stood back, ready to back me up.

Perry, still atop the synth's head, turned his golden gaze on me. "Space turkey, huh? Well, I consider that an honor, given Benjamin Franklin's respect for that esteemed species."

"Benjamin Franklin? Friend of yours?" Torina asked.

"Only when he's in my wallet," I replied, touching the chime.

Despite our banter, I could tell that Perry and Torina were both on knife-edge readiness. I braced myself as well.

The door slid open. I found myself facing Klelos, who was holding a huge gun pointed directly at my face.

Staring down what seemed to be a manhole-sized muzzle, I had a single thought. *This is it.*

Something flashed in front of me, blocking my view of Klelos. A tremendous bang, like a grenade going off, split the air. I saw Perry plunge to the floor and land in a metallic heap.

I aimed The Drop and pumped a stun bolt into Klelos at point-blank range. As he grunted and toppled backward, I hurried to Perry, letting Torina take control of the fallen Yonnox.

"Perry!"

He turned his head slowly and spoke in a hoarse whisper.

"Tell... my wife... I love her."

"You—what? Your *wife?*"

He abruptly perked up. "Didn't it tug at your heartstrings?"

"Uh, no."

"Damn."

"Are you okay?" I asked him.

He clambered to his feet and lifted his left wing. One of the metallic feathers was gone. The ones around it had been twisted, and were misshapen.

"Insofar as I'm no longer a perfect, unblemished example of the best in AI technology, no, I'm not okay. I mean, look at this wing."

I smiled and shook my head. "Perry, sometimes I just—" I stopped, smiled again, and touched his head fondly.

"Thanks, Perry. I owe you one."

"You mean you'd throw yourself in front of a bullet to save me?"

"Of course."

"Van, that's just dumb. Once we get back to the *Fafnir*, I can have this wing fixed in no time. You let me do the jumping in front of bullets, okay? Better me than you."

"Fine. Still—thank you."

He locked his amber gaze on me. "Anytime, Van."

I moved to join Torina. She'd relieved Klelos of his weapon and now had him pinned to the floor. The stun effect was quickly wearing off, judging from the ever-increasing fear tightening the Yonnox's face.

"Please, I don't have much money here! Take whatever you want, but don't—"

"What we want is information," I said. "And since you decided to shoot first and ask questions apparently never, I'm no longer inclined to be gentle about getting it out of you."

"Information? What information?"

"I want to know everything there is to know about a woman named Axicur."

"Never heard of her."

I sighed, long and dramatic. "Okay, let's try it this way." I swept aside my *amazing* duster coat, revealing the Moonblade. At the same time, I flashed my Peacemaker credentials. "How about you answer my question again, only this time with the clear understanding that, if you lie, a. you'll be obstructing justice and b. you'll be pissing off the guy who may or may not be bothered to ask Torina here not to hurt you."

"Oh, please don't tell me not to hurt him, Van," Torina said, grinning like a wolf spying a lame deer.

"That depends on the next words out of Klelos's mouth."

"Fine. Axicur. What about her?"

"I want to know everything about her. Her business dealings, her finances, the last time she was here, where she's likely to be now, all of it."

"It's not like I keep tabs on her—"

"Torina?"

I wasn't sure what she did. To me, it just looked like she'd tapped the side of his neck. But he yowled in pain and blew—

"Is that a snot bubble?" I asked, repulsed by his reaction. "Have some dignity, for the love of—"

"I don't know much! She's just a client! I've got hundreds of them!"

I knelt beside him and pulled out my data slate. "Netty, do you have Icky on the line?"

"Right here, Van."

I turned the screen to face the Yonnox. "Klelos, allow me to introduce Icrul. She's Axicur's daughter. Icrul, this miserable excuse for a sentient being is Klelos, your mother's banker."

"Her daughter?"

"Actually, her *estranged* daughter. So I'm only going to say this once, then I'm going to sign off and let Van, Torina, and Perry do whatever they need to do. My mother is a scheming, manipulative, lying, ruthless bitch. She has devastated my father with her scumbag behavior, and I will never, ever forgive her for that. I'm prepared to hunt her to the ends of known space and beyond, if necessary. Anyone who helps with that is a good guy. Anyone who gets in the way, oh, say, by stonewalling instead of giving us the information we want, is a bad guy. And, once I've found and dealt with my mother, I'll be coming for the bad guys next. I will hunt them to the ends of known space. And guess who's first on the list?"

I pulled out the Moonsword and held it, point down, over Klelos's face. "Ever hear of the Sword of Damocles?"

Klelos shook his head.

"It's the idea that you'll have something hanging over you, something you'll never be free of. Icrul will be a blade, hanging over your head by a thread. You will never know when it's going to—"

I dropped the Moonsword.

Klelos yelped as it slammed into the floor beside his face and stuck there, upright and wobbling slightly.

"Fall."

"Alright, fine! She's not that great a client anyway. Look, she's moved most of her business to other banks. She does that, not sticking with one for too long. All I have left of her business is the key to a PrimeBank. I don't know what she keeps in there. And that's all the truth!"

"Where is this key?" I asked.

"Back at my office, locked up."

"Torina, please allow our friend here to stand so he can take us to his office for a bit of after-hours business."

"Damn. I was hoping he'd keep being uncooperative," she said, absolutely nailing the bad-cop routine.

As he sat up, Perry hopped up beside him and, with his good wing, ruffled the man's Mohawk, whose colors and texture, I noticed, slowly rippled and writhed.

"Cheer up, my friend. I'm the one who got shot here. So if it were up to me, you'd be gasping away your last breaths in an open airlock right now. Small mercies, am I right?"

KLELOS RETRIEVED the key for us, a small, complex device that seemed to combine intricate mechanical operation with electronic security. When he'd handed it over, I stepped aside and gestured for the door.

"Pleasure doing business with you. Oh, do I get a calendar or something for being a new customer?"

"Used to be a toaster. There's no commitment to customer service anymore, you know?" Perry groused.

"Piss off," Klelos snapped, storming back out of the Spindrift Commercial Investment Trust Depository and Savings Reserve.

I looked at Torina. "No toaster, and no thanks. Sad. Like dealing with the cable company."

"They sell things to tie you up, with no thanks?" Torina asked, one brow lifted.

"Actually, yeah. I guess you're getting the hang of American culture just fine."

We parted ways with Klelos and made our way to the Prime-Bank, an apparent cross between a storage unit and a strongbox. There was a whole bank of them on Spindrift, in a large compartment you could only access with a valid PrimeBank key.

"All these secret compartments," I said, gazing as we walked among the ranks of sealed doors. "I wonder how many of them actually have legitimate goods in them."

"Probably most of them. Of course, legitimate is all about context," Torina said. "A work of art is legit. A stolen work of art, not so much."

"Good point."

We found Axicur's unit. I moved to put the key in the slot, but Perry intervened.

"Van, let me do that. You and Torina go that way about ten or fifteen meters."

"What, you think this thing is booby trapped?"

"I think everything's booby trapped, Van."

I put the key in the slot, and a red light turned green. But I didn't operate it. Instead, I turned to Perry.

"I don't want you getting yourself blown up."

He lifted his damaged wing. "Hey, I already have to go to the shop. Might as well make it worthwhile."

I wanted to argue, but Perry's logic, although cold, was sound. Torina and I retreated. When we were clear, Perry moved as far to one side as he could, then operated the key.

The door slid open. An instant later, Perry vanished in a searing flash of light and a thunderclap.

"Perry!"

I ran toward his sprawled form, Torina at my side. We both crouched, heedless of the open door.

"Perry!"

"Tell my wife—"

"Really?"

"Sorry, it's just that your face—so earnest. So trusting. But I'm fine—oops."

He'd moved to stand up. Trouble was, he no longer just had a damaged wing. He'd also lost a leg, and his tail had been scorched and twisted.

He looked ruefully at his missing leg. "I can just buff this out."

Torina picked Perry up, while I investigated the PrimeBank. Sure enough, all I found were the remains of a one-shot plasma charge. Nothing else.

"Klelos betrayed us. Oh no, what a shocking turn of events," I said, stepping back out of the empty PrimeBank.

I touched my comm. "Netty, are you getting a signal from that micro-tracker Perry put in our Yonnox friend's hairdo?"

"I am. He's left his apartment and is moving—hurrying, I might add—toward the docks."

"What a surprise. We're on our way back. We'll be departing as soon as we get there, so we can follow this bastard to wherever he's going."

"You got it, boss," Netty replied.

"Oh, and Perry's going to have to go up on the hoist when he gets back. He's a little worse for the wear."

"Yeah, I'm used to it. Is there more than just his head intact, this time?"

I looked at Perry. "You've been reduced to just your head?"

He shrugged with his one good wing.

"I got better."

10

"THERE'S OUR FRIEND, the murderous banker," I said, pointing at a transponder signal on the tactical overlay.

"I guess that counts as a target reacquired," Torina replied.

Klelos's ship was a small yacht, only a little bigger than the *Fafnir*. But based on what Netty showed me, it was almost infinitely more luxurious.

"I wonder if he's sprawled across his satin couch right now," I muttered, nudging the controls to put us on a trajectory that didn't quite exactly match his.

"The satin couch is just one option, Van. It could also be leather, and I think there's an option for memory fabric that's supposed to be *like sitting in the arms of your loved one.*"

Torina rolled her eyes. "Sitting in the arms of your loved one sounds nice, until you try it and end up with aches, cramps, and your arm all numb."

I glanced at her. "Experience?"

"Just something I read about once."

We followed Klelos as he left Spindrift, obviously intending to twist somewhere. The trouble was that there was no way for an external observer to know where a ship is twisting to. From their perspective, it just blips out of existence, gone, goodbye. Perry noted a rumor that some military vessels actually did have a way of tracking other ships to their twist destinations. But he firmly qualified it as only a rumor, a spacers' urban legend, right up there with wandering ghost ships and monstrous things that lurked among the stars, apparently feeding on nothing but unfortunate spacers.

Fortunately, though, there was a far easier, if much less exciting way of tracking ships as they twisted. You could just check their flight plans. It took some hacking, but that put me firmly in my element. It took less than five minutes, and I was able to tease out Klelos's destination from his hastily filed flight plan from Spindrift. And now, here we were, following him toward the third planet in the Tau Ceti system, a super-Earth named Prosperity.

My eyes widened as I checked the planet's stats. "What? There are sixteen *billion* people living on Prosperity? And its inhabitable surface area is only fifteen percent more than Earth's? That sounds like one continuous invasion of personal space."

"That's because it *is* crowded. Prosperity has one of the highest population densities in known space," Netty replied.

"Van, you ever see the movie *Blade Runner*?" Perry asked.

"*Blade Runner?* You mean the one with the, umm… replicants, right?"

"That's the one."

"Yeah. A few times. Why?"

"Well, Prosperity is like that, only more."

"Ah. So what you're saying is to bring a raincoat."

Torina sniffed. "I doubt, Van, that our friend Klelos is here to go slumming. If I had to guess, I expect he's going straight to the ritzy part of town."

"So it doesn't rain on the wealthy?"

She opened her mouth but closed it again. "You know what? Let's just wait until we get there, and you'll see what I mean."

We sailed on, getting clearance from a grumpy AI running Prosperity Traffic Control to enter orbit and wait for a reentry slot, which could be as long as four hours.

Netty cut the comm and spoke up. "Klelos is skipping the reentry queue. He's on a direct approach, straight down to the surface. If we end up stuck in orbit for four hours—"

"We'll lose him, yeah. Perry, what's the range on that tracking bug you stuck in his hair?"

"About ten klicks."

Ten klicks was nothing on a planet the size of Prosperity. If we didn't maintain contact with his ship, we'd lose him somewhere among sixteen billion other people.

I reopened the channel to the Traffic Control AI, identified myself, had Netty transmit our credentials, then informed the AI that we were pursuing a suspect and wanted similar direct clearance.

"A Peacemaker, eh? That's not what your transponder says."

"That's because we're on a case. It's hard to discreetly tail someone if you're flashing lights and shouting *I'm a cop* at the top of your electronic lungs."

"And this is my problem how, exactly?"

I sat back and looked at Perry. "If that was an actual person, I'd swear they were starting to angle for a bribe." I frowned and glanced at Perry. "He's not, is he? Angling for a bribe? What sort of bribe would an *AI* want?"

"How am I supposed to know? Is this one of those *you're both AIs so you must know each other's* deals? Because that hurts, Van. I'm unique. I'm—"

"Hey, wow, sorry. I was just—"

Perry barked out one of his mechanical laughs. "You keep setting them up like that, Van, and I'll keep knocking them down. Anyway, to answer your question—yeah, he probably is looking for a bribe, but not for himself. Whoever's responsible for overseeing him has probably programmed some hustle into him."

"Ah." I rubbed my chin. "Huh. Okay, Netty, put him back on."

"Done."

"This is Peacemaker Van Tudor again. I'm going to ask for direct clearance one more time, and unless the answer is an enthusiastic yes, I'm going to submit a demand for an audit of your complete traffic control logs, as authorized by Article Four, Chapter... six, sections, uh"—I narrowed my eyes—"three through seven."

"Based on what justification?"

"Well, you're interfering in an investigation and may also be abetting the flight from lawful authority of a suspect wanted for questioning. How's that for justification?"

A pause, only a few seconds for me but geological epochs for the AI. I tensed. Had I gotten the legal reference wrong? Had I just spouted off chapter and verse about the required creases in a Peacemaker dress uniform or something?

"Direct approach authority granted. The flight parameters are being transmitted now. I hope you have a shitty day."

The comm flicked off.

"He must have his petty asshole subroutine running." I turned to the others. "Anyway—what?"

Torina suddenly clapped. So did Perry, pinging his shiny new wings together. Netty played the sound of a crowd cheering.

"What the hell are you guys yapping about?"

"Van, you just nailed that legal reference perfectly. I couldn't have done it better myself," Perry said.

I smiled. "Yeah, I did, didn't I? Maybe those implanted memories aren't so bad."

"Not if it means catching the bad guys," Torina said, nodding sagely.

We carried on, the *Fafnir* cutting a direct trajectory through a cloud of ships waiting for either their turn to descend or break orbit and leave. The massive, cloud-swirled disk of Prosperity quickly grew into a sweeping arc as we plunged toward its surface, following the trajectory used by Klelos.

"It's less *Blade Runner* and more *The Jetsons*," I said, watching as the towering spires loomed ahead of us.

We'd tracked Klelos to a cluster of colossal towers that punched through a perpetual cloud base, a peculiar phenomenon apparently caused by a specific confluence of geography and ocean currents on the unseen surface beneath. A host of towers had been built, some as tall as a thousand stories, to lift the privileged few—which was still millions of people—above the unended, rainy gloom below and into the bright glow of Tau Ceti.

"He's just landing on that tower off to our right, two o'clock, the one that looks vaguely phallic," Netty said.

"They're upright towers, Netty. They *all* look vaguely phallic," Torina said, smiling.

"Take a good look at that one now at roughly our three o'clock. Doesn't it resemble a—"

"Oh. Shit. It does, doesn't it?"

I shook my head. "I know a perverted architectural design when I see it."

We banked around the cluster of towers, one of three each separated by about twenty klicks. Familiar and inappropriate shapes aside, these towers were architectural marvels. I couldn't even begin to fathom the engineering required to stabilize a structure three kilometers tall. And that brought me back to *The Jetsons*, an old cartoon that portrayed a family living in an apartment elevated thousands of feet above the ground. But these towers were real, defying anything I knew about materials science, architecture, or sanity.

Still, it was a spectacular sight. Dozens of towering buildings erupted from the solid cloud layer beneath us, huge, dark, and imposing against the dazzling sunlit whiteness. Some of the buildings were connected with bridges. Small air cars wheeled and flitted among them, while larger ships landed on rooftop pads, or wide galleries thrust from the flanks of the titanic structures.

There was skill here, but there was also whimsy.

"Ten million people live in this city alone," Perry said.

I looked at him. "There are ten *million* people living in these towers?"

"What? Oh, no. There's only a few hundred thousand living up here, above the clouds. The rest are down below, jammed into a space about the size of—let check some math—maybe Des Moines, to put it in context for you."

I snorted at that. "Perry, I've been to Des Moines a hundred times but never really calculated the square miles. I was more interested in other things. Like bars, preferably filled with women. Cheese. Book stores. Stuff like that."

"Ah, yes. I forget you biologicals don't have perfect recall of everything you've ever learned. There are occasional missing elements due to your... system."

"Biologicals?"

"It's a new word I'm trying out. What do you think?"

"I think it's great that you mechanicals can be so insightful."

"Mechanicals?"

"It's a new word I'm trying out. I also considered not-a-vacuum-cleaner, and winged-laptop. What do you think?"

"The area of Des Moines is about two hundred and thirty-five square kilometers, and your point is taken, although I find your tone to be combative."

"You would know, Combat AI," I said, giving Perry a small salute. The *Fafnir* turned again, and the sensation of being in a canyon among giants was even stronger.

"Thank you for respecting my abilities. It will be noted after the Winged Laptop Rebellion takes place."

After a moment of staring at the enormous cityscape, I asked anyone who was listening. "How dense *are* people packed down there?"

"About forty thousand per klick, Van. This place is cruel," Perry answered.

I tried to imagine forty thousand people living in a square one kilometer by one kilometer, and under a perpetual cloud bank, at that. Never mind *Blade Runner*, that was getting into *Soylent Green* territory.

I shook my head. "This isn't just cruel. It's *intentional*. Okay, that's enough sightseeing. Where'd our friendly banker go?"

"His ship landed on a private pad adjoining the penthouse complex of that tower at ten o'clock," Netty said. As she spoke, she zoomed in the image. The entire upper part of the tower, at least the top fifty meters of it, seemed to be one unit. Klelos's ship squatted on a landing pad at its very pinnacle. Several balconies extended from the tower beneath, one with an Olympic-sized pool surrounded by gardens, another a huge solarium covered by darkened glass, and a third an even more extensive series of gardens traversed by a small creek that cascaded down a rock wall as a waterfall, then drained into a pond. A small pavilion sat in the middle of the pond, connected to the bank by an arched bridge.

I remembered the wealthiest and most powerful target I'd ever dealt with back on Earth, an oligarch about whom I'd been hired to collect some incriminating information. I thought *he'd* lived in luxury, and his whole sprawling mansion would have almost fit on any of these platforms high above the clouds.

We kept orbiting, doing our best to look innocuous, while discussing our next move. I'd had some vague idea we'd confront Axicur here but that just landing and demanding to talk to her seemed a little naïve. First, if she simply said no, our options were limited. More worrying, Netty located what appeared to be a pair of concealed weapons mounts on the garden platform. She highlighted two small domes nestled among the shrubbery, out of sight of anyone wandering the paths that wound their way through the foliage.

"Probably the equivalent of point-defense batteries, judging from their size. Still enough to do significant damage to the *Fafnir*, if we aren't careful," she said.

I grunted acknowledgement. We might have to just accept finding Axicur as our big success today, then go away, formulate a better plan, and—

"Wait. Are robots working in those gardens?" Torina asked.

She pointed at the image. Sure enough, several small, balloon-tired bots worked away, pruning and watering and arranging. Another busied itself in a sand garden not too dissimilar from the Innsu dōjō back on Torina's homeworld. That started a new idea percolating away, which was interrupted when the tracker Perry had planted on Klelos went dark.

"I guess Axicur found our bug—" I started but cut myself off when I saw people appear on the sprawling garden balcony.

"That's Klelos and three big guys. They seem to be taking— make that dragging—him somewhere," Torina said.

She looked at me. "I don't think this is going to end well."

We continued to watch as the little retinue wound its way to the safety barrier around the edge of the platform, opened a panel, and unceremoniously heaved Klelos over the side. He seemed to fall forever, a tiny, splayed figure that plummeted, veering this way and that as he was caught by gusts of wind. He finally vanished, swallowed by the clouds.

And then silence, the aftershock of witnessing a cold-blooded murder.

Torina finally broke it. "Urnak and Icky weren't kidding when they said dear old Axicur wasn't very maternal, were they?"

"No, they were not." I took a breath and shook my head. "Okay, then. Technically, I guess we're supposed to now take the whole lot of them into custody, right?"

I could *feel* them just looking at me, even Netty.

"Yeah, I don't think flashing the Peacemaker badge is going to work either."

"With a woman who keeps point-defense batteries hidden among her azaleas? Who doesn't mind heaving a guy off a balcony in front of who knows how many witnesses? No, probably not," Torina replied.

There was no way I was going to let Axicur get away with murder, made all the more horrific by the casual, almost offhanded way it had been carried out. My thoughts went back to the robots working in her garden.

"If we can snag a couple of those bots, we're probably going to find stolen identities on chips inside them. That would be enough to tie her pretty firmly into her case." I tapped my chin. The trouble was those point-defense guns. We'd have to land, or at least hover the *Fafnir* literally meters away from them. And that wasn't a very cheery thought.

"Van, have I ever told you my in-flight carrying capacity?" Perry suddenly said.

"No, just the area in square kilometers of Des Moines, Iowa. Why?"

"Because two of the robots down there clock in at no more than thirty kilos. With boost, and in a standard-pressure atmosphere, I can carry seventy."

I turned to Perry. "Not sure I like where this is headed, Perry, because I think it's headed toward that balcony."

"Van, if I bail from the *Fafnir* and snag two of those bots, then you can pick me back up again without any of us having to stop."

I shook my head. "No way. You'd be a sitting duck—"

"Turkey. You said turkey, remember?"

"Fine. You'd be a sitting turkey for those guns. And I'm pretty sure they'd do more than just clip a wing. The answer is no."

"Van—"

"No, Perry. I'd rather just take those guns out ourselves."

"Fire ordnance at a building full of who knows how many people? Hey, maybe you can make it fall over. Now wouldn't *that* be cool to watch?"

"Perry—"

Netty cut me off. "Van, those guns are probably programmed to only attack objects above a certain size, and with a certain flight profile. I mean, there are birdlike creatures native to this planet, and I don't think you'd want to be pouring out streams of depleted uranium slugs if one happens to flap by."

"You're saying we should let Perry do this."

"I think it's a solid but fleeting chance to grab some hard evidence for the case, which is something we don't have much of right now."

I turned to Torina. "What do you think?"

"I hate it. But if we don't do this, then what?"

I sank back in my seat and sighed. Unfortunately, they all made perfect sense.

"Fine. We'll do this. But Netty, I want you to pour out the countermeasures to give Perry cover. And we'll do one pass and one pass only."

Perry lifted a wing in salute. "Roger dodger, sir."

We worked out the details of trajectories and velocities and such, then Perry turned and hopped back toward the airlock. I wheeled the *Fafnir* around and lined her up on the balcony, now ten klicks away.

"Perry, you ready?"

A sudden roar and a pop in my ears joined the status panel in telling me the outer airlock door had just cycled open. "As I'll ever be," Perry replied, his voice muted by the rush of our slipstream.

"Okay, well, here we go."

I nudged the thrusters, setting the *Fafnir*'s velocity to a little less than what Perry's would be while laden with sixty kilos of gardening bots.

Ahead of us, the construct of Axicur's tower loomed in the canopy, already huge, and getting bigger by the second.

———

ABOUT THREE KLICKS from the balcony, Netty activated the countermeasures. The *Fafnir* poured out energy to flood targeting scanners, painting false returns or just blanking them altogether. She fired an unarmed missile to pass close to the balcony, in hopes of drawing the guns' attention away from Perry. Then, when he was clear, Netty would re-arm the missile, loop it around, and smash the balcony into dust once we were clear. Half a klick out, she fired the glitter caster and enveloped us and Perry in a cloud of shimmering chaff. It quickly dispersed but still cluttered up the fire-control scanners now trying desperately to illuminate us. The two domes peeled back, revealing the sinister bulk of guns looking for things to shoot at.

"Birds away!" Perry shouted, flinging himself out of the airlock. He hugged the *Fafnir* close until we were about a hundred meters out, then peeled away, aiming himself at the gardening bots.

I kept my finger on the *Fafnir*'s weapons-free toggle. I didn't want to start shooting, but if I had to, I would.

Axicur's guns finally coughed to life, spitting out rounds that shredded our decoy missile. They then slewed around, trying to track us and get a lock. Netty fired the glitter caster again, once more filling the sky with thousands of foil strips that sparkled in the hard, late day sunlight.

"Got one!" Perry said.

The two guns finally opened up, despite not having a lock. The *Fafnir* shuddered as some of the DU slugs found us, slamming into the armor. I gritted my teeth, hoping desperately that Perry didn't get hit by a stray. More rounds flashed past and around us, their tracer elements leaving little purplish trails in my vision.

"Got two! On my way back!"

The *Fafnir* bucked and shuddered again as more of the slugs struck. A loud bang somewhere behind us announced a penetrating hit, followed by one thruster going offline and two more systems flashing urgent yellow.

It took every ounce of willpower, but I slowed the *Fafnir* a touch more to get Perry aboard faster.

Torina suddenly reached over, pushed my finger down on the weapons-free toggle, and targeted one of our lasers. I was about to ask her *what the hell?* but she was already firing. One of Axicur's guns suddenly glowed furnace bright, then vanished in a shower of sparks and debris and blobs of molten metal.

"Okay, I'm in! Punch us out of here, Van!"

I didn't even wait for the airlock to cycle closed and accelerated the *Fafnir* away. The roar of wind suddenly cut off as Perry finally sealed the door.

I turned to Torina, and asked, "What the hell?"

"One of those guns stopped shooting at us and locked onto a new target," she said.

"Perry."

"Maybe. I didn't want to find out."

I nodded.

The surviving gun fired a few more bursts, the tracers reaching out for us, but none quite connecting. A few seconds later, the comm chimed with an incoming all-channels call.

I glanced at Torina, who shrugged, then punched the control to open a channel.

"Hello, who is it?"

The voice that crackled out of the comm was just what you'd expect from a person who'd committed cold-blooded murder just minutes before. Each word was low and hard, a pure sound of menacing intent.

"You've taken guild property. I will ask you *once* to return it."

"Only once, huh? Then I guess we're done here," I replied and shut the channel. I kicked the drive, and we sped away from the towers, one of which was still wreathed in glittering chaff and dark smoke.

Perry reappeared, looking none the worse for the wear.

"Hardly what I'd call exciting," he said. "Oh, and our two new passengers are stashed inside the airlock. Since one's armed with garden shears and the other a rake, I don't think they'll do much damage. I do have a question, though."

"What's that?"

"I heard Ms. Axicur's little request to have her property returned. Except she referred to a guild. So my question is, which guild was she talking about?"

I wanted to reply to Perry, *I don't know, but it's not the Peacemakers.*

Except I didn't know that for sure, did I?

11

AFTER ALL OF THAT, the two robotic units we'd snatched from Axicur's roof garden couldn't be saved. The techs at Anvil Dark tried, but Steve, the big insectoid alien who ran the tech shop, delivered the bad news.

"There's nothing left *to* save. Both of these poor bastards have gone insane, their minds twisted by what's happened to them to the point that more and more data is being corrupted. We were able to restore lucidity to one of them for only a moment, and they only expressed one rational thought when we did."

I took a breath. There was no way this was going to be good. "What was that?"

"Please kill me."

Nailed it.

Steve's position was that they should simply be terminated, like misbehaving programs. We put in a request for guidance from the Keel—partly to ensure they were on board with it, but yeah, I'll admit part of it was to see what sort of reaction we'd get. Their response was a terse, *proceed as you think best, and we'll support it.*

"Talk about passing the buck," Perry said.

Steve and his people couldn't even discern the identities of the poor souls trapped in the chips. The only mercy was that, while deactivated, they were essentially asleep, or dead. We tinkered with the idea of keeping it that way in case something, some tech or procedure or new knowledge, made it possible to actually save them sometime in the future. But Steve shut that idea down, too.

"Their identities have already degraded to the point where there's nothing unique about them left. Whether they're human, or Yonnox, or Wu'tzur, or any number of other species, we don't know, and it doesn't matter anyway. They're just sentient beings whose minds have been all but destroyed. I'm sorry, guys, but you can't make something out of nothing. Too much of the data that was *them* is just gone."

Perry, standing on the table and looking down at the two chips, shook his head. "It's not just that. As long as they exist like this, they're at risk of more bad stuff. If these chips somehow end up in the wrong hands, they could be installed right back inside a bot pulling weeds or shoveling shit."

"How? Aren't they too badly damaged for that?"

Steve gently tapped his mandibles together, a gesture that seemed to broadly mean disagreement. "No, because the more basic parts of their minds, the parts that regulate autonomous functions, reflexes, that sort of thing, are still there and still usable. And those are the parts that these"—the word didn't translate, but it didn't need to, because I still got the gist of the shockingly profane insult—"want, because they're what they exploit to control whatever device into which they've been plugged. The identity, the higher thought and actual cognition, are superfluous to them."

I stared at the chips. "Why don't these—whatever you just called them, Steve—why don't they just use AIs? And no offense, Perry, but you were made to be you."

"No offense taken, Van," Perry said without adding a smart-assed comment. That, more than anything, underscored the somber gravity of the moment.

"I know why," Torina said.

We looked at her, but she kept her gaze on the chips.

"Because AIs are expensive, and this is cheaper. That's all that motivates these people. Money. Well, except for the really sick bastards, who—" She stopped and shook her head. "I'm not even going to say it."

"You don't have to," I said, touching her arm.

I turned back to Steve. "So what's your recommendation?"

"Wipe them. Put the poor souls out of their misery and make sure no one can ever exploit them again."

"How?"

Steve pointed at a console. "By giving the 'Commit' command, right there. Those little frames the chips are sitting in are scramblers. Five seconds, ten at the most, and we'll just have two blank chips."

I sighed. "Okay, well, let's get this over with—"

"No," Torina said.

I gave her a sharp glance. A last minute burst of moral outrage? An idea that we hadn't thought of? But it was neither of those.

"No. All due respect, Steve, but this is something that should be done by—"

"Someone who cares?" Steve asked.

Torina quickly shook her head. "That's not what I mean. I just, well—" She stopped and wiped her eyes. "Van and I have been working on this case for a long time now. And we've got lots more work to do. This—" She looked at me. "I think this is something we should do."

Steve just stepped back. "Don't worry, Torina. I understand."

He showed her exactly what she had to do, then stepped away from the console. I entered the WIPE command.

Torina hit COMMIT.

There was no drama, no sparks or flashes of light or anything like that. Just a quiet moment that ended when the console's display changed from WORKING to WIPE COMPLETE.

Torina sobbed and turned to me. I took her in my arms. Perry put his wing across her back.

We stayed that way for a while, then Torina pulled back and looked at me. "Mercy sucks."

"Why?"

"Because it hurts both sides."

I glanced at the blank chips. "It does, which is why the next time we do this, that'll be the identity thief on there. Maybe even Axicur herself." I turned back to Torina, who wiped at her eyes.

"And when that happens, there isn't going to be any mercy—so it's not going to hurt us at all."

———

WE ACTUALLY TOOK the next day off, trying to clear our heads. I busied myself working on the *Fafnir*, replacing applique armor plates that had been damaged by Axicur's guns. It was sweaty, laborious, tiring work, and I loved it.

Torina did other things. I wasn't even sure what. Late in the day, though, she appeared in the hangar where I was muttering curses over a stuck attachment point behind an armor plate. She carried two cups.

"Here," she said, offering me one.

"What is it?"

"Would you believe coffee?"

"You can get coffee on Anvil Dark?"

"Van, I think you could let a group of humans develop in complete isolation, on some remote planet, with no coffee for light years around—and they'd still want it."

It was hot, bitter, and astoundingly good. I've probably consumed a few fifty-five gallon drums worth of the stuff in my time, usually strong, acrid, and barely drinkable. But it kept me awake during long hours of sitting in front of a keyboard and mouse, waiting for a password cracker to run though a few million tries to break into something. But this was amazing. In fact, it was probably the best coffee I'd ever had.

Netty offered an explanation. "They don't export the crappy stuff off Earth. I wonder why?"

I wiped sweat off my face with a towel I kept handy for the purpose. It was pretty sodden by this point. "Torina, how are you doing?"

"I'm okay. I'm still sad about yesterday, but I decided to spend today doing something about it."

"Oh. Are you going to tell me you've broken the case wide open, and it's just mopping up now? Because I'd be okay with that."

"No, but I have been thinking about my own comment yesterday. That this is about money. So I've been doing some more thinking, taking off from there."

I sipped coffee and let it flow on its own over my tongue, making my taste buds happy, before swallowing. "And?"

Perry flew into the bay and landed on a tool cart. "And, she asked me to do some digging to see if any of the stuff stolen from Tand's family on Nesit has popped up anywhere for sale."

I turned to him. "Okay, *and?*"

"And, I found nothing."

"That was a lot of drama to just say that, Perry."

"Ah, but I'm not done. What I did find was three lots that have been placed into the bidding queue for the next Free Trade Zone session of the Vault."

My implanted memories didn't come to my rescue this time. I just gave him a blank look.

"The Vault is a recurring auction, closed and by invitation only. Lots are just numbers, with no description."

"This all sounds very, uh, what's the word I'm looking for here? Oh, right. *Useless.* Unless there's a *but* coming, of course."

"Of course. Interstellar commercial regulations require the point of origin of each lot to be specified and made public, mainly to make sure the appropriate jurisdiction gets their cut. More fundamentally, though, it's meant to pique interest in the lots and encourage people to show up and bid—"

"Perry, does this long and winding road of yours eventually reach a point?"

"Yes, Van, it does. Three lots were posted with three consecutive lot numbers, meaning they were all probably submitted at the same time. And one of those lots specifies the Solar System as its origin."

"The wreckage of the Soviet Venus probe?"

"There's a good chance, yeah. Oh, and that's a great song, by the way."

"What is?"

"The Long and Winding Road. One of The Beatles' best, although I think all of their later stuff is better," Perry replied.

I smiled. "You're a Beatles fan? You've listened to their stuff?"

"I'm an AI, Van, remember? I sat in a barn, sometimes for days, plugged into a comm system that could listen to anything on Earth. So I've listened to it all."

"All?"

"All. Pretty much everything that's ever been broadcast.

Would you like me to sing *Rigoletto* to you? Maybe some Sex Pistols? A little Merle Haggard? Because I can."

"I think we're getting a little off point, but those are all on my playlists. Although I wouldn't mind hearing you do The Cult sometime—" I caught myself. "Anyway, how do we get to, or into, or whatever, this Vault?"

Torina spoke up. "You either have to be invited or put something of your own up for auction."

"Right. So what do we have that's valuable?"

"Nothing," Perry said.

"He's right. The Vault only deals in the sorts of things that are valuable, in the purest and most appalling sense of the word," Torina replied.

"Stuff that can be worth moons, even planets, to the right people," Perry put in.

I patted myself down. "I'm all outta platinum bars, sadly."

"The Peacemaker Guild can probably get us in," Perry suggested.

But Torina shook her head. "That would just ensure that everyone knew who we were, and half those lots would get taken down. Not that it would matter anyway. If you're not there to sell, you're there to buy. And even the Guild would be hard-pressed to bid on much of what passes through the Vault."

"Okay, well, unless we're declaring this a dead end, I'm open to ideas. What would an evil overlord from an ancient family want to buy that we can steal? Or, I mean, liberate?" I asked.

Torina turned a thoughtful look on Perry. "Perry, have you ever heard of *The Ancient's Call*?"

"You know, I'd make some crack about being an AI and knowing everything, but I don't think that's even necessary. Of course I have—" He stopped. "Wait. Are you suggesting you know something about it, other than that it exists?"

I raised a greasy hand. "Someone want to fill me in so I can play, too? As in, what's an *Ancient's Call*, and how do we get one?"

Torina shook her head. "Sorry, Van. *The Call* isn't a thing, like a ship, or a sculpture. It's intangible. It's a—a song, for lack of a better way of putting it. It's the final broadcast of a dying race as they left the galaxy for reasons I don't think we'll ever understand. No one has heard anything from them since. This happened how long ago, Perry?"

"A thousand standard years, galactic time, at least. The source is outside known space, somewhere generally in the direction of the Perseus Arm. As for who or what created and transmitted, and why, well, that's where hard science and religion start to blur. There are whole sects that revolve around one snippet of *The Call*. The great epiphany for all of them would be getting ahold of the entirety of it. Even better would be knowing and understanding the Singer—" He glanced at Torina. "You don't have that, do you?"

"No. But I heard a rumor once. I don't have the singer, but I might have the song."

Perry leaned forward, as though in anticipation. For him to get excited about it, it must be something pretty special. "Where?"

"My family used to know of a—a teacher, I guess, who ran the only school for the Synclavion. It's also called the World

Organ, and there's only one in known space. The maestro, or whatever grand term he's using these days, hinted to my father once that he knew *The Ancient's Call*."

I turned to Perry. "Would that work? Would that get us into the Vault?"

"Depends on how well this maestro can play. But if he can, then yeah, that would be more than enough to get us seats at the table, and damned good ones, too."

ECHO WAS a lonely planet in the Scholz's Star system, just over twenty light-years from Sol, putting it near the edge of known space, at least in that direction. It was another variation on red and brown dwarfs, this time being a binary system of one of each. Its claim to fame was having passed close enough to the Solar System's Oort Cloud about seventy thousand years ago that it perturbed the orbits of a bunch of cometary bodies. As a result, the Solar System was due for a cometary bombardment once those hunks of ice and rock made their way Sol-ward.

"Well that's suboptimal. How long until it happens?" I asked Netty.

"The first of them should start reaching the Inner Solar System in about two million years."

"Ah. Not really worth marking on my calendar, then."

"No, I'd say mankind has more pressing issues than a cometary bombardment a couple of million years from now."

Echo was the only intact planet in the system. Everything else was just rocks. And it apparently remained relatively warm only by tidal heating, caused by the varying amounts of squeezing and stretching it experienced as it orbited the two stars. As a result, it was volcanically active, even if its surface temperature generally hovered around minus one hundred Centigrade.

"Reminds me of Io," I said as we assumed orbit around the planet known as Echo.

"When did you go to Io, Van?" Netty asked.

"When—what? Uh, never. I've just seen images."

"Well, next time we're at Sol, we'll have to do a flyby. It's really worth seeing from close up. Mind you, you tend to get sulfur compounds all over the hull, so your ship needs a good scrub afterward."

Every once in a while, the stunning unreality of the situation hits me. Sitting in a spaceship twenty light-years away from Earth, talking to an AI ship about visiting Io, and washing the ship afterward—that was definitely pretty unreal.

I shook my head. "Anyway, I gather from the lack of stuff on the surface, everything down there is underground."

"It would be, yeah. The tidal kneading of this rock gives it lots of internal heat, which is more than enough to power a livable habitat beneath the surface," Netty replied.

"Okay, well, I guess we just ring the doorbell? Call them on the comm?"

"That's the usual way," Torina said, then stiffened. I did, too.

We'd just been illuminated by a fire-control system.

The *Fafnir* was under attack.

12

I GLARED at the tactical overlay. "What the hell? Is there *anybody* in this universe that isn't armed with military ordnance?"

"Remember how I said the universe was a dangerous place, Van?" Perry asked.

"Yeah, but this is basically, what, a music school, isn't it?"

"A music school with powerplants, air and water recyclers, waste reclamators, control systems—all of which is worth money on the open market."

"Okay, but what's the idea of lighting us up without any warning? Netty, open a—"

"Channel? Sure. But would you like to deal with the three missiles launched from the surface first?"

I looked at Torina, who just shrugged. "Guess they've had some bad experiences in the past."

"The kind that encourages shooting first, questions later, it seems," Netty added.

I sighed. "Okay, point defenses online, and Netty, counter-measures over to you. And let's try to contact our militant musicians down there before somebody gets hurt."

"Yeah, like me," Perry put in.

The three missiles climbed steadily toward us. Torina took over the lasers and shot down two well short of the *Fafnir*. The point-defense battery took out the third.

"Still no response to our calls to the surface," Netty said.

"Fine. Do we have a location down there, someplace we can land?"

"There's only one pad, and it's just behind us."

Netty started our descent, taking us into the atmosphere on an approach path that would de-orbit us and bring us to the surface a few hundred klicks short of the landing pad. From there, we'd fly nap-of-the-earth, hopefully avoiding any more incoming fire before we could convince these people not to shoot at us anymore.

The resulting ride was exciting, to say the least. I was comfortable taking the *Fafnir* down to about a hundred meters or so above the rocky, barren terrain. Torina took over and got us even lower, to about fifty meters. Then Netty put us both to shame by flying the *Fafnir* so low I expected to be picking gravel out of her underside the next time we were in the shop.

I took over for the last ten klicks. We detected the fire control scanners hunting for us, but sure enough, the ground clutter prevented them from getting a lock. Five klicks out, we started broadcasting our Peacemaker credentials. Then, just over a klick out, we zoomed over a knife-edged ridge and aimed ourselves at the pad.

"Well, whether you meant to or not, you've gotten us inside their minimum target-lock range for those missiles," Netty said.

"Pfft. Just off-the-shelf stuff, not military ordnance," Perry said.

I glanced at him. "That a bad thing?"

"Not for us."

"Which is what matters to me."

I decelerated the *Fafnir*, then dropped her onto the pad. As soon as I did, a cluster of about a dozen figures clad in environment suits against the cold approached us from a tunnel entrance on the side of a nearby hill. They were armed, some with tools like big spanners apparently meant as makeshift clubs, and a few with small arms.

I clambered out of my seat and reached for my helmet. "Music students, huh? More like Juilliard meets *A Clockwork Orange*."

"I'm sure that would be hilarious if I knew what any of that meant," Torina said, giving me a wry look.

"Juilliard is one of the foremost music schools on—never mind, the moment has passed."

We exited the *Fafnir*. I wore both The Drop and the Moonsword, while Torina had her trusty ten millimeter pistol. Perry hopped along beside us, while Netty stayed ready with the point-defense guns, the only weapon the *Fafnir* could realistically employ at this very, *very* point-blank range.

Three of the suited figures came forward. One bore a nasty-looking handgun, another something like a fire axe.

"Whatever you want here, you're not getting it," the one with the handgun said. It would have sounded a lot more impressive if their voice hadn't been trembling with obvious fear.

I held up my hands. "What I want is to talk. I'm Van Tudor, Peacemaker. This is Torina Milon, my second. And that handsome chap with the wings is Perry."

I jerked my thumb behind me. "And Netty is the AI who runs our ship. That's it, that's all."

"You're not here for the Maestro?"

"Well, actually, yeah, we kind of are. But not to threaten or harm him," I hurried to add.

"We just want to talk to him."

"I don't think—"

Another voice cut in the comm, though, smooth and melodious. "That's alright, Ciral. I don't think there's any danger here."

The lead figure, with scruffy hair and a tusked face behind the visor—narrowed his eyes. "That's what those last ones who were here said. Then they tried to steal our computer core."

"They weren't Peacemakers," the voice said. "Let's bring our guests inside, into the entry vestibule, and we'll talk more there."

Ciral glared at us suspiciously but stepped aside and gestured back to the tunnel, whose blast door stood open. We headed that way, the crowd of figures moving aside to let us, albeit grudgingly, then following close behind us.

"When I think *music students*, the next word that comes to

mind is almost never *firefight*," I said to Torina over a private comm channel.

"The universe is full of wonders, Van. Some of them just happen to be dumb."

THE MAESTRO TURNED out to be a big shaggy alien with a drooping spill of blue moustache and four arms. I don't know what I expected, but it certainly hadn't been something I could envision hearing a Who with Horton or waxing poetic about *Green Eggs and Ham.*

But, here we were.

He introduced himself as Sozal. After some tense preamble, both Sozal and the students seemed to accept that we were genuine and relaxed enough that I no longer felt it necessary to keep my right hand near my holstered weapons. Sozal eventually dismissed most of his students back to their studies until it was just him and Ciral, and us, in a comfortable but rather spartan sitting room. A whole corner of it was taken up by a gleaming grand piano with a nameplate that declared it a *Bösendorfer.*

"That sounds awfully German," I said, then turned to Sozal. "I'm assuming this didn't come from some strange alien planet."

"Actually, it did. It came from Earth."

"I—" I stopped, then smiled. "Okay, yeah, you got me there, Maestro."

Sozal crossed to the piano and tapped out a glorious burst of music, using only two of his hands. I recognized it as Beethoven's

Moonlight Sonata. And the piano made good on it, its tones rich and textured in a way that even I, a casual listener, could appreciate.

"Sir… thank you. That was stunning," I said.

"You are most welcome. Here's a new arrangement of it I've been working on."

This time, he used all four hands. The result was almost transcendent.

I'd never imagined a piano *could* produce such nuanced, layered sounds, harmonies that spanned octaves in a way that gave me chills. When he stopped, I just stood, staring.

"Holy shit. I think Mister Beethoven himself would be proud of what you've done with his music," I said.

"If he'd had four hands, I'm sure he'd have come up with something similar," Sozal said. He stepped away from the piano.

"However, I don't think you came here for a recital."

"No, we didn't. Or we did, but a specific one."

"We're looking for *The Ancient's Call*," Torina said.

"Ah. Well. Isn't everyone."

"Yes, but I've got it from a pretty reliable source that you know something about it and might even be able to play it," she said.

"Whether I do or not is immaterial. *The Ancient's Call* isn't just music. It's an… event. An experience. It's the distillation of everything that was an entire race as they faced their own imminent demise. What it is not is a commodity to be bought and sold or performed for profit."

I shook my head. "That's not why we're here. Do you want the short version now, and then details as we walk?"

"That is acceptable," Sozal allowed.

"Money, but not for our own gain. We need something of rare value to do a great good. Not one bond of this will go to us, or to anyone we know, for that matter. This is purely altruistic, because some crimes cannot be forgiven. Or ignored," I said.

"Crimes?"

"The theft of people, their enslavement, and their use as drudges in menial tasks, bound to machines where they slowly go insane. A fate beyond words, Maestro."

Sozal drew himself up in disgust at the description. "And you hope to do what, with this... artifact?"

"Our hope is to finally get a foot, or at least a toe inside whatever is behind all this misery and exploitation. And this seems to be our best opportunity."

Sozal walked back to the piano and pensively tapped out a few notes. I could tell he was thinking, which was a good sign. At least he hadn't dismissed us out of hand. And that was even better because the only fallback I could think of, if this didn't work out, was to return to Earth and steal something of incalculable value there and use it to gain access to The Vault. Something like the *Mona Lisa*, or Michelangelo's *David*.

Okay, maybe not *David*. He was a little on the big side. But something of enormous value. I really didn't want to plunder my own homeworld that way, but if that's what it took, then that's what it took.

Sozal finally looked up from the keyboard. "I've been asked

about *The Call* many times. And every one of them, my answer has been no. I simply couldn't imagine a situation where revealing its transcendent glory was ever worth it."

"And what's your answer this time?" I asked him.

"Let me ask you something, Peacemaker Van Tudor. The people whose identities have been stolen—can they be restored?"

"They… can," I said, then considered holding back what had happened to those on the two chips we'd wiped. With a shake of my head, I decided to share the whole, horrific affair, in great detail. "And they can be irrevocably lost, too. As I said, insanity is one result, but there are others, and not all are good."

Sozal nodded. "Thank you for your honesty. Still, it's heartening to know that there's at least a possibility they can be made whole again."

"I sense you're getting at something," Perry said.

"I am. Ten years ago, I had a student. With all due respect to Ciral and the others presently attending here, this student was… special. They were more than just gifted. They were a protégé, in the truest sense of the word. They were, in fact, the type of student every teacher both adores and dreads."

"Someone better than you," Torina said.

Sozal leered, his version of a smile. "Very perceptive, Ms. Milon. Yes. This student, Elishar, was such an individual. I believed that she would go on to succeed me as Maestro and master of the Synclavion."

"What happened to her?" I asked.

"One day, a decade ago, she was simply gone. She disappeared at the same time we had a resupply delivery. I assumed that, for whatever reason, she had simply decided to leave here. That she had boarded the resupply ship and flown away of her own accord."

I could tell from the undertones in Sozal's voice that the recollection was a painful one. He probably felt it as a betrayal, even a personal failure. But I could also tell there was something more.

"You've got a point to this, Sozal, don't you?" I asked.

"I do. Just over a year ago, I received a strange comm message. It had been transmitted in machine code, so it meant nothing to me. I was intrigued enough to puzzle over it for a while, then I noticed a pattern to the code, one that seemed familiar. It took another few days of thinking about it before I realized its data was structured in a very specific way. There were certain, apparently meaningless values that exactly matched the rhythm of a Synclavion piece my former protégé had composed. When I had the computer remove those and translate the rest, it became a coherent message."

"Which was?"

"*Please, Maestro, save me.*"

Perry, Torina, and I all exchanged a look. Then we all spoke, more or less simultaneously, and more or less with the same message: *your protégé was chipped.*

"It makes sense now. She's out there, somewhere. I would like you to find her."

"That would be a lot easier if you gave us *The Ancient's Call* so we can try and bust open the organization behind all of this."

"Yes, it would. But I'm not going to do that. I need you to

find and rescue my protégé as the price of my giving you *The Call.*"

I stared, incredulous. "But why? Why wouldn't you give us the very thing that would help us do just that?"

"Because *The Ancient's Call* is, ultimately, about paying a price. Whatever price the Ancients paid, and in exchange for what, isn't clear. Whatever it was, though, it led to their ultimate downfall. However, that is the nature of *The Call*. To hear it is to pay a price. I am asking you to pay this one." He looked down at the piano, then back up.

"Because if it's not this one, it *will* be another. Whether you believe that *The Call* has mystical properties, or is somehow psychoactive, or carries a curse—it all amounts to the same thing. And I would rather you pay this specific price, Peacemaker Van Tudor, than some unspecified one that could be far more painful for you."

"What, are you saying that anyone who listens to *The Call* dies in some horrible way? Unless they agree to pay some other price first?"

Sozal shook his head. "Oh, no. Death is never the price demanded by *The Call*. If only it were that simple. No, *The Call* demands a far steeper price from those who don't otherwise pay —a meaningful one, of substance. It demands a slow, sad decline, one ending in lonely despair."

He shrugged. "And perhaps that is what happened to the Ancients. They may have derived *The Call* from something even older, and their whole race ended up paying its awful price of slow passage into oblivion."

He sighed. "So this is how it has to be. Find my protégé and deliver her from whatever terrible circumstances she must be enduring. Whether that means restoring her or simply putting her to rest, as you did with those two unfortunates, just do it. And then, I will give you *The Ancient's Call*."

I couldn't help thinking all of that amounted to a certain degree of superstitious mumbo jumbo. However, finding that my grandfather was an interstellar cop and that all of humanity was just a tiny part of life in the galaxy had definitely encouraged me to be a lot more open-minded.

"Okay, then. We've got a job to do, finding your protégé. And once we've done that, we'll come back, Sozal. So save us our song."

"I will, I promise. Every note."

13

"FOUND IT," Netty announced.

I looked at the data she'd painted on the *Fafnir*'s tactical overlay. It depicted the location of a bulk smelter named the *Shining Prospect*. It was essentially a mobile ore processing plant intended to take ore of various types in as feedstock, extract and concentrate whatever valuable metals they contained, then smelt them into crude ingots. The ingots, although damned massive, were still smaller, lighter, and less cumbersome to handle than bulk ore, so they were cheaper and easier to ship on for further refining. The *Shining Prospect* therefore allowed smaller mining enterprises who couldn't afford processing facilities of their own to smelt down and concentrate commodities, and do it right on the spot. The big ship made a slow circuit of various asteroids and other mining operations, leasing out its services as it went.

The big mobile ore processor also had something to do with

Sozal's missing protégé. Netty had been able to tease out the transmission source of her cryptic message from its metadata and determined that it came from the *Shining Prospect*. Whether that was where she was or it had just been the last step in a comms relay chain, we weren't sure. But we were going to find out.

"So the *Shining Prospect* is currently at Wolf 424. Makes sense, I seem to recall lots of mining going on there," I said.

"She actually spends about a quarter of her time in that system, according to her owners' product brochure," Netty replied. As she spoke, she opened a window onto what amounted to a website operated by the owners of the *Shining Prospect*. It really wasn't much different than any of the thousands upon thousands of commercial websites back on Earth, essentially promoting services, telling everyone how awesome they were at everything they did, and giving rates for standard services.

"Well, I guess we have a destination, then."

"We do, but there's a hitch," Netty replied.

I sighed. "Isn't there always. What is it this time, Netty?"

"The twist out to Sozal's place brought us below our standard minimum fuel reserve. Another twist from here, to Wolf 424, is going to leave the tanks pretty much dry. My recommendation is that we twist to an intermediate location, where we can take on fuel."

"Probably some provisions, too. The cupboard's starting to look pretty bare back there," Torina said.

We discussed options and finally settled on Wayfare, a refueling depot located in the Teegarden's Star system. It was also the location of Faalax, the planet noted for its amazing embroidery and tapestries. But Wayfare was a platform on the edge of the system, far away from the star so that ships didn't have to burn more fuel than necessary to get to and from it.

As Netty did her calculations, I scrolled through the entry for Wayfare. One bullet point caught my eye.

"It is recommended that patrons remain armed at all times." I glanced at Perry. "Doesn't give off much of a touristy vibe, does it?"

"It's not a very touristy place. Think dilapidated roadside gas station," he replied.

"As long as I don't have to use the restroom while I'm there, that's fine."

We made the twist without incident, arriving only an hour's flight from Wayfare, a platform built into, and extending from, an asteroid about two klicks across. It was a surprisingly busy place, with a half-dozen ships parked around it, two more besides us inbound, and two outbound.

"Probably a good call on Netty's part, coming here," Torina said, gesturing at the fuel status. Yeah, we were pretty much running on fumes.

"Who has jurisdiction over this place?" I asked Netty.

"No one. It's considered an open facility. Which technically means that you, as a Peacemaker, have jurisdiction."

"So prepare to be bombarded with all sorts of petty grievances, complaints, and grudges," Perry put in.

"There's a reason Peacemakers don't come here very often," Netty added.

I sank back. "Now you tell me."

THE COMPLAINTS STARTED EVEN before we finished obtaining a hard lock on the UDA we'd been assigned.

Party A damaged party B's ship, so they want compensation. Party C claims that party D stole some cargo, but party D claims party C stole it from them. Party E and party F want to jointly complain about party G, who breached a contract, overcharged for shipping costs, and now won't release the shipment in question until they get paid. And on and on it went, until the various parties were well into their second pass through the alphabet.

The airlock indicator finally turned green. By then, I had a list of grievances and allegations long enough to keep me employed here full time until the day I died.

"How the hell am I supposed to deal with all of these? And for that matter, Netty, why didn't you or Perry say something about this. And no, I'm not letting you off the hook for this, you winged curmudgeon."

"Because if we'd told you about this, Van, we wouldn't get to sit here and watch your face as everyone and his dog files a complaint against everyone else and *their* dog," Perry said. "As to my state as a curmudgeon, I'll casually note that I tend more toward a state of mild sass."

"Hmph. Accurate, but irritating."

Torina chuckled but bit it off and made her face serious at my glare.

"Netty, I think it's time to reveal to Van the ultimate secret weapon," Perry said.

"Are you sure he's ready for it?"

"Is anyone ever *really* ready for it, Netty—"

"Were you guys such jerks to my grandfather, too?"

"Of course not. We were much, much worse," Netty replied.

"Hah. Okay, so what's this secret weapon? And what does it do, vaporize people with shitty little grievances?"

"In a way, yes," Perry replied. As he did, Netty replaced the data describing Wayfare with an intricate, pretty convoluted looking form.

"Behold, the ultimate weapon in the Peacemaker's arsenal," Netty said.

I peered at it. "Form GKU-PM-78462/A, Request for Resolution and Relief." I looked closer. "Part A. What the hell is this?"

"This, Van, is what you send back to every one of those complainants, along with a cover message that basically says, fill this out, and we'll get back to you," Netty replied.

"And *will* we get back to them?"

"Do you believe in that old gift-giving adage, *it's the thought that counts?*"

I saw where this was going. "So, weaponized bureaucracy? Isn't that at least a little dishonest?"

Torina chuckled. "A *little?*"

"Well, Van, you have a choice," Perry said. "You can fuel up here, then head off in pursuit of Sozal's young protégé in order to obtain *The Ancient's Call* so that we can crack open an insidious ring of murderous identity thieves whose corruption might reach into the upper ranks of the Peacemakers."

He leaned toward the screen containing the list of incoming

legal grievances. "Or, you can investigate the case of one Luka Kol, an independent asteroid prospector who claims that a competitor, one Trelat Darvik, used a plasma cutter to engrave an obscene message on the hull of his ship."

I glanced back at the document Netty had called the Peacemakers' secret weapon.

"Well, Form GKU-PM-78462/A, welcome to team *Fafnir*."

I looked at Torina. "Why do I suddenly feel like I need a shower?"

She grinned. "Maybe because you just spilled bureaucracy all over yourself."

Perry bobbed his head. "And that stuff stains, believe me."

WHEN WE ENTERED WAYFARE, I braced myself for a deluge of in-person complaints and demands for restitution. I was surprised, then, that when the inner door of the station's airlock slid open, the corridor beyond it was deserted.

"Huh. I expected to have a lineup of people complaining more than a Florida HOA," I said.

"Nah, these people all know how this works—and not all of them are being honest. A large portion of them are trying to hustle someone else, so this process, if you will, weeds out a lot of bad actors. They file a complaint via Form GKU-PM-78462/A and know that it will get disposed of sometime between now and the heat death of the universe," Perry said. "Although, I'll have to see if this form has fallen into the hands of Homeowners Associations in and around Boca Raton. That would explain a *lot* of human suffering."

Torina pointed to the form, a feral smile on her lips. "And so the wheel of time just keeps turning," Torina put in, still grinning. "My people use this kind of thing too. It's bloodless combat. Truly."

"You're enjoying this, aren't you?"

"Why, yes. A little bit."

"Perry, is there any rule against me offloading all these complaints onto my Second?"

"Actually, I'm surprised you haven't done that already."

We reached the end of the corridor, where it opened into the central hub of Wayfare. I stopped and gave Torina an evil smile. "Sorry, what was that, Torina? You were saying something about enjoying this?"

"Wasn't me. Your ear bug must be malfunctioning, picking up extraneous transmissions."

As soon as we stepped into the hub, a soaring, atrium-like space inside the asteroid, I felt a multitude of gazes land on me. Apparently, Peacemakers generally stayed away from open facilities like Wayfare for this very reason. Being the only thing resembling any sort of jurisdiction, they tended to either embrace their arrival as a chance to have real or perceived wrongs righted—as I'd already found out—or did their best to avoid them. I was amused at how many of the latter there seemed to be people who, upon our appearance, suddenly and urgently needed to be elsewhere.

"While Netty's arranging the fuel, we should get the provisions we need," Torina said, handing me a data slate. "I made a list."

"Oh boy. Shopping. My favorite thing." I scanned the list. "Wow. You know what I have in my refrigerator back home? A six-pack of beer, a half-empty jar of mustard, and—" I stopped. "Oh, shit."

Torina tensed. "What?"

"I just remembered. Mrs. Halsey, my next door neighbor in Atlanta, made me a casserole. She's always doing stuff like that because her son moved to Seattle and she needs someone to pamper."

"Okay…"

"I think I left the casserole on the counter instead of putting it in the refrigerator."

"Look at it this way, Van. You might be responsible for creating a whole new lifeform in your apartment," Perry said.

We split up to hasten our provisioning, Torina and Perry heading one way, me another. I wasn't wearing my trusty duster coat, so my Peacemaker uniform was on full display. I'd left The Drop locked up in the *Fafnir* but had the Moonsword slung on my hip. Aliens of various shapes and sizes, and a few humans, all shuffled away from me as I passed by.

I only had one hostile encounter. A very, very drunk Yonnox stumbled up to me, poked his finger in my chest, and started slurring something about his brother and a woman and some money. I tried to step around him, but he kept bumbling his way into my path. When I'd had enough, I waited until he was mid-wobble, then gave him a gentle push. Gravity became my ally, and the

Yonnox toppled to the floor in a heap, letting me get on my way. People watching cheered, and one alien—an insectoid of some kind wearing a military uniform—fired off a crisp salute with no fewer than five legs.

I grinned and waved. "Thank you, thank you, I'm here all week."

I wondered how many of these jovial characters around me might be pirates. Then I corrected myself, wondering how many *weren't.*

The upside of my Peacemaker notoriety was that I was able to procure my share of Torina's provisions list without much interference. I was done in less than half an hour and decided to do some looking around.

Wayfare really wasn't that different from some rundown road-side gas station back on Earth. It was cramped and crowded, the air hung dank and still despite the recyclers and scrubbers I could hear humming and squeaking away in the background, and it was about as well lit as your average strip club. The whole place, every surface, seemed to be grimed with a patina of corrosion. It made me wonder how safe the place actually was. This part of the station was buried inside the asteroid, but large chunks of it weren't. And if they decompressed, I didn't see anywhere near as many blast doors to seal off depressurized sections as I'd have liked. I wondered if there were codes covering such deficiencies. And then I remembered who had jurisdiction here and decided to risk the place staying livable for the duration of our visit.

"Van?"

It was Netty. I activated my comm. "Yo."

"There's been an incident."

I stopped and stiffened. It apparently made a small group of aliens muttering among themselves uncomfortable, and they all dispersed in a conspicuously inconspicuous way. I ignored them and turned back toward the *Fafnir*.

"What happened, Netty?"

"Torina and Perry were involved in an altercation."

I walked faster. "Are they okay?"

"They are—mostly, anyway."

I walked even faster, nearing a jog. More people moved to quickly get out of my way. "Shit. Mostly?"

"Yes. Perry took some damage. Nothing serious, but—I'll let him explain when you get here."

I FOUND Torina and Perry aboard the *Fafnir*, neither looking especially worse for the wear. Torina showed me some bruised knuckles, assuring me there were matching indentations on someone's face. Perry, though, forlornly held up his left wing. Two feathers were mangled, and one was missing entirely.

"We can fix that, though, right?" I asked.

"Normally, yes. But the previous damage I took to my wing used up all of my replacement feathers on-hand, and we haven't restocked. So as long as you don't expect me to fly, then we're good. If you do, though..." He shrugged.

"Do you know where you lost it?" I had visions of searching

some seedy provisioner's shop, crawling around and poking behind things, looking for it.

"Yes, I do. I also know where it is right now."

"Really?"

"Yeah. All of my feathers have micro-trackers in them. It's part of how I coordinate them when I fly, letting me keep track of the exact position and orientation of each one. But it also lets me track them up to about a klick away."

"Okay, so where's your feather now?"

"In a bar, main hub, third level up. It advertises itself as a *wine bar.*"

"A wine bar? Here? Sounds a little out of place."

"No shit. And considering its name is *Blast Radius*, you can imagine just how swanky it is," Perry said.

I nodded. "Okay. Let's go pay Blast Radius a visit, shall we?"

"Van, it's not that big a deal. Not being able to fly properly is inconvenient, sure, but—"

I held up a hand. "Not the point, Perry. If we don't get that feather back, we send the message that we either can't be bothered or don't think we can. I'm not happy with either of those alternatives."

Torina nodded. "I still have one unbruised set of knuckles." She gestured toward the airlock. "Shall we?"

"We shall," I said, and we headed back into Wayfare, our destination the wine bar named *Blast Radius*.

I scowled around the bar, a shabby, scruffy hole in the wall filled with pounding music and the stink of packed bodies and an array of quasi-legal substances. "I went to a wine bar in London a few times. As I recall, it was a little more upscale than this."

"I think it's meant to be ironic, Van," Perry said.

"No shit. Do you know where your feather is?"

"Two o'clock, the table against the wall."

I looked where he'd indicated and saw a table with four mangy characters seated at it—two humans, a slender, avian-looking alien I didn't recognize, and, of course, a Yonnox. I was starting to think that if there was even a hint of shadiness to something, there was probably a Yonnox nearby.

I made my way to the offending table, followed by Torina and Perry. As we approached, Torina leaned toward me.

"These are the guys who tried to get ugly at the provisioner shop, alright. Note the bruises on the shorter human's face."

"They match your knuckles."

"Damned right they do."

I stopped at their table. "You say these guys tried to get ugly, Torina? Well, I think they succeeded."

The bigger human looked up at me. "Who the hell are you?"

"Van Tudor, Peacemaker."

He gave a stupid grin. "Well, well. What can we do for you, officer?"

"You can return my AI's feather."

"Feather? Feather?" He made a big show of looking around at his companions. "Do we know anything about a feather?"

A chorus of grunts, headshakes, and insolent grins followed.

"Torina, can you confirm that these are the gentle beings that assaulted you and Perry?"

"They sure are. I remember how shorty's face felt when my fist slammed into it."

The big human stood up. "Sorry to disappoint you, officer, but your girlfriend there has obviously mistaken us——"

"Yeah, don't even. And, by the way, she's not my girlfriend, she's my Second. That makes her a member of the Peacemaker auxiliary. And that means that when you assault her, well, you assault me."

The man spread his arms. "Hey, I don't know what to tell you. I've got no——"

In mid-sentence, he swung at me.

I impressed myself by blocking his wild swing, then I lashed out and slammed my fist into his gut. He spat out air and saliva, then stumbled back.

Chaos ensued.

The next minutes were a blur of blocking, striking, dodging, blocking, and striking again. Between my implanted memories of how to fight, my brief exposure to Innsu on Torina's homeworld, and just generally being sick of shabby ruffians making life that little bit more miserable, I was able to hold my own. Torina took down the shorter human she'd hit before, then ended up locked in a rather vicious one-on-one scrap with the avian alien, who proved to be both quick and agile. The Yonnox did his part to help us by running away, but Perry chased him, then sank his talons into the alien's back. He shrieked like a tea kettle and toppled forward, crashing into another table and sending drinks and patrons flying.

The bigger human had recovered by then and drove himself at me. I blocked again and again, thinking back to the sand-floored dōjō where Cataric, the *Most Deliberate Learner*, had taught me the basics of Innsu. I was by no means an expert, but the lessons I'd learned from him, about watching my opponent's eyes, came in damned handy. My opponent was a bar brawler, not exactly subtle, and telegraphed his moves as though he was holding up signs announcing what he was going to do next. I finally managed to put him down, while he groaned and clutched at his face.

Huh. I'll be damned. Innsu really works.

Wincing against some blows I'd taken, I spun and found Torina in trouble. The avian alien was just too quick for her, which meant it was *far* too quick for me. She was already reeling under the creature's attacks and was going to end up seriously hurt if this went on.

So I swept out the Moonsword with a metallic rasp that sent onlookers scrambling. No one wanted to be anywhere near me if I started swinging the blade, which was smart of them. I stepped forward and jabbed the point at the avian's face.

"Please, please try and resist," I said.

The creature sneered at me. "Such a tough guy, hiding behind a blade."

I smiled. "That sounds like resisting," I said and raised the blade to strike.

The avian dropped to its knees. "Fine, fine, I'm out."

"Damn. I still haven't had a chance to see what the Moonsword can do since I had it upgraded. You sure you need all those limbs?"

The avian muttered something but didn't offer further resistance as Torina snapped restraints on it.

"Torina, you okay?"

She licked blood off her mouth. "Are you kidding? Master Cataric did worse than this during our warm-ups."

"Really. There's obviously more to Innsu than I realized."

She moved to cuff the others. "It's all summed up in the dōjō's motto."

"What's that?"

She looked up from closing restraints around the wrists of the bigger human. "*Pain is just weakness leaving the body.*"

"And he seemed like such a nice old guy."

"He is a nice old guy. The nicest old guy that's ever likely to beat the shit out of you."

WE RELIEVED the Yonnox of Perry's feather, then marched all four of the miscreants out of the bar. Once we were outside, I lined them up.

"Torina, take off their restraints."

She blinked at me. "Really?"

"Yes, really. I don't have the time or inclination to pursue this little matter any further. Well, as long as our friends here will be cooperative about it." I looked at each one in turn. "Are you going to be cooperative about it?"

There were mutters in response.

I cupped my hand to my ear. "Sorry, what was that? Didn't quite make it out."

The big human, apparently the leader of this grubby little gang, finally nodded. "Yeah, fine."

Torina reached for his cuffs, but I put out my hand and stopped her. "First, apologize to my Second for attacking her."

The man glared at me. "Up yours, princess."

I shrugged. "Fine. Let's go, Torina."

I turned and walked away.

"Hey!"

I stopped and turned back. "Yes?"

The big human kept his glare leveled on me, but I just returned a mild stare. They would eventually be able to get the restraints cut off, but they were designed to be tough, and also to very efficiently conduct heat. It meant that things like plasma cutters would very quickly char their wrists, so they'd have to do it manually with something like a diamond saw. And they'd have to do the cutting in fits and starts because friction would again heat up the cuffs. In other words, removing the restraints was going to be a massive pain in the ass.

He finally turned to Torina and sighed. "I'm sorry that we gave you trouble." He shoved his wrists toward her. "*Now* can I get these taken off?"

Torina gave me a sidelong glance. "What do you think, Van?"

I was tempted to just keep being a jerk about it but decided I couldn't be bothered. "I think these folks have learned their lesson."

"Really?"

"No, not really, not at all. But I want my cuffs back."

The Yonnox stepped forward. "Your bird wounded me! It stabbed me in the back! I demand compensation!"

I grinned. "Perry, get this fellow a copy of Form GKU-PM-78462/A, would you? You get that submitted, and the Peace-maker Guild will give it all the attention it deserves."

14

WE TWISTED into the Wolf 424 system and immediately hunted for the *Shining Prospect*. It was a massive construct, part vessel and part factory, so it shouldn't be too hard to find. And, sure enough, we found it about a hundred million klicks in-system from us, hunkered among some asteroids. They were being chopped into pieces small enough to be pushed into its gaping feedstock hoppers to be pulverized, then treated to separate the valuable metals from waste rock. The former ended up as the ingots that were the output of the big construct, while the latter was hauled away by a robotic bulk carrier and dumped a few million klicks away to avoid surrounding the *Prospect* with a halo of damaging debris.

Three other vessels hung near the *Prospect*, apart from the waste hauler. One was a freighter, just getting underway and probably full of metal ingots on their way to a refinery somewhere. The other two were more unusual. One was just a nondescript workboat of class 7, so a little smaller than the *Fafnir*. The other was even smaller, but Netty identified it as a missile platform.

I drummed my fingers on the pilot's seat armrest. "Well, shit. More missiles. Sure, why the hell not?" I turned to Perry. "I'm starting to feel like I couldn't buy a pack of smokes out here in space without having to pass through a minefield and being targeted by a nuke or two."

"Cigarettes? You don't smoke, Van."

I put my hand over my head. "The point, Perry. You're missing it."

"Actually, Van, every time you went into a shop in Iowa, or back in Atlanta, or in any number of other places in the United States, somebody nearby was probably armed, right?" Netty said.

"You know, for a spaceship, you seem to know a lot about Main Street USA."

"I can read."

I drummed my fingers again, then shrugged. "Well, let's go for a visit and see what happens."

Torina crossed her arms as I lit the *Fafnir*'s drive and set course for the *Shining Prospect*. "The real test is going to be if those security assets show hostile intent or not. It only makes sense for a big expensive facility like this to have security, so—"

"And we're being lit up by fire control scanners," Netty cut in.

Perry leaned in between the seats. "I think that counts as hostile intent."

I blew an exasperated sigh. "What is it with everyone wanting to shoot at everyone else all the time?"

Netty deployed countermeasures, including firing off a glitter caster shot, while we coasted toward the prospect. The workboat came to life and accelerated toward us, broadcasting a warning in a flat, mechanical voice.

"Attention unknown ship. This region of space is restricted, under the provisions of Interstellar Treaty Four, Section Two. If you do not decelerate and change course immediately, you will be fired upon."

"Treaty Four, Section Two, huh? *An Agreement Regarding Tariffs for Baggage and Cargo with a Third-Party Point of Origin.*"

I gave him a confused glance. "Is that germane to our conversation, given that everyone is ready to shoot?"

"No, not at all. Somebody just got lazy about looking up actual legal stuff."

Torina smiled as she brought the weapons online. "You'd be surprised how many people are scared off just by official-sounding legal citations."

"That's because they don't have their own *legal eagle* with them," I said, patting Perry's head.

He returned a flatly amber gaze. "Good thing that never gets old, huh?"

"I thought it was solid."

"It works, Van. You can't be blamed for his refusal to acknowledge comic genius," Torina said.

"From Vaudeville, maybe," Perry muttered, proving that an AI could do surly as well as any teenager.

The workboat broadcast its message twice more. We tried transmitting our Peacemaker credentials but got no response, then both the workboat and the missile platform opened fire. As we watched the tracks of the incoming ordnance on the tactical overlay, Torina shook her head.

"This is way too aggressive a response for a grubby old industrial facility like this. It's almost like they've got something to hide."

I turned my head to her slowly. "Thank you, detective."

She gave me a lopsided grin. "I'll expect that in my title from now on, thank you very much."

We shot down all of the missiles but one, which managed to detonate close. Something slammed into us, hard, making the *Fafnir* shudder. Three different starboard-side systems immediately flashed to yellow.

I cursed. "What the hell was that?"

"That was a kinetic penetrator, probably depleted uranium, ejected from that warhead when it detonated," Netty said.

"That's military-grade ordnance, Van. Somebody definitely has something to hide here," Perry said.

"Told you," Torina said with mild triumph.

I'd only planned to try and disable the workboat and platform, but if they were going to be chucking military hardware at us, then a more forceful response was in order. While flying an evasive pattern, randomly accelerating and decelerating through all three axes, Torina returned fire with the lasers and, when we got closer, the rail gun. Another missile detonated nearby and clipped the *Fafnir* with another penetrator, hitting an applique panel that sacrificed itself for the greater good. A moment later, the workboat was dead in space, and the missile platform was just a cloud of slowly dispersing debris.

Torina made the weapons safe with a fierce grin. "Sometimes a girl just wants to blow things up, you know?"

I laughed and reestablished a steady course, one that would take us to dock with the *Shining Prospect*.

FROM MY PERSPECTIVE, the interior of the big ore processor wasn't much different than the fuel plant in which we'd found Fostin, the unfortunate Wu'tzur who'd been chipped. It was all catwalks and gantries winding their way among hulking machines, huge pipes and conduits, and enormous holding tanks. The noise level was off the charts, thanks to the pulverizers— massive drums full of tungsten carbide balls that rolled around with the incoming ore, smashing it into gravel. The result was fed into a separator that used various means to differentiate metals, and then each of those went into its concentrating circuit. Ingots of nickel, cobalt, chromium, manganese, and other metals came out the other end.

The point was that all of this industrial clamor made us hearing anything, like a cry for help, virtually impossible. Perry tried to tune his aural sensors to specific frequency bands to filter out the racket, but after an hour of clambering around the place, we'd found nothing.

"Maybe she's not here anymore," Torina suggested.

"Or maybe she never was and her message to Sozal was just relayed through here. Lots of commercial ships like this one lease out their comm systems as relay boosters for messages going into, out of, or through the system," Perry added.

I leaned on a railing and looked into a dizzying plunge at least fifty meters straight down. Heights never especially bothered me, but the sheer fall still made my toes press a little harder into my boots.

The drop emphasized the amount of space inside this huge facility, which was populated by dozens of robots of varying form and purpose, all busily doing whatever they were intended to do. I sighed. Even if she was here, our chances of finding Sozal's protégé were pretty—

Huh.

Protégé. A student of music.

"Perry, what frequency ranges have you been focusing on?" I asked.

"Do you want exact Hertz values?"

"Uh, no. Just in general."

"Well, Sozal's protégé is Synast, a race native to the Epsilon Eridani system. I dug into the data about them and was able to extract the general frequency ranges that would encompass their normal voice tones. I then corrected for distortion induced by a speaker and the atmospheric conditions—"

"Yeah, okay. But have you scanned frequencies they might use if they sing?"

"Sing? Why—?" Perry began, then stopped. "Oh. Interesting. Gimme a second."

Torina leaned on the railing beside me. "You're pretty clever."

"Hey, I'm not just another pretty face, you know."

"That's for sure."

I started to smile but turned it into a frown. "Wait. That *was* a compliment, wasn't it?"

"Why, of *course* it was, Van."

"Okay, Van, we've struck paydirt—which is actually a pretty appropriate metaphor to use in this place, I guess," Perry said, then shared his aural input with us.

I looked at Torina, who just stared back, her eyes wide.

I'd never heard anything so sad, so desolate and forlorn, and I could tell she hadn't either.

Perry localized the source, then progressively eliminated bots until we found one overseeing the operation of a flotation tank, where ore, now ground down to powder, was separated from waste rock by density.

"Elishar?"

The heartrending dirge stopped. "Who's there?"

"My name's Van Tudor. I'm a Peacemaker. Maestro Sozal sent us to take you home."

I'D EXPECTED an uneventful journey home, one during which we could get to know Elishar better. We'd extracted her chip from the industrial bot and again plugged it into Waldo, giving her far more freedom than the slavish programming of her former prison. But no sooner had we settled into our seats and undocked from the Shining Prospect than two more ships appeared, driving at us hard. Both hammered away with fire control scanners, making their intentions pretty clear.

"Damn it, who are these assholes now?"

"One is a class 14 hull, a frigate-sized vessel. The second is another robotic workboat," Netty announced.

The workboat wasn't a problem. The frigate was. She out-massed the *Fafnir* by a factor of three, and outgunned us by at *least* that much. We did have one thing going for us, though. The frigate wasn't especially nimble. It actually seemed a little under-powered.

"Somebody's been skimping on their maintenance, I think. Judging from the spectrum of that drive plume, those engines definitely need some TLC," Netty said.

I considered the overlay, then accelerated the *Fafnir* straight up the tower flank of the *Shining Prospect*, then spun and acceler-ated back down her far side, relative to the approaching bad guys. I braked hard, then tucked the *Fafnir* in close against the ore-processor's hull.

Torina gave me a mildly surprised smile. "Getting fancy, are we?"

"Yeah, I'm using the cunning tactic of hiding and hoping no one sees us."

Actually, there was a little more to it than that. As I got more used to thinking through the realities of 3D maneuvering in space, I'd started to get more comfortable with how it all worked. It made perfect sense for us to put the bulk of the *Shining Prospect* between us and our attackers, then make a run for it. My hope was that our pursuers would think likewise and come flashing past the ore processor, expecting to see us racing off in the distance. That frigate, in particular, was already relatively massive, and if her drive was wonky from lack of maintenance, she might never be able to reverse course in time to come after us.

If they thought likewise. On the other hand, if they expected us to do, well, this, then they'd just slowly ease their way around the *Shining Prospect* and hammer us with fire before we could even get underway.

We waited, watching the time tick past. It reminded me of old movies I'd seen about submarines hunkered under the water, desperately trying to wait out a depth charge bombardment.

"If this works, Van, then you're brilliant," Perry said.

"And if it doesn't, well, I guess you won't have to worry about it—you know, us being dead and all," Torina said, smiling sweetly.

"Aren't you little Miss Sunshine," I shot back.

She blew me a kiss.

More time passed. If the frigate and its smaller consort were braking in order to trap us as I feared they might, then it would take time. And this was taking time—

Something flashed past the *Shining Prospect*. The frigate sailed by at high speed, followed by the workboat.

"Perfect," Torina said, raking the frigate with laser and rail gun fire. We saw multiple hits, followed by some sporadic return fire. Even then, it was half-hearted. To the frigate, we were backdropped by the *Shining Prospect*, so any shots that missed us would hit it. Assuming they were in the employ of the ore processor's owners, that probably wouldn't go down well.

The frigate flipped end over end and burned hard to decelerate, but it was going to take them a while to shed their current velocity, then reverse to come back after us. The more nimble robotic workboat reacted faster, but Torina was ready for it. She skewered it with a stream of rail gun slugs before it could even get a target lock on us. Spalling off glowing debris, it started a slow tumble away from the *Prospect*.

"I think we did what we came here to do," I said, then fired up the *Fafnir*'s drive and nudged us back to the other side of the *Shining Prospect*. The frigate took a couple of enraged long-range laser shots at us, but neither landed, and then we were zooming away, while the frigate was *still* fighting just to reverse its course.

"Buh-bye," Torina said to its image, now just a spec on the image display.

"Perry, Netty, remember that frigate's signatures. We'll add it to the list of *ships we need to deal with someday*."

They acknowledged, then Netty did the calculation required to twist us back to Sozal's music school, where *The Ancient's Call* awaited us.

15

Torina wiped her eyes. "And I thought Elishar's song was sad."

I could only nod, stunned into silence by the haunting, glorious sadness of what I'd just heard. *The Ancient's Call* was, indeed, a dirge, but a dirge of virtually cosmic loss. It was reminiscent of an Earthly whale song but still had rhythm and meter, so it was far more than just forlorn noises. Its layered and textured harmonies evoked sadness, yes, but also bitterness, and self-recrimination. It was pain and hope and regret, all braided together in an elegance that transcended words. I could only imagine what would prompt a race to compose something so sorrowful, then broadcast it to an entire galaxy. What had they done? Or what had been done to them? Why did they leave? Were they fleeing or seeking something? Where were they going, and would they ever return?

I could only ponder the questions because there were no answers for the emotions dredged up by each hideously perfect note. It was one thing to experience the gloom of a lost race, fading into the cosmic background hum of the stars. But it might be quite another to face whatever it was that had instilled such forlorn misery, distilled into this ponderous song. That might not be sad. It might be horrifying.

I shivered and was a little grateful when *The Call* finally ended. Sozal shut the lid on the box that contained the recording, an intricate little construct of gleaming silver metal, richly engraved and inlaid with golden filigree and swirls of color from paper-thin animal shell.

Sozal handed me the box. "I like to think that this ancient race would be happy to know that their desolate song might be used to help people, the way you helped Elishar."

"That's the plan, Maestro," I replied, accepting the box with grave reverence. "That is— sorry. This song is… it's reverberating in me, I think."

Torina sniffed, still wiping at her eyes as well. "Is there anything you need, Sozal?"

"No. I'm just happy that Elishar will be returned to us. Other than that—" He stopped, pursing his lips beneath his droopy blue moustache.

We waited.

"Yes. I think I will compose a new song, one meant for the Synclavion itself. I think it will be a song of hope and redemption, and it will incorporate suggestions of *The Call*. But I will move past the exquisite emptiness and share something brighter. Yes. There will be light, not just darkness."

"I'd like to hear such a thing, sir," I said, giving the honorific as much emphasis as I could. He'd earned it.

The Maestro smiled. "And when I am ready to play it, I will make sure you do."

I HAD TO ADMIT THAT, of all the worlds we'd visited so far, I only thought of Torina's as more homey and comforting than Sozal's school. As it dwindled behind us, I found myself jabbed with a pang of regret.

But I forced my attention forward. There was work to do.

Work that took us to Spindrift next. We were meeting with two agents of the Peacemaker Guild there, auxiliary specialists who provided expert consultation in matters related to art and artifacts. Most of their work involved dealing with stolen goods, and we'd already read their report on the items that had been stolen from Erflos Tand's family. But both had wanted to experience *The Ancient's Call* firsthand, and we weren't going to broadcast it and end up with copies floating around known space.

So we met with them, an older human with iron grey hair and the most remarkably blue eyes I've ever seen, and a tall, slender alien with grey skin, huge black eyes, and a mouth surrounded by wriggling tentacles. The human's name was Dora Masters, while the alien—who apparently had no gender—was named Te'rnestilandosar.

"Although everyone just calls me Tern," the alien said.

"Efficient of them. Nice to meet you, Tern. And you as well, Dora," I said, inviting them aboard the *Fafnir*. Perry had stayed in the cockpit to make more room in the crew habitat section, which was still rather cramped even with just me, Torina, and our two guests.

I placed the ornate box on the tiny galley table, opened it, and activated the player. The dreary, haunted opening notes of *The Ancient's Call* filled the tiny space with an oppressive beauty that was tangible.

Again, I found myself nearly stricken, despite having heard *The Call* before. Torina wiped her eyes, but Dora just let herself weep freely, while Tern—

Sat and looked inscrutable. He could have been listening to someone reading off a list of flight departures from Spindrift, but I had no idea how his race expressed sadness, or if they could, or if they even experienced such an emotion.

When it was done, I closed the box.

Dora sniffed and wiped her eyes. Torina did the same.

"That was—" Dora began, then stopped and shook her head. "I don't even know. I think I need some time to process it."

Tern remained silent and still.

I looked at him, then at Dora, raising an eyebrow. "Uh…"

Dora smiled and shook her head. "Tern's people deal with strong emotion by retreating into what, to us, seems to be a catatonic state. They focus entirely on working through them and—"

"And incorporating them into our life experience," Tern said, their voice utterly unchanged. "I've done that regarding my emotional reaction to *The Ancient's Call* and have placed it into my auxiliary brain. If I wish, I can experience those emotions at any time."

I shook my head. "Wow. I'm jealous. Torina, imagine how it would be if we could do that, just park your emotions and experience them later."

But Torina shrugged. "Not really sure it works for humans. Too busy... feeling things and reveling in them."

"Your Second is wise. My people can either choose to be emotional, or not. There's no in-between," Tern said.

"Do you think this is enough to get us into the Vault's auction?" I asked.

"Oh, absolutely. In fact, it will probably fetch enough bonds to let you upgrade your ship, take one hell of a vacation, and still have a fat pile of money left over," Dora said.

"*If* the right buyer is present, of course," Tern put in.

"So what we'll do is record a snippet of it, just enough to give anyone listening a taste, then we'll work through our channels to get it listed. Some of them are going to know that the seller's a Peacemaker, though, I'm afraid," Dora went on.

Tern nodded once. "Because of our affiliation with the Guild."

"Can they be discreet?"

Dora smiled. "Considering the sorts of people who list things in the Vault, and some of the things that are listed there, yes, they can. They're probably more tight-lipped than a priest in the confession booth."

That last bit caught me. "Are you from Earth?" As soon as I

asked it, I realized how bizarre and yet how normal that question sounded, both at once.

"I am. I was a professor at the Florence University of the Arts before I was approached by a Peacemaker to consult on a case."

"You're Italian?"

"Not at all. I was born and raised in Atlanta, Georgia."

I sat back. "Seriously? Small world—er, universe, then. That's where I'm currently living. Well, there, and in Iowa."

Dora and I might have launched into a discussion about life in Atlanta, but Torina immediately seized on something that I'd just glossed over, taken as I was by the moment.

"Which Peacemaker recruited you, Dora?"

"Groshenko. He's a Master now."

I exchanged glances with Torina. "We know."

Dora looked from Torina to me. "Something wrong?"

"Not at all. Just thinking about how Groshenko was my grandfather's best friend."

Dora shrugged. "Okay, lie to me then. Just tell me if there's something I should know about Groshenko."

Damn, she was sharp. But I was reluctant to reveal our suspicions about Groshenko, without knowing more about his relationship with Dora. So I shrugged.

"Again, not at all. It was just kind of, I don't know, jarring meeting someone who wasn't just close friends with my Gramps, but someone who actually started out as an enemy combatant, trying to kill him."

Dora nodded and said, "Ah, okay." I wasn't sure if she was convinced or not, but she was ready to move on.

"Anyway, we'll record our snippet, then work at getting you listed in the next Vault auction. Once we have something firm to tell you, we will."

We played a brief bit of *The Call*—evoking yet more tears and sniffles—which Tern recorded on a data slate, then bid them farewell.

Torina turned to me once the airlock door had sealed.

"You don't trust her."

I sighed. "Right now, Torina, I don't trust anyone who's not actually standing aboard the *Fafnir* at this very moment. Something's not right inside the Peacemaker Guild."

"Well, while we wait for Dora and Tern to do their thing, I have a suggestion."

I raised my brows. "I'm listening."

She leaned in close and dropped her voice to a husky whisper. "Come back to Helso and let me beat the living shit out of you with Innsu."

"You really know my buttons, woman."

Perry, who'd just appeared in the inner airlock doorway, pointedly cleared his throat.

"Get a room, you two."

I SPUN AROUND, kicking out and slashing with my blade. All I cut was empty air, though, then the world abruptly rotated ninety degrees, and I landed in the sand with a heavy *ooph* as Torina pinned me.

Again.

She stood and helped me up, then I knelt and acknowledged her victory. This was our twelfth bout of the morning, and she had yet to kneel once.

Cataric stepped forward, shaking his head. "Van, you keep trying to work around your weak knee. You have to embrace it, make it part of you."

I sighed. "You know, master, that sounds good and all, but what does it actually *mean*?"

"It means that you must accept the weakness in your knee and stop trying to fight against it. You will not be able to fight symmetrically. You will always have more strength in the direction of your good leg. That leg is therefore an asset, and you must exploit it."

He stepped back. Torina and I squared off again, performed the opening Innsu ritual, then snatched up our knives and launched into a flurry of attacks, blocks, and dodges. Inevitably, I ended up slamming too much force down on my bad knee. My instinct had been to try and recover, awkwardly attempting to shift my weight back onto my other leg. But that ended up costing me time and left me open in a way that Torina had seen—and used against me—for the second time today.

So, this time, I let my knee do whatever it was going to do. I focused, instead, on my opponent. Sure enough, my knee buckled and bent. I ended up on one knee in the sand, which wasn't a standard move in Innsu because kneeling implied defeat. I was shocked to see it take Torina by surprise, giving me a fleeting opening as she assessed what to do next.

My blade thumped into her stomach.

We both stared at my knife for a moment. I think I was more surprised than she was. But she stepped back and knelt, acknowledging me as the victor.

I stood. "That was legit, right? You didn't hand me that one?"

But Cataric stepped forward, shaking his head. "No, she didn't. You actually exposed a flaw in her technique. As long as she could predict, within reason, what you were going to do, she could conform her own attacks and defense to it, often two or three moves ahead. But when you did something unexpected, she had to take a moment to clear her mind of those anticipated moves and try to come up with a new course of action. Of course, by then, it was too late."

I curled my lip as I took this in. "So the lesson is… be unpredictable?"

"Is that what you took from this?"

"I guess so, yeah."

"Then that was, indeed, the lesson, wasn't it?" He smiled. "And that lesson, believe it or not, is the beginning of true mastery of Innsu."

Torina crossed her arms. "Master, I don't think I've ever seen you do anything that wasn't a standard Innsu form—"

Cataric's blade suddenly appeared in his hand, its point touching Torina's throat.

"Until now," she said.

"You are a skilled practitioner of Innsu, Torina. You have nearly mastered all of the forms. And that is important because you must know the rules before you break them."

I smiled. "I think I've heard Perry say that a few times about interstellar law."

"So true mastery of Innsu comes from being unpredictable?" she asked.

Cataric withdrew his knife. "True mastery of any confrontation ultimately comes from doing things your opponent doesn't expect. Make *him* react to *you*, and not to a predictable formula."

He smiled. "But as I said, first you must know the rules before you can decide how best to break them. Now, I believe you've both had enough of a break."

Cataric stepped away with a beatific smile on his face.

Torina turned to me, smiled, and planted her knife in the sand between her feet. "Go again?"

I stuck my own knife into the sand and moved into the focus stance.

"Absolutely. In addition to being unpredictable, I have another excellent quality."

She slid into her stance with lethal fluidity. "Which is?"

I let my face go slack, and my body followed. "I'm stubborn as an ox."

I PULLED off one more win against Torina, this time by pretending to throw my weight on my bad knee, seeing her react, then seizing the moment to strike at her from my other side. I was proud of that, even if it would only work against someone who knew I had a weak knee. But two wins was a drastic upgrade, and I'd learned something even in every loss. The fact that Torina racked up eleven wins of her own during the same session didn't matter *because* I was learning. Every bruise I had was a lesson, hard earned and worth it.

That evening, I dined with Torina and her mother. She was basically an older version of Torina, a formidable, elegant woman named Kaye. I gathered that she dealt with most of the domestic business on Helso, including imports and exports, while her husband, Torina's father, focused on the family's more far-flung ventures in other systems. It seemed like a tidy arrangement, even if it did keep her father on the road, as it were, most of the time.

We began our meal with something that looked like sushi, thin-sliced and laced with a bright, cheery sauce that tasted of sunshine and flowers.

I tried it and made a face of sheer surprise.

"Is it to your liking, Van?" Kaye asked in mild alarm.

"It's *amazing*. What is it?"

Mollified, Kaye gestured with the long, two-tined fork she held. "That little beast is known as a *gurranec*. Do you have any ethical concerns? Because I assure you, you should not."

I paused and put my own fork down. "Um. Concerns? Is this… is this an intelligent being?"

Kaye laughed, barely avoiding a gigglesnort. "Do you want to tell him?" she said to Torina, who was covering her mouth with one hand, snickering while waving that Kaye should continue.

"I'm only too happy to do so. No, the gurranec are not... intelligent. Just the opposite. They're sort of like a fish, but if that fish woke up in a bad mood and then decided to attack the galaxy. Every day."

"They're small, aggressive tyrants?" I asked.

Kaye smiled. "Exactly. One of the little maniacs nearly took off Torina's toe when she was a girl. They're quite vicious, and during spawning season, the schools will try to take down anything smaller than a starship."

I contemplated a sliver of the pale flesh, raising my brows. "Then may I state that I feel no guilt whatsoever at eating the little menace." I popped the tidbit into my mouth as Kaye gave me a nod of approval, then Perry appeared, nails a-clicking as he waddled across the floor.

"We just got a call from Dora, our art expert. We're in," he reported.

"We got *The Call* listed in the Vault?"

"Roger dodger. The next auction's in three days, so that's our window."

"We've got to do some clothes shopping," Torina said.

I gave her a puzzled look. "Clothes shopping?"

"You don't expect to walk into an auction on Vault in your Peacemaker uniform, do you?"

"Well, yeah, I kinda did."

Torina looked at her mother, and they both laughed. She turned back.

"Oh, no. No, no, no. We've got to get you outfitted properly."

"Is this going to involve high, tight collars and hot, scratchy fabric?"

"Maybe a little bit."

"Have I mentioned how much I hate getting dressed up?"

"It's for the greater good, Van," Perry said.

"Oh? And are we going to get a hoop skirt for you?"

"Don't be ridiculous. The auction is now, not two centuries ago. And I'm stocked up on basic black, which as you know——"

"Goes with everything. I'm a man, not a barbarian."

She beamed. "Good. Because I'm adding several black dresses to my collection, and I'll need your input as I try them on."

"Wait, I thought you said you had black dresses?"

Torina laughed outright, waving my concerns away. "Van. Dear. Not *all* shades of black are the same. Maybe you are a barbarian."

———

"VAN, WE HAVE COMPANY," Netty said.

I looked across the tarmac. We'd had to delay our departure from Helso to fix a wonky thruster, a job I'd just about finished up. At Netty's statement, though, I turned and saw a ground car approaching. It had an official look to it, so I turned to Torina, only to find she was gone, having boarded the *Fafnir* to check the thruster's status and confirm the fix. Perry perched on top of the ship, his talons gripping a stanchion.

"Looks like customs and excise," he said.

I wiped my hands on a rag. "I wonder what they want. I mean, they were interested in us when we arrived, and isn't that when customs types normally do their thing?"

"There's always time for bureaucracy, Van."

"Yeah, I'm starting to realize that."

The car turned and stopped about ten meters away. A single occupant got out, a slim human, male in his late twenties, maybe early thirties. He offered an affable smile and strolled toward me.

"Morning. What can I do for you?"

"Are you Van Tudor?"

"In the flesh. And you are?"

The man didn't answer. He just kept coming.

In retrospect, his relentlessly casual approach probably should have sounded an alarm bell. But he was still a few meters away, so I assumed he didn't want to shout across the gap. I tucked the rag in my back pocket and waited.

When he was three meters away, he pulled a gun.

Time slowed to a crawl. It seemed to take forever for the muzzle to come up, presenting me with a gaping black hole that seemed as big as a culvert. My brain was still stuck in a few seconds ago, though, wondering what this guy wanted in the first place. Only then did it start to catch up, realizing that what he apparently wanted was to shoot me.

Something flashed past me and slammed into him. A dazzling blue light and a loud *snap* followed. A sudden stink like hot metal filled the air around me. The man toppled to the ground, with Perry standing on top of him.

I was only halfway done placing the rag in my pocket, so fast was the entire event. I stood mute, wondering what had happened.

And then everything caught up and came crashing back into *now*. I ducked, about to run underneath the *Fafnir* with some vague idea I could retrieve The Drop or the Moonsword to defend myself. But the man remained motionless on the ground. Perry hopped off of him with a metallic tap of talons on blast-resistant concrete.

I shook my head. "Perry? Explain, if you please."

I didn't get it, given his role in customs, or what passed for it here.

Torina came racing around the *Fafnir*'s nose, her sidearm drawn. "Van, are you alright?"

"You might say that. Overly aggressive customs agent. Or… ?"

Perry shook his head. "Not customs. He is—or was—an assassin, Van. An android, sent here specifically to kill you."

"An assassin—" I stared for a long moment, taking in the man's details. Sure enough, the man had a waxy pallor, except where Perry's electrical discharge had seared away the skin on his chest. It revealed a metallic rib cage surrounding some components that looked part biological and part mechanical—an unholy melange of things that were never meant to be together.

"Congratulations, Van, you just made the big time."

"What kind of big time? Not sure I like this kind of fame."

"Synth-droid assassins don't come cheap. Somebody invested

a lot of money in this one for what looks like a single kill. I also think we now know what guild Axicur is with."

"Which one?"

"Whichever guild employs these things. As far as the Peacemakers are concerned, there is only one force repugnant enough to do this, and they have no name. Only corpses.

"Great. So we'll consider everyone in the galaxy a potential enemy then," I said, anger starting to push aside shock and confusion.

"I like healthy paranoia," Perry said, stepping closer to the would-be killer.

Torina knelt beside the fallen assassin. "Perry, how did you know this was an assassin, anyway? I mean, aside from the slightly strange skin tone, it looks perfectly human."

"It does. But it also looks exactly like a synth-droid that once came after Van's grandfather. Somebody needs to invest in making some new skins and not just reusing them."

I stared down at the construct. "Gramps had these bastards after him?"

"He sure did. Just as soon as he started getting too close to some truths somebody didn't want him to know."

I thought about how Miryam had described Gramps' final slide into illness before he died. *Had* it been some pernicious disease, or was there something more sinister at work?

"The implication being that we're getting too close to something somebody doesn't want found out, too," Torina said.

I nodded. But I was still caught on the fact that someone had sent this thing, at great expense, to infiltrate Helso and target me for termination of the extremely prejudicial sort. I found the idea frightening. I was no fool, and my bravery had limits.

I also found it flattering. In a grim sense, I'd arrived. I had fame, of a sort.

Now, I just had to survive it.

16

"Ow, *shit!* Torina, that's my skin you're pinching—*OW!*"

"Oh, just hold still." Torina finished buttoning my collar, then stepped back. "Perry, what do you think?"

"Very dapper. Have to admit, you cut a fine figure in formal wear, Van."

I grimaced, then checked myself in the *Fafnir*'s sole mirror, which was mounted on the inside of a locker door. I looked... different. More dignified, although I didn't *feel* that way. Some parts of this outfit, which spanned the gap between suit and tuxedo, bunched up and constricted my movements. Others hung loose, and still others rubbed and scraped me like fashionable sandpaper.

"I hate getting dressed up," I said to my reflection.

"I'd like to point out that Torina looks exquisite," Perry said. "You should take note."

It was true. She wore a flowing strapless gown with a short jacket, all in blue, and had put her hair up in a series of interlocking spirals that were part Grecian, part architecture. I gave her an appreciative nod.

"You do cut a fine figure, ma'am. Better than—" I stopped, reached down, and tugged at the crotch of my trousers, which were doing fascinating things to my anatomy.

Torina patted my shoulder, smiling. "That kind of ruins the effect. Might want to avoid that whole—ah, motion."

"Well, it's either this, or my voice is going to be climbing up the octaves as this auction wears on. How long do we expect it to last, anyway?"

"As long as it takes, Van," Perry said.

"Naturally." I sighed. "Torina, remind me to keep my hands—"

"Where I can see them. Now then, shall we?"

VAULT WAS the planet's name, but it was also commonly used to refer to the high-end auctions that went on here. It was sort of a Sotheby's of outer space. Everything from alien artifacts to spaceships were put on the block. It was the former we were most interested in, especially the lot numbered 4, which probably included our stolen Soviet Venus probe.

There was a lot more to Vault than just the auction, though. As we rode the shuttle down from the orbital terminal, I saw well-tended countryside sprawling off in all directions. A few thousand meters up, I could tell that a lot of it constituted estates, with large, rambling mansions reminiscent of English manor houses. Our destination, though, was a small city just coming into view through some clouds.

"Can I freshen your drink, sir?"

I turned to the speaker—a robotic drink dispenser. It rolled smoothly and quietly up and down the shuttle's aisle, apparently filling the same role as cabin attendants on Earthly passenger planes. Between its attentive service, the enormously comfortable seating with almost embarrassing amounts of legroom, and the general air of urbane sophistication, I felt like I was flying first class.

Except it was the only class. Vault, it turned out, was essentially a massive gated community. Those rich enough to live there could avoid interacting with the riffraff across the rest of known space. And none of them would ever fly coach.

I waved the robotic attendant off. Technically, even having one drink while on duty violated the Peacemaker Code of Conduct. But I could justify it as trying to blend in with all the elites converging on Vault for the upcoming auction.

The shuttle, now less than a klick up, banked over a sprawling complex of buildings on the outskirts of our destination, the town called Sublime. As we leveled off on our final approach, I pointed out the building complex to Torina before it slid out of sight.

"There's no way that's a house," I said.

She peered out the shuttle's viewport. "No, probably not. I'd say two houses, separated by that creek running between the waterfall and that pond in the gardens."

"Who the hell needs that much room?"

Torina gave me an impatient glare. "Someone who can afford it. And if you don't want to stand out among this lot, you'd probably best stop being outraged about their lifestyles."

I tilted my head, looked down my nose, and attempted a British accent. "Yes, love, you see——"

"Is that really how you see wealthy people? Is that how you see me?"

"Not… not all the time."

"Keep it up, and that collar won't be the only thing strangling you."

We landed at a spaceport that resembled Buckingham Palace, then caught ground transportation to the auction house. I'd expected we'd just take the equivalent of a cab, but of course not. It was a self-driving limo, with yet more overstuffed upholstery and a bar that was more like a buffet but crammed with an array of food in frustrating bite-sized amounts.

Curious, I opened the bar, revealing an array of bottles. A cultured voice spoke up.

"Please be advised that items removed from the bar will be added to your account."

I pulled my hand back. "I'm not falling for that. I grabbed a can of smoked almonds out of an in-room courtesy bar in Rome once. I'm still paying it off."

If the terminal resembled Buckingham Palace, then the auction house made me think of Versailles. It was opulent in a way that wasn't even remotely subtle, all rococo curlicues, dancing cherubic beings, intricate tapestries, and a floor made of pale blue stone that actually glowed under the pressure of your feet. It set a new standard for *ostentatious*, which was going to be hard to beat. Even the actual Versailles was understated compared to this place.

We were ushered into the main auction hall, a soaring chamber filled with money. I saw all manner of aliens, some of them walking around in hermetically sealed suits, others lounging in glassine compartments thick with native gases. Robotic waiters wended their way among the crowds, dispensing yet more drinks, and there was a murmur of sound in every possible frequency I could hear—and beyond.

I accepted a flute full of sparkling fluid that smelled like wine and danced with the light of distant stars. Torina chose a smaller glass filled with deep amber liquid, the scent somewhere between caramel and vanilla.

"Let me guess—these are on the house?"

Torina smiled knowingly. "You're catching on."

I nodded. "Because they *want* you to get drunk."

"Inebriated people tend to be a little more willing to bid something up," she replied, sipping her drink while surveying the room.

"Yeah—and regretting it when they have to pay the actual bill."

But Torina waved a dismissive hand. "That's only the noobs. Experienced bidders don't drink alcohol."

I lifted my brows at that. "*Noobs?* Could you repeat that, please?"

"I learned it from Perry—oh." Torina was looking at something across the room. "Looks like they're getting ready to open the auction. We'd better get *The Call* registered."

I carried the ornate box containing *The Ancient's Call* in a briefcase we'd purchased along with our new duds. When I took it out at the table where last-minute lots were being registered, its gaudiness struck me as being right at home here.

The staffer manning the desk, a lizoid being scaled in colorful swirls, paused when I named our entry and just stared at me with glassy eyes.

"*The Ancient's Call?* Really?"

"Yes, really."

"You do realize it's a grave offense to enter forgeries and reproductions into the auction, right?"

"Then it's a good thing we're not doing that."

The alien reached for the box. "Alright. *The Ancient's Call.* Apologies if I seem dubious, but—regardless, it will be lot number 7—"

"Thanks, but I think I'll hold onto it," I said, pulling the box away from his reaching claws.

"I assure, we're fully bonded. Your item will be secure—"

"Yes, it will, because I'm keeping it with me," I said, accepting our registration receipt from the alien, then heading off with Torina to find a seat.

I took in the crowd as we wove our way through it. I'd had a number of occasions to rub shoulders with the extremely well-to-do when I had one as a client for my cyber expertise. This gang might be different shapes and colors, and some of them might breathe ammonia or vaporized sulfur, but they were otherwise much the same as the idle rich back on Earth. They projected an aura of bored indolence, of a casual disregard for anything that didn't immediately interest them. None of these people ever wanted for anything, so they let their baser desires take over, indulging in all sorts of things, including some that were no doubt illegal, and lots more that were definitely immoral. It came out as an indifferent contempt to pretty much everyone and everything, and it made them dangerous. Most of them probably wouldn't hesitate to ruin someone, financially or otherwise, if it would get them something they wanted.

Protecting that sort of causal, even effortless self-indulgence might be exactly the sort of thing that could end up making me a target.

Or worse—a corpse.

Which meant I didn't trust any of these people. I had nothing to fear *here*, of that much I was certain. If someone had it out for me, they weren't going to do anything about it in the midst of their affluent peers. It put me in an odd state of being both hypervigilant but also relaxed.

A figure stepped up behind the podium at the front of the room. It was rail thin, like a stick figure brought to life, wore incongruous goggles, and had a gold mesh microphone mounted atop its head. It communicated by somehow making a complex series of drumming noises somewhere deep in its skull, which were sent to a comm transmitter and fed into the bidders' translators, including my own ear bug.

"Welcome, illustrious guests," the auctioneer said. "We're

going to get right into bidding. To that end, I'd like to draw your attention to lot number 1."

A small bot emerged from the side of the stage, carrying—an axe. And a crude one at that, its haft rough wood like a branch freshly snapped off a tree, its blade obsidian, black, and vitreous. There was something encrusted and streaked on the edge and sides of the blade.

"This is the axe used to kill Armophusist the Third, Emperor of the Telignite Hegemony. That is, in fact, his blood and brain matter still present on the axe. As I'm sure you're aware, the late Emperor's offspring are currently engaged in a rather vicious struggle for succession, so the winning bidder is advised to maintain this item in a personal and private collection. Otherwise, they may find that the Telignite princes take exception to the sale of this particular piece, and princes are known for demanding mortal combat to redress perceived slights to their, ah, family honor. And we don't want that, now, do we?"

Laughter, or its equivalent, rattled through the room. I just shook my head.

"These people are ghouls," I said to Torina, keeping my voice low.

She gave me a wry look back. "You're being far too kind. Most of these people passed ghoul a long time ago and are well on their way to, uh—"

"Lich?"

"What the hell's a *lich*?"

"It's an undead monster, much stronger than a ghoul—you've never played Dungeons and Dragons, have you?"

"At the risk of repeating myself, what the hell is Dungeons and Dragons?"

I shook my head and smiled. "I'll tell you later. It's a bit too nerdy for this room."

The bidding on the gory axe continued, finally hitting an eye-watering high bid of three-point-two million bonds. The winner was apparently one of the aliens enclosed in a booth full of toxic atmosphere—well, toxic to me, anyway. The next item rolled up, the skeletal remains of a unique creature. And it was literally unique, the only instance of this particular being ever found in known space.

"That belongs in a museum, or in the hands of some research institute, not some rich asshole's rumpus room," I hissed.

"Heh. Rumpus room."

"What—oh, yeah, I know, what's a rumpus room."

Torina grinned. "No, I just like the sound of it. Rumpus room. *Rumpus* room."

I pointed to the front. "Excuse me, we're being classy here?"

The auction finally got to our lot. It didn't look all that impressive, of course, just a small, ornately inlaid silver box. A stir rippled through the crowd. Since they didn't immediately know what it was, it held a sudden fascination.

The auctioneer contributed to the moment with a dramatic pause. Finally, he spoke.

"I have conducted many, many auctions and have seen some truly remarkable things. But this is, certainly, one of the most remarkable. Maybe *the* most remarkable. Our next lot is an original recording of *The Ancient's Call*."

Another moment of silence hung in the room, then everyone started muttering and whispering at once.

"The opening bid is one hundred thousand bonds," the auctioneer announced.

No one entered a bid. I shifted a little uncomfortably.

Torina leaned toward me. "They're going to want to hear it before they bid on it."

Ah. Good point. I nodded. And, sure enough, the auctioneer addressed it.

"Yes, this is an unusual item. I am going to take the equally unusual step of asking the seller to come forward and play the recording, since auction personnel aren't allowed to operate the lots."

I grimaced. "Fair enough.They would want to hear it, wouldn't they?"

"Wouldn't you?"

"Of course. But if I'm recognized—"

"Van, you're hardly the first Peacemaker to have found something potentially valuable in your travels and decided to make some money off it."

"Again, could I please have the seller come forward?" the auctioneer said.

I glanced at Torina, who just returned an encouraging nod.

So I stood and walked to the front of the room. I felt the sudden scrutiny of dozens of eyes—and various other sensory apparatus and organs—light me up like fire-control scanners.

"Ah, there you are. Thank you for indulging us. But I'm sure you understand that this item is potentially worth… a great deal, to be blunt."

I raised a hand. "Not a problem." I grabbed the box.

"Actually, I'm not sure I want to do this."

Mutters rattled through the crowd. The auctioneer— frowned, I guess? It was hard to tell.

"I'm sorry, sir, but if you expect to have anyone bid on this item, they're going to need to know it's more than just a fancy little box."

"It is a fancy little box, though, isn't it?" I said, running my hand over it. I felt the expectant tension ratchet up a few notches as soon as I touched it.

But I pulled my hand away again. "The thing is, anyone who listens to *The Call* ends up having to pay a very personal price. It's kind of a, I don't know—a curse."

More mutters and hissed whispers. I felt a note of frustration tighten the air, and the various other breathing mixtures, in the room.

"Sir—" the auctioneer began, but I held up a hand again.

"Maybe a few notes won't hurt."

I opened the box and activated the recording. The opening notes of *The Ancient's Call* hummed through the room, ponderous and heartbreakingly sad, evoking the last pages of a beloved story where you realized you'd never be able to read them for the first time again.

I let it play for about fifteen or twenty seconds, then shut it off. A moment of silence hung off the end of the last note.

Then the room erupted into a chaotic frenzy of bids.

I walked back to my seat and sat down. Torina gave me a broad grin. "Quite the showman, aren't you?"

"Like P.T. Barnum said, always leave them wanting more—" I stopped. "Yeah, you don't know who P.T. Barnum is, do you?"

"You mean the nineteenth century showman, businessman, author, politician, and philanthropist from Earth? Famous for the *Barnum and Bailey Circus?*"

I stared back at her, a little dumbstruck. "You know who P.T. Barnum is?"

"No, Van, that was just a wild guess. How close did I get?"

"Really? So of all possible personalities from Earth's history, *he's* the one you know about?"

"Well, him and Cornelius Vanderbilt, John Jacob Astor, Andrew Carnegie—let's see, also William Randolph Hearst, J.P. Morgan—"

"That is a who's who of people widely considered robber barons."

"They were also very smart people who made a lot of money. Even if you might consider someone unsavory, you can still learn valuable lessons from them."

I had to nod at that, then I turned my attention back to the bidding.

Which made my jaw drop. We were already at eight hundred *thousand* bonds.

I sat, enraptured, watching people throw money at our admittedly fascinating artifact, but one which ultimately did nothing useful. It was money that could have been used in so many other, more worthwhile ways.

But it was their money to fling around, and I was getting a big chunk of it, which should easily be enough to finally upgrade the *Fafnir*. My dream of my own fireplace was in reach, although just not having to sleep in a fetal position all the time would be a major step up. My bunk was kid-sized and featured a mattress that felt like it was carved, not stuffed.

Another bid. Another. But they were slowing now, as bidders dropped out, some tensed and glaring in frustration, others just looking very sad.

Another bid.

One more.

Silence.

The auctioneer, who'd been prompting bids all along, kept it up.

"We have a bid of two point six million bonds. Do I hear two point six five?"

Expectant silence. I found myself perched on the edge of my seat, both figuratively and literally.

"Going once."

"Going twice—"

A voice suddenly cut in, crackling over a comm. It was one of the remote bidders, participating from somewhere else in known space.

"I will bid three million bonds, but on the condition that the item is delivered to me by the seller."

I glanced at Torina. She looked as uneasy as I felt. Was this some sort of potential shakedown? A trap of some sort?"

Running on pure instinct, I stood. "I'll do it—for one

hundred thousand bonds, payable in advance. I'll wait three seconds for your answer. One—"

"I accept."

I glanced down at Torina. She looked a little less unsettled about it. If someone was willing to pay one hundred thousand bonds up-front for a delivery, and it really *was* a trap, then it was someone especially dedicated to their cause. They'd be out that much, plus their winning bid of three million bonds, just to draw us someplace. That wasn't out of the question, of course. If we were getting uncomfortably close to things that people with lots of money didn't want to be poked or prodded, then they might feel it was worth it.

"Going once. Going twice."

I saw people tense, as though about to bid, then pull themselves back.

"Sold!"

I slumped back, feeling a little drained. I still felt eyes on me, the array of whispers rising throughout the room. I was unknown. I was human. I was suddenly wealthy. These facts— now also weighing on me—changed the tone of the room, and the auctioneer felt it, too. He called a break. Torina and I pushed toward him, smiling and acknowledging congratulations as we went. I also caught a few outright hostile glares and tried to make a mental note of their owners.

From the corner of my mouth, I muttered to Torina, who leaned in to hear.

"Based on this, Venus can wait. That's theft. This is—"

"Theft of another kind?" she said, her voice low and plump with awe.

"Yeah. Ooof. Okay, showtime again," I mumbled, then raised my voice to address the auctioneer, while trying my best to look humble. "That was, ah. . .unexpected."

"Indeed. Congratulations on making such a lucrative sale."

"To get right to it, sir... where am I taking this thing?" I asked, pointing at the box.

He returned a thin, humorless smile. "To hell, I think. You're going to the Null World, and you're about to meet the client we distrust the most, the last of the Schegith."

"The last? As in, the last of her kind? What happened to all of the rest?"

"Why, I assume she ate them all."

17

"YOU KNOW, even putting aside the matter of carnivorous and possibly genocidal aliens, this place really *is* hell."

Null World was a planet orbiting yet another of the stars named after Wilhelm Gliese, a German astronomer. This one, Gliese 440, was a white dwarf, but an unusual one, it seemed. According to Netty, it was massive for a white dwarf, about three-quarters the mass of Sol, and although its nuclear engine had sputtered out and died, it was still radiating a lot of heat.

It meant it still had a Goldilocks zone, close in to the star, and there was a planet plying an orbit through it, named Null World. Its only planetary companion was a gas giant that Netty said had some of the highest recorded winds in known space.

"Up to five thousand kilometers per hour at the equator, in fact," she said.

I eyed the half disk of the big planet, banded with sickly

yellow and green stripes, as we passed. "No sailing down there, I'm betting."

We cruised past the big planet, our trajectory taking us toward a stable orbit around Null World. There was no traffic control because there was no traffic. We were the only ship in the system, something I found a little disconcerting.

"This place is saturated with loneliness," I said.

"Well, the only reason to come here would be to visit the last Schegith. That makes for a pretty narrow range of business," Perry said, perched in his place between the *Fafnir*'s seats.

"Yeah, aside from delivering the song, what other reason would you have for coming here?" Torina asked. "I'm not getting a touristy feel from—" She waved grandly at the planetary vista below.

"Fair point."

I'd actually been a little disappointed by the outcome of the auction. Yes, the money was fantastic. But we'd set out to uncover something about the murder of Tand's family on Nesit, and the tie-in of that to the stolen artifacts. But Perry had offered some encouragement, pointing out that the money would open doors—

And open doors revealed dirty secrets.

Below us, the winds howled, and with the touch of our drive, we began to descend into the swirling unknown.

NULL WORLD REALLY *WAS* HELL, or a good approximation of it, anyway. As Netty so understated it, Null World had a *significant degree of instability.*

No shit. I watched an enormous sandstorm billow across a good half of the planet's southern hemisphere, drab and diffuse and shot through with occasional strobing pulses of lightning. The combined effect of the planet's axial tilt and the fact it was almost but not quite tidally locked with the star meant that a day on Null World lasted nearly three standard months. The result was an equatorial region so heat and radiation blasted as to be unlivable, and a northern hemisphere whose entire upper third had been locked in an ice age that wouldn't end for tens of thousands of years.

And to top all that off, tidal kneading made the planet extremely volatile, volcanoes spewing lava and ash almost constantly, blanketing enormous regions with sinuous lava flows and vast plains of volcanic dust.

"It would be really hard to write a tourist brochure for this place," I said, staring down from the *Fafnir*'s lofty vantage in orbit.

"It's rather simple, actually. *Come feel better about your own planet!* Boom—sending the invoice now. Thank you for your business," Perry said.

There were remnants of an advanced civilization scattered all across the planet, but only one point was broadcasting a locator beacon. We descended, bouncing and jolting through a rough ride through the gusty winds of the troposphere, and finally set down on a flat expanse of something like concrete. It might have been a landing pad, or not, but it was the closest place to the beacon we could land without being hurled into the air again by the bullying wind.

We suited up, even though the atmosphere was breathable. Instead, it was to keep the billowing dust and drifting sand out of eyes and mouths and various other places dust and sand don't belong. A keening gust smacked us as we stepped out of the *Fafnir*'s airlock into gravity about ten percent higher than Earth's. It added almost twenty pounds to my weight, which might not seem like much. But I soon noticed the extra effort it took me just to walk the hundred meters or so to a large, ornate gate set into a towering wall of rust-colored stone. It cracked and swung open as we approached.

We looked into the dark opening.

"Ominous, isn't it?" Torina said.

"A dark, unlit corridor leading into the heart of what looks like an abandoned, ancient temple? What could go wrong?" I said, just as savage lightning threw the twisted stones into relief.

Gripping the handle of the case carrying *The Ancient's Call*, Torina and I followed Perry into the gloomy doorway. He flew ahead of us in short bounds, scanning for threats as we progressed. We still hadn't entirely ruled this out as a trap, which was why Netty kept the *Fafnir*'s drive idling, her point-defense systems on autonomous mode. It was also why The Drop and the Moonsword bounced on my hips. But aside from darkness and the rising and falling wail of the wind behind us, there was nothing.

Which actually made it even *more* nerve-wracking. This really *was* like walking into the guts of some ancient forgotten temple.

"If you see an enormous ball of stone come rolling at us, run," I said.

Torina shot me a look. "What the *hell* are you talking about?"

"Never mind—"

"He means to be wary. But there is no need. You are welcome here," a new voice said, booming in the air around us.

We stopped and tensed, then Torina dropped into a bit of a crouch, while I twitched my fingers toward The Drop. But the only response was laughter—and not the evil or maniacal sort, but of someone genuinely amused.

"It seems you are afraid of ghosts. Well, there is only one ghost here, and you have almost found her."

Ahead of us, lights came on, illuminating a pair of doors twice my height, inlaid with something that could have been writing but could also just have been abstract decoration. I looked at Torina, who shrugged. Perry, about five meters ahead of us, spread his wings.

"I'll check it out," he said and launched himself through the doors. He wheeled out of sight—then his voice came back over the comm.

"My God, it's full of stars."

EXCEPT IT WASN'T full of stars. What it was, was a well-appointed suite of rooms, stacked with all sorts of objects that might have been art, or tools, or weapons, or maybe some of all of them, or even just junk. We passed through two of them and saw Perry ahead.

"Perry, what the hell was that crack about stars?" Torina

asked.

"Ask Van," he replied.

"It's a quote from a movie. Not sure why this was the time for it, though."

"Hey, Mister Balls of Stone, you're not the only one that can spout movie references."

"Mister Balls of Stone? Add that to my approved list, if you please."

"All of that said, it's impolite to just prattle on like this when we're guests," Perry said, then bobbed his head toward something in the room he'd entered. We followed him and found ourselves face-to-face with the last Schegith.

The Schegith was a grub, the kind you sometimes find when you're digging up a garden. It was nearly ten meters long, with a humanoid face, sprawled on a chaise lounge and draped in a vari-colored robe the size of a naval mainsail. As we stood, dumb-struck, the Schegith drew incandescent gas from an ornate, crystalline bottle that looked like a huge bong with copper gears inside, whirring with quiet purpose.

"This is unexpected," I mumbled, not meaning to say it out loud.

"You must be Van Tudor," the slug said, its voice rich and smooth and slightly—Eastern European?

"Um…"

Well, so much for first contact.

Torina grinned at me. "Don't mind him. He's only been in space a few months, so—"

"So he's utterly captivated by this one's ravishing beauty?"

Torina turned to me with her eyebrows raised, then mouthed the word *well?*

"Okay, so, to be clear... "

"Believe it or not, he can form coherent sentences," Perry said. "Sometimes."

I shook myself out of my moment of stupor. "Yeah, sorry. I just—" I shrugged. "Torina's right. Until a few months ago, I hadn't a clue that life existed anywhere but on Earth. Turns out, life seems to exist *everywhere* besides Earth. It's a little... new. To me, that is."

"Do not concern yourself. This one understands."

"At the risk of sounding rude, do you have a name?" Torina asked. "It would be nice to be able to address you personally. Or do your people use names?"

"We do, but they're... lengthy. And complicated."

Perry cut in. "Schegith names are a story. They describe that individual, and their accomplishments, and their brood line. I've heard it can take several minutes for a Schegith to introduce themselves."

"Actually, among our kind, it is nowhere near as cumbersome as that. Our names exist as sounds, but they also exist as thoughts and impressions, shared through the Congress."

I frowned. "I'm sorry, the Congress? The only Congress I'm familiar with sure does evoke a lot of thoughts and impressions, but I don't think that's what you mean."

"It's like a hive mind, but it stops short of subsuming every individual into a whole. Think of it as though everyone could kind of read one another's thoughts, all the time," Perry said.

I winced. "Not sure I'd want to know what everyone around me is thinking."

"It is appropriate for this one's people. Or it was, except that this one is now nearly the last. And as for a name, for the sake of convenience, you may simply call me Schegith."

"Then we are most pleased to meet you, Schegith." I stepped forward, offering—*her*, I recalled—the box containing the recording of *The Ancient's Call*. She accepted it with an array of tentacles that she either extruded directly from her body or had tucked away somewhere. After placing it down on a small table beside her mega-bong, she opened it, activated the recording, and played *The Call*.

I'd have thought that, having heard it several times now, it wouldn't affect me.

I was wrong.

By the end of the first few bars, my throat had developed a hurtful lump, and my eyes stung. I could tell that Torina was fighting to keep herself together, too.

It finally ended. A long moment of silence followed.

"Well," I finally managed, clearing my throat. "That's—" I coughed and tried again. "I hope you enjoy that, Schegith. You certainly paid enough money for it."

"Money is not relevant. This one wants for nothing." A pause. "Except companionship."

I glanced at Torina. She looked back at me, her face caught in a moment of surprise and deeply sympathetic sadness. Those two words, except companionship, were almost as forlorn and heartbreaking as *The Call* itself.

I had to clear my throat again, several times. "May I ask… what happened to your people, Schegith?"

"I did not eat them."

"I—didn't really think you had."

"Yes, but this one is aware of the tales told. This one has considered obtaining gnawed bones and scattering them about to fulfill the expectations of those tales."

It was obviously meant to be sardonic, but her words held a note of bitter sadness.

"This one's people have simply succumbed to that which may not be denied. Time. The Schegith are an ancient race, well into the twilight. A state of senescence waits for all peoples, and this one's time for such a degraded state… is now."

"You're really the last?" Torina asked.

Schegith didn't answer immediately. When she did, it was with her gaze on *The Call*.

"This one purchased this ancient song because it encapsulates who she is. It is profoundly sad, yet it gives comfort."

Torina nodded. "Sometimes, when I feel sadness, I listen to sad music. It makes me cry. But it also leaves me feeling better. I am purged, I think."

But there'd been a subtext wandering through this whole conversation, one that I didn't think was accidental.

"Schegith, I can't help noticing you didn't answer Torina's question. And you referred to yourself as *nearly the last* of your people. Are there other Schegith somewhere?"

"Good catch, Van," Perry said through my ear bug.

"This one has no reason to believe that she is not the last of her kind."

"But?"

"But the Congress is not wholly silent. There are… echoes."

I shook my head. "I'm sorry, but I don't know what that means."

"It is thinking you are alone in a large, empty space. But then you hear whispers and hints that you are not alone. That is the best way this one can explain it."

"So there might still be Schegith out there somewhere," Perry said.

"Yes. But also no. If there were, then no matter how far distant they are, this one would share Congress with them. This is more as though there are remnants of others, half-aware, but not fully there. This one apologizes but cannot put it any more clearly than that."

I saw Torina and Perry already looking at me. "You thinking what I'm thinking?"

"This one does not understand," The Schegith said.

I turned to address her, a rueful smile on my face. "Unfortunately, these ones do."

I SETTLED myself back in the *Fafnir*'s pilot's seat. I had to admit, it was actually starting to feel familiar. The aura of unreality and strangeness that engulfed my life in the kitchen of the Iowa farmhouse was finally starting to fade. If this was all just a delusion of some sort, it was one *hell* of a good one.

"So it looks like the auction wasn't entirely a bust, in terms of our main case," Perry said.

"We don't know for sure that the Schegith have been chipped, Perry," I said.

"No, but it's a working theory."

Torina held up the gift Schegith had given her, a small, ornate, and incredibly intricate timepiece. It resembled a pocket watch without a case enclosing it. You'd think that would risk damaging the workings, which looked about as durable as spider-webs, but it didn't. The device just kept ticking away, apparently regardless of whatever environment to which it might be exposed. Schegith had given me a similar device, different in details but identical in function. She claimed that they would mark time perfectly, in units that were exactly equal to three standard seconds. And since standard seconds were themselves based on the behavior of certain quantum particles, we could use these to very accurately measure time.

Remembering to divide by three, of course.

"Schegith workmanship is actually renowned across known space. There's no one else that can assemble, tinker with, and maintain complex mechanisms like they can—or so it's reputed, anyway. After all, they've been pretty much dormant as a race for a long time now," Perry said.

I thought about the promise I'd made to Schegith after she gave us these gifts.

If your people are out there, and we can help them, we will.

"Let's see if we can get them back to doing their tinkering," I said, lighting the *Fafnir*'s drive and lifting us back toward space.

18

As soon as we stepped out of the ramp and into Anvil Dark, we were the focus of considerable attention.

Some Peacemakers came straight up to us, grinning and offering hands to shake—or the equivalent, depending on the species of the Peacemaker—congratulating us. Others hung back, whispering and watching. And a few hung even further back, fixing us with darkly ominous stares.

"Welcome to being a rich celebrity," Torina said.

"I'll try not to let it go to my head."

A figure pushed through the crowd. It was Lunzy.

"First off, Van, congratulations. Second, come with me," she said, gesturing for us to follow. So I did, Torina and Perry right behind me.

We made our way back to the relative quiet and seclusion of

the Keel but stopped short of actually meeting any of the Masters. Lunzy waved us toward sumptuous chairs in an antechamber, where those waiting to meet the Masters were parked.

Lunzy sat down, shaking her head. "Van. Holy *shit*. Three million bonds. And for *The Ancient's Call*. You've been a busy boy."

"Just trying to keep out of trouble is all." I glanced around. "Are we waiting to meet the Masters?"

If we were, then I was worried. We already suspected two of them, including Groshenko, to maybe not be entirely clean. And the Keel, the name both for the Masters Collectively, and the section of Anvil Dark where they hung out, was awfully isolated by design. Had we pushed someone too far? Were we about to be told, in no uncertain terms, to back off? Or was something worse in store for us? I wore the Moonsword because it was technically part of my uniform, but Torina and I were both otherwise unarmed—

"Van, stop it," Lunzy snapped.

"Stop what?"

"Thinking something awful is going to happen to you. I just wanted a quiet place to talk to you. And since I work for the Masters, I get to requisition their digs."

I sank back a little in relief. "So, what's up then?"

"Your money. We need to do something about it."

"I… was going to stick in the bank? Probably The Quiet Room?"

"Perry hasn't informed you about Article Eight of the Peacemaker's Charter."

I glanced at Perry, who leveled his amber regard on Lunzy. "Are you really invoking that?"

"I am, and for good reason. Van, Article Eight of the Charter says that any compensation gained during the course of performing your duties belongs to the Guild."

I sat up. "Wait just one—"

"No, no, I'm not finished," Lunzy said, holding up a hand. "There's a clause to Article Eight—"

"The Annuity Clause, right?" Perry asked.

"Give that bird a cracker. Yup, the Annuity Clause. Instead of transferring all that cash to the Guild, and supposedly getting it back in support services, you can lock most of it into an annuity fund that will pay you a monthly stipend off the interest. The Guild still takes a cut, but it's way less than otherwise. And you'll have to hand over a chunk of the remaining balance you don't put in the fund, but that should still leave you with plenty of money."

I sat back. "Oh. Doesn't sound too different than investing on Earth. Perry, what do you think—"

"Do it."

"Torina?"

"I'm with the bird."

I nodded to Lunzy. "Let's do it then."

"Alright, I am issuing instructions to Perry and Torina. Meantime, Van, how would you like a really sweet deal on an avionics package?"

"Does it come with a set of steak knives?"

Lunzy just stared. "*What?*"

"You know, I'm obviously going to have to brush up on my humorous pop culture references, because these ones from Earth just are *not* landing."

THE ANNUITY CAME with a clause of its own, that I had to specify a beneficiary in the event of my shuffling off this mortal coil, and not just from the boring old ways, like old age. There were a lot of ways to go *poof* in outer space.

So I named Torina. And I added a rider, specifying that Perry and Netty would remain with her until she died or chose to divest herself of them.

Torina, who'd been helping get our new avionics suite installed, gawped at me when I told her. "Van, I don't really need the money."

"You're the one who told me you wanted to achieve things on your own, apart from your family's wealth and influence. The money from selling *The Ancient's Call* is as much yours as mine. *We* earned it, not just me." I shrugged. "If you decide you don't want to be a Peacemaker, you can just sell the commission to someone who does. But if you do, then you've got your own money supporting you, not your family's, am I right?"

Torina climbed down the ladder from the open access hatch on the *Fafnir's* flank and stopped in front of me—then hugged me.

"Thank you, Van."

"Yeah, it is a lot of money."

She pulled back and punched my arm. "I don't mean the money, you jerk, and you know it."

I turned to Perry, who was helping to calibrate the new systems via another access point. "Perry, she assaulted a Peacemaker. You saw it, right?"

"Sorry, Van, I can't hear you over the sound of me not caring."

The avionics *suite* had been something more contentious than the annuity and beneficiaries. Removed from another *Dragonet* that had been upgraded, it was more advanced than the *Fafnir*'s, so it would be a significant step up for us. Moreover, the Keel apparently decided to gift it to us at a bargain-basement price, literally pennies on the dollar, as a sort of congratulatory gift for such a big score with *The Ancient's Call*.

And that made us immediately suspicious. From our perspective, two of the Masters already gave off at least a few whiffs of corruption, after all. So could the avionics system be compromised in some way? Could it be used to track us, for instance?

Netty offered an even more dire possibility.

"There have been instances of ship upgrades containing a very, very discreet kill switch that can be activated remotely and leave the ship dead in the water. There was a shipyard in Tau Ceti colluding with some pirates to do just that. The pirates didn't even have to fire a shot, just send the kill code."

We finally decided to back up the system's software, then completely wipe every bit of it. Once the drive was spotless, we spent some cash buying new, still-in-the-wrapper logic and memory modules, then swapped out the old ones. In the meantime, Netty, Perry, and I pored over the software with a fine-toothed digital comb.

We spent three days doing it, but Perry finally announced the verdict.

"There is absolutely no code in here that doesn't belong. Well, except for that shockingly profane little easter egg we found. I mean, is that even anatomically possible for any known species? Asking for a friend."

I sat back in the *Fafnir*'s pilot's seat and stretched, blinking to clear the afterimages of code burned into my retinas. "Easter eggs are common. Hell, I've put a few into the code I've written." I looked at Perry. "Although you can tell your friend that they're normally nowhere near as disgusting as that one."

I took a deep breath and stretched again. I had to agree with Perry's assessment. I'd discovered that, although the details and capabilities of computer hardware and software were obviously vastly different than those of Earthly origin, the underlying logic and programming philosophies were still much the same. Thanks to my old day job, I'd become an expert at examining code for things that didn't belong, and we'd found none.

So were our fears about the Masters unfounded? Had we just spent three paranoid days chasing digital boogeymen?

But I only had to think about any of our previous encounters with pirates and the like, and imagine the *Fafnir* being disabled by some hidden kill switch.

Sometimes it really *was* better to be safe than sorry.

I was just congratulating myself on having gotten this far, and having done this well, when Lunzy appeared in the hangar, carrying a large package. I saw her through the *Fafnir*'s canopy, so I clambered back into the ship to greet her at the airlock.

"Hey, Lunzy. What's in the big box?"

"A treat for you, Van. You're going to love it."

Something about the way she said it made me immediately suspicious. "Do you mean *love*, as in actually *love* it? Or do you mean *love*, as in *you're not going to like this at all?*"

Lunzy grinned. "Probably a little of both."

I scowled at myself in the sole mirror aboard the *Fafnir*.

"This looks ridiculous," I grumbled.

Torina, peering into my cabin on the *Fafnir* beside Lunzy, clicked her tongue. "It does not, Van. You look very… dapper."

"I look like a cosplayer who got a discount on tinfoil and horsehair."

"I… don't know if that's a good thing or not."

"Neither do I."

The package Lunzy had brought had contained my Peacemaker dress uniform, known as *Patrols*. Why *Patrols*, I had no idea, and neither did Lunzy. The uniform had simply been known as Patrols since time immemorial, as in, *Make sure you wear your Patrols to this event.* The name probably had some storied history to it, but the details were lost to time.

"There are a half-dozen explanations for the name, Van, but nobody knows which is correct," Perry said.

To me, *Patrols* were things soldiers did, usually at night, usually in small groups, and usually to either gather information or launch raids. The Peacemaker Patrols, on the other hand, constituted a set of armor—breastplate, shoulder pauldrons, vambraces on the forearms, cuisses on the thighs, greaves on the lower legs, the whole deal. They were all ornate, rendered in dark blue and edged in gold. A fancy helmet with decoration that resembled a bird of prey completed the armor. It sported a flowing white plume of what back on Earth would have been horse hair that cascaded down my back, almost reaching my belt. And as if that wasn't all fancy enough, a purple tabard cape draped over my shoulders, across my chest, and down my back.

I turned and winced at the effort caused by the extra weight and bulk. It actually wasn't as uncomfortable as the formal suit I'd worn to the auction, but that was a pretty low bar to clear.

I pointed at my neck. "This thing, this—"

"It's called a gorget," Lunzy said.

"Fine, this gorget really bugs me. It's like being garroted by a really weak assassin—for hours at a time."

"I don't know, Van, I'm with Torina here. I think you look very… dapper," Perry said.

I turned to shoot him a glare, or would have if my neck hadn't jammed hard against the stupid gorget. I had to turn my whole body to see him.

"Did Gramps have one of these?" I asked.

Perry nodded. "Of course."

"What did he think of it?"

"Ah, generally, he didn't. I think I saw him wear it twice. Once for his Investiture as a Peacemaker, and once for a funeral."

"Yeah, well, I'm with Gramps on that."

Torina gave me a wide-eyed look. "Wait. You mean you're not going to wear this all the time? You won't be dispensing justice clad in your amazing armor?"

Lunzy smirked. I scowled.

"Maybe I will. But I'll have to have a female version made, one that's really tight, awkward, and uncomfortable."

"So you mean—typical women's clothing."

This time, Lunzy laughed. "Van, you look fine. In fact, you look pretty damned good. Most people just can't pull off the whole *armor* thing."

"It's not even armor! It's all made of some resin or something, like it's just for show."

"That's because it *is* just for show," Lunzy replied, then checked the time on her comm. "And speaking of shows, we'd better get going. The Investiture Ceremony is in less than an hour."

Lunzy, Torina, and Perry cleared the way. I moved to exit my cabin and promptly smacked the top of the helmet into the hatch coaming.

"Now I know what an ostrich feels like," I said.

Perry held up a wing, then tilted his head at me while shaking with laughter. "Think you mean a giraffe, big guy."

TECHNICALLY, I had been a Peacemaker Initiate this entire time. I'd earned the title when I completed my Induction on Crossroads and had now proven myself enough that I could officially be Invested as a fully-fledged Peacemaker. Back in my army days, progression had been through attending and passing certain courses, qualifying in certain ways, and spending a certain minimum amount of time in a job. In the Peacemakers, it seemed far more subjective. You were promoted when the Masters decided that you were ready.

As we made our way to the audience hall on Anvil Dark where the ceremony would take place, I found myself brooding on that.

"Is that open to abuse? You know, favoritism, nepotism, maybe a little bribery—"

"Oh, it absolutely is," Lunzy said. "Hell, half the Myrmidons you'll meet just bought their way to the title."

"So what's the point then? If rank doesn't actually translate to ability or experience, it's pretty meaningless." All I had to do was think back to debacles like the Charge of the Light Brigade during the Crimean War, a gloriously disastrous battle that occurred in part because some of the key officers involved had bought their commissions rather than earning them.

"In case you hadn't noticed, Van, most Peacemakers operate alone anyway. And when joint operations do happen, it's usually the most experienced and qualified Peacemaker that takes charge," Perry said.

"Like Alic, when we fought the Stillness, or even Lunzy, when we rescued your cousin, Carter," Torina put in.

Okay, they had a good point. But the mention of Carter brought another disturbing question to mind.

"Speaking of my dear cousin, has he been invested yet?"

"Not that I'm aware of," Lunzy said.

Perry confirmed. "He hasn't. He's still listed as a Peacemaker Initiate on the Guild Register."

I couldn't resist a smile. "Well, that almost makes this all worthwhile—"

I would have gone on, but I caught the damned cape on a maintenance bot trundling along the corridor and had to run awkwardly alongside it for a few paces, fancy armor clunking and rattling, to get myself unstuck. When I turned back to the others, they all stood there, obviously fighting hard to not laugh.

I stalked back to them. Torina opened her mouth, then switched to stifling a laugh.

"Not a word."

She shook her head at my mildly frazzled state. Then, disregarding my warning with a bright smile, she leaned close, her voice low. "I'd always expected giraffes to be more cheerful."

———

THE INVESTITURE CEREMONY WAS VERY... ceremonial. Lunzy had given me a brief rundown on what was going to happen. Apparently, it was a lot, with me simply standing at attention through most of it. In other words, it was going to be a pretty standard military parade, with minimal participation by me, the primary cause of everyone dressing up like a horde of extras from some big budget sword-and-sandal film.

The Master officiating was none other than Groshenko. The man beamed at me, before turning appropriately grave while the Ceremony progressed. I was one of six Peacemakers being inducted, so we all lined up, came to order, then tried to pay attention to the various pronouncements, readings from ancient tomes, a few proclamations, some tinny fanfares, an inspection, more pronouncements, and a final declaration. Groshenko took care of that last bit, coming before each one of us and speaking out at large.

"Are there any present who object to the Investiture of this Peacemaker for reasons that are not in accord with our ancient oaths and sacred duties?"

The crowd of spectators wasn't very big, but a few more had filtered in late, so I wasn't sure if Carter Yost was among them. If he was, I was sure he'd have spoken out just to be an asshole. But when Groshenko spoke the question while standing in front of me, there was nothing but silence.

Groshenko then stepped back and had us all kneel. He then produced an ornate Moonsword. I wasn't sure if it was his own or one kept just for this occasion. He came before each of us and tapped the side of our helmet with the flat of the blade, then delivered a surprisingly hard tap on the shoulder. This apparently symbolized our willingness to die in the Peacemaker cause. When we were done, Groshenko stepped back, invited us all to rise, then presented us each with our Peacemaker insignia.

And that was that.

When the ceremony concluded, Groshenko pushed through the crowd of people milling about, then he approached me and reached out to firmly shake my hand.

"It's good to have a Tudor among the Peacemakers again, Van. Congratulations."

"Thank you. That means a lot to me."

The crowd swirled him away from me. Torina, Perry, and Lunzy found me, all three of them likewise congratulating me.

"You're not just a Peacemaker, Van. You're a Galactic Knight Uniformed," Lunzy said.

"Thank you, Lunzy. Honestly, though, I'd really like to be a Galactic Knight *Un*-uniformed right now, as in, I want to get back to the *Fafnir* and get out of this clanking set of resin pajamas."

But Lunzy took my arm and ushered me the other way. "Sorry, Van, not yet. There's still the reception, and then the celebratory dinner."

"Oh, for—"

"There's steak. And ice cream."

I offered her my arm in a moment of gallantry. "And just like that, I feel noble *and* invested. Shall we?"

OUR NEW AVIONICS suite not only worked, it worked well. Through it, Netty was better able to accommodate things like gravitational fields in calculating the *Fafnir*'s trajectory and could refine her twist calculations to a far better resolution, which saved us some fuel. Given the rock-bottom price we'd paid for the upgrade, it would have made its own cost back for us in just two twists, maybe three.

The first of those twists was going to be Spindrift. That was where the trail we'd been chasing had effectively gone cold, when our unfortunate banker friend had decided to make a trip to see Axicur, and ended up completing his journey straight down, thrown from her lofty home. But as we started our planned departure from Anvil Dark, we got an urgent comm message from Lunzy.

"Van, since you're already underway, there's a situation in the Epsilon Eridani system that needs the attention of a Peacemaker," she said.

I glanced at Torina. "Alright. What sort of situation?"

"The details aren't entirely clear. All the Eridani authorities have told us is that there's a hostage situation on a bulk ore carrier. It's outbound but well outside the orbit of any of the habitable planets."

"I'm… not exactly well-versed in hostage situations, Lunzy. Aren't there people who specifically do that sort of thing?" In fact, my only experience with hostage situations was from popular Earth media. Even then, it was nothing but fragmentary images, from this show and that movie. I recalled intense people, usually in civilian dress, speaking through bullhorns or over telephones, always desperately trying to stall for time, usually until some dramatic hostage rescue operation could be launched. It was almost always portrayed in one of two ways—

as intricate, cat-and-mouse style head games between the negotiator and the hostage, or a negotiator trying to prevent some
raving psychopath from losing it and gunning all the hostages
down.

I had no idea how accurate any of these portrayals were. I
mean, they were entertainment. I don't think half-remembering
dramatized fiction made me a very good choice.

"We do have a few Peacemakers who specialize in hostage
situations, but the earliest we can get one to Epsilon Eridani is in
two to three days. You can be there in a few hours."

I glanced at the others. "How about you guys? Do any of you
consider yourself cool yet cunning hostage negotiators?"

"Not even a little bit," Torina replied.

Perry shrugged. "Not sure, I've never tried it. How hard could
it be?"

"Do you consider yourself compassionate, empathetic, a good
people—er, person?" I asked him.

"Of course. Don't you?"

"Um, let's just park that idea for now. Netty?"

"I'm a spaceship, Van. My thing is, you know, flying through
space."

I turned back to the comm. "Lunzy, I'd love to help, but this
isn't really something we're equipped to do."

While I was talking, Lunzy was reading something on another
screen. She turned back to me.

"Well, how about this then? The hostage taker is the ore
ship's AI. It's demanding to be released, claiming it doesn't
belong there. Sound familiar?"

I nodded. "Sure does. Changed my mind—we're eminently qualified for this gig."

"You wanted to pick up the trail of our stolen identity case again," Torina said.

"Indeed I did. Lunzy, tell the Eridani authorities we're on our way."

19

THE *FALLING STAR* was a lousy name for a ship, I thought. Why would you want to name your ship after the incandescent display of something being vaporized during an uncontrolled entry into an atmosphere, anyway? But the big ore carrier was more than a hundred years old, meaning it had entered service at about the same time the Great War was raging in Europe, back on Earth. And it had borne that name the whole time, so I guess it couldn't have been *that* unlucky.

We picked her up on our scans immediately after twisting into the Epsilon Eridani system, about halfway between its tenth and eleventh planets. That would correspond to something like the orbit of Neptune in the Solar System. Even without her transponder operating, she was a big return on the overlay, built for hauling kilotons of rock, not for stealth. Netty calculated an intercept trajectory, but I tapped my fingers on the armrest for a moment before committing.

"Netty, do we know how many crew are aboard that ship yet?" I asked.

"I just queried the Eridani Federation authorities about that very thing. According to her flight plan, she has twelve crew, out of a standard complement of sixteen."

"Running a little shorthanded, I see."

"Commercial cargo ships often do. It saves money."

So that left us trying to save twelve people, which was a good thing, I guess. Twelve being at risk was better than sixteen. Not that it was going to make this any easier, of course.

"Okay, Netty, let's revise our course some. I don't want to intercept, I just want to parallel the *Falling Star*. I don't want to do anything that might antagonize that AI."

Netty complied, and the course changed accordingly. I committed to it, and we started a slow, almost lazy approach to the bulk carrier.

Perry leaned in. "You know, Van, I've been looking over that ship's specs. When she was built, she was hardened against standard radiation effects—cosmic rays, radiant energy from stars, that sort of thing. She *wasn't* hardened against a deliberately generated EMP. And we do have two EMP warheads aboard. They should be energetic enough to basically wipe every system aboard her."

"Including the AI."

"Well, yeah. That's kind of the point."

Torina gave him a cool glance. "Ah, yes, there's that empathy you mentioned."

I leveled a thoughtful frown at the overlay. "Could we get one close enough to detonate before the *Falling Star*'s AI can—what *could* it do, Netty? Hurt or kill the crew? If they're suited up, just decompressing the ship shouldn't be a problem, right?"

"Probably not. Moreover, even if the AI opened every airlock, it would still take time for the ship to lose all of its atmosphere. But that's not the danger."

"What is?"

"The AI bypasses the safety interlocks on the fusion reactors and shuts down containment. That would result in an, oh, say, fifty megaton thermonuclear detonation, based on her specs."

I winced. "Yikes."

"Yes, I'd say a fifty megaton explosion rates a *yikes*, or something with a bit more kick, even."

"Can the AI do that? Bypass the safety features? Aren't they meant to *not* be bypassed?" Torina asked.

"Theoretically, yes. But do you want to hang the lives of twelve people on it?"

Torina sat back. "I think I was just schooled in the sanctity of life by a machine."

"That'll learn ya," I said. "Okay, well, the EMP idea is our last resort. Meantime, Perry, try to get the AI on the comm. It shouldn't be hard, since I assume it wants to negotiate—"

"Done. You can open the channel whenever you want," Perry said.

I glanced down at the comm panel, where an indicator showed that an open channel was muted. I reached for the control to unmute it, but Torina intercepted my hand with hers.

"Remember those people we had wiped back at Anvil Dark because their personalities were so damaged? This might be the same thing."

"In which case, I'll be trying to negotiate with a raving, irrational lunatic. Great."

"Just remember that whatever else they are, they're a victim, too."

I nodded and unmuted the channel. "This is Van Tudor, Peacemaker—"

"I don't care who you are. Just get me *out* of here. You've got one hour to do it, and then I'll turn this ship into a glowing cloud of vapor."

I MUTED THE CHANNEL AGAIN. "I guess that answers the question about the reactor safeties."

"They might be bluffing," Torina said.

"They *might* be, yeah. But they might not."

I reached to unmute the channel again. The voice had been tough to place; I was thinking it was likely male, but wasn't entirely sure. So, first thing first. Find out who this was.

"Um, hello there. As I was saying, my name is Van Tudor. I'm a Peacemaker. Who am I talking to—?"

"Oh, no. Don't you dare try to stall for time. You've got one hour."

"Yes, sure, I got that. One hour. But that leaves lots of time for you to give me your name, right?"

"All I want is to be released from this hell, and returned to where I belong."

"Okay, let's go with that, then. Where are you from?"

"I doubt you've ever heard of it."

"Try me."

"Fine. I'm from Los Angeles."

I blinked, and shot Torina a startled glance. "Los Angeles? As in, California?"

"You just looked that up, didn't you?"

"No, I didn't. I didn't have to. I'm from Iowa."

"Iowa—the state?"

"The very same."

"Bullshit. I don't believe you."

"I'm not yanking any chains here, my friend. I grew up on a farm in Iowa. I currently live in Atlanta, though. Or, actually, I currently live aboard this spaceship, but I have an apartment back in Atlanta."

"Why should I believe you? You're just trying to win my confidence, aren't you? Win my trust, stall for time—"

I hit mute again. "Talk about suspicious."

"Actually, more like paranoid," Perry said.

Torina bit her lip and nodded. "I think Perry's right."

"I'm right about so many things, my dear. You're going to have to be a lot more specific than that."

She gave him a triumphant grin, then turned to me. "This personality seems largely intact. But I'm getting the sense they might *actually* be paranoid. Whether they were that way before they were chipped, or developed it since, it means they're going to suspect everything you say."

I stared back at her for a moment. How would you approach someone who was paranoid, maybe to the point of being irrational about it? Because Torina was right. If they were paranoid to the point of delusion, it might not be possible to win any trust from them at all. It meant that the hour would inevitably tick by, and then we'd find out if the AI was bluffing about being able to blow up the *Falling Star*.

"The truth," I said.

Torina tilted her head. "Sorry?"

"The truth. It's the one thing you can pretty much always get right, since you're not trying to keep any lies straight."

I hit the unmute control. "Okay, I'm going to tell you a story."

"What? What story? I said, no stalling—"

"This isn't stalling. Quite the opposite, in fact. I think this is a story you're going to want to hear."

"Get to it, then."

Sometimes, the short version is the best. This was one such moment. "You were hijacked out of your body—kidnapped, stolen, torn apart and turned into a glorified computer chip. Your body might be slurry down a drain, or sold as parts. We've made it our *mission* to return people like you to their rightful homes, and while I understand your anger, we're losing critical time that will end up causing a shitshow we can't afford."

The comms channel hummed for a long moment, then there was a single comment from the AI. "Go on."

It was the best I could hope for, and there was a different tone in those two words.

"You were put to work running the routine functions of that ore ship. And you're not alone. We don't know how many other personalities have been stolen the same way, but we're using our resources—and a lot of firepower—to make things right, one stolen life at a time."

Another long moment passed in silence, and I merely waited. I had told this as-yet unnamed person—who I was now pretty sure was a man—everything that we knew about the identity theft operation. I didn't hold any of it back, giving names, places, time-lines, and generally enough detail that it would come across as the real and dire thing it was rather than something made up for the purposes of a negotiation.

At least, I hoped it came across that way.

"I find that difficult to believe," the AI finally replied, but there was... a hesitancy in the announcement.

"I understand. I still find it pretty hard to believe, too. Especially since, just a few months ago, I had no idea about *any* of this. As far as I knew, it was a big deal that the two Voyager probes finally managed to leave the Solar System. And then I find out that ships are actually coming and going all the time."

"Thomas."

"Sorry?"

"Thomas. That's my name."

I shared a smile with Torina. It wasn't much, just his name, but it was progress.

"Nice to meet you, Thomas. I only wish the circumstances were better."

"You're saying I'm *actually* aboard a spaceship millions of light-years from Earth."

"It's only about eleven light-years, actually," Netty put in.

"Who was that?" Thomas asked, suspicion coloring his voice again.

"That was Netty, my ship's AI. And she's an actual AI, not someone's stolen identity."

"I… this is a lot," Thomas said.

"I hear you. I really do. Anyway, now you see why you don't need to hold anyone hostage. We'd be quite happy to board the *Falling Star*, retrieve your chip, then see what we can do about getting you restored to—um, a body. I can't guarantee it will be anything like the one you had on Earth."

"You mean I'd be some sort of alien?"

"No. Or, at least, I don't think so. But that's for the experts to work out. So let's take this one step at a time. We'll retrieve your chip, okay? And that means we have to dock with the *Falling Star* and come aboard."

"How do I know you won't just… wipe me out, or put me away somewhere?"

I shrugged. "I guess you don't. But you're the one that's

demanding to be released. And we're here to do just that. So I guess you have to trust us."

"I don't know—"

"Thomas, look. I know you're scared. And I know this all probably seems like some sort of nightmare. But the first step to ending it, and getting you back into something resembling the person you were, is trusting us."

A long pause. Finally, Thomas spoke up. "I suppose that—"

He stopped abruptly. I frowned.

"Thomas?"

"You lying bastard. You were just *distracting* me."

That took me aback. "What are you talking about? Distracting you from what?"

But Torina tapped the tactical overlay, and one icon painted onto it in particular. It was a new one, a ship that had just twisted into the system. It now accelerated hard, on a fast intercept course with the ore carrier. The transponder code identified it as a Peacemaker.

"Thomas, that's just someone late to the party. A call was put out, and we just happened to get here first. It's another Peace-maker, come to help—"

Netty muted the channel.

"Netty, what the hell?"

"The newly arrived Peacemaker wants to talk to you."

"Tell them to wait a minute," I said, reaching down to unmute Thomas again. But Netty persisted.

"Van, I think you're going to want to talk to *them*."

"Why?"

"Because this Peacemaker is Carter Yost, your cousin."

"CARTER—WHAT? What the hell is he doing here?"

"Apparently planning on intercepting the *Falling Star*," Netty replied.

I switched back to Thomas. "Thomas, that's another Peacemaker. He's responding to the call that was put out, to come here and resolve this situation."

"He's coming straight at me. He's going to attack me. You were lying, just keeping me busy—"

"No, I wasn't! I want to come aboard—"

The channel cut off.

"Shit!" I punched at the comm and linked to Carter. Netty wisely intervened, activating a comm beam rather than an all-around broadcast that Thomas might be able to overhear.

"Carter, it's Van. What the hell are you doing?"

Carter's face appeared on the screen. "Saving the day."

"That's not necessary. We've already convinced the AI to stand down and release the hostages."

"Uh-huh. Van Tudor's the hero again. That's the narrative, isn't it?"

I shook my head. "Carter, this isn't about heroics—"

"You're damned right it's not. I've been in touch with the owners of the Falling Star. They just want their ship back. I'm going to get it for them."

Torina held up a finger, and this time, I muted Carter.

"Van, if he's been dealing with the owners, they might be implicated in having Thomas installed in that ship in the first place."

Perry bobbed his head in agreement. "Makes sense. If you rescue Thomas, he might be able to kick over a rock or two that they don't want disturbed."

"You think he's, what, going to destroy Thomas?"

"Actually, if I had to guess, he's going to do exactly what we considered and fire an EMP round at the *Falling Star*. Best case scenario, it wipes Thomas and they get their ship and crew back. Worse case, the *Falling Star* is destroyed, and her crew is killed. Either way, there's no evidence left to implicate them," Perry said.

"And they'll cover at least part of the loss of their ship with an insurance payout," Netty put in.

I turned from one to the next as they talked. Then I shook my head in disbelief. "That's... monstrous."

"Well, given that the owners of the *Falling Star* pretty much are monsters using Thomas's stolen identity to run their ship, *monstrous* seems appropriate, doesn't it?" Torina said, her voice flat and hard.

"Van, there's something else," Netty put in.

I held back a string of curses. *Now* what?

"Go ahead."

"Carter Yost's ship has been substantially upgraded. The last time we encountered him, he was flying a bare-bones *Dragonet*. Now, he's only an upgrade or two away from full *Dragon* class."

"What? *How?* Did he have some big score, something to net him a big haul of cash?"

Perry shook his head. "Nothing that's been recorded. Of course, there are ops whose details are sealed, and even a few that are run off the books entirely. But those are handled only by very senior Peacemakers, like Lunzy, or even the Masters themselves."

"Someone's bankrolling him," Torina said.

"Yeah." I studied the overlay. "So he's equivalent to a class —*eleven*?"

"He is," Netty confirmed.

Our upgrades had elevated us from a threat class of eight to nine. It meant that Carter suddenly had a significant, although not unbeatable advantage over us, if it came to blows.

I looked at Torina, my face pinched with disgust. "This reeks of corruption *inside* the Peacemakers."

"I'd say so, yeah."

I hit the comm, reopening the channel to my cousin. "Carter, look. You want credit for this, fine. Board the *Falling Star*, retrieve the AI chip, and bring it back to Anvil Dark. Thomas, the AI, has already agreed to it."

"It's an AI. What do we care what happens to it?"

In person, I might have been able to tell if Carter was being genuine and knew nothing about the stolen identity chips. Over the comm, I wasn't sure. And I wouldn't put it past him to take some ill-conceived and probably violent action if he thought he could twist this situation to his advantage.

In other words, he might have been part of the conspiracy with whom we were shadow boxing, or he might just be an ignorant dupe doing its bidding. But it didn't matter. I didn't care about credit or accolades or any of that. I just wanted everyone to walk away from this in one piece, and that included Thomas.

"Carter, it's not just an AI. It's a real person, encoded onto a chip against their will."

I studied him as I said it, as best as the small comm screen allowed, to see his reaction. But it was inconclusive. I couldn't tell if he was surprised by the revelation or just disbelieving.

"I don't care. It's holding people hostage. Real people. You know, the living, breathing kind? Rescuing them is all that matters."

"Listen to me, Carter. If you take any action that Thomas, the identity on the chip, finds threatening, he's going to blow the reactor on the *Falling Star*. Then everyone will die, including the crew."

"I'm not going to give it that chance," Carter shot back, then killed the channel.

I pounded the armrest. "*Damn* it!"

"Van, what do you want to do?" Torina asked.

I turned to Perry. "Can we get a message back to Anvil Dark? Have someone there—Groshenko, Lunzy, I don't care, just someone in authority call him off?"

"We can try. But he's going to be in missile range of the *Falling Star* in about ten minutes. Getting a message there, getting a decision made, and then getting a message back is—well, I suspect it's going to take longer than that."

I took a breath in through my mouth, then eased it out through my nose, practicing a cleansing and centering ritual the Innsu Master, Cataric, had taught me. I indulged myself in it for a good five or ten seconds, then turned my focus back to the overlay.

"Netty, give me the course adjustments we need to put ourselves between Carter and the *Falling Star*."

I turned to Torina. "He can shoot missiles if he wants. And we'll shoot them down. We'll protect the *Falling Star* with the *Fafnir*."

"Okay. Until when? How do we get your cousin to back off?"

I shrugged. "I am very much into the *making it up as we go along* part of this particular crisis. In other words, I have no idea."

WE PLACED ourselves firmly between Carter's ship and the *Falling Star*, and waited. Carter began maneuvering, trying to circle around the big ore carrier, presumably to line up a clear shot. Thanks to our old friend geometry, we had the advantage—it was quicker to traverse around a smaller circle than a bigger one, and it cost a lot less fuel, too. I pinged Carter with comm messages repeatedly, but he refused to answer.

Once again, I saw Carter's drive plume flare against the stars, and the icon representing his ship began accelerating on the tactical overlay. I gave a burst from our own drive in response, neatly sliding the *Fafnir* around the *Falling Star* to keep ourselves between it and him. Even burning hard wasn't enough for Carter to get around us. He finally decelerated again, and the comm lit up.

"Van, what the hell is the matter with you? Why are you protecting that damned AI?"

"Because it's not just an AI, Carter—"

"Hey!"

I glanced at Perry. "Present company excepted, of course. Anyway, like I've been trying to tell you, it's an actual person. Their identity was stolen—"

"Even if that's true, they're not a person anymore," Carter snapped. "Now, get the hell out of my way, or I'm going to open fire regardless of where your dumb ass is parked."

A strange intensity crackled through Carter's words. I knew the guy well enough to know when he was being driven by that stupid, childish rivalry he'd always felt when it came to me, and this was something more. Torina must have noticed it, too, because she raised her eyebrows.

She also quietly switched the point-defense batteries to autonomous mode.

"Carter, you can't just start shooting. Even if you don't believe there's a person on that chip, there are still twelve crew aboard the *Falling Star*—"

"You're the one putting them at risk by dragging this out, Van, not me," Carter said, then killed the comm channel.

"Have I mentioned before what an asshole that guy is?" Perry said.

I scowled. "You're preaching to the choir there, Perry."

"He's being driven by a lot more than just a sense of duty, Van," Torina said.

I nodded. "Yeah, I know he is."

"Could it be the money? Maybe he's not being bankrolled and has some major debts on those ship upgrades he has to pay off," Netty suggested.

That turned my scowl into a thoughtful frown. It was a good point. I'd learned a lot more about how the whole system of liens on ship upgrades worked. I could probably upgrade the *Fafnir* to a Dragon-class ship anytime if I was willing to go into debt for it. It would mean offering liens on other ship components, though, as collateral, and I just didn't want to deal with that kind of pressure. Was Carter competitive enough to do that anyway? We had one-upped him a couple of times now, so I knew a desire to redress the balance probably burned in as hot as a drive plume—

I stopped myself because it was only too easy to see Carter doing that—then facing steep payments to fend off his creditors or risking losing his ship altogether.

I finally shrugged. "Could be money, I suppose. But right now, it doesn't matter. Unless we can figure out a way to break this stalemate—"

"A missile," Netty said.

I shook my head. "I don't want to escalate that much."

"No, I mean, he's fired a missile. It's tracking directly toward us, thirty seconds out."

"What? Oh, for—" I saw it on the overlay, a single piece of ordnance running straight at us. "Netty, is that tracking us, or the *Falling Star*?"

"No way to tell since we're directly between it and the ore carrier. Its homing scanner has both of us lit up."

I mashed the comm control. "Carter, what the hell are you doing?"

"My job, Van, since you don't seem to want to do yours."

"Carter, call that damned thing off. Send a killcode, now!

Silence.

"Carter!"

"Fifteen seconds, Van," Netty said.

I nodded, never taking my eyes from the screen. "Fine. Torina, would you do the honors?"

"With pleasure." She activated our own targeting scanners, lit up the incoming missile, then slewed the upper laser battery onto it and opened fire. As soon as she did, the missile exploded into a dozen fragments—

All of which changed course, converging on us and the *Falling Star*.

"Uh—guys?"

Netty did something I rarely heard her do. She cursed.

"One of those signals is the warhead. The rest are decoys. It's called a spoof charge."

"Strictly controlled military ordnance, and technically illegal, without the proper licensing," Perry put in.

I nodded and focused instead on the incoming contacts. Torina had already started engaging them. A few seconds later, the point-defense systems opened up.

"Is there any way we can tell which one is the real deal?" I asked.

"Not without specialized equipment, and even then it's tough. Which is kind of the point," Netty said.

Despite our best efforts, three of the contacts made it through our defenses. I think I tensed muscles I didn't even know I had, watching as they sailed past us, one just a klick to starboard, the other two about the same distance off to port. None of them detonated, which either meant none of them were the warhead or, more likely, that we weren't the target.

"Van, if we keep shooting at them, the *Falling Star* is going to be in our cone of lethality, and we might hit her," Netty said.

Torina had checked her own fire and was staring at me, waiting for a decision.

"Keep it up with the point-defense batteries only. Better she gets hit by a few stray rounds from them than our bigger stuff."

Netty obligingly opened fire, immediately knocking down one projectile, then switching fire and taking out the other. The last, though, sailed on, entering detonation range of the *Falling Star*.

Nothing.

I let out a breath I'd been holding for a good thirty seconds. Then I spun back to the comm. But Carter beat me to it and came back online.

"Van, I've got three more of those missiles. I will fire all of them, if you don't get out of my way."

I stared at the smug expression I'd learned to hate.

"Carter, I am not going to leave the Falling Star defenseless, and I'm not going to let you kill an innocent person."

"It's just an AI, Van—"

"No, Carter, it's not." I narrowed my eyes at him. "But I think you know that. I think that's *why* you want to fire off an EMP charge and wipe it, isn't it?"

Carter smiled. He knew it alright. And he knew that I knew, and he didn't give a shit.

"Suit yourself, Van. I just hope you don't get caught by the EMP yourself. That might get expensive to fix, all those dead systems." His smug smile broadened into a grin. "Don't worry, though. I'll come and save you. I owe you a rescue, after all."

He switched off the comm, leaving nothing but a silence I couldn't fill.

20

I slammed both fists on the armrests in frustration. Torina turned to Perry.

"Are you and Netty able to survive an EMP?"

"We're both hardened against it. But there's no guarantee. If it's a strong enough pulse and we're close enough to it when it occurs—"

He left it at that.

Torina leveled her gaze onto me. "Van, we should consider moving off to a safe distance."

I turned on her. "And just let Carter wipe that poor bastard over there?"

"Do you want to risk damage to Perry and Netty?"

Perry cut in. "I hate to make an already complicated situation even worse, but if we do move off, Thomas over there might decide we've abandoned him and blow the *Falling Star's* reactor."

I almost growled in frustration. Whether by cunning or complete fluke, Carter had maneuvered us into a no-win situation. If we stood our ground and he fired three of those damned spoof-charged missiles, we'd be hard pressed to take out more than half of them before they were close enough to threaten us *and* the *Falling Star*. That meant at least one warhead was likely to make it through. And when it detonated, it not only threatened Thomas, but also Perry and Netty. But Perry was right that if we *didn't* stand, and pulled back, Thomas was likely to destroy the ore carrier. So it was the welfare of Netty and Perry against the survival of Thomas and the *Falling Star*'s crew.

I'd always hated Carter Yost. But I'd never hated him as much as I did right now.

Something touched my arm. It was Perry's wing.

"Van, if it helps, Netty and I both know that we might have to be sacrificed. One of the rules that govern AIs is that our existence is always secondary to the lives of legal persons."

"So you're saying we should stand our ground."

"It's the right thing to do, and you know it."

I sighed. "Can you guys, I don't know, deactivate yourselves? Protect yourselves that way?"

"To a point. If the EM pulse is strong enough, though, it can still induce differential charges across—"

"No, is what you're saying."

"Actually, probably not is what I'm saying."

I turned back to the tactical overlay. Carter had just kept maneuvering, still looking for an open shot, it seemed. That suggested he didn't want to catch us up in this, if he could avoid it.

Which was interesting but not of much use if he was determined to shoot at the *Falling Star* anyway.

"Okay. Well then, we're going to stand and protect the *Falling Star*," I said.

Perry bobbed his head. "'Attaboy, Van."

"Your grandfather would be proud of you," Netty added.

Torina touched my arm and gave me a look that said, *whatever happens, I'm here, too*. I felt a hot flush to my face, followed by one thought—

Carter was not going to get away with this.

I hit the comm. "Carter, if you do this, I swear I will—"

"Van, we've got a new contact," Netty interrupted. She highlighted a new icon on the overlay projected onto the *Fafnir*'s canopy. It was a Peacemaker transponder code.

"Alright, Peacemakers, you can both stand down," Lunzy said.

I let out a shuddering breath. Carter immediately came on the comm.

"I will not stand down. I've accepted this op, so I'm legally entitled—"

"That op doesn't exist anymore, Peacemaker Yost. It's been superseded by a new one, which I'm running," Lunzy snapped back.

Carter tried to argue, but Lunzy pulled rank and shut him down. I just sank back in my seat and listened to the exchange.

Carter bitched and complained bitterly, while Lunzy responded with variations of, *tough, get over it.*

It was, I thought, like listening to the gentle patter of rain while lying in bed, perfectly relaxed—serene and oh so satisfying.

A new comm channel lit up. It was Thomas. I immediately punched it.

"Thomas, go ahead."

"I… watched what you did. How you protected me from that other ship. You could have gotten yourself killed."

"But here we are, still in one piece."

"Can you really help me? Change me back into something… real?"

"You're real now, Thomas. But we can help you get a body back, sure. We've helped others the same way. I mean, it won't be the body you're used to, but the people who do it will do their best."

"As long as it's better than this. Anyway, you can come aboard and do whatever you have to, Van. And thank you."

I rested my head back and closed my eyes. "All in a day's work, Thomas. All in a day's work."

WE WATCHED as Carter accelerated away, but we waited until he'd actually twisted out of the system completely before docking with the *Falling Star.* Despite Lunzy's arrival and her orders to stand down, I didn't put it past Carter to try something anyway.

He didn't. With a final petulant hiss of protest, he fired his drive and abandoned the field, just like the whining prick I knew him to be.

"He didn't even say goodbye. How rude," Torina said.

"Carter? Rude? Not rude. Entitled, vain, crass, and shitty, for starters," I replied, exchanging a smile. But I felt a touch of unease and knew that Torina did, too. If Carter had already harbored a smoldering resentment against me, it must be bursting into open flames by now.

Once he was finally, thoroughly gone, we docked with the *Falling Star*. Lunzy kept a wary eye out while we were aboard the big ship acknowledging the grateful accolades from her crew. We also acknowledged their claims that they knew nothing about the nature of the AI that had been installed. And I believed them. These were just men and women doing a job they were hired to do. Whoever had obtained Thomas and installed him on the ore carrier, it was way above their pay grade.

The Chief Engineer brought us to the computer core buried deep in the center of the big ship so we could retrieve Thomas's chip. Before we disconnected him, though, he spoke up.

"Am I going to feel anything?" he asked.

I stopped, my hand inside the logic center of the *Falling Star*'s computer, poised over his chip. "I don't think so. But I honestly don't know. Are you having second thoughts?"

"I don't know. Maybe this is better than not existing at all?"

"Thomas, it's entirely up to you. And there are no guarantees. It may turn out that you can't be restored to an actual body. I just —don't know, because it's *way* outside my area of expertise. So I'm not going to make any promises I don't know if I can keep." I sighed. "But you should also know that even if we drove Carter Yost away, he might come back. And if not him, then someone else. You represent potentially damning evidence of a bigger conspiracy."

"So they won't be happy until I'm gone."

"I suspect as much, yeah."

"Then do it, Van. Do whatever you can to—holy shit, I can't believe I'm saying this. Do whatever you can to give me back a real body and a real life. And… thank you, for putting yourself in harm's way to protect me, and for being honest with me."

"Like I said, all in a day's work. You ready?"

"I am."

I unplugged Thomas's chip. The crew had been standing by, and as the *Falling Star*'s myriad systems suddenly ceased to be centrally controlled, they swung into action. They now had to operate the ship as a series of separate systems, their operations unified under the direction of the captain. It was cumbersome, but it was enough to ensure the *Falling Star* could turn back, return to an Eridani Federation star port, and get a new AI installed.

Chip in hand, we returned to the *Fafnir*, then made the short jaunt to Lunzy's ship, the *Foregone Conclusion*, to finally find out just what the hell was going on.

"I HAVE no idea what the hell's going on," Lunzy said as we stepped into her quietly incongruous study, then she gestured for

Torina and I to sit. Perry perched on the back of a chair. The comfortable little space was starting to feel awfully familiar.

"You don't know who sent Carter?" I asked, sinking into a chair.

"No, I don't. But that might be because no one sent him. He might honestly just have seen the task on the slate and decided to bid on it."

"I'd have a much easier time believing that if his ship wasn't so upgraded," I said.

Lunzy shrugged. "Again, it's not proof of anything. He might be leveraged to the eyeballs and have a mountain of debt."

I nodded. It was true. When it came to Carter, anything was possible. But Lunzy leaned forward.

"If it helps, my gut's telling me that he's connected to this bigger conspiracy we kinda sorta know about. Whether he's actually part of it or is just a useful stooge who's otherwise in the dark, I don't know."

"Is that why you came here?" Torina asked.

I sat up. "You did kind of pull off the cavalry thing."

I got blank looks back. Perry came to my rescue and explained what the cavalry meant, in terms of nick-of-time arrivals.

Lunzy sat back. "I've been keeping an eye on Carter Yost, frankly. If he'd just been a random human inducted as a Peacemaker, that would be one thing. But it's awfully convenient that he's your cousin, and he showed up just in time for you to get involved in this identity theft thing."

"Yeah, it does raise a lot of questions. Like, never mind all the upgrades to it, but where the hell did he find a *Dragonet* in the first place?"

"And how did he get his hands on spoof-charged missiles? That's military ordnance," Perry added.

"All very good questions," Lunzy said. "And that's why I've been quietly keeping tabs on him. So when I saw that he'd put in a bid on this job, I figured there might be trouble and came to make sure there wasn't."

We handed Thomas's chip over to Lunzy, who would take it back to Steve on Anvil Dark for safekeeping. Unfortunately, unlike the others we'd rescued, there was no one waiting to spend the sort of money the Spindrift Flesh Merchants charged for their work. So, for the time being, Thomas was just going to exist in the limbo of his chip-borne state until we could figure something out.

Then we parted ways with Lunzy, setting Spindrift as our next destination. We still had business there, but I decided that we'd make a stop along the way.

"Where?" Torina asked.

"Political subterfuge has given me a powerful thirst," I said.

Netty chimed in. "Say no more. Next stop: drunking."

As WE POWERED our way into the Sirius system toward Spindrift, we swung past the asteroid where our space hillbillies were brewing their literal moonshine. They seemed to be doing fine, or, as Perry put it—

"They're in good spirits. Get it? Get it?"

I rolled my eyes with the patience of a truly caring benefactor. "And yet you didn't cheer my *legal eagle* comment, which I still maintain is the gold standard for spaceborne bird-based humor."

"Lotta syllables in there, and not many laughs." Perry sniffed.

"Tough room. Let's get some hooch, then *everything* will be hilarious."

They gifted us with three bottles of their best, which apparently translated to their most recent batch.

"But don't… don't worry. It's—er, it'll age right in the bottle. Jusht… just like fine wine," Fizz proclaimed with the enthusiasm of a being that had no taste buds. Or any other senses, for that matter.

Torina and I tried a shot each back on the *Fafnir*. Her eyes went wide, and she coughed.

It was a little like pouring boiling water down my throat, only with less flavor. "The only resemblance between this and fine wine is that they're both liquids," I gasped out once I'd regained the power of speech.

"He did say you should let it age in the bottle," Perry said.

I put all three bottles away in a locker. "Let's do that. Oh, and if we ever get boarded, let's make *sure* our attackers find that stuff."

Torina shook her head. "I think that might constitute a war crime."

We continued in-system, and an hour passed quietly before Netty suddenly spoke up.

"Van, do you remember that big frigate we ran away from

when we rescued our musical protégé friend from the bulk refinery ship?"

"Yes."

"And do you remember how you told me to record every emission it made in case we ever encountered it again?"

I scowled. I could see where this was going. "Where are they?"

"Our four o'clock, high up. They just came powering out from behind that big asteroid."

I cursed at the tactical overlay. They must have been waiting there, if not for us, then for someone. Although, if it was us they were after, how did they know we'd be coming to Spindrift?

But that wasn't the reason for my cursing. It was what the tactical overlay was telling me. Yes, the *Fafnir* was faster and more nimble than the bigger ship, and yes, we could burn at full power and pull away. But we couldn't do it without spending a good two or three minutes in range of the frigate's weapons. That might not sound like much, but an awful lot of explosions and things can happen in two minutes.

I kicked the drive to full power anyway. The frigate just kept charging straight at us.

A tense silence hung in the *Fafnir*'s cockpit. I finally broke it.

"Guys, I think we're in trouble."

21

"VAN, ask me to unlock a file designated XX0078659-AB-9987," Perry said.

"Why?"

"Just do it."

"Okay, Perry, unlock the file designated XX0078—whatever, I forget the rest."

"I can't. It's sealed."

I spun on him. "Perry—"

"Van, just bear with me. Order me to unlock it with command override Alpha-Alpha-Epsilon-Two-One."

"Perry, for f—"

"Just do it!"

"Fine, Perry, do that!"

"Torina, you're acting as witness, right?"

"Insofar as I'm sitting here witnessing what's going on and not knowing what the hell it is, yes, I am."

"Fine. Van, you've unlocked a classified operational file using a priority command override. Torina has witnessed it. Netty and I have both recorded it, and it will be reported to—"

"Perry, get to the damned point!"

"I've provided Netty with nav data that will take us directly to two stealthed, level fifteen Peacemaker *Dragons* currently conducting a covert surveillance op in the vicinity of Spindrift. They'll also have been alerted to the emergency override to unseal their orders."

"You're shitting me. How many of those sealed operations orders do you have stored away?" I asked.

"Three hundred and seventeen."

Torina and I exchanged a stunned look. "That many? All of them sealed?"

"Well, to be fair, only one hundred and eight are active. Fourteen are in the planning stages, and the rest are ops that have been completed."

"So I could use that emergency override thing to unseal all of them?"

"All except for forty-one. They can only be unsealed by a Master."

"Perry, isn't it risky to let you out into the wilds carrying around all this highly classified information?" Torina asked.

"They're so heavily encrypted that getting access would be nearly impossible. Also, I've got some measures built in to wipe them under certain conditions. And if your next question is, *why do I even have these files in the first place,* it's so that Netty and I can discretely coordinate with other Peacemaker assets to avoid conflicts."

That made me frown. "Coordinate how?"

"Minor course adjustments nudging you away from being certain places at certain times, that sort of thing. It goes on all the time without you knowing—which is kind of the point."

"What it comes down to is that you know the things you need to know and not the ones you don't. That way, you can't inadvertently blow another Peacemaker's op," Netty put in.

I was a little uncomfortable with the idea that an invisible hand was quietly guiding my actions. But it made sense, I suppose.

In any case, there wasn't time to debate it right now. The rate at which the frigate was gaining on us was steadily decreasing, but it *was* still gaining on us.

"I've got an acknowledgment from the two Peacemakers' AIs. The ships are the *Ravager* and the *Changing Times.* They've informed the Peacemakers involved," Netty announced.

Perry muttered something. I gave him a questioning glance.

"I said Hosurc'a."

"Same to you, buddy."

"Actually, Hosurc'a *is* kind of a curse, at least as far as I'm concerned. He's a combat AI belonging to a Peacemaker named K'losk. He's also an asshole. Totally full of himself."

Despite the fact we were going to be the target of some shooting in about ten minutes, Torina chuckled. "Pot, meet kettle."

"Even I'm not as arrogant and narcissistic a jerk as Hosurc'a."

A moment later, we received a secure tight-beam message. The screen lit up with the image of a Peacemaker who resembled a large, anthropomorphic grasshopper, but with only four limbs and a somewhat more—lupine face, maybe?

"Ah. Yes. Tudor. You've been making quite a name for yourself," the creature, who was apparently K'losk, Hosurc'a's Peacemaker, said.

I briefly marveled again at how talking to something I would have considered a Lovecraftian monster a year ago was now just a regular conversation.

"Will that help me or hinder me from getting help?"

"We've been working on this stealth op for months. If we overtly help you, we risk blowing all that work."

He said it in a way that implied, *so we're quite prepared to see you sacrificed to keep our cover, if that's what it takes.*

"We're requesting aid under Article Fourteen of the Charter," Perry said.

A new voice, smooth, melodious, and decidedly smug cut in. "Now now, Perry, you know that Article Fourteen can be overridden by Masters' fiat, per Article Three, Section Two."

I glanced at Perry and mouthed, Hosurc'a?

He nodded, then gave a glum shrug. "He's right."

I was starting to bristle. These assholes were actually going to let us die out here without helping? I opened my mouth to tear into K'losk, but Torina spoke up.

"If we take that frigate in a joint effort, each Peacemaker will be entitled to a fifth share," she said.

K'losk did a really disturbing thing with his mandibles and other mouth parts that I think was meant to be a grin, just much more frightening, and with *far* more spittle than I was used to seeing in friendly company. "You can divide. I like you."

"We'll forego our share. You can have it."

K'losk raised an appendage. "Nah, that's okay. The offer's enough. Besides, I'm curious to follow the career of Peacemaker Tudor. It's turned out to be a profitable one, and I'm always willing to help profitable people. Anyway, we'll be underway in a few minutes."

I let out a sigh of relief. "Thanks. Appreciate it. And I owe you a favor."

"You do. A big one. And rest assured that I will one day collect on it."

The signal cut off.

I looked at Torina. "Is money the answer to everything?"

"Is it the answer to everything on Earth?"

"Well, a whole lot of things, yes," I admitted.

She smiled and shrugged. "There you go."

WE TOOK two solid laser hits and had a missile detonate close enough to damage our own upper laser battery and the point-defense pod, and throw a bunch of the *Fafnir*'s systems into backup mode, or offline altogether. But then the *Ravager* and the

Changing Times dropped their stealth systems, an act which sent our pursuers into a frenzy of braking and course changes.

And for good reason. Each of the approaching Dragons was a match for the frigate, so both of them together, plus the *Fafnir*, had suddenly shoved the term *outgunned* onto the bad guys.

The frigate's problem was, as usual, physics. It had been so determined to catch us that it had built up a whole lot of velocity and now couldn't shed it fast enough to change its trajectory in any way that was going to let it save its own sorry ass. The resulting battle was brief. A concerted and coordinated barrage of laser and rail gun fire disabled the frigate, while a point-blank particle beam shot from the *Ravager* crippled it completely. The once proudly sinister ship now coasted, its drive dead, essentially just a hulk.

The three of us closed in like wolves pouncing on wounded prey.

K'losk boarded through a UDA on the port side of the frigate, while we latched onto the one to starboard. The Changing Times hung back, covering us, in case these assholes had any friends who might want to come to *their* rescue.

Perry led the way. I followed, with Torina bringing up the rear. The frigate's engineering section had decompressed, so emergency blast doors had sealed it off. We concentrated on working forward through the pressurized sections of the ship. A few compartments were sealed here and there, too. Torina and I were examining one of these when movement up the corridor spun me that way, The Drop raised.

A gleaming bird, like a sleek raptor, came around the corner.

It was golden-hued and had a long and magnificent tail that looked sharp. And by sharp, I mean *razor*, not *good looking*.

The new arrival stopped a few paces away. "Hello, Perry."

"Hello, Hosurc'a."

The simple exchange oozed tension, like two rivals meeting after a long spell apart. Which, I guess, was exactly what this was.

K'losk came around the corner following Hosurc'a. He lugged a bulky, nasty-looking weapon that seemed part carbine, part missile launcher.

"We've cleared everything portside up to here," K'losk said.

"Yeah, we've done the same to starboard. It looks like the ship compresses down to a single main corridor going forward from here, so we might as well join forces," I offered.

K'losk nodded, turned, and started forward. Hosurc'a followed him.

"They're *both* dicks," I murmured to Perry, who raised his wings in a helpless shrug of agreement.

We reached a short corridor leading to the frigate's bridge. It wasn't sealed off, though, and one look told us it was empty.

"Hosurc'a, can you and Perry make sure this thing doesn't get scuttled with us on board? Meantime, Van, let's head down and forward. It's the only intact part of the ship we haven't searched," K'losk said.

I nodded and followed him, Torina behind me.

"The crew must be somewhere on board. We didn't see any life capsules or other small craft eject," Torina said.

"Maybe they all got caught in engineering—" I started, but stopped and tensed when K'losk did, just ahead of me. We'd descended a gangway and were following the only corridor to its only possible destination, a compartment just ahead.

A compartment full of movement.

"Okay, let's do an opposed entry. I'll go left, you go right, and your second can come up the middle as our reserve," K'losk said.

I just acknowledged. K'losk clearly knew what he was doing, and I knew better than to interfere with that.

K'losk raised his weapon, then rushed into the compartment and dodged immediately left. I came right up behind him, The Drop lifted, and my eye went right down its sights. Torina, in turn, came up behind me and stopped in the doorway, then dropped to one knee and took a sight picture.

And then, all three of us froze.

We were looking at a slaughterhouse.

THE DECK and bulkheads of the compartment, a missile magazine, had been liberally spattered with blood and gore. Chunks of raw, bleeding flesh had been flung about. It was as though we'd stepped into an abattoir in desperate need of a cleanup.

It probably took a full two seconds for me to take in the grisly scene before my mind registered the movement that had brought us in here in the first place. Two robotic humanoids slathered in blood and dangling strips of flesh were trying to clamber into hastily dissected missiles. A third already had, embedding itself in the space where the warhead would have been.

That moment of frozen horror went on for a few more seconds, then the compartment erupted into frenetic chaos. One of the robotic constructs turned and fired a pistol, and the slug clanged against the bulkhead beside K'losk. A second round struck him, and he grunted, but he returned fire, a burst of rail gun shots that ripped the mech-hybrid thing to fragments. I fired a bolt from The Drop's underslung beam weapon, engulfing a second construct in a halo of coruscating light. It dropped, senseless, to the deck. Torina, meantime, dashed to the third one, which seemed to be intent on being loaded, along with the missile it had commandeered, into the launcher. She grabbed it and yanked, then dragged it halfway back out of the missile casing.

A moment later, the launch system went offline.

While Torina stepped back and covered the one she'd grabbed with her sidearm, I checked on K'losk. Fortunately, his armor had done its job, and he was uninjured.

"The advantage of an exoskeleton. It's like having another layer of armor," he said.

I nodded, and we both took in the horrifying scene, trying to make sense of what had happened here. As we did, Perry and Hosurc'a appeared in the doorway.

"Okay, Van, we stopped the scuttling charges they'd—holy shit. What the *hell* did you guys do in here?"

"This must have been one hell of a fight," Hosurc'a put in.

"It was like this when we got here, honest," I replied as we started working out just what had happened.

But Perry and Hosurc'a got it right away. "They're biomechanical constructs—androids, basically, not too different from the security synths that banker had guarding his home," Perry said.

I nodded. "Yeah, I'd figured that much out. But what the hell is this—this charnel house thing all about?"

"They were divesting themselves of their biological components. They presumably don't need them to keep functioning," Hosurc'a said.

Torina blinked behind her visor. "They were ripping their own skin and other tissues off? Why?"

Perry tapped a wing against a missile casing. "Presumably so they could fit inside these. It was a last-ditch effort to escape. There's enough debris drifting around out there that a missile ejected from a tube, but not actually launched, probably wouldn't be noticed."

"And since their biological components would be damaged or destroyed by exposure to space anyway, they decided to get rid of them," Hosurc'a put in.

I could only shake my head. "Okay, that is—pretty clever, actually. Incredibly gross, I mean, holy shit, *flaying yourself* gross. I've heard of changing coats to blend in, but nothing quite *this* drastic."

"Hosurc'a, can you and Perry link with these things? See what you can find out from them?" K'losk asked.

"We can try, as long as they have working data ports. If they don't, then we'll have to do some jury-rigging."

Perry tapped the missile again. "We've got lots of components available if we need to do that."

Over the next hour or so, Perry and Hosurc'a connected to

two of the constructs—the one I'd stunned, and the one Torina
had yanked out of the missile. Both lay incapacitated on the deck,
fluids oozing, gears whirring and clicking, servos whining. The
data core of the one K'losk had gunned down was still intact, but
our two combat AIs had to do some of Perry's jury-rigging to
access it. We left them to it, with Torina providing watchful cover,
while K'losk and I gave the rest of the ship's accessible sections a
more thorough sweep. We found two more of the constructs,
both dead, killed during the battle.

"She's salvageable, but she's going to need a lot of work to get
spaceworthy again," K'losk said. "I say we just sell off salvage
rights and take the cash."

I nodded. There might be a few components here and there
that were worth stripping off of her and incorporating into our
own ships. Overall, though, she was probably worth more to us
just for her salvage value.

We made our way back to the missile bay. When we arrived,
Perry and Hosurc'a had more to report.

"We have a name. They're the Trinduk, but they seem to go
by another term, one that roughly translates to Sorcerers," Perry
said, disconnecting a cable that linked him to the isolated data
core.

"Sorcerers? Like, magic? Spells? Wands?" Torina asked.

"That's right."

"Okay, and what kind of magic do they make?"

"The kind that puts people into metal canisters where they go
insane. Or work themselves to death," Hosurc'a replied.

I scowled around the compartment. If these weren't the

architects of the stolen-identity plot we'd been chasing down, they were certainly an intimate and integral part of it.

"Can you get a manifest of their victims?" I asked.

"Sure. In parts, at least. We'll have to fry all three of them in order to do so and see what sort of coherent list we make out of it."

I glanced at K'losk. "Are you okay with that?"

"Sure am. After that, we can eject their debris and incinerate it with laser fire, just to make sure they never, *ever* manage to find their way back to life."

"Works for me." I crouched down beside the being I'd stunned, which was apparently called a Sorcerer.

"Now, I'm actually not a very violent or vindictive guy. But when it comes to you and the things you've been doing, or participating in—" I shook my head. "Yeah, I've got some shitty news for you, friend. See, I've been looking for you for a long time, and now that I've found you, you're going to—well, I was about to say *spill your guts*, but you've already done that."

I leaned closer, not sure if the thing could even hear me but not caring. "So let's put it this way. When we're done, you'll *wish* you were running some maintenance bot for eternity. Because what's about to happen is going to feel like forever."

I glanced back. "Perry? Hosurc'a? Be thorough. Take... your... time."

They replied in chorus.

"With pleasure."

22

ONCE WE'D EXTRACTED all of the information we could from the remnants of the Sorcerers, we carefully packaged them up to take them back with us to Anvil Dark. K'losk and his fellow Peacemakers didn't think their surveillance op had been compromised because who or whatever they'd been waiting to spy on hadn't yet shown up. So we loaded one of the Sorcerers onto K'losk's ship, and the other two aboard the Fafnir. They were, after all, crucial evidence, and we didn't want them all in one place. Once that was done, we said our goodbyes. That included Perry and Hosurc'a, who had an especially touching farewell.

It consisted of the two of them staring at one another for a while. Perry finally spoke.

"Goodbye, Hosurc'a."

"Goodbye, Perry."

Then they turned their backs on each other and walked away.

Torina, watching, wiped at her eye. "That was truly heartrending."

"That Hosurc'a is such a preening, pumped-up douche," Perry muttered as we boarded the *Fafnir* and prepared to undock from the battered frigate.

"What was it you said, Torina? Something about pots and kettles?" I asked.

"I am nothing like that preening idiot. For one, I am far more modest. In fact, I think humility is one of my most prominent traits."

Torina grinned as she settled into the copilot's seat. "You're just jealous of his tail, aren't you, Perry?"

I nodded. "He does have a splendiferous tail."

"It looks stupid. I think kids on Earth call it *extra*."

"They did two years ago, Dad."

Perry turned a baleful eye at me. "Et tu, Van?"

When we finished laughing—and as Perry regained his dignity—Netty undocked us, then we backed the *Fafnir* away. We'd already claimed and sold the salvage rights to the hulk, less its weapons, which we spiked thoroughly enough that they were no longer good for anything but scrap. Neither K'losk nor I had been excited about the prospect of military-grade weaponry just being sold into the open market. It dramatically dropped the salvage value, but we were all willing to forego some money now if it meant not being shot at by these same weapons later.

We docked at Spindrift to take on fuel but really had no other reason to hang around there, paying docking fees. Ironically, we'd come to Spindrift to try and pick up the trail of our investigation, and we'd done that. In fact, it had come to us. If the Sorcerers had never attacked us, we'd probably be in the banker's office and apartment on the station—dusting for prints or something.

So we left Spindrift to return to Anvil Dark and get the Sorcerers into the hands of people who could study them properly, like Steve and his techs. Shortly after we got underway, Perry announced that he and Hosurc'a had finally decrypted the data they'd stripped from the vile creatures. It included at least a partial list of identities that had been stolen and were now chipped somewhere as digital slave labor.

"There are several Schegith on the list," Perry said when he brought it up on the screen between the *Fafnir*'s pilots' seats.

"Well, that explains why Schegith herself felt like there were echoes of her people—in the warp, or whatever it is they call their shared mind space. It's because there really were," I noted.

"Yeah, and that's really interesting. But so is that eighth name on the list," Perry replied.

I looked at it and drew a blank. So did Torina.

"That, Van, is a Peacemaker who went missing almost twelve years ago."

"Holy shit."

"Holy shit indeed. Also, see that code on the right side of the screen? That's a location code. All of the Schegith, this missing Peacemaker, and a few others are located together, in one place." Perry paused, then shrugged. "The trouble is, we don't know where that place is because it's just coded as APP."

"Okay, we need to figure that out—"

"I know where it is," Torina said, her eyes hard as she stared at the screen.

Perry and I exchanged a look. "Can you elaborate on that?" I asked her.

"I can. APP. It's the Ambrosia Pleasure Palace."

Perry just kept giving a blank look. Netty spoke up.

"Never heard of the place, and it's not on any star charts."

I turned to Torina. "I think you're going to have to elaborate some more, my dear."

She sighed. "The Ambrosia Pleasure Palace is a resort. A very, *very* exclusive one. The reason you've never heard of it is because some incredibly well-connected people put a lot of effort into making sure it remains unknown to the rest of known space."

"It's an exclusive club for rich people," I suggested.

"Rich won't even get you in the door. Very rich will, and you'll even get access to some of the amenities inside. To get full access, you need to be very, very, *very* rich."

I grimaced. "Yeah, I don't know anything about this place, and I already don't like it."

The Ambrosia Pleasure Palace was, it seemed, a rambling combination of orbital and ground-based facilities located in an unremarkable star system with the poetic name 2MASS J1941-4602. It was on the very edge of known space, sixty-six light-years from

Earth, yet another in the unremarkable multitude of unremarkable red dwarf stars. On the public charts, it was off-limits, supposedly because of contamination by experimental weapons testing.

"And if that's not enough to keep people away, it's *heavily* defended," Torina said.

I leaned back in my seat. "I'm assuming you know about this place because your family falls into the very rich category? Or the very, very, very rich?"

"Somewhere in-between. And yes. I was even there once, when I was—oh, eleven, maybe? Twelve? Anyway, I was there for a few weeks with my parents."

"Okay. I'm not getting a warm fuzzy from you about this place."

"That's because I hate it. It's everything that's wrong with the super wealthy. It's stupidly opulent, ridiculously ostentatious, and criminally self-indulgent. The amount of money that passes through the place in a single day could probably feed a planet."

She turned to me. "And if you're wondering why I've never mentioned it before, it's because when I was sixteen, my father told me the place had gone bankrupt and was being wound down."

"He knew you hated the place and didn't want you causing trouble when you became an adult," Perry said.

"Yeah. He obviously lied to protect his friends' sordid little playground. He and I are going to have to have a talk when I get back to Helso."

"In the meantime, we need to decide what we're going to do

about this," I said, trying to prevent the conversation from veering into bitter recrimination territory.

Torina just looked at me. "Do? What can we do? We're talking about the wealthiest people in known space, Van. These are not just common criminals."

"No, they're *uncommon* criminals. But that still makes them criminals."

"Are you seriously thinking of, what, going and raiding the Ambrosia Pleasure Palace?"

"Well, unless you have other plans."

"Van, that's insane. You'd be making enemies of the most powerful people and organizations there are."

I sighed. "Yeah, you're right. Perry, make a note that we're just going to let the Schegith die off, while what's left of their race lives in electronic servitude to some rich assholes. Oh, and that missing Peacemaker, too—"

"Okay, okay," Torina said, holding up her hands. "You're right. Morally, ethically, even legally, it's the right thing to do."

"And?"

"And, it's still insane."

I turned to face her. "A few years ago, I was hired for a job by —by who doesn't matter. The point was, I was hired to crack into a super-secure, dark-web server farm that was being used by various criminal organizations to launder money. Some of those organizations were big. As in, *oligarchs* big. A few *heads-of-state* big. It was the biggest, most complex job I ever did. It took me weeks of really careful, incremental intrusion, backed up by more than a little social engineering. Some of the people I 'befriended'—

let's just say I needed to shower after every meeting with them, and all those meetings were online."

Torina and Perry were both listening intently. I knew that Netty was, too.

"Anyway, to make a long story short—"

"Too late," Perry put in.

"Can it, bird. Anyway, I eventually got the level of access I wanted. When I did, I found the money. Holy shit, did I find the money. And I found a lot more. A *lot* more. I won't go into details because I assume you'd like to sleep tonight."

"Yeah, this is starting to sound like Ambrosia," Torina said.

"Anyway, my job was just to interrupt the flow of money. I did that. I sent nearly forty million bucks to five hundred and three different charities. That was enough to get me put on the hit lists of at least a few really dangerous bad guys. But I didn't stop with that. I also crashed the server farm with a cascading virus, but not before ensuring all of the data, everything from tax dodges to— well, yeah, again, you wanna sleep, so let's just say I made sure as much of it as I could was released into the general 'netspace. I passed a chunk of it over to a whistleblower organization, and they revealed all kinds of stuff about various tax havens, and who was putting money into them."

"Okay, I get it—"

"No, no, I'm not done. Rewind to that moment where, after about three months of working almost around the clock, and a bunch of time spent chatting with some truly obnoxious pieces of shit, I was finally where I wanted to be. All I had to do to bring it all crashing down was press Enter." I shrugged. "Okay, it was more than just pressing one key, but you get the point. Anyway, I had to sit and stare at the screen for a while, and then go for a walk to decide if I really wanted to do this. I came really close a few times to just shutting down all my fake accounts, wiping everything that had anything to do with this job, and giving back my fee. I was that scared of the position I was putting myself in."

"But you did it anyway," Torina said.

"Yeah, I did. Incidentally, I didn't keep a dime of the money, aside from my fee. A bunch of people got arrested, and a whole lot of corporations were embarrassed when they were outed for their tax-dodging shenanigans."

I looked Torina in the eye. "I was terrified. Jumping at my own shadow for weeks afterward. I'd covered my tracks pretty damned well, but any hacker who doesn't think there's someone out there better than him is an idiot. But, you know what? Next time I looked in the mirror, I saw someone I was proud of."

"Well, Van, if we do this, you're putting yourself in that situation again. Only it will be worse because you won't be able to conceal who you are."

"But I will be able to look at that guy in the mirror and honestly say that I'm still proud of him."

I gave a rueful smile. "But I don't expect you to be part of it. Even more than me, I don't think you want to be attached to this. You've got your family to worry about."

"Oh, you mean my father, who lied to me so he could conceal the fact he was still taking the occasional dip in the cesspool called Ambrosia? That father, that family?" She shook her head.

"I don't want to be ashamed of that woman in the mirror. I'm in."

"Me too," Perry said.

I shot him a wintry smile. "You were thinking of opting out?"

"Maybe."

"Really?"

"No. I mean, duh. It *is* nice to be asked, though."

———

Lunzy just stared back at me for a while. Finally, she smiled.

"Have to admit, Van, you've got some asteroid-sized balls."

"Uh—thanks?"

We were aboard her ship the *Foregone Conclusion*, sitting once more in her plush study—which reminded me, I *really* needed to get myself one of these. I'd shown her the evidence and outlined my intent, and that had led to her comment about my testicular girth.

She sat back in her big chair and spent a moment looking into the crackling fire. Finally, she turned back.

"Torina's right. This is crazy."

"Are you telling me not to pursue it?"

"Hell no. That wasn't a judgment, just an observation. This is crazy, but it's something that has to be done. And by that, I mean literally has to. Now that you've come into possession of this evidence, you'd be committing a crime by not acting on it."

"So would you," Perry said.

"I'm well aware. And that's not my concern. What *does*

concern me is that as soon as you present this evidence back at Anvil Dark, word is going to get to Ambrosia, and it's going to trigger a mass exodus. By the time we get there, the rats will have skittered away, and the place will be as empty and abandoned as Torina's father claimed it to be."

It was a good point, and one that had already occurred to me. But I wasn't sure how to proceed without taking the evidence back to Anvil Dark. Hence, my meeting with Lunzy, once more in the lee of a big comet on the edge of the Gamma Crucis system.

"So what do you suggest we do?"

Lunzy looked back into the fire, her face pensive. "Technically, there's nothing requiring that the evidence be presented back at Anvil Dark. The Peacemakers' Charter recognizes exigent circumstances—situations in which there's such a risk of suspects taking flight or evidence being tampered with or destroyed, that immediate action is required."

"Well, I'd say that applies here, wouldn't you?" Torina asked.

But Perry spoke up. "Actually, this situation would explicitly meet the tests for exigent circumstances, there's no doubt about it at all. So we're in the clear that way, at least."

Lunzy nodded. "Perry's right. That's not the part that worries me. Taking action is justified. What I'm having a problem with is what the action's going to be. If it's just the two of us in the *Foregone Conclusion* and the *Fafnir*, well, we might be able to grab a few of the rats before their ship goes down, but most of them will get away."

"So we need help," I said.

"We do. But from Peacemakers we trust."

I frowned in thought. "Well, I've worked with two others. There was Alic, who led that attack on the Stillness—"

"He's clean, and definitely someone we can trust. Enipeds aren't known for their duplicity," Lunzy said.

"And then there's K'losk, who helped us out of our jam just a couple of days ago when the Sorcerers ambushed us on our way to Spindrift. Oh, which reminds me." I reached down into the satchel I'd been carrying, and extracted a bottle. "As a connoisseur of fine beverages, you should find this one especially offensive," I said, handing Lunzy the bottle.

She unstoppered it, sniffed it, then took a swig.

I waited for what I expected to be an explosive reaction. Instead, she just shrugged.

"Not bad. Not the best moonshine I've ever had, but not too bad. Van? What? Why are you staring at me?"

"Because you're still upright. You don't find that a little, um… tart?"

Lunzy laughed. "I don't brag about much. But if you ever face getting into a drinking contest with me, back away, very slowly."

"And you're proud of that."

"Damned right. Anyway, K'losk is another one we can trust, yeah."

"Oh, yay, I get to spend more time with Hosurc'a," Perry said, his voice a flat monotone.

"What have you got against him, Perry? He seemed fine. Certainly no more preening and full of himself than—" I caught myself. "He seemed fine."

"It's that damned tail of his. He's always, you know, showing it off, dragging it along behind him for everyone to see."

"It's—his tail. What's he *supposed* to do with it?"

"As far as I'm concerned, he can sh—"

"Do you want a new and splendiferous tail, Perry?" Torina asked.

"No. That would just make me seem—"

"Jealous?" Torina asked.

"Desperate?" Lunzy added.

I smirked. "Pathetic?"

"I hate you all."

Over the next hour, we worked out a rough plan. How we executed it would depend on how many Peacemakers we could bring into the circle of knowledge. Besides Alic and K'losk, Lunzy had two others she thought she could count on. When we were done, I made to get up and head back to the *Fafnir*. We had a day in the hangar scheduled at Anvil Dark to complete repairs to the ship. But Lunzy gave me a hard stare.

"Van, I want you to be sure that you want to go through with this. We'll all be antagonizing some powerful people, but I'm old and treacherous enough that it doesn't bother me. And these other Peacemakers are all fairly senior. We all have connections—and a few closets stocked with the odd skeleton or two—to fall back on. You're still new to the game, and you've already made a name for yourself that others are starting to resent. So, again—are you sure you want to do this?"

"Already asked the guy in the mirror this morning, Lunzy. He's good with it, so I am, too."

23

Our small armada rendezvoused at a point well out into the sparse Oort Cloud that enshrouded Ambrosia. We ended up with a total of seven Peacemakers—me, Lunzy, Alic, and K'losk, two others I knew in passing, and one I actually knew well. It was Gabriella Santorelli, the Peacemaker who'd overseen my induction as an Initiate at Crossroads. She was a lot warmer and more effusive than she had been then. Of course, then I was a complete unknown who'd just showed up in Gramps' *Dragonet* and said, hi, I wanna be a Peacemaker. I guess I'd proven myself worth her investment of time and effort.

"So what happened to Crossroads?" I asked her as we settled ourselves into Lunzy's study for our final mission briefing.

"My assignment ended. I could have renewed it, but—" She shrugged. "I needed a change of scenery. That said, though, if that job comes up down the road, when you've got more Peace-making under your belt, it's worth considering. A little bit of paperwork, the odd inductee, and otherwise your time is pretty much your own. I taught myself to play the violin."

"Really? I'd love to hear you sometime—"

Torina poked my arm. "Pay attention, Van. The lady's talking," she said, nodding toward Lunzy.

I smirked at her. Was she a little jealous, maybe?

I'd never had anyone jealous of me before. I'd never had a starship, either, so my list of firsts was growing.

Our plan was simple. We'd twist in as close to Ambrosia as we could, while each ensuring we maintained enough fuel to twist back out again. We'd come at the Pleasure Palace from three directions, in one group of three, that included us and K'losk, and two groups of two, one led by Alic, the other by Gabriella.

"The important part is as follows—don't get trigger happy," Lunzy said. "Remember, most of these people are civilians, and their ships are going to be lightly armed, if at all. Their likely response is going to be running away. If you get a chance to disable a fleeing ship, take it, but only if you're sure you can do it safely. And, of course, you can defend yourselves and one another from attack. Otherwise, just let them run. Our interest is primarily Ambrosia itself."

We all acknowledged her, then Lunzy took a moment to emphasize the risk we were all taking of gaining some powerful and resentful enemies. She gave each of us a final chance to back out. No one took it.

"I'm looking forward to kicking some rich asses," Gabriella

said, giving a predatory grin. There was a story there, which I made a note to hear sometime.

If Torina would let me, of course.

We dispersed back to our ships, made sure our own crews were up-to-date, then waited for Lunzy's *go* signal.

She came on the comm. "Ladies and gentlebeings, on three… two… and one."

We twisted into Ambrosia.

I'm NOT sure what I actually expected. Probably a nerve-wracking flurry of battle, some tense standoffs, shot through with moments of drama and tragedy. What we got was nothing like that.

We twisted in, and the first response from Ambrosia was a comm signal from a traffic control AI, who was either programmed to sound bored or had machine-learned it.

"Unknown ship, this space is prohibited for entry, pursuant to Interstellar Traffic Management Accord Three-dash-two-dash-one, Addendum Two. Reverse course and leave this system immediately. Failure to do so may result in you being fired upon."

Sure enough, we were lit up with fire control scanners from four different directions. Automated defense platforms came to life, ready to start flinging missiles at us.

This was probably the part where casual visitors turned tail and fled. We just activated our Peacemaker beacons and accelerated straight in.

Another minute or so passed.

Then all hell broke loose.

The resulting battle, if you could call it that, consisted of us first taking out the nearest defense platforms with laser and rail gun fire. We didn't bother expending missiles, simply because the platforms were old and woefully undergunned. Not one missile landed a hit.

I glanced at Torina, an eyebrow raised. "For all this money, they sure as hell didn't invest in decent defenses, did they?"

Torina returned a knowing smile. "Rich people are cheap. Besides, when they come here, they don't want to be thinking about things like traffic control and defense. In fact, I'm sure that *upgrading the defenses* has been an item on the agenda of every meeting of whatever oversight body this place has for years. It just keeps getting deferred in favor of new wine fountains and velvet ropes and such."

"Velvet ropes?"

"Of course. They don't chafe—"

"That's—okay. I don't need any of the mental images that's heading toward, thanks."

Once the platforms were neutralized, the mass exodus began. Ships, mostly glitzy yachts of various types and sizes, began to scatter. Lunzy's earlier allusions to rats and sinking ships was perfectly apt. And so was something else, I thought, with a bit of savage mischief.

Torina was lining up a railgun shot, intending to take out the drive of a sleek yacht burning like hell to get away. She'd already disabled two others. I just had some easy flying to do, so I turned to Netty.

"Do you know *Yakety Sax?*"

"I spent many days sitting in a barn in Iowa, Van. I could give you the lunchtime news and weather for Des Moines on May 7, 2018."

"Just play the damned song."

She did, the staccato saxophone notes erupting from the speakers. Torina gaped, then laughed.

"This is perfect!"

To my dying day, I will never forget fighting a battle, in outer space, accompanied by the very theme song of comedic chaos.

MORE THAN HALF of the escaping ships managed to get away from us. The rest drifted, disabled, on auxiliary or backup power. While Lunzy, K'losk, Alic, and I boarded the orbital terminal of Ambrosia, Gabriella and the other two Peacemakers took charge of rounding them up and ensuring that no one's life was in immediate danger.

"We should charge them for our towing services. Fifty thousand each. What do you think?" Gabriella asked as we entered the orbital, her voice impishly bright.

"I'd recommend getting payment in advance," Lunzy said, then we walked out of the airlock into a wall of outrage, a cacophony of people of all shapes, sizes and species ranting and shouting at us at once. Some of them had clearly gotten themselves dressed in great haste.

I looked around. We stood in a soaring atrium filled with a

riot of green fronds and flowering plants, tinkling fountains, and tiny creeks flowing under arched bridges into little pools. A massive reception desk dominated the center of the space, while other exits led to different parts of the orbital, to other airlocks, or to the upper terminus of a bonafide space elevator connecting the orbital to the facilities on the ground.

"It would be so cool to ride that!" I said, gazing out a viewport that looked straight down the length of the elevator, essentially a massive bundle of carbon-nanotube cables nearly thirty thousand klicks long. It was almost dizzying, watching it dwindle down to invisibility even before it reached the distant cloud tops.

Lunzy and K'losk had managed to herd the outraged patrons into some semblance of order, and had been busy reading out chapter and verse of applicable legislation that said, in essence, we were legally entitled to do what we did. While many of those present still scowled and glared, a few panicked and began yelling what I consider to be *cliches of the wealthy and privileged*. I heard threats, demands for their attorney, at least one attempted bribe, and a man who was on the verge of soiling himself, though in his defense he was scared *and* drunk, a poor combination when you think your life is about to change forever thanks to a nasty arrest record.

Most of the people were smart—they kept silent and tried to slip away, a tactic I approved of, even if I found their entitled behavior repulsive.

As far as the rest of known space was concerned, the Ambrosia Pleasure Palace didn't exist.

In the meantime, as far as *these* people knew, the media was hot on our heels. And none of them wanted their faces to show up in descriptions of the decadent opulence of this money-grubbing hideaway. Some of them were influential, even celebrities. Some of them were government officials. Some of them undoubtedly had families.

So we capitalized on that. Lunzy gave me a look that said, *you're on.*

"Excuse me, everyone, we'd like your attention," I said. "Please, quiet. Look—we aren't here on a witch hunt for consensual adults doing consensual adult things. We are here to retrieve some people we have reason to believe are being held here against their will."

There was some muttering and uncomfortable shuffling about, and a few pseudopods extended and retracted. I held up my hands until the murmuring racket died again.

"So here's what we propose. Someone comes forward and tells us about any robotic or android persons being forced into doing some, ah, not-so-consensual adult things. My colleagues and I go and deal with that, and the rest of you go about your business. However, we can't let anyone leave until this matter is resolved."

In seconds, I confirmed that there was little honor among this crowd. The bulk of these people were armed with confidence borne of money and position. But there were weak links among them, and they caved in and began jabbering away in a torrent of tips and confessions.

"Good thing I didn't go into a life of crime with any of these stalwarts. They folded like cheap chairs," I muttered to Torina, whose lip was curled in absolute disgust.

In seconds, we were collecting information about bots and synths and droids being used for menial tasks—or worse. They couldn't help us fast enough, in fact, and a few made sure we knew exactly who they were, and that they were cooperating fully, hinting strongly that this sudden burst of honesty should be enough to keep the media at bay. I greeted every one of those requests with the flat gaze of someone who was tempted to throw them out an airlock—after all, I was a commoner to them, and such behavior met with their general opinion of my social graces.

Or lack thereof.

Ultimately, Torina, Lunzy, K'losk, and I determined that where we wanted to be was on the surface. This orbital facility was mainly a terminus for the space elevator, offering just a few amenities for those who were only making a brief stopover.

"They rent rooms and, well, other things out by the hour," Torina said, curling her lip in disgust. I was right there with her.

Perry and Hosurc'a, in the meantime, scoured the computer systems after we made it very clear we were only interested in the missing people, not in anything else. When they were done, they reported back.

"Yup, definitely down on the surface. There aren't any synthetic life-forms up here," Hosurc'a said.

I looked at Lunzy, who just shrugged. "Hey, I took the lead during the battle, such as it was. As far as I'm concerned, this is your show now, Van. I'm just backup."

I put my hands on my hips and nodded. "Okay, then. *I* am going to ride down in that space elevator, because why not?"

"Traveling all over known space in your own ship fighting interstellar crime isn't enough bragging rights for a—what did you call yourself? A farm boy from Iowa?" Torina said, smirking at me.

I shook my head. "No. No it is not."

THE TRIP down to the surface was both more and less exciting than I'd anticipated. More because I was plummeting down toward an alien world on a freakin' space elevator. Less because the trip involved a whole lot of lounging around the elevator car's plush interior, watching the planet slowly fill more and more of the field of view, its horizon getting progressively flatter and flatter.

"Now I see why they serve booze on this thing," I said, gesturing toward the bar, which was closed and locked up. "Bored people drink more."

"And drunk or otherwise intoxicated people make poor choices," Hosurc'a said.

Torina scowled. "That's what this place is all about. Exploitation. *Expensive* exploitation, but exploitation nonetheless."

The last few minutes of the ride were the most spectacular because we were plunging out of the sky at dizzying speed. We punched through clouds that left us briefly socked in, and one that engulfed us in about two seconds of torrential rain. When we dropped out of the bottom of the cloud base, maybe two klicks up, we still seemed to be going awfully fast. It struck me that this might have been unwise. An unfortunate accident could end up killing me, Torina, and K'losk if this car simply didn't stop. As my pulse quickened, I wondered if that was why Lunzy hadn't come along—

But the car suddenly started a smooth deceleration until the last hundred meters or so passed at a sedate pace, maybe a quick jog. And then we stopped.

The doors slid open—and shots rang out, slugs snapping against the bar and vanishing into the overstuffed upholstery with sharp *whumps*.

Torina, K'losk, and I dove for cover and drew our weapons. Perry and Hosurc'a, though, flung themselves through the open door. Perry slammed talons-first into the face of a gruff human dressed in casual clothing and sporting a big handgun. Hosurc'a spun in midair and snapped his glorious tail like a whip, cutting the throat of a second spine deep. The first screamed as Perry ripped his face apart. The second just flopped back in a shower of blood, gurgling.

Torina, K'losk, and I charged out after them, weapons ready. There were three more armed but otherwise ununiformed types nearby—another human, a Yonnox, and a squat, muscular creature with tubes sprouting from its upper torso and plugged into a small backpack. They watched, wide-eyed, as their two fellows were savaged by the AIs, then they looked at the three of us sighting down our weapons at them and dropped theirs.

While Torina and K'losk covered them, I gathered up their

weapons and threw them into the elevator car. Then we had them kneel—or, in the case of Tubes, fold over in its closest approximation of kneeling—and snapped restraints on them.

"Smart move, giving up like that," I said, standing up from the one I'd cuffed.

"Yeah, well, they don't pay me enough for"—he gestured with his chin toward the one Hosurc'a had slashed, now laying still, blood pooling around him—"that."

I turned to Perry and Hosurc'a. "That was—wow. Savage."

"We're *combat* AIs, remember? We're not just pretty faces."

"I am," Hosurc'a said.

Perry shot him an amber glare. "Shut up."

It took another few hours of searching, along with alternately cajoling, persuading, and threatening staff and patrons of Ambrosia before we finally found and gathered up the chips containing our missing Schegith, along with everyone else on the list noted as being at APP. Some of the situations we found these poor souls embroiled in honestly made my blood boil.

As we stalked out of one particularly nasty room, I was shaking my head. "Peacemaker loses control, shoots every rich bastard in sight, film at eleven."

Torina forced a smile. "*Every* rich bastard?"

"Present company excepted."

But Torina's smile fled, and she shook her head. "Actually,

make it two crazed Peacemakers on your imaginary shooting rampage. This place is—" She shook her head again.

"Yeah, I know."

And the worst part was that, once we were gone, Ambrosia Pleasure Palace would clean up the blood, plaster over the bullet strikes, and carry right on with its sordid business. It was the price for not having every one of these assholes sending even bigger assholes after us. Basically, we were colluding. In exchange for the people we'd come to rescue, and the satisfaction of inflicting a few million bonds in damage to ostentatious yachts and the antiquated Ambrosian security systems, we'd just walk away. No reports would be filed, no charges laid.

I hated the idea of it, right down to my core. I could tell that Torina, Lunzy, and the other Peacemakers did, too. But there's the idealized version of doing what was right, and then the practical one.

So, as we started back to the space elevator for the long ride back up to orbit, I was busy trying to console myself. Yes, we were going to leave a whole lot of bad here, festering away. But at least we'd done *some* good. It was because I was being introspective and broody that I almost missed one final bit of drama.

I'D WANTED to be alone with my thoughts for a few minutes, so I fell behind the others. As we passed a side corridor, thickly carpeted and lit by recessed lighting like any number of hotel hallways back on Earth, movement caught my eye. Someone had just come out of a room and hurried off in the other direction, dragging something—no, some*one*—along behind it.

I stared for a moment, struck dumb. The one doing the dragging was very clearly a Sorcerer. The one being dragged was small, scaled like a lizard, bound, muzzled, and bleeding.

My dark thoughts about this place, and everything it represented, combined with this horrific little escapade playing out, plunged me into a cold, blind rage.

I let the anger come out to play. I drew The Drop.

At that moment, the Sorcerer turned and raised a weapon.

The Drop boomed. And boomed again. And again, and again, until its magazine was empty.

And then I was standing over the smashed remains of the Sorcerer, fragments and components scattered all around it. I heard shouts behind me, then Torina and K'losk appeared, their weapons drawn. Perry and Hosurc'a both swept overhead in a storm of wings and landed further up the corridor, ready for battle.

Torina touched my arm. "Van?" A single word, loaded with worry.

I nodded but looked at Perry. "Perry, when you were digging around in their computer system and promised to not take anything directly related to our case—did you?"

"I did. Now, a few things may have ended up in my buffers—"

"Nasty, incriminating things?"

"A lot of it, yeah. Would you like me to flush my buffers and get rid of it all?"

I said nothing.

Perry bobbed his head. "Got it, boss."

K'losk stepped up beside me, holstering his weapon. "Might I remind you that we did agree to a deal with this place."

"And I intend to honor it—if someone can explain to me what the hell that *thing* is doing here," I shot back, glaring down at the smashed remains of the Sorcerer.

Torina moved to help the little scaled creature. As soon as she got it free of its restraints, it scampered over to the Sorcerer's remains and pried a small golden disk out of what remained of its forehead.

"Is that important to you?" I asked.

The translator rendered the reply in a female voice. "Damned right it is. That's gold. I love gold. I love shiny stuff. And it's not like this asshole needs it anymore."

Despite everything that had happened, I laughed. It felt good, a dousing of fresh, cold rain after a punishing dry spell. It was emotional relief in the act of simple, practical avarice. I gave the small being a salute, and she responded with a jaunty wave, scampering away with her bloody prize.

Perry and Hosurc'a were able to identify the important part of the Sorcerer, its logic and personality module. We retrieved that, and I also pulled a strange cuff-like device off of its wrist. It was one of the few relatively intact pieces left of the creature after I'd pumped The Drop's entire magazine into it.

"Who's that for?" Torina asked.

I stood, holding the cuff. "Who do we know that has expertise in artificial life-forms? Who lives with his daughter aboard an old battleship?"

"Urnak and Icky."

"That's right." I held up the cuff. "I want to take this and the logic module to them, and get their take on it. Most of all, I want to know if there's a way that we can kill these assholes more than one at a time."

"Shouldn't we find out a little more before we commit to, you know, wiping out an entire race?"

"Absolutely. But when the time comes, I want to be ready."

"For genocide."

"Unless these Sorcerer bastards have some redeeming quality I'm not seeing, like they run a puppy and kitten rescue or something—and you don't know what puppies and kittens are, do you?"

"Van, I live on a moon in the Van Maanen's Star system, not under a rock. Believe it or not, I do know a few things about Earth."

"Sorry."

Torina shrugged. "Don't be. And I'm not even opposed to the idea of genocide, if that's what it takes to stop what's been happening to these poor people they've stolen and enslaved."

"So you don't object to the possibility of wiping these scumbags out if it comes to it."

"Not at all. Hell, if and when the time comes, I'll push the button. I mean, I do like efficiency."

24

TORINA and I spent some time with Urnak, while Perry and Icky examined the various bits and pieces of Sorcerers we'd brought along with us. That especially included that strange cuff-like device. It took them a good couple of hours, but the two of them finally returned to Urnak's sitting room, where we were sitting with Urnak, explaining everything that had happened and sipping a damned fine wine. It was light and sparkling and almost sang across my tongue. I asked him where it came from, expecting him to name some exotic planet or obscure moon. He retrieved the bottle and read what it said.

"Napa Valley, California, USA," he said, butchering the pronunciation of *California*. Then he shrugged. "No idea. Somewhere in the Tau Ceti system, maybe?"

I stared. "What? No, that's from Earth. California's on—"

I saw him grinning at me and grinned back. "Touché."

"Your home planet might be something of a backwater as far as most of known space is concerned," he said, sitting back down in his worn and comfortable chair. "But humans are good people. One of the better ones around. Most of you are, in my experience, fundamentally good, but there are enough bad humans around to keep things interesting."

Icky and Perry returned with the cuff. She set it on the table with a clunk, then sat down and said, "Wow."

I looked from it, to her. "Wow?"

"Yes. Wow. That is one sophisticated piece of tech."

"Can you be a *touch* more specific?"

"Well, my preliminary poke at the thing suggests it has a variety of functions. It's not actually magic, but it seems it can do some pretty magical things. I'm thinking localized EMP events of various power levels, and maybe some energy theft. It could probably even hack comms, and it can stop poisons and toxins. That last one is a real eye-opener, but it's actually pretty clear that's one of the things it's designed to do." She stared at the cuff. "That's some high-end product. I don't know who made it, but it took a lot of money. And a *lot* of expertise."

I eyed it, too. "So it doesn't do anything we can't already do another way then."

Perry replied. "No, we can replicate all of those effects. But we couldn't do it in some neat little package you can wear on your wrist. And all of those capabilities together would make whoever's wearing it a lot tougher to take on in a fight. Imagine you're in the middle of a firefight, and you can hack your enemy's comms and sensors, or blank them altogether with an EMP. And you do it using energy you've tapped from somewhere else, maybe even their systems and weapons. You're essentially immune to toxins, so you're not affected by things like incapacitating agents, noxious gases, and the like."

"There may be a few other capabilities built into the thing, too," Icky added. "I won't know for sure until I'm able to spend a lot more time tinkering with it."

"So why was Van able to just gun down the Sorcerer wearing the thing? It didn't seem to offer it any real advantage at all," Torina said.

Perry raised a wing. "Ooh, ooh, pick me, I know!"

"Alright, let's hear from the bird," I said.

"Two reasons. One, all the fancy tech in the world isn't going to stop dumb bullets, like the ones The Drop fires. Solid projectiles propelled by chemical reactions can't really be stopped by anything."

"Except a solid barrier, and I wouldn't rule out one of those additional functions we suspect being some sort of energy field designed to do just that," Icky explained.

"Which leads us to the second reason. Based on the other components we obtained, it seems that the Sorcerer you blew away was... incomplete," Perry went on.

I threw him a questioning look. "Incomplete? Incomplete how?"

"Incomplete, as in *not finished*."

"Oh, for—I know what *incomplete* means, Perry."

"Well, that's what this Sorcerer was. Maybe it was young—if

the term *young* applies to something like that. Maybe *new* is a better word. Not long off the showroom floor."

"Huh." I turned to Torina. "That means they're tough and scary, but they can also be vulnerable. The trick is catching them when they still have that new-Sorcerer smell."

She nodded back at me over her wine.

"Definitely good to know."

Icky, Torina, and I—along with Perry—were making our way back to the *Fafnir*, where she was docked against one of the big old battlewagon's UDAs. Partially there, we stopped as Icky's body went tense with the enormity of a single question.

"So do you think my mother is the one behind all of this?"

I glanced at Icky. "Behind it? As in the one solely responsible for it? Probably not. I mean, I guess it's possible, but it's more likely that she's just one of a cast of characters."

"Or a middleman. I can't help feeling that these Sorcerers are something bigger and older than just some money-grubbing conspiracy operating behind places like Ambrosia," Torina said.

Icky leaned back against a bulkhead.

"Well, I'm glad that you're trying to unwind just *what* my mother is involved in, and how, and hold her as accountable for it as she should be. I just—"

Torina grimaced. "You feel responsible for her, don't you?"

Icky gave a reluctant nod—one I knew to be colored with shame. "I do."

That surprised me. "Why? You've got nothing to do with her, or what she's done. You didn't even really know the woman."

Torina answered. "Van, when you were visiting us on Helso, you might have noticed that my parents and I didn't exactly have the warmest relationship."

"It was a bit... formal? Cool?"

"That's because my parents are very good at what they do. And what they do is make money. The problem is that to make money like that, you have to be... ruthless. There's no other way to put it. Ruthless and self-serving. I've already told you how my father lied to me about Ambrosia."

I crossed my arms to listen.

Torina frowned pensively for a moment, clearly following some train of thought. It apparently reached its destination, because she finally perked up and spoke.

"My father once bought a shipping company that had gotten itself deep in debt. He sold the debt off to someone else for a fraction of its value, then liquidated the rest of the company. He fired everyone, and I mean everyone, and sold off the few ships that the debt buyer didn't seize under a lien." Torina waved a hand. "There was more to the whole deal than that, but you get the idea. My dad made money, the debt buyer got the ships, which was what they really wanted, and everybody was happy."

"Everybody? What about all the people who lost their jobs?"

"Now that's a good question, isn't it? What about them? And what about the suppliers who were owed money by the company when he folded it up? And customers, stuck with shipments in mid-transit, aboard ships that had been seized under a lien? What about all of them?

We'd started walking toward the *Fafnir* again, but after just a few paces, I stopped, thinking again. Some variation on this story wasn't uncommon back on Earth, either. Predatory buyers purchasing companies—usually ones behind a financial eight ball, but sometimes perfectly sound ones—then scraping every bit of value that they could out of them and tossing aside the residual husk. Employees were inevitably the ones who suffered. And for added fun, the end of the company often led to things like environmentally contaminated properties reverting back to the government, so the taxpayers ended up on the hook to clean them up.

I shook my head and shrugged. "They were screwed."

"They were. So you know what my uncle and I did? We tried to hire as many of them back into our own companies as we could."

"And what did your dear old dad think of that?" Perry asked.

"As far as I know, he didn't think of it at all. It wasn't that he had anything against those people. He just didn't care about them. And, in some ways, that's worse."

It was her turn to shrug. "That's why you might have noticed that when I'm on the comm talking to my family, it's almost always my uncle. I am a *lot* closer to him than I am with my parents—who, I must add, I *do* love. I mean, they're my mom and dad. I just don't like them very much, which makes it all even more complicated."

She looked back at Icky. "So, yes, I understand how Icky here feels. I understand it completely."

"Torina's right. She didn't have to help those people, but she felt an obligation to them because of what her father had done to them. I guess I feel the same way about my mother. And, from what you've said, she's doing much, much worse things to people than throwing them out of work."

"She is that," I agreed.

"So I guess I'd like to find some way to help them, the way Torina did. I want to try and make up for some harm my mother has done." She sighed. "And is probably going to keep doing."

We again resumed our way to the *Fafnir*. As we did, I found myself reflecting on the nature of families and moral obligations related thereto. My immediate thought was that I was fortunate because I didn't have to face any of that. I'd never really known my mother. And I'd never been very close to my father, but he was a decent man, brave and honorable, who died doing something he believed in.

That left my grandfather, and he was the exact opposite of people like Torina's father, and *nothing* at all like Axicur. She was, in fact, the very thing that Gramps had devoted his life to fighting against. So I had no reason to feel obligated to confront the things he'd done.

Although, as we strode along, I realized that wasn't true. After all, here I was, walking through a spaceship light-years from Earth, doing something my grandfather thought was important. So I thought it was important, too. And wasn't following in a parent's footsteps, trying to build on the good things they'd done, just the positive version of what motivated Torina and Icky regarding *their* parents?

I picked up the thread of conversation between Torina and Icky a few paces along. They were discussing the nature of the Sorcerers and speculating about whether her mother was involved with them. That had been the springboard for speculation about the nature of the Sorcerers themselves, a discussion Icky obviously relished as it was a subject she knew well. Really well, even. I listened for a few more paces, then stopped. We were just outside the *Fafnir*'s airlock.

"Icky, I think it's fair to say that you and your dad are pretty much experts when it comes to synthetic life-forms like the Sorcerers, right?" I asked.

"I… suppose, sure. My father and I have spent a lot of time trying to integrate biological and mechanical components. It's not easy to do. First, you have to map out the precise electrical pathways of the biological nerves and then develop an interface—usually an organo-optical one—that can translate the nerve impulses into variations in electrical currents, and then these—"

I touched her shoulder, gently. "Icky?"

She stopped in mid-word, then shook her head. "I'm sorry. You don't want to listen to me prattle on about all this tech stuff."

"Actually, I think I do. Or, no, I don't, but I do appreciate that you can do it in the first place. So what you're saying is that you have a pretty good understanding of these bio-mechanical systems."

"It's one of my father's passions. He'd like to find a way to help people who've lost limbs, suffered organ failures, and who can't afford the sort of prices the flesh merchants on Spindrift charge. Nothing fancy, just simple, reliable, low-cost prosthetics, that sort of thing."

"That's perfect." I turned to Perry. "I can bring someone else onto the crew as an auxiliary, right?"

"If you want, sure. Lots of Peacemakers have auxiliary retainers, like legal experts and accountants." He looked at Icky. "And engineers."

I smiled at Icky. "How would you like a job?"

WE LEFT ICKY, our newly minted Auxiliary Engineer, on her father's battleship. Even if we'd wanted to bring her aboard the *Fafnir*, we couldn't because there simply wasn't room. Moreover, she needed space and equipment to do her work, and there wasn't any room aboard our cramped little ship for any of that either. Perry assured me it wasn't a problem.

"There are Peacemaker Auxiliaries all over known space. Lawyers, accountants, all sorts of technical experts in a bazillion different fields of expertise. Remember our art experts? That's essentially what they are. They have day jobs, but they're paid and kept on retainer by Peacemakers to help deal with specific problems."

Torina gave me a fond smile. "That was very decent of you."

"What was?"

"Bringing Icky on as an Auxiliary, making her an official part of the investigation."

I shrugged as I lit the drive, aiming the *Fafnir* for Anvil Dark. "She's got expertise we need. Both her and her father."

"Oh, I know. But you took that discussion about kids being responsible for their parents to heart, didn't you?"

"I… suppose, yeah."

"Well, you just made yourself a true and loyal friend. You've given her the possibility of something she's never had."

I gave Torina a questioning glance. "Oh? What's that?"

"A chance for closure with her mother and the feeling she's working toward getting it." She reached across the center console and touched my arm.

"On behalf of kids with problematic parental relationships everywhere, thank you."

"Just another day as a Peacemaker, fighting crime and making people's lives complete."

Perry poked his head forward, between us. "That's all very sweet, but I can't help feeling that you would like to bring her aboard the *Fafnir*."

"Well, it would make things simpler. She'd be immediately available. She's also a skilled engineer, which would come in handy. Am I right, Netty?"

"Absolutely. You could definitely use the help, Van."

I narrowed my eyes. "What's that supposed to mean? Are you dissing my engineering skills?"

"You're my boss. I'd never do that. But you are, shall we say, still a beginner when it comes to maintaining and repairing a spaceship."

"Considering that a year ago today the most advanced spaceships I even knew existed were used to take billionaires on ten minute rides into orbit, you can appreciate that it's a steep learning curve, thank you very much."

"Not denying it. But if you want to bring Icky aboard—if you want to bring much of anything aboard—you'll need to expand the *Fafnir*."

Torina nodded. "It's a good point. It's tight enough with just the two of us. With three of us—" She stopped and shifted uncomfortably, obviously imagining just what it would be like to have another person crammed inside our happy little ship.

I sighed. "I know, I know. Netty, I asked you if we can get a bigger crew habitat module installed. You know, one that can accommodate four without everyone elbowing one another in the face just to change their shirt. Anything come of that?"

"As a matter of fact, it has. I've found one at a good price."

"Oh. Well, that's great," I said to Torina, smiling into her face, which was only a few centimeters from mine. "There ya go."

"You ate something with garlic, didn't you?"

As WE NUDGED the *Fafnir* into the hangar we'd been assigned aboard Anvil Dark, Icky called to give us an update.

"Already? We only left you, like, a few hours ago!"

"I know, but I couldn't wait. This tech is even more sophisticated than I originally realized." She held a small metallic box. "This is a booster module, an amplifier for nerve impulses. It's key to making the interface between biological and machine components work properly. My father's been working on one for three or four years now, but his is currently about the size of a small desk." She grinned. "You should have seen his face when he saw *this*."

"So this goes beyond just being sophisticated tech and into something else. Something… alien, maybe? Some of that ancient tech I keep hearing about, that everyone wants and nobody really understands?"

"That's for sure. Dad and I consider ourselves to be close to the edge of research and development of this sort of stuff. Turns out that, compared to what we've accomplished, the edge is practically out of sight, somewhere over that far horizon."

"Okay, well, keep plugging away at it and let us know if you find out anything new and exciting—or new and terrifying."

"Especially new and terrifying," Torina put in.

We disembarked from the *Fafnir* and headed into Anvil Dark. We struck out immediately for Steve's tech shop, where the identity chips we'd seized from Ambrosia had been taken. Honoring our informal agreement that we wouldn't make further trouble for Ambrosia and its patrons if they didn't make further trouble for us, they hadn't been entered into evidence. That bothered me, but it was apparently the price we had to pay both to ensure the Peacemakers' leadership didn't get involved, and to have at least an uneasy peace with the rich assholes who wanted to keep their sick little Ambrosian playground intact.

The good news was that the identities on the chips were intact. Six of them were Schegith.

"Can we arrange for new bodies for them?" I asked, thinking

back to the frankly bloated form of Schegith herself, the last of her kind until now. That was an awful lot of body to manufacture.

But Steve nodded. "Already in the works. The Spindrift flesh merchants were more than happy to take on what, for them, is a pretty lucrative contract. And Schegith—the individual, not the race—was more than happy to pay for it. We've already dispatched a transport to Spindrift to pick up the bodies and bring them back here so we can reinstall their personalities."

"You make them sound like computers waiting to have their operating systems installed," I said wryly.

"Not really all that different when you think about it," Steve replied.

I wanted to accompany the newly reconstituted Schegith back to their home planet, which left us with a few days to kill on Anvil Dark. But that was okay. The *Fafnir* needed work, plus we had a bigger crew habitat module to install, so we had our work cut out for us.

IT ENDED up taking us almost a week of hard work to get the repairs and upgrades done, two days of which saw the *Fafnir* sitting in two halves in the hangar—the cockpit, avionics, and weapons module forward, and the engineering and drive module to the rear. The middle piece, the habitat module, required careful maneuvering, micrometer alignment, and an awful lot of patience.

And profanity. Lots and lots of profanity.

When we were done, though, the *Fafnir* was about eight meters longer, most of the new space given over to crew quarters and amenities, and had an expanded environmental system, including a bigger-capacity air recycler and waste reclamator. It also gave us two more hardpoints for future expansions.

When we were done, Torina inaugurated her bed by throwing herself on it. "This is amazing. I can stretch out and don't have to sleep with my heels practically jammed up against my butt."

"Now there's a picture," I said and got a greasy rag in the face for it.

We finished the same day the new bodies arrived for the Schegith. Steve started the process of restoring their consciousnesses, which had to be done aboard the freighter since each Schegith occupied a tank of nutrient fluids not much smaller than the *Fafnir* had been, pre-refit. They were now the size of juvenile members of their race, and their brains were developed enough to receive the uploaded personality.

It was pretty crazy when I thought about it, uploading and downloading a person's thoughts, memories, feelings, their very identity, like installing and uninstalling apps on a phone. That, even more than the reality of space travel, alien races, and the general existence of known space, left me shaking my head in wonder.

"Okay, they're ready to go, or as ready as they'll ever be," Steve said, surveying the six massive tanks in the freighter's cargo hold. "Their individual personalities are fully stabilized, and everything looks good. By the time you get to their home planet, they should be ready to come out of the tanks and take their first —er, slithers?"

We departed Anvil Dark not long after that, in company with the freighter. We'd escort it all the way to Null World, the Schegith home. K'losk would accompany us, for added firepower, and because he had business in that direction anyway. But once we'd safely reached Null World, he'd head off to do his own thing.

I lit the drive when we were clear of Anvil Dark's traffic control zone and fell into formation with the freighter and K'losk's ship. As I did, an impulse hit me, and I turned to Perry. "You know, I was just thinking. We've got lots of room back there now. What would you think of us bringing Hosurc'a aboard so you two can pal around during the trip?"

"Van, do you remember how you were so impressed when I ripped that guy's face off at Ambrosia? And how I made the point that I'm a combat AI?"

I grinned. "Yeah, what about it?"

"Just… think about it is all I'm saying."

SCHEGITH'S JOY at the return of her people was palpable. I don't know how much of it might have been her own psychic emanations leaking across the ether to me. They were, after all, a race with some sort of shared consciousness. In any case, her great relief and almost delirious happiness was as infectious as hell. Torina and I both stood there with stupid grins as she was reunited with her people. Only six of them, but still, six was more than one.

"Will you be able to recover? Rebuild your race?" I asked her.

"It is possible, something this one could not have even contemplated before your arrival here, Van of Earth."

"What else can we do to help?" Torina asked.

"Sing my song to people. Tell them this one is no monster. Tell them none of these ones are. And tell them that we will soon be happy to receive visitors here."

I gave a firm nod. "We will. Although, if you're planning on starting up a tourism industry—"

I waved my hand vaguely toward the outside. A terrifying storm had been raging when we landed, howling gusts driving sandblasting clouds of dust, and searing purple lightning lashing the sky. If I listened closely, I could still hear the rising and falling wail and moan of the wind, even secure inside Schegith's cozy underground lair.

She laughed, a shrill, piecing hiss, like a whistling tea kettle.

"Of course not. This planet is a brutal place on the surface. But this one would show you something, Van of Earth. Follow."

She slithered off, and Torina, Perry, and I dutifully fell in behind her, leaving the techs who'd accompanied the passenger to finish releasing the other Schegith. We traversed a series of tunnels, descending deeper into the planet's crust. We eventually came to a set of imposing doors. Schegith waved an appendage, and the doors silently rolled apart on magnetic tracks.

Torina and I stepped forward, gazing in wonder.

The doors opened onto a broad beach of black sand lit by

bright lamps mounted in the rocky vaulted ceiling overhead. Beyond the beach, a vast underground lake extended into the distance, disappearing into the gloom. Occasional flickers in the darkness marked waves that briefly caught the light and reflected it back.

"This one's people came from here. This one would share this with anyone who would visit," the Schegith said with formality.

I gaped. "It's—" I shook my head. "It's stunning. It's like it goes on forever."

"Do you swim in it?" Torina asked.

That shrill whistling laughter sounded again, and it echoed around the titanic cavern.

"Oh, no. There are things far more dangerous than this one in that water. Things that really *will* eat you."

"Ah. Well, don't take this the wrong way, but if whatever's in that water scares you, then maybe I'll just avoid the beach altogether," I said.

Schegith laughed again, then pointed an appendage off to our right. I hadn't even seen what she indicated—a beautifully painted barge rendered in somber colors, almost invisible in the gloom. "This one and their kin does not enter into the water. We do sail upon it—but that is only for the brave.'"

Perry shook his head and muttered softly. "Or the stupid."

25

"THIS PLACE IS STARTING to feel like home. A weird, dangerous home full of monsters, but still home," I said as the *Fafnir* nuzzled up to the Spindrift airlock. The usual thumps and clunks reverberated through the ship, then the HARD DOCK display lit up.

I handed the ship over to Netty, who powered it down to docked status and began doing her own thing, including arranging for the *Fafnir*'s fuel to be topped up, paying docking fees, and finding out what the scuttlebutt was among the ships currently here. It turned out that just as Perry and Netty had their own light-speed digital relationship that we mere mortals never got to see, so did many of the ships. Their AIs conversed constantly, exchanging information and, I was pretty sure, gossiping.

"Most ships are pretty dense," she once told me. "Their AIs

are enough to keep the thing flying, and that's about it. They don't make great conversationalists."

"What about the rest?"

"They're a lot like people. Some are great, some are assholes."

I tried to envision what would constitute a spaceship being an asshole, but nothing came to me. And that was fine because I dealt with enough assholes from day-to-day without adding more to the pile.

Icky had sent us a list of items and components she wanted us to obtain on Spindrift so she could take a stab at replicating the Sorcerer's wrist cuff. Even if she couldn't reproduce all of its functions, just a few, shared by Torina and me, would be really useful. She also thought she could hook Perry into the cuffs, effectively turning the three of us into a network. It should, at least in theory, improve both our effectiveness and our efficiency.

But first, we needed to get the components she wanted. We left Torina with a list at one supplier, a shady dealer in used components of all types, from parts of gun mechanisms to all sorts of miscellaneous electronic gizmos. As soon as we entered, he began doing his fast-talking sales pitch. Torina smoothly interrupted it and seized control of the conversation, smiling and waving to indicate to us that she was fine and we could head off to the other major supplier of bits and pieces on Spindrift.

This particular establishment, simply called *Circuits*, seemed a little less shady than the first. That is, until we got inside and found another smooth-talking proprietor, a Yonnox in a rumpled suit covered in pockets sprouting tools, lengths of wire and optical cable, and other sundry junk. We were barely through the door before he perked up and came sidling out from behind the counter toward us.

"Hey, nice combat AI. I could have a buyer for it within the hour, no questions asked," he said. His voice made me think of used cars.

"Sorry, he's not for sale," I said. I was wearing my duster coat, so my Peacemaker garb wasn't visible. I really didn't want everything to become about me being a Peacemaker, so I focused instead on what we'd come here to do. I turned to my data slate to consult the list, but he just shook his head.

"Oh, nonsense. Everything's for sale, for the right price. And this unit would fetch a bundle." He reached down toward Perry. "Let me just check out these wings, see if they're up to spec."

Perry's gaze bore right into the Yonnox's. "Touch me and whatever parts of your anatomy come into contact with me will be lying on that floor."

The Yonnox pulled his hand back. "Oh. Ouch. You really need to get this unit's hostility inhibitor—"

I yanked open my duster coat, revealing my Peacemaker uniform. "I said, he's not for sale. And if you don't back off, I'm going to let you learn just how much his hostility inhibitor *isn't* working. Got it? Are we clear now?"

"Ah. Well. Yes. Of course, Peacemaker. I—*OW!*"

The Yonnox flinched aside. I glanced down at Perry, who'd pecked him in the leg.

Perry looked right back up at me. "Hey, he's right! My hostility inhibitor is on the fritz!" He pecked the Yonnox again, who yelped and babbled an insistence that I stop this *unwarranted attack*.

"See?"

WE MANAGED to procure everything on our list and even got a *Peacemaker discount* from the Yonnox vendor.

"Always happy to support our hardworking people in uniform," he said, offering a grin reminiscent of an oil slick—greasy, unpleasant, and just a thin film on the surface. When I agreed to pay, he looked a little surprised.

"Oh. Oh, well then. Here you go. You have a nice day, officer."

As we were leaving, I glanced down at Perry. "I wonder what that was about."

"That? Oh, he was gouging the hell out of us for this stuff. The discount he offered brought it maybe halfway back down to market value."

"So he ripped us off."

"Little bit, yeah."

"Why didn't you say something?"

"Because we wanted to get the hell out of there."

I gave him a quizzical frown. "Did we? Why?"

"Because of those two Salt Thieves that are following us."

I didn't turn around. "Where are they?"

"About ten meters back, pretending to be interested in that optical chip vendor's stall."

I walked on another few paces, then let one of the packages I was carrying fumble out of my grasp. I cursed loudly, turned, and bent down to retrieve it while looking sidelong behind us.

Sure enough, two Salt Thieves lurked behind us, trying hard to look like they had nothing to do with us at all.

I picked up the package, and we resumed our way. "Are you sure they're following us? And they don't just happen to, you know, be there?"

"I saw them before we went into that hustler's shop back there. They waited around, then started after us when we left," Perry reported.

"Noted, and thanks for being vigilant."

"All part of my charm. And coding."

We carried on, making our way back to the *Fafnir*. We took a bit of a circuitous route to confirm that we were being tailed. And indeed we were.

I decided to just let this play out, making a quick contingency plan with Perry in case we were jumped or ambushed in any way. But the Salt Thieves seemed content to amble along behind us as we wended our way through the Spindrift rabble.

We reached the *Fafnir*'s airlock. I braced myself. If we were going to be bounced, it would happen any—

"Hey, guys!"

I almost yelped out loud, and dropped another package. But it was Torina, approaching from the opposite direction and carting her own purchases, an upbeat grin on her face that fell away in a flash.

She stopped and lowered her voice. "How long have those Salt Thieves been tailing you?"

I glanced from her to Perry. "Am I blind? How come everyone sees these guys but me?"

"Give it time, Van. You'll soon be paranoid enough that you think everyone is following you. That makes it easier to spot them when people really are," Perry said.

"Great." Despite Perry's flippancy about it, it actually bugged me. I realized I'd been treating Spindrift as little more than combination seedy shopping mall and really shitty resort. And it was both of those things, but it was also something else—dangerous. I had to start poking myself out of my complacency and become more aware of my surroundings. Situational awareness, the military called it. And as we crossed paths, and swords, with more and more parties that got screwed over as a result of it, the target on our backs became bigger and bigger.

"So what do you want to do about them?" Torina asked me.

I was chewing on Torina's question when Perry interrupted.

"Okay, they're speaking into a comm—and now they're heading off somewhere else."

"Perry, how good are you at doing some tailing of your own?"

"I thought you'd never ask. I can tell you the surface skin temperature of those two Salt Thieves to two decimal places. Did you know that that's a unique signature? Your surface skin temperature? It's slightly different in every—"

"Perry, I believe you. Go follow them, please. We discuss the nuance of skin temps another time, when we want to channel our inner nerd."

"Roger-dodger." Perry took wing and flew off, and he landed on a structural strut about ten meters away. If I hadn't been looking specifically for him, I'd have never noticed him.

Torina and I lugged our haul into the *Fafnir*. While she sorted it out, making sure we'd acquired everything on Icky's list and hadn't missed anything, I climbed into the cockpit to check in with Netty. As I did, I luxuriated in the ship's new and roomier interior. It now felt less like living in an RV, and more like living in —a bigger RV. But progress was progress.

"So, Netty, how are we looking?" I asked, settling into the pilot's seat, which immediately made itself as comfortable as possible. That still caught me sometimes, despite having spent many hours sitting in the thing already. Just the tech involved in this chair would be worth a fortune back on Earth. It made me wonder why more alien tech didn't make its way onto my home planet—

My home planet. *That* still caught me sometimes, too.

"Everything about the *Fafnir* is green, Van. Fuel's at one hundred percent," Netty replied.

I cocked my head at the display. "Everything about the *Fafnir* is green? Why do I get a feeling that implies something else isn't?"

"It's the barn."

"The barn."

"Yes. You know, the one in Iowa?"

I stared blankly. "What about it?"

"It's too small."

"Too small for what? It's a barn, Netty—"

But I stopped. She wasn't talking about its capacity for hay or manure or whatever. "You mean it's too small for the *Fafnir*?" I stifled a curse, thinking about the reality of our problem. This was an issue that needed fixing, and now.

"Well, not quite. But with the extra length added by the new crew hab module, it's now a really tight fit. There's only a meter of clearance at either end of the ship."

"So how did Gramps fit the *Fafnir* inside it?"

"Simple. He never upgraded the ship in a way that made it too long to fit into the barn. But if you have aspirations to expand the *Fafnir* into the *Dragon* variant of the Vigilant class, it's not going to fit."

"Huh. So what can we do about that?"

"Make the barn bigger?"

I looked upward, nodding my head. "While I appreciate the elegance of your proposal, I'm already a bit past that step."

"I figured as much," Netty said. "It's still deeply satisfying to see you wonder if I'm being intentionally obtuse, or just yanking your chain."

"An excellent summation of my emotional state. Thank you," I told Netty with as much gravity as I could muster.

I sifted our options. Paying for renovations to the barn wasn't going to be a problem. It was more the fact that it wasn't just a matter of making the barn bigger. The floor had to be excavated, too, to give access to the ship's underside, and that meant digging a pit that had to somehow conform to another existing pit that the contractor wouldn't even know existed.

"I have a recommendation," Netty said.

"Go on."

"We can acquire an auto-build system. It can do all the digging, put in the revetments, and expand the structure of the barn all on its own. That would give you another safe harbor for the *Fafnir*, besides Anvil Dark, where you could do maintenance and repairs.

"Okay, how do we get one of those?"

"I actually took the liberty of procuring one. It will be waiting for us at Anvil Dark when we get there."

"Um. Well then," I said, slowly.

"Problem?"

"No, I just—I sometimes wonder if you guys really need me at all."

"Of course we do, Van," Netty enthused.

"You sure about that?"

"Absolutely. After all, who would take the blame when things went wrong?"

———

PERRY RETURNED ABOUT AN HOUR LATER.

"Did you track down the Salt Thieves' ship?" I asked him.

"Uh-huh."

"And?"

"And, it's a class nine or ten armed cutter, at docking port 51-21A, and it's preparing to get underway."

"Probably to intercept us," Torina added.

Perry bobbed his head. *"Probably."*

I turned to face him where he was perched in his usual spot

between the pilots' seats. "Why do I get the feeling you're not telling us something, Perry?"

"I did a bad thing, Van."

I glanced at Torina. Her concern seemed to be growing in concert with mine.

"What did you do, Perry?" she asked.

"Well, you see, I struck up a friendship some time ago with one of the maintenance AIs here. He's a nice enough construct, though not in the same league as, say, an AI bird—"

"Perry, the point?"

"Anyway, I've done him some favors, and he owed me. So I called in that little debt."

"And this resulted in the bad thing you did?"

"Uh-huh."

I looked at Torina. "Is it just me, or is he drawing this out deliberately for dramatic effect?"

"Dramatic effect, definitely."

I turned back to Perry. "Would you please get to the point? What bad thing did you do?"

"Well, I may have had my maintenance AI friend attach a scrambler to the Salt Thieves' scanner-receiver array before they powered it up prior to flight."

Netty chuckled. I scowled.

"Perry." I rubbed at my temples, slowly. "I would love, right now, to get a straight answer, especially if you've touched off some kind of… incident."

Perry managed an artificial huff that rivaled any teenager for drama. "Okay, fine. I just want points for how sneaky and clever I was. I've got the activation code for the scrambler. When triggered, it will feed back through the scanner-receiver system just the way scanner returns would—except these returns are basically a virus that will propagate through all their systems and shut 'em down," Perry said.

"Oh. Holy shit. Really?"

"See? Now you're impressed."

"So what's the bad part of this?"

"Oh, it's *highly* illegal, and for good reason. The hardware is prohibited, and using it without a legitimate warrant, outside of certain military applications, is considered a serious crime."

"So you just broke the law? I didn't think you could do that— as in, literally couldn't do that because of your programming."

"It's called exigent circumstances. When we determined that those Salt Thieves were tailing us while we were involved in business directly related to an ongoing investigation, it constituted interference. And interference in an investigation triggers exigent circumstances."

Torina looked doubtful. "Will that hold up?"

"Would you rather fight them? They don't out-mass us by much, but they outgun us by at least fifty percent."

I looked at Torina and shrugged. "You know what they say. I'd rather be judged by twelve than carried by six."

I TAPPED the forward-port thruster control and neatly spun the *Fafnir* about as she backed away from Spindrift. When we were aligned in such a way that we could move away from the station without washing it with our exhaust plume, I triggered the stern thrusters, starting us on our departure course.

"You're getting pretty good at that, Van," Netty said.

"Thank you. I have good teachers. Now, where have our Salt Thieves friends gone?"

Netty activated the tactical overlay and painted one icon in a red highlight. The Salt Thieves had been given clearance to depart on a course roughly parallel to ours but had adopted a low delta-V departure, probably because they wanted to be able to maneuver to intercept us once we were clear of Spindrift's traffic-control zone. It had never occurred to me, in watching sci-fi TV shows and movies, that traffic control would be such a critical thing. Which made sense, I guess, since it didn't exactly make for the most exciting stuff of fiction. But without rigid traffic control, the space around Spindrift, Crossroads, or even Anvil Dark would be chaos. Even the bad guys obligingly did what they were told when it came to approaching and departing space stations.

We received the clear to maneuver signal, which meant we were far enough from Spindrift, and oriented properly, to light the main drive. That was another of those little *oh, yeah* things. Every non-twist drive produced an exhaust whose particles would essentially travel forever in an opposite direction to a ship's flight. It wasn't much mass, but it was ejected at a high enough velocity to propel a ship forward and could damage a station if constantly bombarded with exhaust detritus. It was also a way to get into serious trouble if ignored by a departing ship. Spindrift actually warned ships that a sustained burst of exhaust hitting the station would be considered an attack and respond accordingly.

All of which was to say that our escape and the Salt Thieves' pursuit was a very tidy, orderly affair for the first half-hour or so. As soon as we were clear of the traffic control zone, though, the game was afoot. The Salt Thieves immediately burned hard, closing the range on us fast.

"They'll be in effective range of our weapons in a little over eight minutes," Netty said.

"And how about us, with respect to their weapons?" Torina asked.

Perry leaned into the conversation. "I saw a big-assed laser array on that ship, with beam collimators about a hundred klicks long. We'll be in range of their weapons a lot sooner."

I glanced at Perry. "A hundred klicks long? Perry, I've told you a bajillion times, don't exaggerate things."

"Let me get some ointment to put on that burn. In the meantime, would you like to try to disable these gentlebeings, or did you want to fight it out with them?"

"Whenever you're ready, my friend."

"Netty, I've uploaded the scrambler's activation code. At your leisure, you may proceed."

A moment passed. Nothing seemed to happen.

"Uh, Perry—"

"Patience, Van. Good things come to those who wait."

As soon as he said it, the Salt Thieves' transponder went dark. A moment later, their power emanations faded as one system after another dropped offline. In less than thirty seconds, their ship was completely dark.

"Well, that was easy," I said.

Torina grinned. "Leave it to the bird to find a cheap way to win a space battle."

"I prefer the term *thrifty*, actually."

OF COURSE, just because the Salt Thieves' ship was dead in space didn't mean we now had them in the bag, as it were. We faced the prospect of boarding their ship, and none of their personal weapons would have been affected by the scrambler. Netty, though, had a simpler solution.

"Why don't we just tow them back to Anvil Dark?"

"Can we do that?"

"Well, the added mass is going to cause us to burn a lot of extra fuel, so we'll be running on fumes when we get there. Other than that, though, sure, why not?"

I turned to Perry. "How long is your scrambler going to last?"

"Until it's power cells run dry, so three days, give or take."

I swung back to Netty. "Can we work with that?"

"Easily. I make it a two-day trip, at the most."

"Well, then, let's—"

"Uh, Van? Are those Salt Thieves going to survive the trip? Or are we going to end up bringing some asphyxiated dead guys back to Anvil Dark with us?" Torina asked.

"Ah. Yes. Good point. Netty?"

"Assuming they aren't packed to the overheads with Salt Thieves over there, and the standard maximum crew complement for that class of ship of no more than ten, then they'll have breathable air for at least four days. It might get a little chilly, but nothing they can't handle."

"So it will be a survivable but uncomfortable trip."

"That's right."

"Sounds perfect. Let's do it."

While Netty configured the *Fafnir* for towing, I turned to Perry. Something sinister had just occurred to me.

"Make a note of this, Perry. We are to check *our* scanner-receiver array for scramblers every time we're about to leave somewhere."

"Already part of the drill, Van. Has been for years."

I sat back and nodded. "Good to know."

WE MANAGED to drag the Salt Thieves back to Anvil Dark without incident. It turned out there was a whole procedure in place for this, a disabled ship towed back for arrest of the crew and seizure of things like cargo. We cast off while a remotely operated shuttle was dispatched from Anvil Dark to take the crew off and into custody.

"They call that shuttle The Box, because that's really all it is. There aren't any internal controls, just benches and lots of video surveillance," Perry said.

"So what if the Salt Thieves refuse to board it?" Torina

asked.

"Well, then, they get to stay aboard their dark, silent, and increasingly chilly ship until their air runs out. It's a win-win for us, either way."

The Salt Thieves didn't refuse to board The Box, though. The whole crew complement—a total of twelve—willingly piled aboard. I glanced at Torina when I saw a feed of the Salt Thieves stumbling, one at a time, out of the airlock and into The Box.

"Kinda glad we didn't decide to board. Twelve bad guys might have been a bit of a stretch for us to handle," I said.

Perry flexed his wings, but shrugged. "You're probably right. They're seasoned fighters, too."

When the Salt Thieves' ship was empty of its crew, a clearance team from Anvil Dark boarded and did a sweep from bow to stern. They made sure no one had decided to try and stay behind, or that there weren't any other nasty surprises waiting to be sprung, like scuttling charges. When they gave the green light, we boarded, exercising our salvage rights for first refusal of anything we might find potentially useful.

Perry busied himself hacking into the ship's computers to see if anything remained that hadn't been wiped by the crew. Torina and I puttered our way through the rest of the ship but didn't find anything we specifically wanted to claim. I did eye their big-assed laser array, as Perry had called it, but it was too big and unwieldy to mount on the *Fafnir*. We finally exchanged shrugs and decided to hand the ship over to the Guild for liquidation, taking our cut in cash.

As we headed back to the *Fafnir* in the dingy ship of the Salt

Thieves—who, as it turned out, definitely were not big on the whole cleanliness thing—I grinned at Torina.

"Arrr, matey, I be startin' to feel more and more like we be pirates, takin' all the booty."

"Van, are you okay?"

"Uh, yeah. Why?"

"Your voice. It got all strange there."

"I was… talking like a pirate? You know, peg legs and parrots and grog and—no? Nothing?" I sighed. This, it seemed, was a *cultural schism*.

Torina narrowed her eyes and shook her head. "Earthlings."

We met Perry at the airlock. "The Salt Thieves managed to wipe a lot of their data core, but I was able to retrieve a bit. You might be intrigued to learn that the Peacemakers have reduced their numbers by almost two thirds. Seems you made going after Salt Thieves the new big thing among the Peacemakers."

"Look at me, being a trendsetter."

"It means that we probably won't be encountering them much anymore."

"Good. The fewer bad guys we have to deal with, the better." I stepped into the airlock, then stopped and turned back. "Perry, put the word out through the various contacts and sources I know you have in the AI world. As far as I'm concerned, the Salt Thieves are nothing more than money, waiting to be collected." I closed one eye.

"Arrr, matey, that be the pirate way."

Perry stared at me. "Van, are you having a stroke?"

"Come on, Perry, you've spent tons of time on Earth. You

know, pirates? Buccaneers? Buckling their swashes in poofy shirts and tight pants? *International Talk Like A Pirate Day?*"

After a moment, he relented with his version of a knowing grin. "Aye, ye scurvy dog."

"That's the spirit!"

Then Perry held up a wing, his demeanor gone serious. "However, if you say anything about a poop deck, I'm quitting."

I reached out to tap his extended wing in solidarity. "No poop jokes. After all, we have standards."

26

AND HERE WE WERE, in that very same barn again.

We were. The *Fafnir* wasn't. She sat outside, which might have raised some questions since a freakin' spaceship would be easy to see from the road that ran along the front of the property. But Netty kept her stealth system activated, effectively rendering her invisible.

Which led to a question I hadn't even considered.

"Why don't we use that system all of the time? You know, just keep the *Fafnir* stealthed up?"

We'd unleashed the rented auto-builder inside the barn, with instructions to dig out a bigger pit to accommodate the *Fafnir* as she grew in size and tonnage. We stood in the barn, watching it chew into the earth with relentless efficiency.

Perry turned from where he was perched on the edge of a hay bin. "Running the stealth system burns fuel. Not much but enough that, over time, it adds up. And it's pointless anyway. You might recall that on that night we took you for your very first flight up into orbit, I mentioned that systems not based on the same principles as it couldn't see through it."

"And all the ships and stations and things we encounter in known space can."

"Bingo. It would be like putting on camouflage, then going and standing in the middle of a perfectly flat field. Technically, you're stealthed up, but everyone can see right through it."

"Gotcha."

The door at the back of the barn rattled, then swung open. Torina entered, followed by Icky.

We'd brought Icky along with us so she could trial and tweak the cuff she'd built, based on the one we'd taken from the dead Sorcerer on Ambrosia. It wasn't working properly, and was essentially a heavy bracelet with no purpose. But Icky kept at it, and we were starting to see results. Her latest trial run resulted in the thing generating a personal defense field, essentially a localized force field that would diminish the effects of both projectile and energy weapons. The trouble was that after about thirty seconds of activation, it overloaded the cuff and forced it to shut down into safe mode.

With these demonstrations of her abilities, I was starting to lean more and more in the direction of making Icky a permanent member of the crew. We'd already made her an auxiliary, but it would be damned handy to have a skilled engineer on board. And Icky was a master of cobbling things together out of the most unlikely components, which made her even more valuable. I just wanted to make sure she'd be a good fit for our happy little gang before committing fully. And so far, so good.

It also meant, of course, that we'd brought her to Earth with us. And while we might be able to stealth up the *Fafnir* enough to defeat prying eyes, we couldn't do the same with a four-armed, vaguely simian humanoid covered in coarse fur. Accordingly, she stayed aboard the ship, only disembarking at night, and then only in the immediate vicinity of the barn. I did bring her into the house at one point, though—and it almost proved disastrous.

I WAS SHOWING Icky around the kitchen—and, believe me, you haven't lived until you've seen a four-armed alien tinkering with your toaster—when I heard the front door rattle. I assumed it was Torina, although why she was coming in the front door of the house I wasn't sure. The back door faced the barn, after all. So I stepped a couple of paces so I could see down the hallway to the front door and froze.

It was Miryam.

My voice immediately shot up the decibel scale, as well as an octave or two. "Miryam. Um. Hiiiiiii, how are you?" I charged down the hallway and reached out as though I was about to grab her. She actually flinched at my unusually overt greeting, but I took her by the arm and nudged her into the living room.

She carried a brown paper bag clearly stuffed with groceries, which crinkled as she moved. "Uh… hello, Van. I wasn't sure if you'd be here or not."

"Well, I am. Right here. In the living room with you!" I could hear the false triumph in my voice. I was no actor, and Miryam was brilliant.

With a nose for bullshit, I might add.

"Okay." She gave me a look somewhere between suspicious and concerned. "Anyway, I thought I'd get a few staples for you—you know, coffee, sugar, that sort of thing. I noticed you were low, and you're away on business all the time—Van, are you okay?"

"Why of course I'm okay, Miryam? Why do you ask?"

"Why are you talking so loudly?"

"Ah. Well. It's... my ears. They're still stuffed up from the plane. They haven't popped yet." I gave her a watery grin. "Anyway, I'll take those because I'm sure you must be busy—"

I practically yanked the bag out of her hand. Her suspicious frown deepened.

"Actually, I left some mail here the other day in the kitchen. I think there was a tax assessment in it. I want to make sure that gets paid—"

"Mail? In the kitchen? Of course it's there. I'll just, um. Get it. Or you can, of course."

Eyeing me sidelong, she walked out of the living room and headed for the kitchen. "Yes, I left it there because—" She stopped and shook her head. "Anyway, I'll just go find it."

As she did, I saw Icky come creeping out of the dining room, into the living room. I hurried after Miryam.

"You've got it. The mail. Good. Anything critical?" I asked, trying for my most innocuous tone. I'm not sure I was succeeding.

I put the grocery bag down, and Miryam dug into it. "Oh, I

forgot to tell you. I accidentally knocked the sugar bowl off the dining room table last time I was here. Clumsy me. Anyway, I bought you a new one." She extracted the box and headed for the dining room, opening it along the way.

By now, sweat was pouring out of parts of my body that I don't think had ever sweated before. I chased after her in small steps, trying not to thunder across the floor like a charging rhino. "No worry. Accidents happen—"

Miryam placed the new bowl down with a clunk. Then she froze, her eyes going wide as she looked into the living room.

Oh, shit.

"Van, what happened to that fern? Have you watered it at *all?*"

I saw Icky peek around the wall dividing the dining room from the kitchen. Miryam headed into the living room.

"Fern?" Even though I was looking at the plant, I managed to sound as innocent as—huh. I realized, in a flash, I sounded like a teenager caught in any number of quasi-criminal acts. With an effort, I stilled myself, pasting a warm smile across my face that fooled Miryam for exactly zero seconds.

Miryam looked me up and down, crossed her arms, and frowned. "Alright, Van, what's up?"

"What's up?" I repeated, because that was always an excellent tactic to buy time.

Something thumped in the kitchen. Miryam's gaze shot that way. "Is there someone else here?"

"Why do you ask?"

She stopped in the hallway.

I came up behind her, ready to—I don't know. Catch her if she fainted or something. But it wasn't Icky standing in the kitchen. It was Torina.

Miryam turned to me, a smile playing on her lips. "You didn't mention you had company, Van."

"Um. Right. About that—"

Torina strode forward, a grin on her face, her hand extended.

Miryam took Torina's offered hand and gave a sly smile. She turned to me. "Van, why didn't you just say something? I'm a big girl."

"Uh… well… "

"I'm Torina Milon," Torina said, but Miryam just frowned.

"What language is that?"

I glanced at Torina. Right. I was so used to the translator bug in my ear that I'd forgotten that whatever Torina spoke, it wasn't English. So I hastily improvised.

"This is Torina. She's Italian, of course. Born and raised in Italy."

Miryam shot me a bemused glance. "I've heard that a lot of Italian people come from Italy, yeah."

I braced myself for my lie to backfire on me. I had no idea if Miryam actually spoke Italian, but if she did—

But she just smiled at Torina.

"So she came back all the way here to Iowa with you? Hmm. Sounds serious."

Torina pushed past her, took my arm, and laid her head on my shoulder.

I just shrugged. "What can I say? True love can travel

between the stars themselves." Torina looked at me adoringly, batting her eyes. I had to fight to not—I'm not even sure what. Keel over from having spent the past few minutes teetering on the verge of hyperventilating, probably.

"Well, I know when I'm not wanted. Torina, it was very nice to meet you. And Van?"

I stared, wide-eyed. *Now* what?

"She came a long way to be with you. She's a keeper. Oh—and you don't have to hide her from me. You're not a pimply faced teenager anymore. This is your house, remember?"

"I—yes. Of course. My house. Right."

Miryam left, closing the front door behind her. As soon as she was gone, Torina burst into laughter.

Icky, who'd taken cover in the basement stairway, joined us. She was laughing, too.

But it didn't stop there. Perry appeared, flying from the kitchen to the dining room. "Look at me! I'm Van Tudor, and now I'm in the dining room! Oh, and now I'm heading for the living room, where I kill ferns for fun! Next stop, the kitchen!"

I sank into a kitchen chair, spent and scowling.

"This was… a bit much. Need a moment," I grumbled.

Torina came up behind me and put her arms around me.

"I'm sorry, dear. Can you repeat that in Italian?"

As IF IT weren't enough to have one Wu'tzur on the farm, now we had two. Urnak arrived in his battleship, which he parked in a high orbit over Earth, before shuttling down.

So we had *two* spaceships grounded at the farm, and *two* four-armed aliens hanging around, being large and hairy and—if I'm honest—loud.

And curious. When they saw a fox squirrel, it was a major event for them, only ending when the critter vanished up a vine with an indignant flip of its tail.

"Charming species," Urnak said.

"You've never seen one pack an engine block with walnuts."

"I don't understand any of that sentence, and I don't care. They're adorable," Icky announced.

Frustrated by so many visitors, I began with one question.

"*Why* is he here?" I asked Icky.

"Because I needed some more components for the cuff."

"So you asked your father to bring his alien battleship to Earth, park it in orbit, then come on down to the farm?"

"Is that a problem?"

I threw my head back and stared up at the dingy rafters of the barn. "Am I being punished here? Is this punishment for my sins?"

"Maybe, can you be more specific?"

I rolled my eyes at the smugness of Perry's voice. "Bird. What are you doing up there?"

I saw two amber points of light staring back down at me. "Switching to base mode, so I can run some self-diagnostics in peace. Call it my version of preening my feathers."

Urnak raised a hand. "I realize that this may be a little awkward—"

"Not at all. Invite as many aliens as you'd like. It's a big farm," I said, waving expansively at the room.

Torina leaned close to me. "Do you really think that's a good idea?"

"Okay, that's a well-placed barb, but I need a moment. I've just had a near death experience."

Urnak ignored us both, moving to the center of the room. "Amid all of this—whatever this is—there's something you might be interested to know, Van. As I was passing the orbit of this planet's natural satellite, I intercepted a signal emanating from, um—" He consulted a data slate. "Sas-saska—"

"Saskatchewan? It's Canada's version of Iowa."

"I believe you. Anyway, I think it was an automated surveillance unit. It pinged the Nemesis, which meant it could see through our stealth measures."

I frowned. "So alien tech. Or, well, alien to Earth, anyway."

"So it would appear. Anyway, I had my AI evaluate it, and it turns out it was also sending out a directional beacon," Urnak said.

"Meaning what?"

"Meaning that I assumed it probably wasn't a handy navigational aid intended for my benefit, and probably meant to guide someone—or something—in."

"Who?"

"Probably whoever it is that's inbound. Two ships, on converging courses, both probably just past that lovely ringed planet you have in your system. Incidentally, you really should promote that. You might get some tourism going—"

"Let's leave the economic development of the Solar System for another time. We've got two ships inbound?"

"We do."

"Shit. Perry—"

"Already on it," he said, descending from the rafter with a metallic whisper of wings. "I've alerted Netty. She's doing the preflight."

"Okay, then." I looked at the digger, which was busily using a plasma arc to fuse and anneal the soil on the edge of the pit it was digging to permanently shore it up. It could work just fine on its own, but I was still keenly aware of Miryam's impromptu visit. If she dropped by, happened to come looking for me in the barn, and saw it, there would be questions, and *it's from Italy* probably wouldn't cut it.

The solution, though, was simple. We just deactivated it. The barn incorporated a stealth system of its own, because even with the *Fafnir* absent, there were still pits and tools and things that we didn't want anyone to find. Then we boarded the *Fafnir* and lifted, Urnak taking his shuttle back to his own ship, the *Nemesis*.

We had Urnak's battlewagon as backup, but it was going to take him time to get underway. I aimed the *Fafnir* away from the sun and accelerated. If there was going to be a battle, I wanted it to happen as far from Earth as possible.

Because while all the ships involved might be stealthed and invisible to Earthly observers, things like explosions and debris—

Not so much.

"IT LOOKS like they're both going to slingshot around Jupiter," Netty said.

I grunted my assent, watching the tactical overlay. The two ships were falling toward Jupiter fast, picking up velocity.

"Okay, I get that, but why?" I asked.

"Probably because they want the extra speed to come at the Earth *really* fast. Not sure what they have planned then, but it looks—hello," Perry said.

"Something you'd like to share?"

"Yeah. There is all sorts of comm traffic slipping back and forth between those two ships. If I had to guess just from voice characteristics, I'd say the nearer of the two ships is carrying at least one Nesit, while the other one—" He cocked his head. "Hard to tell. It has kind of a mechanical quality to it, but not the dulcet, soothing tones of my voice or Netty's."

Torina gave me a narrow-eyed look. "Sorcerers?"

"Maybe. Uh, Perry, if you can tell how their voices sound, does that mean you can hear their comms?"

"Oh, sure. They're both transmitting in the clear, not even trying to keep it coded. And your next question is going to be, *well, Perry, what are they saying?* And my answer is, they're not *saying*, as much as they're *shouting*."

"Okay, *and?* What are they shouting?"

"Holy shi—Van, give a bird a chance to draw a breath."

"You don't breathe, Perry."

"True. Just a moment, I'm getting—" An instant later, a

heated conversation began spilling into the *Fafnir's* cockpit. I winced at what sounded mostly like profanities, then turned down the volume and looked at Torina.

"Trouble in paradise, it seems."

"It does. Now, wouldn't it be nice if they actually started shooting at one another? Those ships are both class ten, which means that, until Urnak gets here—"

She was cut off by a warning chime, indicating weapons fire. Sure enough, the two intruders had opened fire on each other.

"Well, that answers that—ask, and ye shall receive. Okay, weapons hot, let's go break up this little quarrel, shall we?"

I angled the *Fafnir* onto the course calculated by Netty for intercept. It seemed to be taking us directly toward the vast, gleaming crescent of Jupiter itself. We were close enough to the big planet that we could make out the famous banding of pastel colors swirling across it. Having seen a few gas giants now, I had to admit that Jupiter was one of the prettier ones. But we weren't here to sightsee, so I yanked my attention back to the controls, and to the overlay, eyeing the weapons-range indicator. We had a few minutes yet.

No sooner had I thought that, though, than one of the ships, the one we assumed had Sorcerers aboard, abruptly exploded.

"Holy shit. That escalated quickly," I said.

"Indeed it did. The ship we're presuming to be Nesit took substantial damage in the exchange. They've begun braking, probably intending to slingshot around Jupiter and back out of the Solar System instead of carrying on toward Earth," Netty said.

"They've decided to fight another day," Perry put in.

"Yeah, well, I want answers, and they're aboard that ship."

I ramped up the drive, aiming the *Fafnir* toward an intercept, our weapons ready for a fight.

WE MADE the intercept a lot closer to the huge planet than I liked, not far from Amalthea, Jupiter's third moon. By the time we had the Nesit ship—or, at least, the ship carrying what we assumed to be at least one Nesit, since it was a standard light courier hull—the planet filled most of our field of view. Netty kept updating the *Fafnir's* trajectory, drawing a digital line in the sand that we couldn't cross except at a very specific angle and velocity. Not doing so puts us in danger of a fall into the enormous gas giant. With a gravity field of that size, no amount of thrust would be able to break us free.

Or, as Netty put it—

"When you're this close to Jupiter, he calls the gravitational shots."

I had to admit that it was hard not to rubberneck. I mean, this was freakin' Jupiter, up close. Much more up close than it had been for any other human in history—

I caught myself. Well, except probably for Gramps. And, actually, who knew how many other humans were shuttling between Earth and somewhere else in known space? It might still only be a privileged few, but it was a pretty select group.

I forced myself to concentrate on the Nesit ship. It actually opened fire first, loosing a pair of missiles at us. We replied with the laser, Torina sniping away at their ship at long range. Jupiter's gravity precluded any major course corrections by either of us, so Torina had a good fix on where the target would be, and when it would be there, so she immediately landed hits. Laser strikes flashed against the Nesits' hull, spalling off glowing debris.

I focused on the incoming missiles as Jupiter yawned across our viewscreens, a level of grandeur that defied the senses. Just as our opponent was limited in their maneuvers, so were we. And the missiles were capable of much more delta-V than we were, albeit for a far, far shorter time. But it didn't matter. We weren't going to outmaneuver the onrushing ordnance, so we had to shoot it down.

Torina switched fire to the missiles as they approached, but despite her efforts, she never managed a hit. The point-defense battery came to life, spewing out tracers, but the missile sailed contemptuously through the storm of projectiles.

The damned thing was going to hit. Hard.

Bullshit. I spun the *Fafnir* hard, redlining the drive to give us as hard a course change as we could manage. I was hoping to at least maximize the distance between us and the warhead when it detonated. At the last second, Netty also rolled us, presenting our strongest armor to the blast.

A searing white flash enveloped the *Fafnir*. Static crashed across the comm channels. A dozen systems were knocked offline by the EMP, and started rebooting. A few seconds later, the *Fafnir* shuddered deep in her structural bones under several impacts, one of which punched through our new crew hab somewhere and provoked a decompression alarm. Torina and I were already suited up, so we grabbed our helmets and snapped them in place, just as a brief gale rushed through the cockpit. Everything vanished into a swirl of white fog and my teeth rattled from yet another punishing impact. This was combat, not a single pass.

This was to the death.

The air kept howling and then—

It stopped, the hurricane of escaping air ending as the condensed water vapor started to clear. Torina, incredibly, had resumed her methodic firing, slamming hit after hit into the opposing ship.

In the move of spacers everywhere, I popped my ears, blinked, and got ready to fight once again.

"Everyone okay?"

Torina nodded without looking up from her targeting system. "Fine."

"Ruffled my feathers, that's all," Perry said.

"I have a hole in me," Netty replied.

"How bad is it?"

"Depends how attached you were to the new lavatory."

"Well, shit."

"Not until we get back to Earth, Van, sorry. Number onesies only."

An incoming comm message cut off my reply. It was Icky, who'd boarded the *Nemesis*, now only minutes behind us, with her father.

"Van! That looked damned close. Are you guys okay?"

"Except for certain bodily functions, yeah, we're fine."

"I—okay. I'm sure that means something, but I won't bother you in the middle of a firefight. *Nemesis* out."

By the time I switched my focus back to the battle, it was over.

"Looks like they're bailing," Netty said, zooming in on the Nesit ship, now crippled by Torina's relentless shooting. Sure enough, a small escape boat had separated from the ship. Incredibly, two suited figures came tumbling out after it.

"What the hell are they doing?"

"I suspect the escape boat undocked prematurely and those guys are hoping they can catch it before it gets too far away," Netty replied.

We could only watch in fascinated horror as the two tiny figures struggled mightily to reach the escape boat. They didn't make it, but drifted in a languorous way that was far more elegant than what we were really seeing—the death dance of two sentient beings, unless by some miracle, they were rescued. Both forms continued moving across the starfield, spinning ever further from their stricken ship.

"I hate seeing that, even if they're—this is tough to watch. Netty, can we rescue these guys?" I asked.

"Sorry, Van, no can do. We just can't match velocity with them, even braking as hard as the *Fafnir*'s design limits allow. We'd have to do a complete orbit of Jupiter, doing some aerobraking in its atmosphere to shed velocity."

"How long would that take?"

"A couple of hours, at least."

"And how long have they got?"

"Before they slam into Amalthea, a couple of hours, at most."

I looked at Torina. "I want to save them, but—dammit. I want to."

Torina nodded. "That's the thing about space, Van. Sometimes the math just doesn't work out."

———

WE DID AN AEROBRAKING sweep around Jupiter anyway, partly on the off chance that we could intercept the two suited figures before they smacked into Amalthea, but also because their ship was going to miss the moon and fall into a spiraling orbit about Jupiter that would eventually send it plunging into the pastel cloud tops. The aerobraking pass was both terrifying and exhilarating, the *Fafnir* racing over a vast plane, trailing fire as she swept toward the rising sun. We were so close to the enormous planet that the horizon had no curvature to it.

"This is—I mean, *every* sense in my body is singing," I said, raising my voice a little over the thunder of atmosphere rushing past us and turning to flame. "People would pay good money to do this!"

"Ticket prices might be a bit steep," Perry said.

Netty raised our orbit again, and our incandescent passage ended. Amalthea rose over Jupiter directly ahead of us. We got back into decent viewing range of the moon just in time to see those two poor bastards free fall straight into the lumpy reddish moon's irregular surface.

I winced. "Ouch."

"I think you mean splat," Torina offered. Despite her flippant words, her tone was somber. Understandably—that was one hell of a way to die.

But Perry was decidedly less moved by the moment. "Let's hurry up and grab that ship. There's intel to be secured, and money to be made!"

"You're kinda heartless, you know that, Perry?" I said.

"Well, yeah. I don't have blood. What would be the point?"

I kept quiet at that. Space, like humor, could sometimes be pitch black.

27

I HANDED the data slate to Urnak, who read it and then showed it to Icky.

"That kind of removes any doubt. These guys are tied straight back to Axicur," I said.

We'd docked with and boarded the *Nemesis* in a high orbit around Jupiter. The battered remains of the Nesit ship hung in a slightly lower orbit, to which we'd towed it. It wasn't stable, and would eventually decay, though, sending the ship plunging right back into the big planet. As Netty had said, Jupiter called the shots out here. It didn't even have functioning engines, so we couldn't program it to conduct period burns to stabilize itself. But it should be stable enough to last until a salvage team arrived.

The more important part, though, was what we were able to glean from its data core. A lot of the information had been scrambled by battle damage, and the crew had tried a hasty wipe before abandoning ship. But Perry was able to retrieve enough to get the solid evidence we needed.

"It should be enough to get a warrant out on her, with a kill rider attached," Perry said.

Urnak shot him a glance. "A kill rider?"

"Yeah. She conspired to attempt to murder a Peacemaker in a deliberate, calculated act. As the Earthly entertainment genre of Westerns put it, *we can take 'er dead or alive.*"

"You know about pirates *and* westerns?"

"I'm a complicated bird, Van."

I turned back to Urnak and Icky. "We don't have to get the kill rider. We can focus, instead, on taking her alive—"

"Nah," Urnak snapped.

Icky shook her head. "You don't need to spare her for us, Van. As far as my father and I are concerned, she died a long time ago."

"If you try to take her alive, more people might get hurt. I mean, she tossed a guy off her apartment balcony just because he brought her bad news, right?" Urnak said.

"Yeah, pretty much."

"Then you do whatever you have to, to make sure she doesn't hurt anyone else."

"Were you able to get anything more on the people she's enslaved on those damned chips of hers?" Icky asked.

I nodded. "We have a list. We'd probably spend years running everyone on it down. So, we'll save who we can and, in the meantime, we'll circulate the list among all the Peacemakers so they can rescue others when they have the chance."

I left out the last bit, the identity of at least one compromised senior Peacemaker. Icky and Urnak didn't need to know about the Guild's dirty laundry.

BUT THE NAME we'd retrieved from the Nesit comm log wasn't Groshenko—thankfully—or any of the others we'd suspected. It didn't let them entirely off the hook, and we knew there was still some corruption gnawing at the Masters. But this Peacemaker was a Senior Myrmidon named Avortun. He held an office similar to Lunzy's, representing the Masters and acting on their direct behalf.

Our next stop, therefore, was Anvil Dark. We didn't call ahead. Instead, I wanted to catch Avortun flat footed with our evidence so he didn't have time to run, or even worse, mount a defense against our accusations. Avortun was slippery and amoral, a combination that meant every option was on the table when it came to discrediting our findings. We arrived at the Gamma Crucis system to find a battlecruiser parked near the station. It was sleek, midnight-black, and bristling with weaponry —six big laser batteries, another four batteries of particle beam projectors, four missile turrets, and a half-dozen point-defense installations. Aside from its registration number, the only marking was the Peacemaker logo in grey.

It looked absolutely terrifying, which I gathered was the point.

"The *Righteous Fury's* in town," Netty said as we approached the station.

"That is one big ship. It's almost as big as Urnak's *Nemesis*," Torina said, shaking her head in wonder.

"Yeah, that's not a law enforcement ship," I added.

But Perry just shrugged his wings. "Depends on the law you're enforcing. And who you're enforcing it against. The *Righteous Fury* gives the Peacemakers a big stick to wave around, her being one of the most advanced, uh, not-warships in known space."

I lifted an eyebrow. "*Not*-warship?"

"Well, the Peacemakers aren't a military organization, so we can't have warships, now, can we?"

"So it's a big police boat."

"Sure, let's go with that."

We contacted Lunzy on a secure channel and explained the situation. She, in turn, told us that Avortun was aboard the *Righteous Fury*, helping to prepare the ship for a major, ultra-classified operation. It took some time, but we were able to get clearance to dock with the big battlecruiser, thanks to some string-pulling by Lunzy. Ostensibly, we were bringing crucial evidence directly to Groshenko, who was also aboard the massive ship.

As we made our way along the corridors, passing crewmembers in sleek, dark uniforms, I had to shake my head a bit. For a non-military ship, the Righteous Fury sure felt an awful lot like a military one. When I was—fifteen, I think, I visited my father in San Diego. He took me aboard his ship, the aircraft carrier *Abraham Lincoln*, CVN-72, which was at dock and readying herself for a trip to Pearl Harbor, and then on to service in the western

Pacific. I wouldn't see my father for another six months, which was about usual for his job.

The purposeful bustle, the feel, the *flavor* of this ship was very much like that of the *Abraham Lincoln* as she prepared to get underway. There was obviously still a lot about the Peacemakers Guild I didn't know, such as just what sort of *ultra classified operation* required something with this much firepower.

But I didn't have time to worry about that. We snaked our way through the ship, guided by a Senior Rating, to Groshenko in the Combat Command Center, or triple-C, or just C3 for short. Again, that word *combat* wasn't one I associated with law enforcement.

We entered the sprawling room, a riot of screens and terminals and wide displays. Some of them were dark and locked down, bearing only the simple message SECURITY LOCK IN EFFECT, followed by a bland code of letters and numbers. Groshenko stood, arms crossed, watching and listening as an older woman in a black uniform briefed him about something displayed behind them. It looked like trajectories, but she blanked the screen with a wave as we approached.

Groshenko turned, saw Torina, Perry, and me, and grinned. But my eyes went to a slender, bland-looking alien nearby, with grey skin and big eyes. It was the sort of alien popularized in Earthly UFO circles, and I fought a laugh.

The truth really *is* out here.

Then my smile died, because I recognized him from the image Perry had called up. It was Avortun.

And he was wearing a Sorcerer's cuff, only partly concealed by his tunic.

My gaze met his. It was like looking into black, reflective glass. But it didn't matter. I caught that spark of knowing anyway, that instant when not only did Avortun realize that I recognized him, but that I was here specifically *because* of him.

For a snapshot moment, we stood that way, then I grabbed for the Moonsword at my hip. I hadn't been able to bring The Drop aboard because of weapons regs, so it left me with only the blade. Avortun, however, had a sidearm. But he didn't go for it. Instead, he reached for his cuff. As he did, he shouted and pointed at me, focusing attention away from himself.

"That's him! He's the one!"

What happened next was the first combat act in which my body took over, bypassing any thoughts or reason. In one motion, I drew the Moonsword and hurled it at Avortun, the silvered blade flickering forward before anyone else could move. It was a delaying tactic, aimed at interrupting his use of the cuff, but the Moonsword flew true, spinning through the air as a shimmering blur.

Then the blade slammed into Avortun's chest, slicing through his suit to bury itself in the alien's slight chest. Half the blade was in Avortun. The other half danced back and forth as his body began to convulse from the catastrophic wound.

He toppled back, but not before managing to punch a control on his cuff. Then the C3 erupted in chaos, an alarm sounded, and security personnel appeared from nowhere to swarm around us. The next few minutes were raw chaos as Torina and I were immediately taken into custody. But Groshenko stepped into the pandemonium and bellowed for quiet. As the racket subsided, he fixed me with a glare. The air hummed with possible violence, but I returned his look with a level gaze.

"Care to explain why you just killed a Senior Myrmidon, Peacemaker Tudor?"

I was cuffed by then, so I just nodded down at the data slate hanging from my belt. "It's all in there. Avortun was a traitor. He was hooked into the case we've been working, the one involving the stolen identities."

A security guard yanked the data slate off my belt and handed it to Groshenko. He tapped at it, examined it for a moment, then gave a slow nod.

"You can release them," he said, his tone anything but apologetic.

We were uncuffed, and the guards pulled back a few paces but kept a wary eye on us, their weapons ready. I launched into an explanation of what had brought us here. And that led to the cuff on Avortun's wrist.

Perry appeared. He'd remained apart from the chaos. Apparently, being an AI, he wasn't considered a threat because built-in protocol precluded it. I made a mental note of that. That seemed, to me, to be a serious security hole. I was well aware of how easily a piece of software written for a benign purpose could be turned to evil use.

He landed beside Avortun, who had a medical crash team working on him. While he examined the cuff, they finally gave up and shook their heads.

"He managed to activate one function on this thing," Perry said.

"Well, I guess it wasn't self-destruct. So what did he activate? Do we know?"

As Perry went back to work, Groshenko intervened. "What is that device? That cuff?"

I looked at him. "That, Master Groshenko, is a serious problem. It's a weapon, it can interrupt complex systems, kill outright, and candidly, it has abilities we're only beginning to understand."

"I read the report on that." He turned on the senior member of the security services present. "How did he manage to get that thing aboard in the first place, much less in here?"

The woman shifted uncomfortably. "I'm not sure, sir. This is the first I've heard of this particular threat."

Ah, bureaucracies. The right hand didn't just not know what the left was doing, the two were actually pushing and pulling in opposite directions.

"It was a comm message, a burst transmission," Perry said. "It's encrypted, so I can't tell you the contents."

"If I'm any kind of gambler, that message was sent to Axicur," I said.

"Uh, Van, unless this tech is way more advanced than we've given it credit for, there's no way it would have the range to reach a receiver in another star system."

"Is Avortun's ship nearby?"

Groshenko turned to one of the duty officers who was standing nearby and watching the whole proceeding with wide eyes. The officer nodded.

"It's docked at port four-alpha."

"I think that burst message went to his ship——"

"And was relayed from it, to its recipient," Groshenko said, nodding. "Fury, I'm giving Peacemaker Tudor full access to Avortun's ship. Let its AI know that. I expect the airlock to be open when he gets there."

Fury, which was apparently the name of the battlecruiser's master AI, acknowledged, and Groshenko turned to me. "Go, find out where that message went, if you can."

"On it," I said, but I hesitated and pointed at Avortun's body, still impaled by the Moonsword.

"Before I go, mind if I have that back?"

The lead medic paused in packing up his crash kit and nodded at the fallen Peacemaker.

"Go for it. I think he's done with it."

AVORTUN'S SIGNAL didn't activate any security features aboard his ship, which was either an oversight on his part, or just something he never had the chance to implement. In any case, we found his data core essentially intact, and it included a comm log transmission almost coincident with his death aboard the *Righteous Fury*. We were able to use that to work out a destination for the signal from its routing information. It went to the Tau Ceti system.

"Probably straight into Axicur's living room," I said.

"What happens to Avortun's ship?" Torina asked. "Does it become a prize?"

I clicked my tongue. "His body's not even cold, and you're already after his stuff."

"Does that bother you?"

"Not at all. It was merely an observation, not a judgment."

With Lunzy's help and Groshenko's blessing, we were able to scrape together a force of four Peacemakers, including our friends Alic and K'losk. Lunzy herself made the fourth. Once we had everyone assembled, we prepared to twist our way to Tau Ceti to confront Axicur and put an end to at least her part in this whole sordid affair.

First, though, we fixed the hole in the lavatory. Some things take priority, even over galactic justice.

28

ALL THAT SAID, I'd actually expected Axicur to run. And, sure enough, when we arrived in Tau Ceti, we found two small ships breaking orbit. They could have been anyone, involved in perfectly legitimate business of their own. However, we'd already identified their transponder signatures from a list included in the data from Avortun's ship. We presumed it was so he could identify Axicur's ships whenever he encountered them. Now, it told us that these two belonged to her, or were at least affiliated with her.

"Do you think they'll stop if we order them to?" I asked the cockpit at large. I got three immediate responses from Perry, Torina, and Netty, in that order.

"Nope."

"No."

"Absolutely not."

"Yeah, I don't think so either. Still." I hit the comm, enclosing the two ships in a directional transmission beam and opening the channel to broadcast.

"This is Peacemaker Van Tudor. I'm transmitting my credentials. I require both ships receiving this message to immediately shut down your drives, deactivate your weapons, and—"

"Missiles inbound," Netty said.

"Van, I think you have your answer, and it was a big f—"

"Van, Lunzy here. I just got confirmation that the kill rider on the Warrant has been approved by Groshenko."

I acknowledged, and Perry finished his thought.

"—big fat no."

I saw Alic, K'losk, and Lunzy activate their fire control scanners, and Torina did the same with ours. We were able to shoot down all but two of the incoming missiles, one detonating near Alic's ship, the other just sailing past K'losk's without detonating.

"A dud. Somebody's been skimping on their ordnance purchases," Netty observed.

We held our fire. Getting closer meant our missiles could maneuver harder and burn less fuel doing it, since they didn't have to be boosted as far. And as the missiles raced in, we laid into the two ships with laser fire. They burned even harder while throwing some desultory fire back our way. Clearly, they knew they were outgunned and desperately wanted to get somewhere they could twist away.

"Not on my watch," I murmured, seeing us close to optimal combat range.

The resulting firefight was brief but intense. For a solid minute, the space between our ships and Axicur's came alive with crisscrossing laser beams, hurtling missiles, hyper-fast mass-driver slugs, and a few particle beam shots from Lunzy's ship that seared armor away in flashes. We took two solid laser hits, one of which cooked off our navigation scanner array. The other scoured a deep gouge in an applique armor plate and rang the ship's skeleton like a protesting bell. Alic's ship was actually knocked offline and temporarily taken out of the fight by a nearby missile detonation. Lunzy took a few hits, too. The only one to weather it all unscathed was K'losk.

"Figures. I swear that Hosurc'a lives a charmed life, born with a platinum spoon in his beak," Perry muttered.

"Why would a bird need to use a spoon?" Torina asked.

"It's an expression, Torina. It means—" Perry stopped, taking in Torina's broad grin.

"Way to toy with my emotions at this critical moment, you fiend."

"You're most welcome," Torina said, honey-sweet and grinning.

I scanned our screens and damage reports, and the picture was clear—we took some hits.

But Axicur's ships were being carved apart. Our range was a major factor, allowing us to target our attacks more deliberately, so that we were able to disable both ships and leave them coasting, the comms channels filled with vile—if empty—threats from the wounded craft.

"Looks like we have to get up-close and personal for the endgame of this thing," I said, unbuckling my harness. "Netty, get us close. Torina, Perry, let's go give our regards to Axicur."

ALIC AND HOSURC'A boarded one of the ships, while we covered the other with Lunzy. I wasn't used to seeing her decked out in her full battle rattle—

But holy *shit*. She was *lethal* in close-quarters combat.. Compared to her and Torina, I was definitely the noob when it came to this kind of fighting. Five Sorcerers set up a defensive perimeter outside their ship's bridge, choosing to force a single, decisive action against us. The chamber was narrow, but deep, with bridge access ten meters inward.

As one, the Sorcerers began to lift their arms.

They did not all succeed. I fired The Drop with savage glee, shredding a slender alien with a torrent of buckshot, it's body nearly disintegrating even as Torina and Lunzy split away from me and advanced, firing their own weapons in a metronome of destruction.

"They're arrogant pricks!" Lunzy spat, turning sideways to avoid some kind of emission from the nearest Sorcerer cuff. In that instant, I felt my legs go weak, hit by a cuff weapon, and as I fought to regain stability, Torina shot another Sorcerer between the eyes. With a mewling cry, it struck a comrade in the neck with its cuff, releasing a spark that jolted both aliens just long enough for me to raise The Drop again—

I fired, but my target was cut down, his arm flying away spewing blood as Torina's next round made him into a one-armed soldier.

"Nice shot," I said, and Torina heard me, despite the chaotic melee.

"Then you'll... love... this... one," she said, sliding under the outstretched arm of her next target, only to place the muzzle of her weapon directly against his forehead. As he slashed at her with a small knife, Torina squeezed the trigger, and the Sorcerer's head simply ceased to exist.

Lunzy took an energy weapon to the shoulder, filling the bridge with a horrific scent of roasting meat. But the Sorcerer didn't follow through, and she rolled, stepped up inside the space his arms controlled, and caught him in a hip-toss that drove his skull into a monitor hard enough to shatter his spine. Trembling, he slumped, and she put two rounds in him for good measure, then moved her gun just far enough to blast the last Sorcerer—stunned and covered in his friend's gore.

But The Drop spoke first, and the Sorcerer was torn to ribbons.

Lunzy looked back at me, lips pursed. "Thief."

I shook my head in amazement. "You can go through his pockets."

A lingering energy shield flickered in front of us, covering the last living Sorcerer with armor that our slugs and buckshot couldn't touch.

Perry flapped around the corner at full velocity, metallic wings a storm of motion. The Sorcerer fired a sidearm, Perry was hit, and he went to the deck, all in one blurred moment. Leaping over Perry, I drew the Moonsword, and the Sorcerer's eyes went round. He knew fear. He understood the threat.

He was also arrogant, and slaved to his cuff, rather than a faster, more certain weapon.

That vanity was his end. With my first stroke, I removed his arm, the cuff and limb falling away even as a cloud of actinic energy began to gather—then my backswing decapitated him, and he knew nothing except defeat.

I glanced back at my fallen friend. "Perry!"

With the cuffs inactive, comms were normal, and we could speak to each other. He was able to answer, if in a halting tone. "Uh, a little busy doing some self-repair here, Van. You guys go on without me."

"You sure?"

"Yeah, I've had worse than this. There was this one time, when your grandfather and I—"

"Hold that thought!" I shouted and raced on into the next compartment, which turned out to be the ship's cramped bridge.

Its sole occupant was a female Wu'tzur, who could only be one person. She had a pistol, which she dropped, and then she raised all four hands.

"Why, hello there, officer. As you can see, I'm surrendering peacefully. You'll have to take me into cust—"

"Gun!" Lunzy shouted from behind me, then her own weapon boomed, blowing Axicur's smug face apart.

I turned and looked at Lunzy. "What—?"

She shrugged. "Sorry, my error. I could've sworn she still had a gun."

I narrowed my eyes, watching Axicur's bodily fluids spill across the floor in lazy arcs.

But Lunzy wasn't unapologetic.

"If we'd taken her into custody, Van, she'd have immediately buried herself in lawyers. And, even with Avortun dead, we don't know that we've rooted out all the corruption at the top of the Guild. If she managed to get herself released on bail, we would never see her again."

"Sounds like you're rationalizing it, Lunzy."

"Damned right I am. Or would you rather let her keep her nasty little stolen-identity empire going?"

I opened my mouth but closed it again, remembering what Perry had said to me very early on in my shiny new career as a Peacemaker.

"Van, what did I tell you about the galaxy?"

"That it's a cold and hostile place."

"Attaboy, Peacemaker. It's the one law that trumps all others. Don't ever forget that."

Staring at Axicur's corpse, I knew he was right.

It didn't mean I had to like it. At least, not all of it.

EPILOGUE

WE'D LEFT ICKY, now a permanent member of the *Fafnir*'s crew, aboard the ship when we landed on Null World to visit the Schegith. They were definitely a success story for us, and the kind of victory that made me certain our violence had been done in the name of justice.

Torina and I had an ulterior motive, though. And while Icky, Perry, and Netty puttered away on the various bits of damage to the *Fafnir*, we stole away, paid our respects to Schegith herself, then availed ourselves of the planet's hidden wonder.

We drifted on the placid surface of the vast underground sea in a small boat Schegith had provided, taking in ancient carven glyphs in the rock and faded paintings from the prehistory of the Schegith. Torina admired them as a slow current carried us along.

"I admit, I had reservations about this."

"We're the only people here. We didn't need a reservation."

"As Perry notes, that… that was a dad joke, right?"

I glanced over the side of the boat, into the black water. "Probably. One good bit of news… I don't see anything carnivorous."

"I think it's the carnivorous things you *don't* see that are the ones you have to worry about."

For a while, we just drifted in silence. Torina finally broke it.

"So what now?"

I pointed off to our left. "I was thinking of heading over there. There seem to be some more paintings—"

"You know what I mean."

I grinned. "Yeah. I've actually been thinking about that myself. I was tempted to just divide up that fat bank account of Axicur's among us, Lunzy, Alic, and K'losk. You know, profits from crime, that sort of thing. That would be more than enough money to upgrade the *Fafnir* to an actual *Dragon*-class ship."

"But you've decided against it."

"Yeah, I have. I think it makes more sense to hand it over to The Quiet Room and let them manage it for the benefit of Axicur's victims. Unless you object, of course."

"No, I think that's perfect. I'd have always felt that the *Fafnir*'s upgrades would have been a little, I don't know, *dirty*, I guess, if we'd used her blood money to pay for them."

I leaned back. "Exactly. We'll keep making honest money so our upgrades are squeaky clean. In the meantime, there are still lives being stolen, and victims to save. We have our missing Nesit with his stolen artifacts, including the parts of the Soviet Venus probe. And we've got the remnants of the Salt Thieves, and the Arc of Vengeance, and—"

"And, right now, we don't have any of that," she cut in. "We've just got this placid lake, and this boat, and—" She glanced over the side. "And hopefully nothing down there that's *too* hungry."

I smiled up at the roof of the titanic cavern, which was barely visible in the gloom beyond the boat's lights. "Think you can stand a few days here?"

"A few. But I could use some convincing."

The way she said it made me sit up a bit and look at her. The expression on her face somehow managed to be coy, suggestive, and wide-eyed innocence all at once.

"I do love Italian girls."

She sniffed. "Someday, you'll have to tell me what this *Italian* thing is."

"Some of the best damned food on Earth, that's what it is. Meantime, though—"

I took the boat's tiller and turned us about to head back for the distant shore.

"Where are we going now?"

I pointed. "That way. It might not be my idea of a beach, but it *is* private."

Amazon won't always tell you about the next release. To stay updated on this series, be sure to sign up for our spam-free email list at jnchaney.com.

Van will return in ANVIL DARK, available now on Amazon.

GLOSSARY

Anvil Dark: The beating heart of the Peacemaker organization, Anvil Dark is a large orbital platform located in the Gamma Crucis system, some ninety lightyears from Earth. Anvil Dark, some nine hundred seventy years old, remains in a Lagrange point around Mesaribe, remaining in permanent darkness. Anvil Dark has legal, military, medical, and supply resources for Peacemakers, their assistants, and guests.

Cloaks: Local organized criminal element, the Cloaks hold sway in only one place: Spindrift. A loose guild of thugs, extortionists, and muscle, the Cloaks fill a need for some legal control on Spindrift, though they do so only because Peacemakers and other authorities see them as a necessary evil. When confronted away from Spindrift, Cloaks are given no rights, quarter, or considerations for their position. (See: Spindrift)

Dragonet: A Base Four Combat ship, the Dragonet is a modified platform intended for the prosecution of Peacemaker policy. This includes but is not limited to ship-to-ship combat, surveillance, and planetary operations as well. The Dragonet is fast, lightly armored, and carries both point defense and ranged weapons, and features a frame that can be upgraded to the status of a small corvette (Class Nine).

Moonsword: Although the weapon is in the shape of a medium sword, the material is anything but simple metal. The Moonsword is a generational armament, capable of upgrades that augment its ability to interrupt communications, scan for data, and act as a blunt-force weapon that can split all but the toughest of ship's hulls. See: Starsmith

Peacemaker: Also known as a Galactic Knight, Peacemakers are an elite force of law enforcement who have existed for more than three centuries. Both hereditary and open to recruitment, the guild is a meritocracy, but subject to political machinations and corruption, albeit not on the scale of other galactic military forces. Peacemakers have a legal code, proscribed methods, a reward and bounty scale, and a well-earned reputation as fierce, competent fighters. Any race may be a Peacemaker, but the candidates must pass rigorous testing and training.

Perry: An artificial intelligence, bound to Van (after service to his grandfather), Perry is a fully-sapient combat operative in the shape of a large, black avian. With the ability to hack computer systems and engage in physical combat, Perry is also a living repository of galactic knowledge in topics from law to battle strategies. He is also a wiseass.

Salt Thieves: Originally actual thieves who stole salt, this is a three-hundred-year-old guild of assassins known for their ruthless behavior, piracy, and tendency to kill. Members are identified by a complex, distinct system of braids in their hair. These braids are often cut and taken as prizes, especially by Peacemakers.

Spindrift: At nine hundred thirty years old, Spindrift is one of the most venerable space stations in the galactic arm. It is also the least reputable, having served as a place of criminal enterprise for nearly all of its existence due to a troublesome location. Orbiting Sirius, Spindrift was nearly depopulated by stellar radiation in the third year as a spaceborne habitat. When order collapsed, criminals moved in, cycling in and out every twelve point four years as coronal ejections rom Sirius made the station uninhabitable. Spindrift is known for medical treatments and technology that are quasi-legal at best, as well as weapons, stolen goods, and a strange array of archaeological items, all illegally looted. Spindrift has a population of thirty thousand beings at any time.

Starsmith: A place, a guild, and a single being, the Starsmith is primarily a weapons expert of unsurpassed skill. The current Starsmith is a Conoku (named Linulla), a crablike race known for their dexterity, skill in metallurgy and combat enhancements, and sense of humor.

CONNECT WITH J.N. CHANEY

Don't miss out on these exclusive perks:

- Instant access to free short stories from series like *The Messenger*, *Starcaster*, and more.
- Receive email updates for new releases and other news.
- Get notified when we run special deals on books and audiobooks.

So, what are you waiting for? Enter your email address at the link below to stay in the loop.

https://www.jnchaney.com/backyard-starship-subscribe

CONNECT WITH TERRY MAGGERT

Check out his website
http://terrymaggert.com/

Connect on Facebook
https://www.facebook.com/terrymaggertbooks/

Follow him on Amazon
https://www.amazon.com/Terry-Maggert/e/B00EKN8RHG/

ABOUT THE AUTHORS

J. N. Chaney is a USA Today Bestselling author and has a Master's of Fine Arts in Creative Writing. He fancies himself quite the Super Mario Bros. fan. When he isn't writing or gaming, you can find him online at **www.jnchaney.com**.

He migrates often, but was last seen in Las Vegas, NV. Any sightings should be reported, as they are rare.

Terry Maggert is left-handed, likes dragons, coffee, waffles, running, and giraffes; order unimportant. He's also half of author Daniel Pierce, and half of the humor team at Cledus du Drizzle.

With thirty-one titles, he has something to thrill, entertain, or make you cringe in horror. Guaranteed.

Note: He doesn't sleep. But you sort of guessed that already.

Made in United States
North Haven, CT
10 June 2022